CRITICS RAVE ABOUT SIMON CLARK!

"I'm going to seek out and read everything Clark writes. He's a true talent."
—Bentley Little, *Hellnotes*

"Not since I discovered Clive Barker have I enjoyed horror so much."
—*Nightfall*

"A master of eerie thrills."
—Richard Laymon, author of *The Cellar*

"Clark has the ability to keep the reader looking over his shoulder to make sure that sudden noise is just the summer night breeze rattling the window."
—CNN.com

"Simon Clark is one of the most exciting British horror writers around."
—*SFX*

"Clark may be the single most important writer to emerge on the British horror scene in the '90s."
—*The Dark Side*

"Watch this man climb to Horror Heaven!"
—*Deathrealm*

"Clark writes with compelling characterization and indelible imagery."
—*DarkEcho*

HORROR IN THE TOMB

Luna's cries brought Doctor Paul Marais back to the castle crypt. Beech went with him. As they descended into the crypt they heard thunderous pounding—a fist striking the inside of the marble tomb.

Saiban came partway down the steps into the shadow-filled void where a copse of stone pillars supported the vaulted ceiling. The man screamed: *"Marais! You told us she was dead!"*

Groans boomed through the stonework. A deep sound that throbbed with immeasurable pain. Paul approached the tomb in which Dominion had placed the corpse just hours ago. He could see that the statue carved in veined marble vibrated from the onslaught from beneath the slab. Saiban clamped his hands over his ears.

Paul caught Beech's eye. "Will you help me move the lid?"

"No!" Saiban's howl merged with the groans pulsing through the crypt. "For God's sake, don't let her out!"

DEATH'S DOMINION

✠

SIMON CLARK

LEISURE BOOKS   NEW YORK CITY

For Janet

A LEISURE BOOK®

November 2006

Published by

Dorchester Publishing Co., Inc.
200 Madison Avenue
New York, NY 10016

ISBN 0-8439-5493-0

The name "Leisure Books" and the stylized "L" with design are trademarks of Dorchester Publishing Co., Inc.

Printed in the United States of America.

Visit us on the web at www.dorchesterpub.com.

DEATH'S
DOMINION

1

FIRST LIGHT

Hard to kill . . .

Today. He opened his eyes to find that the morning had gone all wrong. Instead of daylight falling through the vast windows that were always open wide to the blue skies, there was darkness. He still didn't fully understand the meaning of "light" and "dark." Beyond the windows the sky was black. Inside his bedroom, he could barely see the outline of the television on the wall, or his sun hat suspended by its peg behind the door.

The morning was every which way wrong because that door didn't open as it should to admit a figure with a smiling face. A comfortingly familiar figure that brought his food.

The sense of wrongness wouldn't leave. Because instead of birdsong and the soothing hum of voices in the hallway an odd silence dominated his world. The child reached out for the reassuring presence of the bars around his bed. It took a moment for him to find them because this blackness getting in the way of his eyes meant he couldn't see the sheltering frame around his mattress that kept him safe. Nevertheless, his newly born fingers found the smooth bars soon enough.

"Ah?" Although he couldn't yet frame the sound into a coherent word, he succeeded in adding the rising inflection so it sounded like a question. "Ah? Ah?" *What's happening?* Again, he couldn't articulate the confusion, but the sounds he made were infused with the note of asking what had gone wrong with the world.

What could he do? Maybe if he waited long enough the friendly blue sky would return to his window. Then not long after that the smiling face would appear to feed him. After all, this is what he'd always known. It was beyond his understanding to imagine circumstances would ever change.

Then he did hear. It was a sound loud enough to startle him. He'd heard a door slam before. That bang he'd just heard was a bit like the slam of a door. Only it had been a lot, *lot* louder.

It happened again—that bang. But before the sound he'd heard a scream. It had been at such a volume that it made him flinch. The bang came again . . . and again . . . then a voice that shrieked, *"No!"* Another slam echoed down the hallway. So many slamming doors . . . Only they didn't *really* sound exactly the same as a door crashing shut. Just as the morning being all wrong, there was a pervading wrongness about that sound, too. Quickly, he reached out a hand, grabbed the bars, and pulled himself into a sitting position. No sooner had he accomplished that than the door burst open. With it came a spill of brilliant light, followed by a figure he recognized. It was the happy lady that brought him his food. Only this time there was no smile. Her eyes were very wide; the expression on her face alarmed him. For some reason she wore a pair of hands on each shoulder. Was this a funny thing intended to make him laugh? But her expression frightened him. Especially the way her normally friendly eyes stared at him. And the hands on her shoulders belonged to arms that pulled her back through the doorway (though she didn't want to go).

He heard her shouting, "Don't hurt him! Whatever you do don't hurt him . . . he's not like the rest. Do you hear? He's not like the rest—he's different!"

She'd only been gone for a moment when he heard the sound like a slammed door. After that, he didn't hear her voice.

With the door partway open, light flooded into his room. He could clearly see the frame around his bed and his sun hat on its peg. A smell also reached him. A spiky smell, which made him so uneasy that he climbed over the bars that enclosed his bed. His feet pit-pattered on the tiled floor as he scampered to the door to find out what was making all that sound.

Blood.

A word without meaning. Blood . . . blood . . . blood . . . It ran through his mind like music. He couldn't link the word with all that red stuff on the walls and floor, and the red juice that poured from the crevice in his feeder's shoulders where her neck had been. Her head, he noticed, lay near his feet. Its eyes wide open.

"Uh." She always looked at him when he made that sound. "Uh-uh." So why didn't she look at him today? He crouched down to touch his feeder's face. The red juice transferred itself from her to his finger.

"Uh." A sense of profound sadness engulfed him. It was if the darkness beyond his window had somehow found itself into his body. Why didn't the lady move? Why had her head moved away from her body?

Dead, dead, dead . . . That had no meaning either, yet it set up a chanting resonance inside his head. The sense of internal darkness intensified. For a while his eyes locked on the still face of the lady. *Dead, dead, dead . . .*

"Uh!" He pushed the head with his knuckle. It rolled over so it faced away from him. Trembling now, he rose to his feet. Instinct drove him to find other people. He pictured smiling faces and knew the reassurance such faces would bring. The hallway was empty apart from the lady. There were sounds, however, coming from the far end where there were a pair of doors. Even though he wasn't strong and not yet sure of his balance he managed to reach the entrance by supporting himself with the wall.

Unlike the hallway this big room was full of people. For a moment he watched because what took place had no meaning for him. Men and women sat on a line of chairs in the center of the room. More men in gray clothes walked along the seated people and they placed a big fat red necklace over each head. Then the men in gray moved back to the wall.

Oooh . . .

So this was where the sound of slamming doors came from. He watched without any reaction as a blossom of flame erupted from each necklace. Then, one after another, the seated people fell off their chairs, and just like with the feeder lady their heads came away from their bodies.

Blood, blood, blood . . .

They no longer moved.

Dead, dead, dead . . .

Again, those words without meaning swam through his mind. And when he watched the men in gray who hurried another group of people forward to sit in the same chairs, another strange word infiltrated his mind: soldiers.

Still too weak to do anything but watch he witnessed a second batch of men and women in pajamas decapitated by red necklaces of high explosive. The torn, bloody bodies formed mounds on the floor. The men in gray shouted to another group to hurry in. Each seated individual was garlanded with a red tube around the neck.

Didn't they know what would happen to them? There were no words at his disposal to shout a warning, but a forceful "Uh!" burst from his lips.

The men in gray noticed him now. One of them carried a sticklike object. He pointed it at a lady in white who was dressed the same as a feeder. The man ordered her to perform some action.

She came forward to take the child's arm. She smiled like his feeder lady, who now lay back in the hallway. In that soothing way she said, "You come with me. I want you to sit with the others."

She's terrified. Her mouth is bleeding. They've beaten her . . . This time the words appeared to form some connection. They made him anxious. Rather than these events being inexplicable, and having nothing to do with him, suddenly he was part of all this. Instead of walking obediently with the lady as he would do normally, he stopped dead.

"Please, child." She gently pulled at his arm. "We have to sit in these chairs for the men." She smiled, yet her eyes glittered with tears. "I'll sit next to you and make sure you're all right."

"What's the holdup?" one of the men barked.

"Nothing, he's coming," she told him. "He'll do as I say."

"He better."

Men in gray yanked the red necklaces down onto those already seated. They were pliant and accepting . . .

. . . when they should be refusing to do this. Don't they know what the necklaces will do to them . . . ? The words began to assume meaning now. *This isn't right. The men in gray are hurting these people . . .* He tried to tell the feeder lady this, but all that came from his mouth was "Uh . . . rrr."

"I told you to make the bastard sit down." This came as an angry shout from one soldier. He lifted the stick-shaped thing and struck the feeder lady on the side of the head. Her smile melted as the pain blasted through her.

"Your turn, handsome."

The child realized that a thick red necklace had been dragged down over his head to encircle his neck.

"Do the nurse as well," called another of the soldiers.

The lady pressed her lips together to stop herself from crying as a soldier slammed the red loop over her head. No . . . this is wrong. He knew he was too weak to stop the soldier, but he tried anyway. He raised both his hands and gripped the soldier's muscular forearms in each fist.

"Lieutenant? We've got a live one here," the man shouted. "Will someone take care of him?"

The feeder lady pleaded, "My dear, accept your fate. You mustn't fight them. Come sit with me, there's a good child. It'll all be over in a second . . . No, don't resist . . . *you're not allowed to hurt them.*"

The soldier's face darkened with fury. "Hurry up! Someone stick a bayonet in the bastard!"

"That's a good boy," the lady said as the child released his grip on the man's arms. "Let the soldiers do what they have to do."

The soldier, who was hauling the strawberry-colored necklace over her head, cuffed her with his fist. "Stand still!"

The child watched. This time the sense of wrongness overwhelmed him. He knew he was no match for the man but pushed him anyway. To the child's surprise the man fell onto the mound of headless corpses. And he clutched his chest as if that little push had hurt him.

"No, listen to me, child," the lady begged. "You must not hurt them. Do as they tell you."

Why he hadn't noticed he couldn't tell, but he saw a

pair of soldiers gripping his arms. For a second it puzzled him that they were panting as they tried to pull him backward. With a sweep of one arm he sent them both tumbling across the room. The child was weak—he knew he was weak—so why did the men shout in pain as they threw themselves onto the floor?

Another man in uniform ran at him with a stick . . . no, not a stick, a rifle. The rifle had a knife blade fixed at the end. He jabbed it at the child's stomach. It didn't hurt. It felt like a gentle prod. The child reached out one arm, spread his fingers across the man's face, then pushed. This time the force was greater. And away went the man to crash back against the wall. He didn't shout like the others had done. He just lay there, while blood trickled from his nose.

All this appeared to happen in a leisurely way. Nothing had been rushed, although now the child realized the other soldiers were running toward him. Why did they appear to move so slowly? One raised a submachine gun. Lights flickered at the end of the tube. The child felt a stinging sensation in his chest. Angry now, he snatched the machine gun from the soldier; one of the man's fingers snapped away from his hand where it caught in the trigger guard. As the man screamed the child hit him in the face with the gun. The metal object disintegrated on impact, while the man's lower jaw ripped clean away before the force of the blow. The disfigured man went whirling away in a geyser of blood, and ruby drops moved in slow motion through the air.

The child noticed that the men and women who'd previously been sitting dispassionately were now on their feet. Some started to remove the red necklaces. A number of soldiers were fleeing, while others were screaming in panic into their radio mics. "Backup urgently needed . . ." He sensed rather than interpreted the meaning of the sentence. More troops swarmed into the room. These wielded bulky weapons that they fired at their victims. People in pajamas toppled as huge-caliber bullets smashed their bodies.

The feeder lady grabbed the child's arm as she fell dying. "Run!" she screamed. "Get away from here!"

Through the window he saw the blue sky at last replacing the blackness. This was the only thing he could see that held a promise of friendly reassurance. The child must take his chances in that welcoming azure glow. With tracer shells flashing by his head he launched himself through the glass in the hope there was a power that would raise him up into the safety of that serene, blue world.

2

SHADES OF FRANKENSTEIN

A great, dark pounding roar. That sound became his world. There was sound, nothing but sound—no sight, nor touch, nor smell. The child didn't know how long he'd been walking when the rolling waves of thunder inside his head started to recede. At long last he began to see the dark, vertical columns that were clad in a multitude of soft forms. They were the most brilliant green he'd ever set his eyes on.

Trees . . . leaves . . . The words slipped into his mind. Their meaning was difficult to grasp. These giant forms were strange yet familiar at the same time. For a moment he was hypnotized by the vivacious emerald hues. "Ah . . ." He reached up to grasp the delicate greenery. Some of it came away in his fingers. It filled him with curiosity. He examined it closely, seeing the gloss on the green surface, and the veins running through its flesh. He sniffed it. Chlorophyll . . . rather than a word it was a sound in his mind; the sound itself was associated with green. He smelled the fistful of leaves again; a subtle fragrance of something akin to mint. He sighed. "Ah . . . ahhh . . ." He allowed the emerald shreds to flutter away from his fingers.

The child touched his ears. The thunder had gone now. When his eyes were open he saw this lush, billowing thing that generated the word *forest*. Above him, blue sky. Birdsong. Tiny creatures, far smaller than birds, hovered over yellow flowers with a buzzing sound. Their wings were iridescent rainbows of color; he was conscious of blood flowing through those transparent membranes. A breeze gently caressed his hair. This was a warm, friendly world. And yet . . . and yet, when he closed his eyes that dark thunder returned. Images spat through his head. Men in gray. Slamming door sounds. Red necklaces that exploded . . . tore away the heads of those apathetic men and women. Violence. Blood. Death. Why did he see one set of images with his eyes open? And another chaotic mix of images with eyes closed?

Memory . . .

"Uh . . ." Eyes open. Much better. He liked the blue sky. Birds glided through the air.

Gun . . . Lady dying . . . "Run, child, run!" Yes, he'd run. *Men firing their guns at him. Into the window*—smash! *Then over the fence. "Run, child, run . . ."* His eyes watered with the effort of keeping them open so he wouldn't be forced to see the terrible pictures inside him. Birds are good to watch. He locked his gaze onto a black one with a yellow beak as it soared out of the blue to alight at the top of the tree. It perched beside a nest that contained squeaky creatures. *What's in there?*

A moment later he gazed into the nest of woven twigs. Three little balls of speckled fluff cheep-cheeped away as hard as they could. Their beaks were open. Each creature had bright eyes that shone like black gemstones.

In surprise the child looked down at the ground from where he crouched on the branch. It was an astonishing distance to where he'd been standing in the grass just a blink of an eye ago. He must have climbed up here to see the chicks in the nest. Only he hadn't been aware of doing so. From this height at the top of the tree he could see the forest stretching away. Beyond that were rectangles of gold (fields . . .); there were houses clustered by a lake.

"Dotty . . . Dotty . . . Didn't you hear me?"

He looked down as a tiny figure approached through the trees.

"Dotty! I can't keep up. Slow down!"

From his treetop the child watched the figure on two legs pursue another figure on four legs.

"Dotty!"

Instinct prompted him rather than curiosity. Effortlessly, he dropped from branch to branch. A second later he landed lightly on his feet in front of the two-legged figure.

"Oh! You shocked me!" The girl regarded him with huge brown eyes. "What were you doing up that tree?"

A nest . . . chicks . . . He knew what he wanted to say. All that escaped his mouth, however, was another of those grunts. "Uh."

"Aren't you tall? You're bigger than Jason and he's bigger than my dad." She yelled, "Dotty! Where are you?" Her eyes searched the woodland. "Where's that bad dog gone? He knows I can't run as fast as him." She folded her arms and made a stern face. "But he does it every time. Dotty!"

He turned his head. The sound of the dog running through undergrowth came to him with so much clarity he could picture its paws moving from the crunch of dry grass to a subtle thud of paws on bare earth.

"Dotty. You'll get it from me, if you don't come back

now." She puckered her lips and blew. Her mouth emitted a faint rushing sound. "One day I'm going to learn to whistle. I'll whistle as loud as Jason. That'll teach Dotty—because he's a bad dog!" She looked the child up and down. "You're just like me, aren't you?"

He checked his arms. They were longer than the girl was tall.

She continued in a chatty way, "You're wearing pajamas like me. Though you've got shoes on your feet. Look at my doggies." She was clad in comical puppy bedroom slippers. Two big cartoon eyes peered from beneath floppy ears. "My dad says I've got to make 'em last because he doesn't know how long the market's going to stay open. It better, 'cause they shut up the supermarket last week. Now we've got to go round the farms to get food . . . and that takes ages . . . ages and ages and ages." She stared up at him. "Who shot you?"

"Uh?" As he ran his fingers over his chest he recalled the soldier who fired the submachine gun. The white cotton top had three holes punched through to the skin underneath. Surrounding the holes were black burn marks. He slipped a finger through the torn material to explore the wounds in his flesh. They were wet. Each one contained a pellet of some hard material.

The girl moved closer to scrutinize the three holes. "Doesn't it hurt?"

"Hmma . . ." Neither agreement nor disagreement with her question. Only a sense of a bafflement.

"When my dad shoots rabbits they drop down dead. Why aren't you dead?"

"Naa-a."

"You should go to the hospital . . . you don't want to wind up dying on me, do you, now?"

Hospital. The word meant nothing, but it fired images through his head like those bullets had struck his chest.

Hospital—corridors, beds, low voices in a darkened room, displays of moving lights on monitors.

"Listen." The girl pulled his arm. "Dotty's crying. Can't you hear him?" With another shout of "Dotty!" she ran toward the trees. "I don't know where you are!" A note of distress ran through her voice. "*Dotty!*"

The girl was running the wrong way. He couldn't tell her, but he made a growling sound to catch her attention. Then he loped toward where the dog was crying. Beneath the cries he detected a strange humming sound, not unlike the buzz of the insects. He didn't need to glance back to know that the girl followed. Her feet clad in the comical puppy slippers swished through the grass.

In seconds he'd raced through bushes, blasting a pathway through with his body. Within a few paces he was clear of the bushes to find an open expanse of ground enclosed by posts linked by wires. The dog stood on the far side of the fence. Its nose was close to it as it peered through. The animal quivered and there was a smell of singed fur. On top of the dog's head was a burn mark. He looked from the seared skin to the wires that linked the posts. The buzzing came from there. Electricity. In his mind's eye he saw the dog racing under the live fence, its head catching it and taking a hard enough jolt to cause a small burn. The creature was bright enough not to repeat the exercise and now stood at the other side of the fence, unable to return to its mistress.

"Dotty! You silly boy!" The girl ran forward to grab hold of the wire.

In a split second he'd yanked the girl back from the wire that sizzled with voltage. Then he reached over the barrier without touching, scooped up the dog, and placed it at her feet.

The girl, meanwhile, clutched the back of her neck. "Ouch. You big idiot. You hurt me, pulling me like that."

Tears filled her eyes. "You really hurt me!" Sobbing, she ran back through the bushes. "You bully. I'm going to tell, I'm going to tell!"

In a blaze of motion he caught up with her. He reached out his hand, with its fingers splayed.

"I'm going to tell . . . you're going to be sorry!"

The dog barked.

Stop her telling! The command came as an instinct, rather than words. In his mind's eye he saw himself pressing his hand against the girl's mouth. It would be so easy to stop her telling anyone. Just a little pressure . . . he could make the dog silent, too. Dotty would never bark again. Then this green forest would be tranquil, just as he liked it.

"Nnn-errh!" He slashed aside a low branch that would have struck the little girl on the head. Then he stood there, holding on to it. Confusion welled up inside him. He knew he could stop the girl. But something about that course of action filled him with a dark fog of terror. Pain, hurt, blood . . . Concepts of right and wrong meant nothing, only the idea of stopping the girl like he'd stopped the soldiers sickened him. Instead of pursuing her he stood there, the branch gripped in his hand. The girl ran as fast as she could in her puppy slippers. Dotty sped alongside her. Soon they vanished among the trees until all he could hear were the sounds of their feet.

It didn't take long. The men arrived in a truck that bellowed clouds of blue smoke into the forest. The child watched their arrival. He sat placidly beneath the vast branches of the tree, enjoying the warm breeze. Now this snorting beast in green metal lumbered toward him. Immediately, the men saw him. They shouted. They gestured wildly. Then the ones standing in the back fired at him. Tracer rounds approached in a graceful arc. The first bullet ripped a fist-sized hole in the earth nearby. The second pecked out a streak of creamy white timber in the trunk.

The child had done nothing to anger them, so why this? More bullets smacked through the leaves. Once the truck stopped jolting on the rough ground, that's when their aim would become true. Smoothly, he rose to his feet; then with fluid grace he loped away into the forest. Once he entered the dense stand of trees the men were forced to leave the vehicle as there was no space for it to pass between the trunks. They pursued him on foot. For a while he was convinced they'd catch him, but he found it simple to outpace them. Soon they tired and were forced to stand panting, their rifles hanging limply from their hands. For some reason he didn't become breathless like them. Later, he even doubled back out of curiosity to watch them from behind a bush as they moved in a line. Constantly, they called to one another.

"See anything, Jack?"

"There's broken grass by that oak."

"If you see it, aim for the head. They can take a helluva lot of lead in the guts before it slows 'em down."

"Maybe someone ought to go back for the dogs?"

"Don't worry, we'll flush it out before long."

"Did you see the bastard? Did you see the size of it? I wouldn't even come up as high as its elbow."

"Fancy a scrap with that monster, Greg?"

"We won't get that close. Just blast it the first chance you get."

Some of the men laughed as they trudged up the slope.

"Don't let them scare you, Greg. It might decide to run, but it won't attack us. It's their nature. They can't fight back."

At that moment one pointed. "Hey . . . this looks like it!" They rushed toward a clump of alder where the undergrowth had been trampled. The child knew from the scent reaching his nostrils that the trail had been made hours ago by a hefty four-legged animal that bore a strong odor of musk.

As he watched them go he suddenly stiffened. The sense came to him of being watched. He whirled round to find a figure standing by a tree not twenty paces from him. A growl burst from his lips. He raised his arms in readiness to protect himself.

The figure stepped forward. "It's not safe to hang around out here. Follow me." When the child didn't respond the man smiled as he shot wary glances in the direction of the trail the hunters had followed. "It's OK. You're the same as me." He paused. "You're one of us." When the child didn't respond the man approached with his hands held out at his sides. His voice was gentle. "Don't be afraid. Now . . . what's your name?" A pause filled with forest birdsong. "OK. Maybe you're a little shy. Do you want to know my name?" He smiled. "I'm a doctor . . . I'm Dr. Frankenstein."

The child stared at the man as he indicated his own clothes. They were green surgical scrubs with a red badge stitched on the right breast.

"Dr. Frankenstein?" The man rubbed his jaw. "I guess you're not completely back with us yet, otherwise you'd appreciate the hilarity and acute wit of my joke. Dr. Frankenstein? Get it?" He sighed. "This is going to be harder than I thought." He took a deep breath. "Look. I'm not going to hurt you. I'm a friend. *Frr . . . iend*. Understand? Frr . . . iend good." He clicked his tongue. "And you won't appreciate my witty film reference, either, will you?" Slowly he approached. "You've still got your wrist tag. I just want to take a little peep. No . . . steady, pal. I'm not going to do anything unpleasant. My name's Dr. Marais . . . Considering the circumstances call me Paul. My, my, someone's taken a dislike to you already. I'll look at those slug pecks as soon as we're safely out of here. Come on, pal, you've got to let me . . . before those men come back and blow us to buggery . . . uh . . . relax . . . let me look at the . . ."

The child noticed the thin yellow strip around his wrist as the man took hold of his arm. The child moved back, dragging the man forward.

"My good heavens, you're a strong one, aren't you? It's OK, relax. I just want to check the . . . *My God. So it's you!*" He gave a low whistle, then quickly scanned the wrist tag. "You're the talk of the staff room, old pal. You woke up too soon. No one's ever recovered consciousness in the wonder tub before. That, my friend, is why you're special. See here?" He ran his finger over the black marks on the wrist tag. "You shouldn't even be out of bed yet. And I've been chasing after you through this bloody forest for the last two hours. Those gunshots were a dead giveaway that someone was enjoying a good old-fashioned monster hunt. But no pitchforks and blazing torches for us, eh?" The man cocked his head to one side. "You can hear the tramp of feet, can't you? That's the sound of doom approaching. D-O-O-M in capital letters. And this time I'm not joking." The doctor tried to tug the child along, but he remained statuelike under the tree. "Come on. I'll take you to the others. Where you'll be safe? Do you follow what I'm saying?"

Voices grew louder as the hunters emerged from the other side of the clearing. They hadn't noticed the pair yet.

The doctor whispered, "If you don't come with me now, then we're both dead . . . to be more exact, dead again." The doctor looked the child in the eye. "You've got to trust me. OK?"

There was something in the tone of the voice that the child recognized. At last he allowed himself to be led away.

3

BURN, MONSTER, BURN

"Monster," he said, "I'm going to tell you exactly what I'm going to do to you"—the man consulted his wristwatch—"in precisely forty-five minutes."

There were six other men in the barn with Elsa as she sat on the high stool in its center. The men were dressed in farmers' work clothes, mainly denim with heavy-duty boots. A couple wore leather jackets in honor of the occasion. The five watched the sixth man as he spoke. "Sit there. Don't move. Listen to what I say. When we're done with the other one you will walk with us to the field opposite these barn doors. You will not speak to anyone. There's a post in the field. When we reach it you will be fixed to it by chains. You will not call to anyone in the crowd. Wood will be piled around you. There's no gasoline to spare so it won't be as quick as you'd like. But seeing as there's been no rain for a week the kindling will be dry." He held her gaze. "When everything's ready I'll start the fire. If you take my advice you'll breathe the smoke. That way you might lose consciousness before flames reach you. Understand?"

Elsa didn't nod. She merely looked him in the eye.

One of the younger men spoke up. "But do these things feel pain?"

"There's one way to find out," said another. He held a lit cigarette in front of her face, then put it against her chin. She maintained eye contact for a moment before the pain made her flinch.

"Oh, the bitch felt that."

"She's not even a bitch, she's a monster."

"I'm not a monster," Elsa countered.

A youth sang out, "It speaks! It speaks!" Then he laughed before tugging her long hair. The force of it almost toppled her back off the stool. His face reddened with excitement as he pulled at her nurse's uniform. "C'mon! Let's see what you've got under there. They say you lot have got three tits."

"Imagine that sitting astride you, Robbie—she'd break your fucking spine."

Robbie stopped tugging her uniform. "You might be a necrophile but I'm not."

"No, you're in love with Mrs. Hand and her five lovely daughters."

The men laughed as the youth flushed with embarrassment.

"Stop picking on the lad," one of them said. "He's just got a bad case of stagnation of the virginity."

One of the men leered. "He could break himself in practicing on this one." He stroked her thigh. "Before she burns."

"I told you," the youth spat back, "I'm not a necrophile."

"OK. Calm down."

Elsa looked at the man who spoke. It was the same one who'd detailed her execution plan. He seemed to be the one in charge.

"Emotions are running high. So let's not start falling out among ourselves."

"He started it," Robbie grumbled. "I'm not sticking it in no monster." In a sudden burst of bravado he grinned at his tormentor. "I wouldn't even stick yours into her, Bill. And that's been up every pig in the village."

"Still . . . I've never seen one of these naked before." Bill prodded Elsa. "It wouldn't hurt to take a look, would it?"

"Call it for scientific purposes." Robbie sounded excited.

Elsa turned to their leader. *He'll say no*, she told herself. *He'll know better than allow them to become a frenzied mob.*

He shrugged. "It can't do any harm. It's not as if she can complain to anyone."

They rushed at her and started to pull at her clothes. *Don't struggle . . . if they want to do this, then you must let them.* Muscular fingers nipped her breast. She let out a cry. This only seemed to excite the men. Hot breath panted in her neck as they hauled her top up toward her shoulders.

A female voice cut through the hurly-burly. "Five minutes until they light the first fire. Anyone who wants to watch should get themselves out there now."

Startled, the men jumped back as if nothing had been happening. The leader wiped a bead of sweat from his forehead as he said, "Ma, what're you doing out this time of night?"

"The same as you lot. This is the first time in my life I've got a chance to see one of these animals go up in flames. Mark my words, Cullum, I'll not miss this."

Elsa watched the elderly woman approach. Her white hair had been tied back so tightly it pulled her eyes into narrow slits. She used a cane to help bear her weight. As much as age, the lines around the old woman's mouth revealed years of arthritic pain.

"Cullum? What are you doing, then?"

"Ma? Nothing. We were just—"

"I'm not bothered about this one. I'm asking if you're going out into the field to watch."

Elsa realized that Cullum was the woman's son. She detected that his exasperation at being treated like a little boy was tempered with deep respect.

Cullum spoke gently. "We're guarding her . . . it . . . until they're ready."

"I'll stay with her. You get yonder."

"Ma?"

"The creature's not going to do anything. They aren't capable of hurting people. It's not in their nature." The old woman jabbed the ferrule of her stick into Elsa's stomach. "You won't touch me, will you?" Another painful jab. "See that? Got a stomach as solid as an oven door. Strong as an ox. But she won't hurt me any more than a fish'll jump out of a river and walk."

"Ma—"

"Now, you go watch the other one roast. I'll bet you a month's pension that she'll dance in them flames an hour or more before she drops."

Outside, the crowd of people grew excited. Elsa could hear raised voices. There were elements of anxiety and fear, but there was an elation, too. Homo sapiens had won. After years of humiliation . . . *imagined humiliation*, that is, they were exacting their terrible revenge. The men in the barn stared in the direction of the barn door. They were like children eager to see a show.

"Why are you waiting?" the old woman asked. "Go on, before you miss it."

"But you wanted to watch, too."

"I know every knothole in this barn. I'll see what I want to see from here."

Cullum couldn't stand still he so badly wanted to be out there. This would be the biggest event in their lifetimes. Even so, he was uneasy leaving his mother in the company of the thing they called "monster."

"Ma, why stay here with this thing? You can see for yourself what it is."

"I know. That's exactly why I want to give it a few home truths." She viciously jabbed the walking stick into Elsa's stomach. "Did you hear that? You're going to hear exactly what I think before they roast you!" With that she struck Elsa so forcefully across the arm with the cane that even the men flinched. "Now, be off with you, Cullum. And take your friends."

Neither Cullum nor anyone else wanted to argue with the ferocious woman.

"I'll have to lock the door behind me, Ma," Cullum told her.

"Then mind you lock it!"

Eager to be out of the barn, the men unbolted the door before pouring out into the night. In the field an upright post had been set in the earth. Milling around it were dozens of men, women, and children. Many carried candles burning in lanterns. The glow illuminated figures that carried bales of sticks toward the post. The barn doors closed on her captors. From the expression on their faces they fully expected the old woman to have mutilated Elsa by the time they returned. Once the doors were padlocked from the other side the woman approached Elsa. Her gray eyes studied Elsa's face. "Yes, I know your kind. I know what you're like." She nodded at the closed door. "Did they rape you?"

Instead of replying Elsa asked, "Why don't you go watch my sister burn?"

"But she's not your real sister . . . not your *blood* sister, is she?" She sniffed. "But you sort call each other brother and sister like you belong to one big family, don't you?"

"What do you know about my *sort*? You don't know anything about us."

"And you know nothing about me, young woman."

Young woman? What happened to the insults? Elsa looked more closely at this veteran of the remote farming community. The lined face softened.

"I'm eighty-five years old. Sixty years ago I worked in one of the cities on the coast. Back then your kind and mine got on. Oh, we lived in separate communities, we never became what you'd call friends, but we could ride in the same bus together without getting into a war about who sat where." She limped to the barn doors. "All that's changed of course." With her back to Elsa the woman leaned forward so she could see through a knothole in the timber. "Your . . . 'sister' is at the stake. Did you know her well?"

"Enough."

"Then stay on your stool. There's no need to see this."

For whole minutes there was silence in the barn. On her stool Elsa sat with her back hunched and her arms across her stomach as she watched the back of the woman's head. Her silver hair developed a golden halo. Elsa realized that was the light of the fire shining through the knothole. Outside, the crowd had fallen silent . . . only it was more than silence. It was the suspenseful pause of people waiting for a momentous event. And what they tensely bided their time for happened. Voices rose. A wild exclamation of surprise. The sound alone could have been from a crowd when their team unexpectedly scored a point. Elsa knew what was happening. Even though she could see nothing but the horizontal tracks of firelight coming through the narrow gaps in the barn's planking, she had to force herself not to imagine Lorne burning alive. Her lovely blond hair would go first . . .

Elsa couldn't remain silent. "So do you like what you see?" No reply. "Is my sister dead yet?"

The woman stared through the knothole at the "monster" burning in her own dozen cubic yards of hellfire.

"In half an hour they're going to do the same to me. Are you going out there with the rest of that pack of fools to watch? Because when I burn I won't keep quiet. I'll curse them! I'll curse their moribund farms! And I'll curse you!"

For a moment there was no movement in the barn. From outside came sporadic bursts of shouting, even applause. Elsa still refused to imagine what provoked the celebrations.

Then without turning to look back at Elsa the woman spoke. "Fifty years ago I gave birth to Cullum. I had a difficult time. It had just gone two in the morning and the hospital was short staffed. There'd been flu going round. I'd been in labor eight hours and Cullum just wasn't coming. The only specialist neonatal doctor was one of yours. Already by then they weren't allowed to deal direct with human patients; they were restricted to teaching, and that remote treatment they used to have back then. But the short of it was my baby would die inside me. The Saps had given up on me, but one of your kind—those we call monsters now—didn't quit. She delivered Cullum and stayed with him until he was breathing like he should. You saw yourself my only son grew up as strong as anybody else's little lad." In the gloom the lines of firelight seeping through the boards revealed themselves as a brilliant golden latticework.

"So who's to blame?" Elsa asked. "How did our relationship become so poisonous?"

"I don't know, lass." The woman sighed. "What I do know is this. Up that ladder is a hayloft. Behind the bales you'll find a window. Climb out onto the roof. You can work along the cow shed, then drop down behind the wall. That lot won't be able to see you from over yonder. Follow the river upstream. You'll have a better chance in the hills. And don't think of trying to save your sister. Take it from me, she's dead."

There was a pause as Elsa stared in disbelief.

"Run, lass. They'll be back in five minutes."

"You mean you're giving me permission to—"

"Go on with you, girl! Get out of my sight!"

Elsa slowed to a walk. At the side of the nighttime river that gurgled its way through rocks she looked back. Beyond the silhouette of the farm's chimneys, there was a copper glow in the air. The yellow firelight had turned red. A blood red that hemorrhaged into the night sky.

A murmur escaped her lips. "Sister, I'm sorry . . ."

The sound of carousing reached her. The death of an innocent woman had made the farming community glorious. They exulted. A chorus of cheers reached her. *Keep moving*, she told herself. *When they find you've gone they'll come looking for you.* If they caught her now they'd redouble their efforts to inflict humiliation and pain on her. She'd often heard the taunt "Dead meat don't hurt," but what did they know?

As she waded across the river she looked toward the rising belly of a hill. And then for the second time in her life she heard the faint song of the ancient dead. It came as an indistinct nocturne on the night air. . . .

4

I, GOD SCARER

They walked through the nighttime forest. To the child it was a world every bit as rich as the forest by day. Above him, through the branches, he glimpsed a spray of silver lights against darkness.

"Stars," Dr. Paul Marais pointed out.

The world was rich with subtle colors, animal scents, the piping of fluttering leathery creatures that flew something like birds; he heard the scrape-scrape of burrowing creatures in the soil beneath his feet. He was even conscious of the tidal flow of sap through tree trunks. There were times he paused to savor the wonder of it all. Paul, however, prompted him to keep moving through this richly textured nightscape of smell, sound, and sight.

"You're going to be sick of the sound of my bonny Scottish accent," Paul whispered as they walked. "But I'm trying to wake up your mind. We've got to get all the mental connections firing so you remember who you are . . . what you are. You have to learn about the circumstances . . . the shitty circumstances, I might add . . .

that brought us out here to the middle of nowhere. And you have to understand what happened to the world. That and why we don't belong in it anymore." He paused. "No, don't watch the fox cubs; listen to me. Do you remember your name?"

Name? Something moved inside his head. A stir of understanding. "Uh . . . muh . . ."

"Name . . . your . . . nay-murr."

He clenched his fists with the effort. "Ch . . . ch-kurr . . ."

"Go on, my friend, you can do it."

"N-chur . . ." He redoubled the effort. "*Child.*"

"Child?" Paul Marais clicked his tongue. "The ward staff call all the Transients 'Child.' It's endearing and they don't have to remember everyone's name."

"Child!"

"Ssh . . . keep it down. We're not out of the woods yet. Figuratively or otherwise."

"Child."

"OK. Very good. It's a start. But keep moving." Paul glanced back the way they'd come. Hundreds of tree trunks marched away into the darkness. "We've probably lost the hunters back there, but it's open season on us now. There'll be more out with guns. They won't want to miss any of the fun."

"Nnn . . . guns . . ." The child touched his chest. It was still sore.

Paul gave a low whistle. "You took three big ones in the ribs, didn't you?" He shook his head in wonder. "You're a lucky man to be still vertical." His teeth gleamed as he grinned in the gloom. "What I wouldn't give to look under that skin of yours. No wonder the folk in Birthing couldn't stop themselves telling everyone you're the bloody modern miracle."

A breeze moved through the forest. A sizzling sound

rose from the leaves, while the trees appeared to nod their shaggy heads in acknowledgment of the doctor's statement.

"I'm a city boy," he said. "Forests make me itch. There's something uncanny about them. Too much life all in one place. See, I told you you'd get tired of my voice. But I want to see the light of consciousness blazing from those two eyes of yours, my friend. Show me that fucking window of the soul. Do you hear?" He sighed. "You're hearing, but you've still to find the on-switch." He clicked his tongue. "Now I'm babbling . . . OK. We need to find the others." A grunt escaped his lips. "If they haven't been caught."

They walked beneath the trees. The only sounds were ones expressed by the natural world around them. The child couldn't even see any houses, although he did detect the faintest whiff of coal smoke from a distant dwelling. To his right an owl sped from the darkness to snatch a mouse from the grass. Nearby, larger beasts lay grunting in half slumber in the undergrowth. At that moment, there was a sense of peace. And despite the death of the mouse in the owl's beak, a tranquility held sway over the nocturnal forest. A sense of natural order; of primordial rhythms adhering to their proper course. The child felt himself fall into step with this heartbeat of nature. The disturbing images of death and blood in the building just hours ago receded. He was no longer alone. This figure in green clothes strode beside him. The man spoke constantly, yet it was a soothing voice that rarely rose above a whisper.

"You don't remember your name yet? No? You will soon enough. It's written there on your wrist tag. I won't tell you it. You need to remember yourself if you're going to claim it as your very own . . . in here." The man tapped his own temple. "I don't know what happened to you before the transition. *Transition?* What euphemisms we create, eh? You might recall being in hospital. Some patients experience terror, others serene acceptance. Then you went through the transition process . . . and you became what you are now. Years ago they called us Frankenstein monsters. Personally, I prefer the name that some prankster painted on our wall. *God scarer.*" They followed a brook that sang through a jumble of pebbles. "So, what's it like to be a God Scarer? I've been a fully fledged God Scarer for twenty years. I like it. It's got to be better than being dead. Which we are of course. I carry my death certificate in my wallet. On dreary days it cheers me up. Yours'll be back at the Transit Station. Although I'm sure it will have been burnt to the ground by now. Along with most of my colleagues and patients."

"Dead?"

The doctor glanced at the child with a raised eyebrow. "Yes. Dead. Dead as nails. The terrible crime they—*we*— committed was our complete dedication to humanity. Of course, we had the temerity to be like Lazarus. We rose from the dead. You have to admit it doesn't seem at all fair, does it? Did we God Scarers ever hurt anyone?"

The child stopped. "Frankenstein."

"Aye, we're the big, bonny children of Frankenstein." The doctor gave a grim smile. "Yes. Good old bloody up-to-his-elbows-in-cadaver-guts Frankenstein. Victor Frankenstein was fiction, of course, but in essence the process became fact. Science showed us the way to reanimate a corpse. Moreover, it improved on the original." He sighed. "That's right, pal. We're dead men walking. OK . . . Keep up, my little God Scarer. We've got to find somewhere safe. If we don't, we'll wind up dying all over again. Once is enough for me."

* * *

Paul whispered: "It's no good. We can't go any farther. We'll have to find another crossing upstream."

The child watched from the cover of the massive oak. All around him was the living, breathing world of the forest. Stars shone from a sky that was as black as the pupil of an eye. He'd enjoyed this walk with the man. Now they couldn't go on. Even though Paul had, until this point, relentlessly urged him to keep moving quickly. Why couldn't they continue? He saw nothing to prevent them. The child took a step forward.

Paul grabbed hold of his arm. "Not that way. Don't you see the soldiers? There's three of them. Over the far side of the river. They're guarding the bridge." He clicked his tongue. "Aye, they're waiting for us, my friend." He stepped back under the trees. "So, that's not the way for us. It might be a bit of a hike, but there's bound to be a crossing up . . . No. *Listen to me.*" Once more Paul tugged on the child's arm. "Stand still, laddie. You can't cross the bridge. We're God Scarers. They'll spot us in a second. And see those weapons? Submachine guns. They make piles of nicely diced monster flesh."

"Uh . . . uhh . . ."

"Try and understand what I'm telling you. We can't cross the footbridge. They'll kill us if we do. And, no, we can't fight them. Even if they didn't have guns we have vowed—every man jack of us—we've vowed never to use violence against a human being. If they strike us we never retaliate. *Do no harm to humanity. Do not allow harm to befall humanity due to your action or inaction.* That's our law. The God Scarer law."

For a moment the pair stood beneath the sheltering arms of the oak. A light nighttime breeze stirred the leaves so it sounded as if the mighty tree whispered to them; a primeval language of the natural world.

Gently, Paul Marais pulled the child in a direction

away from the footbridge. "That's it, pal. This way. We'll find a way back to our brothers and sisters. Nice and easy does it. Quiet as a mouse, eh? We don't want to attract the soldier men's attention."

The sound of the river sliding across the gravel played on the child's mind like a song. He glanced back to see the bridge spanning the black waters. Built of white timber, the guardrails gleamed like twin rays of light as they ran from this bank to the next. The child turned.

"No, this way, sonny. Remember what I told you? Soldiers? Guns? We don't want to—*hey*." The whisper almost became a shout. "Oh, bollocks. No . . . don't you dare . . ."

The child started to move. Part of him was dimly aware that Paul had tried to hold on to him, but the child effortlessly shrugged free. Now he loped out of the forest toward the footbridge. He needed to cross the river. That's why he was here. Instantly the three soldiers on the far bank saw him. A second later electric light blazed across the water to illuminate him. Shouts reached his ears.

"Do you see it, Corporal? It's from the Transit Station."

The three men ran onto the narrow bridge to block the child's way. Behind him, Paul yelled at him to return to the trees. Although the child couldn't say why, he knew he must cross the bridge at all costs. His feet made a muffled pounding as he ran on soft earth. Ahead of him, three men in their gray uniforms were already on the bridge. Two of them carried objects that emitted a bright yellow light. The other carried a long-barreled weapon. At the halfway point across the river the three stopped. The youngest appeared to waver.

"Don't worry, Robson," called the leader of the group. "God Scarers can't hurt anyone. It's inbuilt. They're not allowed to harm a human being."

The child's feet hit the boards of the bridge with a sound that boomed like thunder. It was enough to make the soldiers flinch.

"Stop! I know what you are. I order you to stop. You must obey me!" The soldier called to the one with the rifle. "When it stops shoot it in the head."

"Yes, Corporal!"

The soldier aimed the rifle as the other two shone their lights in the child's face. At either side of him the white handrails blazed with reflected light. Behind him Paul Marais had stopped running toward the bridge; his body language broadcast his sense of resignation at the imminent destruction of one of his kind.

"I ordered you to stop," bellowed the corporal.

The child ran faster. The timber structure trembled under the force of his pounding feet. The soldier that was nearest, the one with the rifle, lowered it. Pure fear at the sight of this colossus racing toward him froze his limbs.

"Snap out of it, Kruger! It won't hurt you. It's impossible!"

A dawning of understanding. The child saw fear on the man's face. It paralyzed him. He was incapable of using the rifle. Or so it seemed. At the last moment the man raised the weapon.

Paul screamed, *"No! Don't fight them! You're not allowed. You can't— Oh, God!"*

The child saw the soldier's trigger finger whiten as the pressure increased. A split second later the child's fingertips swung to brush the end of the gun muzzle. To him it didn't seem a forceful blow, he only meant to push the rifle aside. Yet the second his fingers struck it the steel barrel bent out of shape. The momentum of his action tore the rifle from the soldier's hands. By now, the man howled in terror and disbelief. Another split second later the child had grabbed hold of the man's tunic, hoisted him the air, and hurled him into the river.

The corporal who'd been last on the bridge threw his flashlight aside in order to swing the submachine gun from his shoulder. He'd have managed to fire a burst, too, only the young soldier panicked. He pushed by his superior with a screaming *"Get out of the way! Let me through!"* Then he fled for the far bank.

The corporal recovered his balance. He dragged the bolt back on the weapon. Another second and the corporal would have emptied the magazine of .45 caliber rounds into his attacker's chest. But there wasn't a second to spare. The child still ran forward. At the same time he swung out his arm. His palm slapped over the man's face, his splayed fingers closed over the scalp. He could feel the bristle of razored hair under his fingertips. He even felt the press of the corporal's two eyes bulging out into the palm of his hand. The child still ran forward. He carried the man like a doll, the legs swinging as the feet parted company with the decking.

Paul's voice carried over the water. "For God's sake! Don't hurt him. He's a human being. You mustn't do anything to cause injury!"

The corporal still carried the submachine gun in one hand. When he fired off a short burst the child closed his hand. The man's skull did nothing to prevent the spasmodic contraction. The child's fingers simply passed through the man's head. Blood squirted between the fingers. That and pulped bone and clear brain fluid. The soldier suddenly hung limply in his hand. The child flung the corpse away over the rail. It fell into the water with a dead-sounding splash.

The way ahead was clear. He loped across the bridge to the pastures at the other side. The third soldier didn't interest him now. The man had fled into the night.

When the child reached the pasture he stood there in lush grass and wildflowers that reached up to his knees. He savored the scented air coupled with the sudden peace of the night. Above him, stars burned with a serenity all of their own.

A little while later Paul Marais joined him. For a moment he was out of breath, and then he spoke: "Are you special, like they say? Or are you a *real* monster? Our kind have never killed a human being before." He took a deep breath. "Now you?" He wiped his hand across his face. "For God's sake. Just tell me what made you kill that man."

The child turned his face upward to bask in falling starlight. At that moment he understood. "I know my name." Deeply he inhaled the scent of dew forming on the grass. "I am Dominion."

5

PREY

"Follow the river upstream. You'll have a better chance in the hills." Elsa heeded the woman's advice. Within moments the village was out of sight. All that betrayed its position was a bloody red glow in the sky where the fire that consumed Elsa's sister blazed.

She only had a vague idea of the terrain in this part of the country. For the last three years her kind had been forbidden to leave the grounds of the Transit Station. So the hills she now approached had only been a series of blue-green mounds on the horizon. Eyes that were sensitive enough to rely on starlight alone revealed the dirt path running alongside the river. As far as she could tell there were no people nearby. The rustling she could hear in the forest came from the animals that lived there, not the footfalls of man. Bats swung out of the night sky. Their ultrasonic piping reached her ears. She could differentiate the notes, and even something of the emotion they conveyed—the gratification of finding plump insects, or the warning that a tall creature roamed close to the water.

From the milky haze on top of the hills came the song of the ancient dead. Elsa had heard it before. It was just days after she woke up after her transition. At first she believed it had been a symptom of making that journey from life to death, then back to life again. But nobody she confided in had experienced anything of the like. The sound had continued for hours until it had very gradually become attenuated and then died completely away. As a child she had loved to ride in her father's boat. On one occasion at anchor she'd gazed down at her reflection in the water. Until that moment she'd only viewed the sea as an ever-shifting horizontal plane. A vast "surface" with nothing beneath it. But that day was uncannily still. The ocean didn't even wrinkle. They could have been drifting on cooking oil. The sunlight must have reached a critical angle because at that moment, as she leaned forward on the gunwale, she looked past her reflection with its wide brown eyes. She realized she was gazing down into the depths of the ocean. And down there was another world. There was an entire topography of hills; there were deep, shadowed canyons through which fish glided. The sense of revelation had been profound. Elsa never saw the ocean in the same way again. It was the same with that faint nocturne she heard now, the soulful voices that sang a melody that she found more haunting and moving than she could say. The voices climbed the musical scale and then gently descended. Just as she'd once viewed only the surface of the sea before that singular day on the boat, her intuition revealed with such breathtaking power that she was only hearing the surface of the song. Elsa sensed there was an entire universe of meaning beneath that melody.

Nobody else had heard the songs of the dead, so as her convalescence progressed she'd stopped mentioning it. By the time she'd left she pretended to herself that she must have imagined it. Only now it was back. This time stronger. As if the song contained a message for her, and her alone. At that moment she decided she had to search for the source of the music. After all, there was nothing to go back to. She'd worked at the Transit Station for three happy years. Now the army had stormed it and killed its occupants. If the building was still standing the authorities would never permit it to reopen. Even before the onslaught local children had been painting *Castle Frankenstein* on its walls with their parents' blessing. She'd been fortunate to escape with a fellow nurse. For an hour or so they'd walked toward the coast in the hope they might find a way of escaping the country. Although it wouldn't be lawful for a member of the public to kill a Transient, not a single police officer would consider arresting a "monster killer." If anything the killer would be feted as a hero.

So the farmers caught Elsa and Lorne. Then took them back home to burn them in the field opposite the barn. If it wasn't for the woman who believed she owed a debt to the monsters for safely delivering her only son, Elsa would be nothing but smoking bones by now.

Elsa moved if she walked in her sleep. The darkness, the dogged rhythm of her stride, the exhaustion, they all contributed to her slipping into a state of only part wakefulness. So when she saw the gray shape drift by in the river it took a while to register what it was. When she did she bounded down the bank onto the shingle bed to look more closely. The gray smudge in the waters wore army fatigues. Her oath had commanded her not to harm humanity, it also commanded her with equal vigor to safeguard it. So, without hesitation, she waded through the water with enough force to create a huge churning wake of foam. Elsa reached out a powerful arm, grasped the jacket collar, then surged back to shore, her feet splashing through the shallows. In the reeds, ducks protested noisily at being disturbed. Seconds later she hauled the figure onto the grass slope, then knelt down to check for signs of life. When she saw the state of the head she knew it would be a waste of time to continue. The skull had been crushed with so much power flaps of bone hung down onto the earth. The face was no longer recognizable as human; merely a ruinous stew of red and black shapes in a chaotic Dali-esque montage. The head wound—and what a damnable head wound—didn't appear to be the result of a gunshot, although her nostrils detected the sharp smell of cordite. The soldier had either fired a gun recently or been very close to someone who had. Nor did the damage suggest a fall. The entire skull had been compressed with such force that the head's contents had squirted out through lesions in the skin. She checked the uniform that bore the twin stripes of the rank of corporal. Civilized morality dictated she should discover his name and telephone the police. Only the price of doing that would undoubtedly be her life. After a tussle with her conscience she pulled the corpse to the path where it would be found. Then after covering the man's ruined face with his own handkerchief she continued walking.

Barely an hour after leaving the cadaver she reached a footbridge. Immediately she noticed that a flashlight lay in its center. It still blazed its beams across the boards. After checking that no one was nearby she ran to the fallen light. Another flashlight lay close by. This one had been crushed. Either it had been deliberately smashed or a heavy individual had unwittingly stepped on it. Certainly it wouldn't have been run over by a vehicle as the bridge was too narrow to allow anything other than people to cross. A brassy gleam caught her eye. She picked up a spent ammunition cartridge. It smelled of cordite smoke, so it had been fired recently. Instantly she pictured the corpse of the soldier. He'd smelled of gun smoke, too. She took another dozen steps. Now there was a spatter of blood on the timber pathway. The way it had coagulated into such a dark, tarry mass suggested it to be human blood. Her nerve endings tingled. So what had happened here? It connected with the mutilated corpse downstream. But her senses suggested her own kind had passed across this bridge recently. She couldn't smell their trail, but it was as if they'd left a trace of their passing in the very timbers. *Yes, I'm guessing that they came here. Yet they'd never kill a human being. It's simply not possible.* However, she'd heard rumors among fellow medical staff who oversaw that Frankenstein procedure for reanimating the dead. In the last few months there were whispers of unusual anomalies occurring in the bodies of Transients. Normally, the dead returned to life like freshly minted coins. Each one with the identical biological characteristics, if not identical appearance. That's why they called each other brother and sister because they belonged to the same postmortem clan. But one old doctor pointed out that "Mother Nature will never be denied her right to make changes to living creatures. Evolution is subversive. In most cases it will sneak those subtle biological changes in through the back door."

As she crossed to the bridge to the other side Elsa stopped to grasp the rail as the revelation struck. Intuition spoke to her so loudly it took her breath away. The death of the soldier? The ability to hear the music of the ancient dead? In some mysterious way they were linked.

We, the God Scarers, are changing. Only we never realized how much. Human being recognized the change. That's why they want to destroy us. They aren't envious. They're frightened.

6

THE STONE SISTERS

Dawn haunted the horizon like a ghost. The whiteness of it manifested itself on top of the hill they now climbed. From a deathly predawn hush the forest slowly awoke. Birds called from the trees. Rabbits emerged from warrens to smell the air. Danger or safety? Their sensitive nostrils appeared to sift those scents from the atmosphere. A deer trotted through the bushes to their left—a splash of gold against dark greens.

Dr. Paul Marais walked hard to keep up with his charge. When Dominion stopped climbing the hill to gaze back at daylight creeping into the valley, he took his chance to hammer the point home again.

"Dominion. Listen to me. I've told you this over and over. You *must not kill*. Do you understand me?"

Dominion said nothing. The light touched grass in the hollows, turning it from black to emerald. Ants emerged from their nest to begin the day's labors.

Paul pressed his argument. "Our people have never killed their people. Never, ever. Do you follow? If a human being decides to destroy us, so be it. We must not fight back. Get the rule through that skull of yours: *Do no harm to humanity. Do not allow harm to befall humanity due to your action or inaction.*"

Dominion watched a pair of blackbirds feeding their young in a nest.

A sigh escaped Paul's lips. "It's important you understand, Dominion. Back there you threw a soldier into the river. You might have caused his death. Worse—far worse—you knowingly and purposefully crushed the second man's skull. You killed him. I—I can't add enough weight to this statement: That is wrong, so profoundly wrong. You *must* not kill." Paul grasped the massive forearm. "Talk to me, Dominion. Do you understand? Hey . . . talk!"

Dominion looked into the face of the man standing there in drab-green surgical scrubs. The man's eyes searched his face as if he needed to see some flicker of understanding.

The words still didn't come easy. "Ah . . ." The word escaped with a sighing whisper. "Soldiers . . . they would hurt Dominion. They would make death."

"Yes, they would 'make death.'" Paul mimicked the slow words pushed with so much effort from Dominion's lips. "That's OK . . . Well, it's not OK, but that's what we spawn of Frankenstein, we God Scarers, are resigned to. Our philosophy is writ in stone. It's etched into our bones. We never kill. If the guys return with flamethrowers we don't fight them." He grimaced. "We let nature take its course. Do you follow?"

Dominion gave a single shake of his head.

"Listen to me, Dominion. If you try to take another life, then I will kill you myself. Got that?"

Another emphatic shake of the head. "You ran."

"I agree. When the shooting started at the Transit Station I ran like a frightened rabbit. That's the instinct for self-preservation. We still have it, Dominion, despite being a bunch of dead men walking." He clicked his tongue as the implications sank in. "In the cold light of you know what?" He indicated the gray dawn. "I figure now that it might have been wisest to simply stand in line like the rest, and let them stick that exploding necklace over my head."

"You belong in life."

"Belong in life? A nice way of putting it. You're right, Dominion. I love this." He nodded at the tree-covered valley where herds of deer drank at the river. "But I won't kill for it."

"Doctor. You are the same as Dominion."

"No, pal. You're wrong. Dead wrong."

"You will fight for life."

"Think again. I'm nothing like you." Paul continued up the hill. "Something went wrong in the Regenerator. You really are a monster." Grim laughter burst from his mouth. "You, Dominion, are a monster's monster. You are Frankenstein's darkest nightmare."

They walked toward the summit. By the time they reached the hilltop the sun had lifted its red, burning eye over the horizon. As its rays touched the trees it released their aromas to the morning air. At this altitude there was a fresher scent of pine. Behind, and below them, the valley bottom had become a jumble of copses, fields, and faraway houses. The river threaded its way to a sea that revealed itself as a misty flatness in the distance. As they approached the summit of the hill with its patches of wind-bent trees and bushes, Paul held his arm out toward Dominion with a palm raised. A command for silence.

"See that circle of standing stones?" Paul whispered. "That's where I left them." His face darkened. "Our bonny little party of survivors." He scanned the nine columns of blue-black stone. "Nine Sisters stone circle," Paul grunted. "Bronze Age people erected these to prove to the world that they were capable of creating something immortal. A monument to their lives that would remain long after they'd melted into the soil. Isn't it an exquisite metaphor, Dominion? Because here we are, three millennia later. We were created by those folks' descendents to be immortal. A monument to the lives of *our* mortal creators." He shook his head. "While you enjoy the irony of it all I'll scout round to see where our band have vanished to. Stay here, please. And for God's sake don't hurt anyone."

Dominion stood on the highest part of the hill. The valley spread beneath him. An early morning mist clung to its hollows. He allowed the sights, scents, sounds, and the feel of the place to flow through him as he remained statuelike, a flesh-and-bone, dead-and-alive colossus dominating the crown of the hill. Even the stones of the standing circle appeared lesser in stature to him. Although he did not examine the stones closely he sensed that they hadn't occurred naturally, and the arrowhead shapes of blue-black rock had been embedded there a long time ago. By now sunlight touched them. Their surfaces glinted, while the shadows they cast drew nine long blades of black across the ground.

The buzz of honeybees nudging among the wildflowers reached his ears. He smelled dew mingled with the musky odors of animals scurrying in the undergrowth nearby. The sunlight falling on his skin warmed it. The gunshot wounds in his chest were barely a tingle now. The brightening of the world from night into day had a symmetry with the dawning of understanding inside him. He knew his name wasn't "child" now. It was Dominion. He remembered the calm of the Transit Station before the soldiers stormed it. And he recalled snatches of what had happened before. There was an immersion in a brilliant blue. Like the heart of a star it shone through him even though his eyes were closed. Its intensity seared him. Whether it hurt him or not, he couldn't be sure. But there had been such a concentration of emotion and physical feeling that he'd been driven to scream himself awake.

He studied his hand. No flaws marked the skin. Each pink nail was smoothly rounded. Didn't he have a scar across his left thumb? A childhood accident when he used his father's modeling knife to make arrows for his bow. He examined his thumb. There was no scar now.

Dominion allowed his hand to return to his side. Paul had asked him to wait there, so that's what he'd do. He allowed his mind to submerge into the world around him. Once more he sensed the currents of the universe flowing through his flesh. When he closed his eyes he fancied he could hear the Aeolian hum of atoms in the Nine Sisters. The atoms vibrated at a distinct pitch to those in the natural earth in which the stones stood. It gave them a slightly different . . . taste? No, not taste. That wasn't the right word. Something *like* taste. A unique signature that made them stand apart from their surrounding environment.

Then the world shifted. Its rhythms altered. He sensed a taste—that word again—another taste . . . a flavor, that told him someone was coming. Rather than concentrating on what lay inside him, and how his instinct related to his surroundings, he allowed his mind to rise to the surface of things again. Dominion opened his eyes a fraction. Through the slits he watched the woman approach.

Slowly, in a way that was nearer to a glide than a walk, she entered the space between the circle of upright stones. There she made her way to the tallest stone that towered over her. Then she listened. Every so often her eyes would close as if to hear some distant music.

At last she emerged from the stone circle. He sensed her watching him for a while before she asked the question: "Do you hear them?"

He continued to look out across the valley as the sun rose. When he didn't answer she approached. He noticed the way she appraised the bullet wounds in his chest, plus the rust-colored stain on his right hand.

"You killed him, didn't you?" She stared in horror. "You murdered the soldier. Look at his blood." She grabbed hold of his hand and raised it to his face.

Dominion remained there like a statue that could be as ancient as those standing stones that had withstood the forces of nature for the last three thousand years.

As she held his hand she grasped the wrist tag. "Dominion?" She looked troubled. "It says here you were at the Transit Station. But you only made transit a few days ago. You shouldn't be able to walk this far yet. Who brought you here?" She shook his wrist as if to snap him out of the trance. "What made you murder the soldier?"

In a blur of movement his fingers splayed out as he gripped her jaw. Then he tilted her face up toward his. "I am Frankenstein."

Even though she couldn't move her head she retorted, "You're not Frankenstein . . . Frankenstein never existed."

"I am God Scarer."

"No."

"I— Monster."

"You're not a monster. You're one of us. And this time next year, there won't be one damn Transient left on this planet." Again she tried to break free. "If you're going to crush my skull—*do it*. Because there's no rule against killing our own kind."

Dominion studied her face for a moment. Her expression puzzled him. "You are hurting?"

"Hurting! You're breaking my damn neck!"

Dominion released her. Once more his arms returned to hang limply at his side as he gazed at the play of sunlight in the valley.

Rubbing her neck, she glared at him. "What are you doing here anyway?" When he didn't answer she said, "Call me insane but I could hear singing. It came from up on the hill. And guess where it's loudest?" She nodded at the stone circle. "Only you don't hear them, do you? That makes me a lunatic. No wonder with the madness of the last three days. I saw people butchered at the Transit Station. I fled with my friend, but the mob got us. If I hadn't escaped I'd be dead, too. They burned Lorne like she was a piece of garbage. But what's the point in telling you? You're still gaga from transition. Hell. You shouldn't even be on your damn feet. Never mind running round the countryside murdering human beings. The world really has gone crazy . . ."

"You're not going to get much sense out of our brother, Dominion, here."

Dominion watched as Paul Marais emerged from the bushes. Seven individuals followed him. They wore tired, hunted expressions.

Paul shook his head. "Dominion. I should be surprised—nay, astonished—that you've managed to conjure up another fellow God Scarer. But a wee birdie tells me that you, old pal, are going to be the fount of one surprise after another."

7

This, Our Monster Law

As the sun rose over the hilltop, there was one of those significant pauses. One that had the potential to be filled with a laugh, a scream, a gunshot. There was only this overwhelming sense that a change would occur with shocking suddenness.

She looked at the group of men and women—of God Scarers—that stood there scared themselves. Behind them, with an eerie note of coincidence, or even destiny, exactly the same number of standing stones that composed the Nine Sisters reared out of the earth. They shared the same circular distribution. Nine figures in a blue-black stone. In turn, alongside them, their strange doppelganger: nine figures that science had brought back from the dead.

The uncanny voices she'd heard since escaping being burned at the stake rose in volume. *There's a purpose to this*, she told herself. *I'm meant to be here and so are these people*. That song she heard inside her head threatened to shake her brain from her skull. She had to do something. She sensed that the ancient standing stones—maybe even the very universe would explode if she didn't.

"I'm Elsa." The words felt as if they blurted crazily from her. The faces that regarded her suggested they didn't hear the tidal wave of voices that reached into her soul to shake her heart. "I was at the Transit Station."

"So were we." The moment the man in green surgical scrubs spoke the singing stopped with a suddenness that felt like a drag of claws across her nerve endings. If she flinched he didn't notice: "I'm sure I've seen you before in the coffee bar. My name is Dr. Paul Marais." He spoke with gentle Scottish accents that were easy on the ear.

Elsa strode forward with her hand extended. *This is screamingly insane and normal all at the same time,* she told herself. *Here we are, survivors from a massacre: We're acting as if it's a staff meeting.*

She shook hands. "Dr. Marais."

"In the circumstances, call me Paul." He gave a tired smile. "This isn't a place for titles. Good to see you're in one piece, Elsa." He nodded. "You've already met the big guy. He's—"

"Dominion. Yes. I read the wrist tag."

A red-haired woman in a nurse's uniform looked taken aback. "Dominion? Why was he allowed to choose a name like that? It'd never be allowed on the register."

Paul sighed. "I know. Humanity would see Dominion as controversial. Whatever interpretation you put on it, it hints at domination. Language these days is elastic anyway. They call us Transients, to denote we're the product of a Transit Station. Of course, Transient means short-lived. Ephemeral. Now we have Dominion here. And as for me I can't help but think about that Dylan Thomas poem: 'And Death Shall Have No Dominion.' Anyone here believe in destiny?" Paul gave a bitter laugh. "Dominion is going to be full of surprises. And it isn't just going to be his rule-breaking name. Isn't that so, Dominion?"

Elsa saw that Dominion didn't move. He continued to gaze down into the valley as if he saw things there that no one else could.

Maybe I hear things these people can't, she told herself.

Paul cleared his throat, perhaps noticing she appeared distracted. "Elsa. Allow me to introduce you to our party."

"Party?" This was the redheaded nurse again. "We're all that's left out of more than two hundred people at the Transit Station. You saw what happened to the Newborns. They wrapped explosive round their necks and blew their fucking heads off." Her voice had risen to the point that when she stopped speaking the silence seemed unnaturally intense. Even the birds stopped singing.

Elsa saw Dominion had not moved. He stood a good head taller than anyone else in the party. His new growth of hair showed as a blond furze on his gold-brown scalp. He wore the sweatshirt and sweatpants that served as pajamas for the "Newborn," the newly reanimated dead as they convalesced at the Transit Station. His almond-shaped eyes were deep fathomless black rather than brown. Her gaze was drawn back to the bullet holes in his chest that showed as pink wounds through the punctured fabric of the sweatshirt.

Elsa was first to break the silence again. "So what's Dominion's story? By rights, he shouldn't be walking round the countryside so soon after transition."

"Because Dominion here woke up in the Regenerator. As far as I know that's a first."

The group shot startled glances at Dominion. "So this is the guy?" said one. "Everyone's been talking about him."

"The one and only. Our new pal Dominion. Monster

or miracle? You decide." Paul held up his hands. "No doubt Dominion here's going to be the topic of our conversations for a wee while to come. But in the meantime we should finish the introductions. Elsa, this is Beech."

The redheaded nurse nodded at Elsa.

Then Paul introduced the others in quick succession. Most were from the medical team with the exception of three Transients who'd passed all their individuation tests, and were due for repatriation. Paul finished by adding, "What we need to do now is find some cover. We stick out like the proverbial sore thumb. And once I've taken care of Dominion's injuries we've got a decision to make."

"And that is?" Elsa asked.

"We've got to decide whether we want to survive . . . or simply give up and die."

The shock? The trauma? The post-massacre malaise? Maybe the arrival of Dominion was the catalyst for change. Elsa watched as the group went from mute fear to nothing less than a pyrotechnic display of arguments and accusations.

"You said we'd be safe once we got clear of the Transit Station."

Paul held up his hands. "I never said that. *Safer* was the word I used. There—"

"What we have to do is find a phone. Then we call the police, tell them we're turning ourselves in. They won't harm us."

"Want to bet?"

"And what are we going to eat out here," the redhead demanded, "roots and beetles?"

A thin man with mournful eyes shook his head. "There is no escape. We know humanity wants us dead. We should surrender ourselves to that fact."

"You mean just give up?"

"There's nowhere else to go. There are no hiding places."

Elsa detached herself from the group to join Dominion. He stood impassively gazing into the valley where deer drank at a stream.

"Dominion," she began, "do you just see animals down there, or do you see something else?"

He said nothing. His black irises followed the movements of a fawn dipping its muzzle into the water.

"You know something?" she continued. "What brought me up here was the sound of singing. I followed the sound from way down there . . . down where my friend was burned alive . . . you can still see the smoke from the fire. When I heard the music I figured there was nothing else to do but to find where it was coming from." A breeze stirred the grass. "Want to know something else? For some reason, when I hear the singing I'm convinced it's the voices of people who died thousands of years ago. What do you make of that, Dominion?"

Again no reply, or even a hint that he'd heard what she said.

Despite his silence she found she couldn't stop the flow of speech. "So I hear songs from dead mouths. What does it mean? I can't say. All I do know is that when I walked toward the source of the music it brought me here. To these standing stones. And to you." By now a huge stag had joined the herd of deer. It raised its head to call out down the valley. "Do you think our arrival made them argue." Elsa nodded back at the group of survivors who yelled at each other. Paul was trying to placate the angry men and women. "They don't know whether to try and find somewhere safe, or to hand themselves in. Of course, if they do, they'll be tied to a stake and burned alive. No one wants our kind now. They're hell-bent on making all God Scarers extinct."

Members of the group spilled away. "Elsa, you remember me. I'm Xaiyad. We used to live on the same floor at the Transit Station. Will you explain to this idiot"—he indicated one of the physios who glared at him with his arms tightly folded—"that the locals don't find us physically repulsive. It's because the rest of the world imposed economic sanctions on this country, and for the last twenty years run its industries into the ground—that's what's turned the Sapheads against us."

"Sapheads?" Elsa echoed. "Didn't we decide years ago that to call Homo sapiens Sapheads was insulting?"

"Call them anything you like these days," Xaiyad retorted bitterly. "When they get their hands on us they'll still rip us apart whether we're polite to them or not."

"That's just the point," continued the second man. "You just steamroll through—"

Paul appeared. "Show us some mercy, guys. I need to treat Dominion's wounds. Then we should get out of here."

Someone snarled, "Leave it here."

"It?"

"You said yourself it killed a soldier. Something went wrong during transition." The man tapped his temple. "Wrong here. This thing will be a liability."

"Thing?" Elsa turned on the man. "This *thing* is the same as us. In humanity's eyes he's a monster. Just like you and me!"

Paul approached Dominion. "OK, my wee pal. I'm going to take a look at those wounds. Are you all right with that? You're not going to pull my head off for my troubles, are you?"

Elsa turned away from the bickering men. "Paul. I'll help."

"Thanks. But stay clear of the big guy's arms. To look at his impression of a statue now you wouldn't believe it but when the spirit moves him he's bloody fast."

"I can handle it."

"And those not so wee fists of his are like sledgehammers. I can vouch for it."

As Paul gently examined the seemingly immovable Dominion she asked, "What made him kill the soldier?"

"Self-preservation."

"We're not allowed to harm a human, even to save our own lives."

"I know that. Dominion here is a law unto himself."

"How bad is it?"

Paul whistled. "I'd like to peel back that skin and take a look at what wonders lie within. I know our bonny clan is hard to kill, but these three bullets have only penetrated the skin and subcutaneous layer. They're not lodged in the chest muscle."

"So Dominion is different from us?"

"You mean an evolved version of us? You've been listening to the same gossip as I have." Paul shrugged. "Search me. From the look of these slugs I'd say they were handgun fare, from either a pistol or a submachine gun. They might be low velocity compared with a rifle, but even so . . ." He whistled. "I'm having no luck shifting them." He wiped his forehead. "Here I am, on a hilltop trying to squeeze bullets from flesh like they're nothing more than metallic blackheads. But no go."

"Can you leave them in there?"

"I could. My guess is that a guy like Dominion won't fall prey to infection any time soon. But I wouldn't want to risk it."

"What do you need?"

"To remove bullets? A scalpel would be useful. The surrounding tissue has begun to close over them." He grunted. "Although where we find a scalpel up here is anyone's guess." He glanced up at Dominion. "At least our patient is placid. For now."

"I'll take a look round," Elsa said.

"Ah, you must have been a Girl Scout in a previous life."

"Something like that," she replied as she walked away.

If anything, she volunteered to search for a tool that would remove the bullets from Dominion's chest because she wanted to escape that quarrelsome bunch on the hilltop. By now they were debating that their very act of escape from the Transit Station massacre might be construed as an act of violence toward humanity.

As she moved through the bushes she spoke the familiar mantra aloud to herself: "Do no harm to humanity. Do not allow harm to befall humanity due to our action or inaction. This is our monster law." *Maybe we're all entering the valley of personal madness*, she told herself. *Our ethical arguments become a flight from reality.* Right now, however, Elsa wanted to concern herself with solving practical problems. She needed to find some implement to allow Paul to remove the bullets. What they did then to save their skins was another matter.

Elsa scanned the ground for a sharp enough object. A piece of broken glass maybe. Or even a sharp enough twig. The branches on the bushes were green and pliant. They wouldn't be any use. And she could see no glass. The area consisted of grasses, wildflowers, and bushes mixed with prickly yellow gorse. The only man-made objects were the standing stones of the Nine Sisters. If this had been a popular place for humankind three thousand years ago, they shunned it now. She didn't see so much as a cigarette butt. Elsa tilted her head to one side. Even though she concentrated on the sounds around her—the birdsong, the buzz of insects—she couldn't hear the song of the dead. It had fallen silent again. A mental aberration, she told herself. *Your friend died on a pile of burning logs last night. Any wonder you're hearing things?*

She paused. A different sound reached her ears now. The faint musical notes of water trickling over stones. In a few steps she'd found its source. Surrounded by lush ferns, a spring poured water out of a cleft in the rocks. Elsa crouched beside it. First, she cupped her hand to contain some of its crystal waters; then she tasted it. Sweet and cold, as if it had passed through a subterranean ice field. A lovely taste. She devoured more. Then, after wiping her lips on her fingertips, she looked down into the small pool that had received the trickle of spring water. This might well be the source of fresh water for the ancient people who'd erected the circle. She could picture muscular figures quenching their thirst after laboring over the blue-black stones three thousand years ago. After hours of hauling rock this spring must have seemed like a slice of heaven. They'd have relished the flow of ice-cold liquid down their throats. She imagined the Bronze Age men and women gathered round here at the end of their working day to talk, enjoy the spring water, and take pleasure in the sight of the sun slipping down toward the horizon. After resting for a while they'd gather their belongings and head back to their village for a meal, then to sleep.

Elsa leaned forward over the pool that was no larger than a tabletop. For a second she studied her reflection. Her widely spaced eyes were calm after the madness of the last seventy-two hours. Her long hair spilled forward, tips touching the surface of the water. When she looked through the surface membrane of the pond her eyes focused on the stones at the bottom. She dipped her hand into it and dug down into the stones. A moment later she brought out a handful. It occurred to her there might be a shard of glass that Paul could use as a blade to prise the bullets from Dominion's flesh. All she could see, however, were pebbles as water trickled through her fingers. The pebbles were a dull red, but there were splinters of flint in there that showed as silvery flakes. She repeated the action, allowing her fingers to act as a sieve. At the third attempt she looked at what lay there in her hand and said to herself, "This will do."

A few minute later she passed what she'd found to Paul.

He looked at her in surprise. "Elsa? Is this what I think it is?"

"A lucky find."

"I'll say." Paul held up the flake of glittering stone to examine it. "A flint arrowhead. It's the first time I've ever held one. Look at the workmanship. They knew what they were doing three thousand years ago, didn't they?" He smiled. "Knapped to perfection."

"I don't know how sharp it will be."

"If it was used to tip an arrow it should be . . . uh . . . trust me, it's sharp. Very sharp." Paul had pressed the ball of his thumb onto the arrowhead's point. He showed her a nick in his skin that oozed blood. "What would our bowman from prehistory say if he knew that their flint arrowhead would be employed to operate on not only a man—but a man brought back from the dead?" He chuckled. "Please forgive my melodramatic moment, Elsa. But extracting bullets from one of Frankenstein's progeny on a hilltop sort of excuses me, doesn't it?"

Elsa smiled. "You're forgiven."

"Now if you could lift up his sweatshirt to expose the chest? Then I'll begin. . . ."

Dominion didn't so much as murmur as Paul held the sliver of ultrasharp flint between his thumb and forefinger. Expertly he sliced four radiating lines in the skin.

That done, he forced his fingers against the now star-shaped wound. A glittering slug of metal slid outward until it bulged proud of Dominion's flesh. Paul pinched the firearm round between finger and thumb and pulled it clear. That done, he tossed it into the grass.

"Number one." Paul cut more radiating lines away from the second gunshot wound. A trickle of blood ran down Dominion's gold-brown chest.

For the first time since this bizarre operation began Dominion grunted. Elsa saw it wasn't the pain. The towering man had looked down into the valley and seen something.

Dominion spoke a single word. "Man."

Elsa followed his gaze. "Paul. There's a couple of men on horseback. They're following the same path we used last night."

Paul checked for himself. "A scouting party. Do you see rifles?"

Elsa nodded.

"Me too." As he skillfully worked with the stone blade he called across to the group of men and woman who still earnestly debated their fate, "There's a scouting party headed this way on horseback. I estimate it will take me around ninety seconds to finish up here with Dominion. Once I've done I intend to flee. Because I've been given a second chance at life on this planet, I don't intend to throw it away. Whether you surrender yourselves to those guys or come with me is up to you." The doctor glanced back before returning to work on the bloody holes in Dominion's chest. "It's time you people made your minds up."

8

HIS DEATH

Dominion walked down the other side of the hill. Here there was low yellow scrub. Very little in the way of trees. Mostly stunted oaks with gnarled limbs. At times he knew he walked with his kind. At other times he was no longer aware of their presence. The men and women had no more, nor no less, a significance than the grass he strode through.

At one point a woman with copper-colored hair touched his arm. "Does it hurt?" When he didn't answer she said, "Your chest, Dominion, does it hurt?"

"Don't waste your time." These words came from a long, thin man with deep-set eyes. "He's not made all the neurological connections yet. If he ever will."

"He will," the red-haired woman countered. "And probably faster than you and me if he woke up in the Regenerator."

"Have you seen? He's still got human blood on his hand. The transition was an aberration. He should have been destroyed."

"You're beginning to sound like the Sapheads. Why should we be destroying our own when humanity is doing their level best to hound us to extinction?"

"We've only ourselves to blame. We were too superior for our own good."

"In six months' time that's going to be academic because there won't be a single God Scarer left on the planet."

Dominion paused. "God Scarer?" He grunted as understanding began to flow. "I scare God?"

"Sure you do, buddy. We all do."

The red-haired woman urged him on. "Keep walking, Dominion. We've got to find somewhere safe."

Dominion looked back the way they'd come. The pathway made by wild animals snaked back up the hill toward the Nine Sisters stone circle. "Men on horses. They hurt us?"

A thickset man chipped in, "Don't hold your breath for gifts of chocolates." He sounded grim. "Didn't you know it's hunting season for the likes of us now? No, I don't suppose you did. You still haven't fully clicked into the socket."

The redhead scowled. "Leave him alone, West."

But the man called West continued in something close to a bitter rant. "They say 'ignorance is bliss, but preindividuation is Nirvana.' Isn't that so, Dominion, old buddy?"

The man slapped Dominion on the back. As he drew his palm away Dominion's shot his hand back to grip his wrist.

"OK, you big cheese. I was just being playful. Savvy?" West's eyes narrowed. "You can let go now. Hey! You don't know your own strength."

"Serves you right." The woman spoke with satisfaction.

"Dawn, make him let go of me. He ripping my arm out."

Dominion saw the pain brighten the man's eyes. "I can hurt you?"

"Yes, yes! You can hurt me! Satisfied?"

Dominion released the man's arm. West rubbed his wrist while shooting pained glances at him. "You want to watch that temper of yours. We God Scarers have a reputation for a mild temperament. . . ." West noticed the rest of the group had stopped moving.

As Paul hurried along the path to catch them up the redhead asked, "What's wrong?"

"Lerner's gone back to the stone circle."

"What?"

"He's convinced he can negotiate our surrender with the horsemen."

Dominion sensed an intense emotional shock running through them.

West shook his head. "There's no way we can wait for him?"

"No. The horsemen are likely to catch us if we do. You've got to keep moving."

"Well, what are we waiting for?"

"*You* keep moving. Beech, will you take care of Dominion?"

"Sure, but you can't seriously expect to go back for Lerner?"

"If there's time I might be able to convince him to come back with us before the men reach him."

There wasn't time. Elsa had joined Paul for the run back to the standing stones. Just a hundred paces away from them they crept into the bushes as the two horsemen reached the hilltop. Lerner held his arms apart to show he didn't mean harm. Even with their sharp ears Elsa couldn't hear what passed between Lerner and the two men. All she was certain of was that they spoke a few words to each other. Lerner had a broad open face that was as benevolent as that of a saint depicted in the old stained glass windows found in churches. His wispy hair blew in the light breeze.

Both men carried rifles. One drew back the bolt and fired into Lerner's chest from a range of a dozen paces. He took a step backward. One knee buckled but then he recovered his balance. Lerner still spoke to the men in what appeared to be a calm way to persuade them to hear him out. The other horseman fired into Lerner's mouth. The gentle giant of a man turned slightly. Elsa saw blood streaming from his mouth down the white shirt. Instinctively she rose to her feet to help the wounded man.

Paul grabbed her. "No," he hissed. "Don't let them know you're here."

"But you've seen what they've done to him?"

"What can we do to help? You know we can't fight them. If we try and take Lerner away they'll turn the guns on us."

The men fired in quick succession now. Chest, stomach, thighs, arms, shoulders, face. The high-velocity rounds smashed into Lerner's body. The impact made him flinch. One round found its way through the man's torso to erupt from the other side and splash into the dry earth with a puff of dust. Slowly, Lerner sank to one knee. He supported his weight on one hand while he held the other arm above his head. A signal that he meant no harm, and wanted to talk.

Paul closed his eyes as he whispered, "We're hard to kill; we're not indestructible."

Elsa shook with disgust and anger at the scene of bloody murder in front of her. The stones of the Nine Sisters formed a mute audience for the spectacle. How many times had they witnessed violent death in their three thousand years?

Now, if they had eyes to see, they would witness the men dismount from the horses, then advance on Lerner to beat him with the butts of their rifles. When that failed to finish him, even though his head was bleeding from a dozen cuts, one of them drew a hunter's knife from his boot and labored to cut Lerner's throat. Still, the giant of a man held up one arm. It was his only act of defiance. He could have brushed the men away like ants, but she knew he wouldn't break the monster law. *Do no harm to humanity.* He didn't even attempt to run away. Nor did he push away the knife that sawed at his throat. More blood gushed down the front of his shirt. Eventually, however, the horseman gave up. His arm must have been aching and he was clearly breathless. The cartilage protecting Lerner's trachea was far too tough for a mere knife. By this time the other hunter had reloaded his rifle. At point-blank range he fired into the back of Lerner's head. One of the rounds even ricocheted away as a red spark.

"Dear God." Paul bowed his head in a mixture of disbelief and pure grief.

Elsa gulped. "Maybe they'll give up and leave him?"

Paul shook his head.

Meanwhile, Lerner forced himself to stay sitting upright. His head had sagged forward until the chin touched his chest. Even so, he still held one arm up. Whether it was a plea for them to stop or a gesture of defiance she couldn't tell.

The next half hour unfolded in a dreamlike way. The men tethered the horses near the stones, and then they diligently collected dry branches. They even came within twenty paces of Elsa and Paul's hiding place, but the men were too focused on their task to search for any more of Lerner's kind. By turns, Elsa wanted nothing more than to creep away from the despicable scene unfolding in front of her. Yet there was a chance the men would move on after all and leave their victim wounded but alive. And then, in a dark burst of passion that shamed her, she longed to hear Dominion's feet to come pounding along the pathway. Guilty, but ecstatic, she saw in her mind's eye how the giant figure would smite Lerner's attackers. The sheer lust to witness these two men suffer appalled her. *Vengeance is impossible. We must accept whatever humanity chose to exact.* Whatever she longed for amounted to nothing. When the two men had piled dry branches around the kneeling figure of Lerner with his massive arm still raised they lit the fire. She and Paul watched. What else could they do? Perhaps they owed it to him to witness the dignity of his death so they could tell the others.

The fire was a pyramid of chrome lights. Sticks popped in the fire. Smoke drew a filthy black smear across the blue sky. It was only as the flames themselves began to die down that Lerner's arm sagged, then slowly sank down into the heart of the fire.

9

ATTACK OF THE FEARLESS CORPSE KILLERS

"If we don't keep moving the same will happen to us as happened to Lerner."

"What's the point?"

"Do you all want to be burned alive?"

"Whatever we do, wherever we go, they'll catch us in the end."

It had taken two hours to catch up with the group after she and Dr. Paul Marais had watched the horsemen build a fire around Lerner. The image of the man's arm raised above the flames had seared itself into her memory. Once the rest of the group heard the circumstances of Lerner's brutal slaying they'd stopped walking. Their pessimistic spirit held them captive as much as any prison.

With the loss of Lerner they were down to eight. Dominion stood beneath an oak tree. He gazed up into the branches. Perhaps he saw things the others did not. Just as Elsa had heard the mysterious song of the dead. He stood there, immobile. He shared the stillness and the strength of the oak tree that soared into the sky a hundred feet above him. She found her eyes traveling over the musculature of his body. The transition process from death to life often resulted in flaccid muscle. The Newborns tended to be weak for the first month of their new lives, but Dominion's balance was as perfect as the aura of physical strength. Elsa watched his dark eyes searching the branches. A shaft of light pierced the leaves to glint on the blond hair that bristled from his dark scalp. He, alone, appeared unperturbed by their circumstances. Now, here a bunch of frightened God Scarers, fleeing from their would-be executioners, were preparing to surrender themselves to their fates.

A defeated expression haunted West's face. "We could work our way to the coast."

"Why?"

"If we turn ourselves in to the authorities in one of the bigger cities, at least they'll deal with us in a civilized way."

Paul was scornful. "Want to bet?"

Another added, "The Saps blame us for the collapse of their economy."

"What do you suggest? Emigrate to fucking Mars?"

"We could find a boat."

"And then what? If you can sail the thing, where do we go?"

This seemed to be become the eternal topic of conversation. Elsa listened to the same replay of arguments. The group had split down the middle into two factions. Those that wanted to flee into the hills, or some hoped-for place of safety across the sea. The others talked about surrendering to the police. But their idea of what happened to them then was nebulous beyond belief. Somehow they clung to the faith that humanity wouldn't harm them. Paul remained steadfast. He insisted they shouldn't throw themselves at the mercy of human beings. Elsa, for one, relished her second chance at life.

Paul insisted, "We can keep clear of the patrols. If we just keep walking."

Saiban, this was the thin man with mournful eyes, shrugged, helpless. "Where do we find clothes to protect us from inclement weather?"

"We can find clothes," Paul countered.

"And food?"

"There's got to be something we can eat."

The redhead, Beech, joined the argument. "I'm all for getting off this stretch of dirt, but no Saps are going to sell us food."

"Beech, we shouldn't use the derogatory term Sap." Saiban was troubled. "They are Homo sapiens. Human beings. They—"

"It's not blasphemy to call them Saps. You might think humans are superior to us, but let me tell you, Saiban, they don't sit on clouds dealing out thunderbolts to any of us God Scarers who bad-mouth them."

Saiban's gesture spoke louder than words: *What's the point in talking?*

Paul checked his watch. "It's noon. We can still make another twenty miles before sunset."

"Yes," Beech said. "But which direction? Do any of us really know this area?"

One of the nurses added, "And what if the weather breaks? We need shelter."

Once more Elsa found herself surveying this group of individuals. They were all tall. Normally they could be described as handsome; an artist would call the woman Junoesque; on the whole they stood taller than a human male. Now they were tired, their faces haggard, while the skin around the eyes was puffy. Only Dominion appeared impervious, even with the bullet wounds in his chest. The movement of the branches held his attention. As the arguments rumbled along their course she heard the breeze sighing down the gully. Water tumbled over the rocks in the stream. Birds circled high overhead. At that moment it seemed to Elsa this would be her life from now on. She'd spend her days with this bunch of men and women from the Transit Station as they trudged the land in a perpetual search for somewhere to live. Not that any place would be safe. Not in this country anyway.

Just listen to them, she told herself. *They're ready to debate until hell turns to glacial.*

Saiban had returned to his old stance of negotiation with humankind. "Surely, we'll be able to talk to them."

"Lerner tried. They won't listen." Paul appeared worn down by the arguments now. How long until he simply struck off on his own cross-country?

"That's because we haven't spoken to anyone in authority."

"You really think they're going to let us live?"

"If we can find a phone. We don't have to—"

"They'll trace the call."

Elsa chipped in. "There are abandoned boats on the coast. Ever since the shipping companies collapsed they're—"

"So we hop on board and hoist the anchor?"

Elsa found her anger rising as she met Saiban's perpetually mournful gaze. "We can try."

Paul broke in, *"Dear God in heaven, we've got to try."*

"It's that or we'll wind up dead," Elsa said.

Saiban came as close as he could to a smile. "Yes, dead again. You'd think we'd be used to it by now."

This fatalism stirred up Beech. Her red hair flashed in

the sun as she verbally lashed out. "How are we going to survive with that kind of pessimism, Saiban? Why don't you go throw yourself on the mercy of—"

That's as far as she got haranguing Saiban. Dominion lashed out, seized her by the long red tresses, and dragged under the trees.

Beech cried out in shock. "What are you doing? Leave me alone."

West gulped. "My God, he's going to kill her."

Paul called out to the others, "Stop him . . . all pile on him. He'll be too strong for us to tackle him one on one."

They'd barely taken a dozen steps when a cracking thud split the afternoon air. Elsa spun round. The open space between the trees where Beech had stood remonstrating with Saiban suddenly blossomed with fire. Particles that sounded like hail rattled through the branches.

"They've found us," Saiban cried.

"Grenades," Elsa shouted. "Get right under the trees. Where they're thickest."

And that's where they found Dominion. Above them, a hundred feet of dense branches—layer after layer of woody limbs reached the top of the gully. By this time Dominion had released Beech. Strands of copper hair still clung to his fingers.

"Christ, you fucking monster, you nearly ripped my head off." She pressed her palm to her head as her face creased with pain. "Never do that again. I swear I'll—"

"Beech. Shh." Paul put his finger to his lips.

"Dominion just saved your life," Elsa added. "Didn't you hear it?"

"Hear what? All I heard was my own damn hair ripping from my scalp."

Paul shushed her again, then pointed upward. "Saps," he whispered. He glanced round. The rest of the beleaguered party were there.

A human voice floated through the canopy of green. "See them?"

"They ran into the trees."

"You going to try another?"

There was laughter. "Just you try and stop me."

A pitter-patter sound followed. The noise of a heavy object falling through leaves. Elsa with the rest of the group found themselves staring up into the branches. They knew what would happen in the next five seconds.

Elsa found herself counting. One, two . . . In that steel shell that would be no larger than an apple an internal fuse would be burning toward explosive. Three, four . . .

Whummp!

Layers of thousands of leaves muffled the explosion. Even so, everyone flinched. A moment later mangled twigs, bark, and pulpy gobs of mashed leaves dropped down onto them. Elsa glanced round to make sure everyone was all right. Dominion stood there, like a statue, simply staring upward. He sensed the men standing on the cliff top almost directly above them. It was from there that they tossed grenades down into the gorge.

Paul whispered, "Everyone okay?" There were terse nods. Even so, West had a flesh wound to his head where a piece of shrapnel had found its way through the foliage to puncture his scalp.

Again Paul murmured to reassure them, "They can't see us now. Keep still, and . . ." He held his finger to his lips for silence.

A whispered voice reached them. "You know, they looked as if they were going farther up the gorge."

The next time an explosion reverberated against the walls of the chasm it was far enough away for none of the shrapnel to reach them. A couple of minutes later another grenade detonated, but clearly it was a good hundred paces away.

"They're moving away," Paul whispered. "They don't know where we are."

"For now." Saiban was grim. "But they'll come back. And if it isn't them it will be other men." The melancholy in his eyes deepened. "They'll never give up."

For ten minutes they sat in silence as the thunder of bursting grenades receded into the distance.

At last Paul grunted, "OK. Let's go."

Beech shrugged. "Where?"

Paul didn't reply. He merely trudged along the stream downhill. Elsa fell into step behind him. The others did the same. Their pace was mechanical. Dark clouds slid over the sky. It felt as if the jaws of a giant trap were slowly—yet implacably—closing in on the them.

10

TIMES OF THUNDER

Elsa stared in disbelief. At that moment the urge to laugh and to cry rose in equal measure inside her. They had followed the deep gully downhill after the grenade attack. No one had been seriously hurt. A few grenade fragments had found their mark, resulting in minor injuries. West suffered a scalp wound that trickled blood into his left eye until it was ringed a deep crimson. From that eye came the never-ending trickle of a red tear, as if for all the world her fellow God Scarer wept blood.

As they'd followed the gully, between two high rock faces that transformed what had been open countryside into a jail, that's when even the natural world turned against them. A dark slab of cloud filled the sky. Although it threatened rain, no raindrops fell. Even so, it began to thunder. An ominous grumbling that continued without pause across the mountains. With that dry thunder came gusts of wind that blew grit into their eyes, making it difficult to see. Then came the torture of the descent. The oaks, elms, and birch gave way to thornbushes that dragged bloody furrows in their bare hands and faces as they forced a pathway through.

West, with his blood-filled eye from the grenade splinter, tugged a thorn from the side of his fist. "See what happens to monsters when they defy God?" A bead of scarlet crowned on his hand.

No one commented.

We poor bastards, Elsa told herself. *We poor, miserable, God-shunned wretches. We're traumatized from the attack last night. We haven't slept in twenty-four hours. We haven't eaten. All we've had to drink is stream water. Lorne was burned at the stake. We've been hunted by men with bombs. Now this . . .* Elsa plodded alongside the stream. Constantly, they had to push aside the mass of branches that bristled with flesh-ripping thorns. The trees resembled sea urchins rather than vegetation. Black spines punctured fingers, hands, faces. Briars dragged at their shins, stinging nettles prickled any bare skin they touched. When Elsa checked her reflection in the stream as she took a sip of water she noticed blood oozed from her earlobe where a thorn had spiked the fleshy part of her ear.

When they had respite from the thorns they were forced to climb over moss-covered boulders. Now this miserable bunch of survivors, refugees, call them what you will, repeatedly lost their footing. Each fall produced a crop of skinned elbows, bruised limbs with a whole panoply of grazes, wrenched muscles, and painful jolts.

After the torture of the gully they found themselves halfway down a hillside. Immediately they recognized the valley in front of them with a river that wound its way down to a town that stood on the coast. Her eyes absorbed distant rooftops. On a cliff above the ocean stood the box shape of an ancient castle. She, along with the rest of the group, turned to look upward. Perhaps a hundred feet above their heads was the plateau where the stone circle stood: the Nine Sisters Bronze Age monument where they'd met just hours ago. A dozen paces from that would be a mound of ash that shrouded the burnt body of Lerner.

Paul's eyes bled pure defeat. "I'm not going to state the obvious."

"I will." Saiban's voice deteriorated to a rasp. "After walking for hours we've come full circle. We're back where we started."

Beech sighed. "We know that. Do you have to . . ." Even the redhead was too exhausted to argue. She sat down on the hillside to stare out over the valley. It had become gloomy now. A shadow-filled rift in the earth. Dry thunder clumped away in the distance as if monstrous feet stamped in anger.

West blinked a blood-rimmed eye. "Thunder speaks. You know what it's saying?" His face was grim. "We belong dead." His laugh came as a bark. "We belong dead. Don't you love a timely film reference?"

When his shoulders began to shake she thought he would burst out into manic giggles, but he put his head down. He stood like that for a long while, one hand covering his mouth. No one stared at him, but they couldn't avoid the wretchedness of his grief. It was a strange, dry weeping. A barren, painful dryness that seemed to find its counterpart in that dry thunder that beat through the air. And even though the sky grew darker it didn't rain. Not one drop.

So we've come to this. Forty-eight hours ago she had led a busy, fulfilled life at the Transit Station. She took care of her charges—the men and women who'd been given the chance of a second life after their old one either petered out in a hospital bed or was snatched from them by any of the million or so day-to-day accidents that can rob an individual of life.

Elsa clenched her fists as thunder raged at them. "I swam too far from the shore . . . I didn't know how there was a riptide."

West still sobbed into his hand. Thunder crashed against their heads.

"I was swimming with my husband." Elsa couldn't stop the words. "We tried to stay together. My body was the only one the coast guard recovered. Richard must have stayed with me as long as he could . . . the riptide was like white water. You couldn't . . ." Her voice dried. "Too strong. That's all."

"Elsa." Paul placed his hand to her shoulder; a gesture of affection.

West lifted his head. "I know we're not supposed to talk about our past lives, or . . . or how we died . . . to hell with it. Why should we trap ourselves in all these rules? *We can't do this . . . we can't do that . . . always defer to humanity . . . never answer humanity back . . . always step aside. . . . always yield; they have right of way . . .* it's a fucking cage. You know what?" His voice became raw as grief turned to anger. "I overdosed on aspirin. Do you know what a fucking mess that is? You don't fall asleep and *oh so* gracefully slip away. You wake up after they pump your stomach. You're wide awake. At first you feel OK. Only the damage has been done. Blood vessels rupture and you bleed from every orifice—eyes—" He stabbed his finger at the blood streaming from the head wound into his eye. "Yes, just like this. And everywhere else, too. Ears. Nose. Mouth. Navel—and yes . . . Yes! Every hole south of the equator, as well!" He raised his face to the sky as he gave a grim laugh. "I'm a suicide. A successful one at that. Suicides are rejected from the transition program. My mother bribed the doctor to report it as an accidental overdose, so I got the Lazarus treatment. Mother wasn't going to allow me to escape her as easily as that."

Saiban wrung his hands. "It's our law. We never tell anyone how we died."

Beech pushed her hair from her eyes. "I proved that riding my motorcycle at ninety on a wet road at night won't get you gold medals in common sense." Her glare challenged Saiban to stop her. "Go on, Saiban. Report me for confessing that I died by blasting into someone's garden wall. Either way, we're all heading for the chop."

The others in the group all began to speak.

"I died in a fire."

"Heart."

"Cancer. Ten years, four operations. Sacks of chemo."

"Thrombosis."

Elsa knew this was a radical break from traditions. *We Frankenstein monsters . . . we God Scarers . . . whatever you call us. Until now we never admitted to anyone how we died. Yes, it's on record. But the records are confidential.*

"My wife's name is Sonia."

"I had a partner. Khan is—or was—a musician. I don't know whether he's alive or dead. I underwent transit fifteen years ago."

"I've four children. One was a baby when I died."

Saiban clenched his fists. Thunder backed his voice like a rumble of drums when he shouted, "Shut up. You mustn't do this. We never do."

"No," Paul said at last. "We never admit how we died. And we never speak about the people we left behind. It's considered impolite among our kind to discuss the people we loved in our first life."

"We mustn't start now." Saiban glared at each in turn. "There's good reason for not raking up the past. We all know it won't help. All it does is bring pain."

Elsa realized that apart from Saiban only Paul hadn't mentioned how he'd left his old life. Nor had he mentioned a past partner, nor family. At that moment the sense of their place in the world returned with a violent abruptness. Here they were, on the hillside. Above this bleak, exposed place clouds pressed down from the sky, as grim as the roof of a tomb. Thunder muttered angrily in the distance. Here, nine men and women of her own kind slipped once more into an exhausted silence. Their faces bore scratches from slithering down the thorn-filled gully. With the exception of Dominion, of course. He was unmarked.

Why have I forgotten about Dominion? He was with us during our cowardly skulk through thornbushes. And yet for the last half hour he seems to have slipped away from our group. As if that huge physique has become transparent. He must have been there of course. Only for some reason I never noticed him.

Not only were the survivors too tired to move, there seemed no point in walking again. They didn't know the terrain. If they trudged on, it might take them into the arms of their tormentors, or another five-hour walk might simply result in a dispiriting tour of the hills before the path brought them back full circle to this rocky hillside beneath the plateau on which the stone circle gazed bleakly into eternity.

Even so, Paul tried to encourage them. "It's time we moved on. We're too exposed here."

"What's the point?" West radiated defeat.

"All it needs is for another search team to ride by. We're sitting ducks."

Saiban responded with, "We should surrender to the police."

Even though Elsa couldn't see the sun she guessed it must be low in the sky. Already gloomy due to the cloud, a deeper darkness crept from the sea and flowed over the coastal land like an incoming tide to engulf the valley.

"We shouldn't stay out here all night," Paul said. "We need to find shelter."

"Surrender." Saiban nodded at the town.

"We can't give in. If we hand ourselves over to the police they'll turn us over to the mob," Elsa told him. "I've seen it happen."

"They'll do what they want to us in the end."

"We can't admit defeat." Even though Paul uttered the words Elsa heard resignation in his voice. "They don't have the right to slaughter us."

Saiban shook his head. "Legally, we're not alive, remember? All of us have death certificates. Humanity can't be culpable for killing what's already dead."

Even the thunder appeared to mutter in agreement. With the encroaching darkness came chilling currents of air that made Elsa shiver as they flowed round her. And although she suspected that perhaps half of the group didn't relish the idea of surrender to the humans, there was no willingness to move on. Bruised, exhausted, traumatized, their faces raked with bloody scratches—even the strongest had no heart to continue running for their lives. Far away in the bay a ship sounded its horn. The long drawn-out note could have been the despairing cry of a lost soul.

We lost souls. We the defeated. We, the soon to be dead again. Elsa despised this litany of thoughts. What could she do? Everyone on that cold, bleak hillside felt the same as her. *Where can we run? Where can we hide?*

It might have not been then that Dominion spoke. She might have lost herself in her pessimistic reverie before she realized that the figure that towered above them had begun speaking. The voice was low; a near monotone.

". . . forever. How much is a bird in the sky? Today, I've seen trees, stones, water, cloud. Heard the thunder. Birds? How much? Mice? How much? Foxes? How much? Thunder. No rain."

"Dominion's the lucky one," West grunted. "His brains are pulp. When they find us he won't feel a thing."

Dominion's insane. That's why he's talking nonsense. Elsa told herself this, but something about the rhythm of his words, and their clarity, forced her to listen.

As Dominion faced the darkness in the valley his soft voice pulsed on the air. "Last week there was nothing. I ate silence. I lived in darkness. The world stopped turning. I wondered what it would be like if I opened a door and I found my father and his father and his father talking . . . So I opened the door and I found them talking and they told me to hoard shit. Don't flush it, keep it. Shit is better than gold. Don't abandon your shit. Keep it safe. Hoard it. You must treasure excrement because it's heaven-sent."

A nurse in surgical scrubs shook her head. "He's no miracle. Whatever happened to him in the Regenerator caused his psyche to flame out."

"No," Elsa hissed. "He's not mad. Listen to him."

"Shit is gold. Keep it safe. Gather it in a heap and make it grow. Make it grow gold; make it grow your house; make it grow the clothes you wear."

"He is insane," added the nurse. "Then, some of us are well down that route already."

"I listened to my father and his father and his father . . ." Dominion's voice quickened. "They told me to keep the shit in secret places. Pile it higher and higher. Keep it growing because there's gold inside. In every brown orb is a nugget of gold." He spoke louder. "My family were poor. All my ancestors could afford were fields that were stones and everything they planted died. My family lived with hunger . . . what they had most of was the excrement that filled the dung pits. They dug all of it out, and they spread it on their field. The next year they were first to market with more onions than they could carry. After that they were never poor again."

West raised his head. "Am I imagining this? Or did Dominion just tell us his ancestors got rich by growing onions in their own shit?"

Beech clicked her tongue. "Wake up, Westie. That's exactly what he said."

"Hell's bells." West displayed a streak of dark humor. "If he's getting his synapses together ask him if he knows a good place to hide. Anywhere, as long as it isn't in his grandpa's dung pit."

Paul hoisted himself to his feet. "We should find shelter. There's bushes back there that at least . . . uh, what's he doing now?"

Dominion strode forward to stand on a boulder that had a commanding view of the valley.

"Dominion?" Elsa called out in a low voice. She was still wary of hunters being within earshot. "What is it? Can you see anyone?"

West added, "Tell me you see a nice deep cave where we can squirrel ourselves away."

Dominion turned to them. "No . . . Don't hide. Go down to the town. Take what you need."

The command stunned them. The group looked at one another in disbelief.

"Go down there?" West appeared breathless at the very idea. "Go into the lion's den? You are crazy after all."

"*Dominion—no.*"

The huge figure didn't pause. He began to stride down the hill toward the coastal town. Elsa realized she didn't know the name of the place even though she lived just a few miles from it. Now she could only dimly make out the gray smudge of buildings nestled between two high cliffs. On the north side stood what must be an old fort or castle. Scattered below, the houselights twinkled. Now that town was Dominion's destination. The towering figure with the uncannily straight back and gigantic stride forged through ferns and stinging nettles. Right at that moment it seemed impossible anything could stand in that formidable creature's way.

For a moment the group watched Dominion plow downhill through the vegetation as if an elemental force drove him.

Go down to the town. Take what you need. His words reverberated inside her. Go down to the town? Insanity. They'd be slain the moment they entered the place. It would be suicide. You might as well throw yourself off the cliff top into the ocean. And yet she realized she was already following him. *Go down to the town. Take what you need.*

Saiban called out, "Elsa. Don't go with him. You don't know what he's going to do down there."

Already Saiban's was a lone voice. One by one the rest of the group followed. They moved as if they'd been mesmerized. It was an act of insanity . . . but what else could they do? Where else would they go? Up here in the hills was a slow death. Down there would be different. But whether it was a fast demise . . . or something else she didn't know. Elsa's heart hammered furiously. Fear or excitement? Again, she couldn't tell. As she forged her way through stinging nettles she passed a board fixed to a post. The years had taken their toll. It was submerged by plant growth. The flat panel had cracked. Moss had formed a green rash across it. But she recognized it as an information board provided for tourists when they still visited the area. Although it was faded by years of ferocious weather she made out a map. It showed the town on the coast where they were now headed. Scaur Ness. On the cliff top, a dark oblong labeled the Pharos. That must be the castle. They now followed a long obliterated path toward it. On the way they'd pass features with strange names that assumed a forbidding aspect to Elsa. Mulgrave Moor, Stanghow Crag, Thorngrove Wyke, Throstle Nest, Haggaback House, Stony Marl, Dalby Head, Warsman Snout. The dark rhythm of the place names shared a symmetry with that pulse of dread she felt in her heart. The names possessed all the resonance of a primeval rite.

Elsa knew this was it. She'd passed the point of no return. She'd resolved to follow Dominion into town. Whatever happened then was in the lap of the gods.

11

THE TOWN OF SLEEP

Forget stealth. Subtlety? Out the window. This was no
creep into town as thieves to quietly pilfer what they
needed. This was blitzkrieg. Dominion strode into the
harbor town. He marched along the main street. His feet
thudded on the pavement; the only sound in the sleeping community. Elsa and Paul did their best to keep up
with Dominion's relentless march. They were perhaps
fifty paces behind him. The rest of the group followed in
a straggling line. They were in a daze. No one expected
Dominion to arrive like he owned the place. To Elsa's relief there was no one about. The townspeople all seemed
to be in bed even though the church clock had still to
sound the midnight hour. To her right lay the glistening
pool of the harbor, where a motley array of fishing boats
dipped on the tide. Farther to her right the cliff that
dominated the town soared two hundred feet into the air.
On top of that loomed the formidable mass of the castle,
or the Pharos as it was known. Even though it was night

she could make out its powerful towers that thrust upward like muscular limbs.

From a distance Scaur Ness appeared picturesque. Close up, she saw that economic ruin had left the town a desolate place. Trash littered the street; in the alleyways that led into the back lanes rats gnawed on bread crusts that spilled from entire mounds of household refuse that hadn't been collected in weeks. Half the streetlights didn't work. What were once quaint cottages with red-tiled roofs were dilapidated—an oddly pathetic sight that tugged at her heart. Many of the stores were boarded up. A bankrupt gas station could only boast a tangle of weeds growing on its forecourt. More rats squeaked among the filth. Now that they were in the midst of the populated district Elsa couldn't avoid the stink of the drains that were pungently in need of maintentenace.

Ahead of her Dominion bore down on the town's center. "Wake up!" His voice was thunder, while echoes duplicated the command, *Wake up . . . wake up . . . wake up . . .*

Behind her, she heard intakes of breath as the rest of the group reacted to Dominion's roar.

"Wake up!"

"My God," Beech hissed. "What's he doing?"

West's voice was grim. "If he wants all the Saps to know we're here he's doing a grand job."

Saiban hung back. "He's insane. We should never have come here. We could have negotiated a surrender. We could have turned ourselves in and—"

"Wake up! Wake up! Wake up!" Dominion's voice battered the town.

Saiban clammed his mouth shut. His frightened eyes roved over the dense pack of houses as lights flared in bedroom windows.

"Wake up!"

Elsa glanced at Paul. His eyes were wide with shock.

"Why did we follow him?" she asked. "We're as crazy as he is."

"Watch him. Dominion knows what he's doing."

Beech joined them. "He's waking the whole place, that's what he's doing."

West moved back against a wall. "He's off his skull. Keep back, they'll start shooting at us."

"Just wait." Paul's voice was fierce. "Dominion's onto something. This has a purpose."

"God help us if you're wrong."

Dominion stopped before the old houses that ascended row after row up the hillside. They formed his own personal audience of bricks and timber.

"Wake up! Wake up!"

By now faces could be glimpsed behind windowpanes as people peered out to see this man-shaped typhoon that had roared into town.

"*Wake up!*" The bellow reverberated through the alleyways. Dogs started barking. "*Wake up!*" As the echo of his wake-up call faded he strode toward a car, reached down with his massive hands, grasped its bodywork beneath the doors, then lifted. With a strangely bovine groan the vehicle rolled onto its side.

"Maybe we should leave Dominion to it?" West suggested. "We don't want to spoil his fun." He wiped a fear sweat from his brow. "What do you say to making a run for it before the townsfolk start taking potshots?"

"Wait," Paul hissed back. "See what happens next."

"You're as crazy as he is." West backed off to where the rest of the God Scarers hid in the shadows.

In a break between the houses a cemetery ran uphill to a church built of gloomy stone. Dominion walked with all the dread purpose of Satan himself sweeping into his private realm. He smashed open the iron gates. After that he surged through the graveyard. His massive arms swung out punching the heads off statues that adorned the tombs. He bellowed, "Wake up! Wake up!" as he toppled monuments to the dead who lay rotting in the ground beneath his pounding feet. Whether he called to the cadavers lying in their coffins or to the citizens of Scaur Ness Elsa could not say. Nevertheless, she glanced across at the houses. More lights came on in bedrooms. A yellow radiance fell on the harbor waters to illuminate the rotting hulks of ships. In the windows she saw silhouettes of heads as a startled populace tried to figure out who this man was with a voice of thunder. She saw Dominion seize an angel in white stone that must have weighed two hundred pounds. He hoisted it above his head, then hurled it into a storefront. It crashed through the shutters in an explosion of shattered glass.

"He's not done yet," Paul murmured. "Keep watching."

Dominion then attacked a pyramid-shaped tomb. He wrestled with an object before wrenching it away from its brackets. Elsa saw he'd torn a cross from the stonework. The thing was almost as tall as he was. And when he hoisted it onto his shoulder to carry it back through the cemetery the ringing clang the shaft made when it struck against tombstones told her the massive cross had been wrought from iron.

Elsa shook her head. "A great time to find religion . . ." Her stab at black humor was intended to ease her growing sense of alarm. It didn't work. She felt sick with fear. Why had she followed Dominion? She must have been infected by his madness; it was the only answer. Now Dr. Paul Marais, standing there in his green surgical scrubs, watched with such an expression of awe shining on his face he could have been witnessing the Second Coming in all its shining majesty with a choir of angels to hallelujah the appearance of the Godhead.

*But no ... we are a bunch of scared monsters—
Frankenstein's bastard progeny—cowering in a filthy, run-
down, bankruptcy-ravaged town at the edge of the sea. And
any second now its inhabitants are going to realize what we
are. Then they'll start killing.*

In the meantime Dominion obeyed some dark, indomitable instinct. He crossed the road from the cemetery with the cross on his shoulder. So old, even the
ironwork had become gnarled like the limbs of ancient
tree, the cross sparked on the blacktop each time it
clipped it. Still, nobody from the town challenged Dominion. It seemed as if everyone knew he would do
something. They were held in a spell of anticipation.

Dear God, just what would that instinct drive him to
do next? Elsa found herself holding her breath. By this
time, Dominion had reached the car. He swung the cross
from his shoulder; then as if he wielded a spear he drove
it into the car's fuel tank. Gasoline hemorrhaged from
the gash in the tank. It spilled onto the road to flow
along the gutter. The next moment he used the cross as a
club. He swung it against the torn fuel tank. A thunderous *clang* reverberated through the canyons of trash-
filled streets. The second time he struck the car so hard it
shuddered like a wounded beast. Sparks jetted from
where the metal struck metal. The third time Dominion
smote the car as it lay there the sparks ignited the gasoline. Instantly a ball of fire rose into the night sky. It illuminated the houses in a sickly yellow light. A second
later the burning fuel in the gutter sent a line of fire running along the road.

Dominion threw the cross into the blazing car. The
force of the impact pierced the bodywork. The cross jutted out of the vehicle at right angles, a cruciform shape
bathed in the incandescent light.

As the God Scarers followed Dominion they clearly

wished they were anywhere but here. Next stop for the giant figure was a grocery store. He shouldered open the locked door. Once in the store he ripped a drape from a window and threw canned food into it. Elsa and Paul arrived to find the store's owner race in in his pajamas from an inner doorway.

"Stop that . . . get out of my store. Do you hear?" The white-haired man flung himself on Dominion.

Dominion flicked him away as if hardly noticing him. Winded by the blow, the man leaned back against magazine racks that held just a handful of dusty journals. Before he could recover, another figure darted from the same inner doorway that the man had used. It was a woman in her twenties. She wore a white cotton nightdress. Her black hair tumbled down to her waist in wild curls. In the gloom her eyes flashed as bright as splinters of glass. Elsa recalled Dominion's handiwork in the form of the soldier's crushed skull. She pictured Dominion sweeping the woman's beautiful head from her shoulders with one powerful swipe of his arm.

"Stop!" The woman grabbed hold of Dominion's upper arm.

His gaze swept down to meet her eyes. Elsa anticipated the woman to fall back before such a glare as that, but the woman stayed her ground. Instead, she put her open palm on Dominion's hand.

"You must let me help." She picked up a case of cans and tipped them into the drape that Dominion had spread out across the counter.

When she stood back he gathered corners of the fabric to create a massive pouch for the food. After picking it up he walked past the dazed storekeeper and back out into the street, where he thrust the makeshift bag into Paul's hands. That done, he walked in that purposeful way along the road that separated the harbor from the tiers of houses.

Elsa and the rest followed him. What could they do? They couldn't flee so easily now that the townspeople had started to emerge from their homes. Behind them, the storekeeper stumbled through the wrecked doorway of his shop.

He cried out: *"They've taken my daughter . . . Do you see! They've got Caitlin. For God's sake help her!"*

Caitlin didn't need God's help. She didn't need anyone's help. Because Caitlin walked behind Dominion of her own choosing. She was a wiry, determined-looking woman with black hair that swished down her back. Her slim legs emerged from the bottom of the cotton nightdress to gleam nakedly in the meager lights of the town. When her father called she didn't look back. Elsa saw that no matter how much the rough road hurt Caitlin's bare feet she wasn't going to slow down. Not for one bloody minute.

12

THE PHAROS

The town had woken. Everywhere, houses had lights shining from windows. Men and women were spilled out into the street. His legs carried him forward. He hadn't planned this. He operated on pure instinct.

To his right the cliff face soared high over the town. On top of it stood the castle. An enormous structure of stone blocks. Its impassive face had brooded over the town for centuries. That was his destination. For all the world it could have been whispering his name . . . Dominion . . .

Ahead of him the road split into two. The left fork carried on by the harbor. The right fork arched over the water to be carried aloft by an iron bridge to the other side. Behind him were his own kind. They were exhausted and they were frightened. With them was the woman in the white nightdress—a human. In front of him a group of men had formed a line across the road. They'd hastily dragged on jeans, T-shirts, sweaters. The laces of the boots were untied. In the gloom he saw that they'd armed themselves with what they could. Some had shotguns. The rest carried axes, hammers, iron spikes. Dominion's sharp senses were alert to every sound, odor, and movement. The car he'd set alight still burned with a snapping sound as windows shattered; the tires bursting with the heat sounded like rifle shots. In this mix of sounds he heard the claws of the rats as they scuttled through the drains beneath his feet. Gulls shuffled restlessly in their nests among the chimneys. The unusual noises had unsettled them. He also heard the murmur of the men forty paces in front of him.

"You know what they are, don't you?" one grunted to another.

"They'll have got away from the Transit Station. Some of them are wearing hospital fatigues."

Dominion didn't flinch. He walked straight at them.

One bearded man held up his hand. "That's as far as you go."

Dominion kept walking.

A thickset man in an unbuttoned shirt gestured with his shotgun. "You've got to do what we say. You stop where you are. Do you hear?"

A boy called from a doorway, "Who are they, Dad?"

"A bunch of God Scarers."

A woman called from the house, "George? What are you going to do to them?"

"What do you think? Get the boy inside."

From the direction of the house came the sound of the boy protesting. "No . . . I wanna watch!"

Another man shouted from the line, "You lot . . . hey, you fucking monsters. I'm talking to you. Go stand by that railing."

The God Scarers stopped dead.

Dominion didn't pause. If anything he moved faster.

A number of the men in front of him appeared uneasy at the sight of this colossus bearing down on them out of the night.

The man in the open shirt called out to steady their nerves, "Don't back away. They're God Scarers. They can't hurt us. It's impossible for them to harm a human being."

Fifteen paces away.

"Shit." One of the men fumbled with a rifle.

"I'll drop the big one." The man called George raised his shotgun. The weapon discharged with a dull *thump*. Buckshot stung Dominion's chest. Behind him the human girl shouted. When he glanced back he saw a red stain appear on her arm.

Dominion lunged forward.

"Oh, Jesus Christ," was all the man managed to say before Dominion knocked him to the ground. The other man with the gun quit struggling with the faulty firing mechanism. He flung it aside and ran. Those that stayed found themselves tossed aside as if they were nothing more substantial than dolls. One brawny man struck Dominion on the shoulder with an iron bar. As he raised the club for strike number two Dominion gripped the man's fist that held the bar and squeezed. He heard the bones in his attacker's hand break. When the man screamed in pain he let go. The man stumbled away into the night clutching his injured hand to his belly.

With the exception of the men lying semiconscious on the pavement, the way was clear.

"I told you to bring the food." Dominion glared at Paul.

Paul nodded and picked up the makeshift bag made from the drape. Cans clunked together. The group, however, still didn't move. All, that is, except the human girl. She followed him despite blood pumping from the wound in her arm where the ricochet had caught her.

Dominion turned to Paul again. "You are a doctor?"

"What of it?"

"Then you can take care of her when we get there."

"But she's—"

"Start walking," Dominion told them. "We're nearly there."

With that he crossed the bridge. Ahead of them a flight of steps that had been cut into the cliff face ascended to the castle. Dominion began to climb.

No one challenged them. No one got in their way. Back in the streets the people tended to their wounded neighbors while others gathered in groups to talk. No doubt asking one another what they should do next about this midnight invasion of monsters into their town.

13

TRESPASS

Dominion might have exerted an irresistible pull for all they could do to resist. He climbed the four hundred or so steps to the castle. It loomed above them into the night sky. A dark monument to oppression against a darker firmament.

Behind him climbed the girl in the nightdress. Even though she'd been wounded by the buckshot, with blood forming a sleeve of glistening red on her left hand, she refused to pause. Sheer willpower drove her on. Then came Elsa, Paul at her side. The rest of the God Scarers followed in a bunch behind them. Any time now Elsa expected a hail of gunfire directed at them from the town below. It fell eerily silent, however. Either stunned into inactivity by Dominion's audacious invasion of their sleepy backwater, or they reasoned that to fire on the monsters might result in the death of one of their own. Caitlin appeared to be wayward, probably the local wild child, but nobody back there wanted her dead.

Elsa glanced back down the stairs that had been

hacked into the cliff face in an elongated Z. Four hundred steps that carried them high over the town. In the gloom she could make out the glistening pool of the harbor. Beside it flames still danced on the car Dominion had put to the torch. The town itself lay in the cleft of a valley. On the high ground at either side of it empty moorland appeared to roll away into infinity. But as Dominion ascended the last few steps to the top of the cliff her attention was drawn once more to the Pharos—the castle that stood on the highest point above Scaur Ness. At the head of the steps a paved area extended fifteen paces to a massive portcullis of crisscross steelwork that was set into the castle wall. The wall, in turn rose, forty feet above them to the battlements. At either end of those a tower rose another twenty feet. Dominion paused.

"Don't fail me now, my wee chappy," Paul murmured to himself in his soft Scottish accent. "You came here for a reason. Don't let go of it now."

As Dominion gazed up at the vast expanse of granite blocks the girl from the town caught up with him. Blood still dripped from her fingers. Red smears violated her white cotton nightdress. She was panting, and yet her face shone in triumph. Her expression screamed to the world that she'd witnessed a miracle.

She gazed up at Dominion in awe. "I'm glad what you did to the town. I loved it when you set fire to the car. And when you smashed your way into my father's store I thought my heart would burst with excitement. Just explode right in my chest! I've never felt like that before. You should have seen the expression on those idiots' faces. They deserve it. You've brought more life to this dump in five minutes than they ever did in their whole lives!" Even though she laughed, tears slid down her face. "You were a bolt of lightning!"

Dominion still remained in the same posture. He gazed at the castle with those dark eyes.

Once more Paul murmured to himself as if in prayer, "Dominion. Don't fail me now. You came here for a purpose. What is it? What did you plan to do?" He glanced back as if expecting to see a mob crossing the bridge intent on hacking the monstrous intruders to pieces. "We are depending on you, you bloody miracle of science, you. Without you we're going to wind up dead again."

A sea breeze poured across the battlements. A ghostly sigh rose, then fell. Elsa felt the cold air reach through her clothes to touch her skin. A sapping cold that had the deathly essence of the tomb about it. *Then all of us here apart from the girl have cheated the tomb. Now it's found us. It's reaching out to us. Science robbed our graves. They resent being empty; they want us back.* Those morbid thoughts worked away deep inside. They were little seeds of death. In the distance she heard the undulating voices of the ancient dead. The voices appeared to rise out of the earth before sinking beneath the sod again. That was never hallucination, she told herself. She really did hear something that nobody could ever hear. *There's a reason I'm hearing the songs of the dead. Just as there's a reason Dominion brought us here. He's establishing neural connections now. He can form words. His thought patterns are becoming rational.*

The words gushed from her. "Dominion. Don't forget why you brought us here. Something woke you up in the Regenerator. Maybe it was a premonition. You saw what you'd do in the future. And that you'd bring us here to the castle. Whatever happens now don't let that vision slip away from you."

Dominion stared up at the towers. Nobody moved.

Elsa's voice surged into a shout. "An instinct woke inside you . . . it's like you realized a truth . . . some great truth that shook you awake before it was time. Now there's a danger as your conscious mind takes control that you'll forget what you had to do. Dominion. Close your eyes. See that vision again. Remember what is it you have to do!"

Dominion stared; a giant of a man frozen in a statue-like pose.

"Dominion. Close your eyes. Think! Why are you here?"

He closed his eyes. The next second the eyelids snapped back to reveal a pair of blazing eyes. In a surge of movement he almost leaped at the portcullis. With both hands he hauled at the steel gate. Padlocks snapped at its base. Slowly it began to rise, guided by the grooves cut in the stone archway.

"Help him!" Despite her injured arm Caitlin ran forward to grab hold of steel bars that were as thick as her wrist. With all her strength she heaved at the recalcitrant gate that had been designed by the castle's builders to keep the enemy at bay.

Elsa stood alongside Caitlin. She gripped that icy steelwork and lifted, too, straining every muscle. Paul joined them. A grimace distorted his face as he helped force the gate upward. Metalwork screamed as it forced its way through runners that hadn't been used in years.

Paul bellowed back, "Everybody!"

A moment later the Transit Station's survivors joined in. Everyone with the exception of Saiban. He cast mournful glances down into the town. He might have been inwardly debating the merits of descending the steps to abandon himself to his fate in the darkened streets.

Then they were inside.

"Saiban . . . you've got ten seconds!" Paul yelled the words as they struggled to prevent the portcullis sliding shut to cut them off from the outside world. "Saiban!"

For a moment it really seemed as if he would remain outside the castle. The weight of the portcullis would soon defeat them. Any second it would crash back down to the stone slabs.

Dominion spoke. "You might want to die. But one day our survival might depend on you."

Saiban flinched. The words struck him hard. For a moment he stared at Dominion as the relentless force of gravity dragged the portcullis squealing downward, inch by inch. A second later he made a decision. As the portcullis's descent quickened he ran at the gate, ducked, and he was inside.

Now the group released the tons of steelwork. With a resounding crash that must have rattled dishes in cupboards across the town the portcullis slammed back down to earth.

14

HER FLESH

God Scarer tableaux. Aren't we magnificent? These thoughts ran through Paul's mind as the nine survivors from the Transit Station seated themselves at tables in the cafeteria—a disused and profoundly neglected cafeteria at that. The men and women he saw in the light of what had been decorative candles looked as if they'd been dragged through a whole forest of thorn. They were disheveled, most wore surgical scrubs that were distressed to say the least, ripped at shoulder and knee; smeared with dirt from scrambling down the gully. Their bodies revealed an array of minor injuries. Blood oozed from cuts. Bruises mottled skin. Dominion, alone, appeared as indomitable as ever. His injuries were more like a hero's medals. An aura of invincibility haloed him. He walked slowly around the cafeteria to gaze at the vaulted ceilings and the hefty stone pillars that supported them. His domain.

"Paul . . . Paul?"

"Sorry. I'm good at self-obsessed reverie."

Elsa set three bottles on the table where he sat. From each one protruded red candles; the word REJOICE was printed horizontally on them in gold.

"That's all I can find now," she said. "So at my count we've about twenty candles."

"Until we find more, we best not burn them all at once."

"Did you have any luck?"

"I found a first aid kit in an office behind the reception area. It's all pretty basic—bandages, sticking plaster, sterile wipes. But if—"

"Quick. It looks as if you'll need it now." Elsa indicated Caitlin where she sat cradling her arm that had taken a hit from the shotgun blast.

"Damn," Paul hissed. "I forget that human beings are on the fragile side."

Elsa prevented Caitlin from tumbling off the cafeteria chair as she slumped forward. The girl was clearly faint from the blood loss. It took a determined effort on her part, but she roused herself from the torpor, then lifted her head.

Her voice came as a whisper. "We made it, then. The Pharos?"

"Funny name for a castle. How are you feeling?" Clearly she suffered the early signs of shock. Normally, Paul would have touched her forehead to gauge her temperature. It was a gesture to reassure the patient too. Only this was a human patient. His first.

"The Pharos?" With an effort she stopped herself fainting away again. "Lighthouse. At least, hundreds of years ago it was . . . I mean . . . as well as being a castle."

"Caitlin. It is Caitlin, isn't it? Look, my dear, I'm going to have to take care of that arm of yours. You're bleeding."

"Scottish. You're one of them and you're Scottish."
She managed a smile. "Weird."

"Aye, weird. But they have Scottish God Scarers too.
In fact any nationality and race you care to mention.
Can you flex your fingers for me? There . . . good. Now
make a fist. Good, good. Well done."

"You can't do that!"

Paul looked up to see Saiban rising from his chair with
such an expression of disbelief splashed across that
mournful voice that he fully expected the man to start
howling the place down.

"Saiban. The lady has been shot."

"Good grief. You mustn't touch her. It's not allowed."

"Yes, yes . . . we sons and daughters of Frankenstein
shouldn't touch a hair on a wee human head. But what
do you suggest?"

"She's losing blood, Saiban." Elsa glared at the man.

Paul pulled back the sleeve of Caitlin's nightdress.
"See? Bullet wound to the crook of her right elbow. I'm
guessing no serious damage. She will need—"

"No." Saiban's face quivered with anger. "I won't allow
this. None of us will. No Transient must touch a human
being. It's forbidden."

"Saiban. I must treat her. The wound is still bleeding.
Look for yourself."

"Then ask her own people to care for her."

Beech shouted across the cafeteria, "So they can kill
us? We're safe in here."

"Safe?" Paul murmured. "Hmm, that's debatable." He
glanced across at Dominion, who lightly ran his hand
across one of the walls as if gauging its strength. Strong
enough to withstand an artillery barrage? It might come
to that. He turned his attention back Caitlin. "Keep your
hand held up. Like you're taking an oath of allegiance.

That's it. Keep your elbow slightly bent. We need to stop the bleeding."

"Dr. Paul Marais, I order you not to touch her. She is human."

"You're right, Saiban. I'm a doctor. She needs my help."

"Then call a human doctor. You are not permitted to touch her."

Dominion spoke as if only half aware of the conversation. "Treat her."

Saiban shook his head. "Don't listen to Dominion. He's insane."

"You followed him here, Saiban."

"Only because I thought we could negotiate with the authorities. Maybe the local mayor."

Caitlin roused herself. "The mayor is my father." Her face was gray. "Rather than talk to your kind, he'd have stuck your heads on spikes." Blood loss made her laugh sound like that of a drunk. "Heart of gold, my old daddy."

"Caitlin . . . Caitlin?" Elsa shook her gently to rouse her. "You need that wound treated. It hasn't stopped bleeding yet."

Paul crouched beside her to look up into a face framed by the mass of black hair. He reached out his hand as if to brush back the hair from her eyes.

"Marais." The note of warning in Saiban's voice turned it into a snarl. "I'm warning you. I'm your superior."

"You're in admin, Saiban," Elsa told him.

Beech added, "And if you hadn't noticed, that place you administered has been burnt to the fucking ground."

"Listen to me." Saiban's voice rose to a screech. Despite everyone's exhaustion, heads snapped up to look at him. "Our laws are sacred to us. If you try and touch the woman I will stop you myself. By force if necessary."

"Take a big gulp of reality, Saiban." Paul glared at him. "Just look at us. We're refugees. We've got nothing. I can do one useful thing in my life right now. An injured human being is slowly bleeding to death. I can help her."

"*Marais*—"

Paul still held back from touching Caitlin. Gently he asked, "Do I have your permission to treat you?"

Her reply was heartfelt. "Of course you can."

"It will mean touching you."

"So?"

"You realize what I am?"

"Uh." This question of his puzzled her. "You're a God Scarer, aren't you?"

"That's right. I was human, like you. I died. Then they resurrected me."

"Like the Frankenstein story. I know . . . ouch. It's hurting, Paul."

"Marais. It's not allowed."

"Paul . . ." Caitlin sounded dreamy now as her blood pressure dropped. "While you're not allowed to hurt us . . . doesn't your law say that it's wrong to allow something bad to happen to us? This is bad, Paul. It hurts. I want you to put it right."

"Anything you say, Caitlin."

Paul eased back her sleeve with one hand, then cupped his hand beneath her elbow. That first touch of human flesh struck him with the force of a lightning bolt. He hadn't anticipated the eruption of emotions. He knew he masked it. He held it all in. Not a flicker. Not a tremor. Just the coolly professional actions of a doctor working on a patient, but inside himself his nerves had become incandescent.

Saiban lurched forward. Paul knew that this man with the long, mournful face, who constantly bleated defeatism, was going to attack him. However, Beech and Elsa moved to block the man's way. When he tried to shove through they grabbed Saiban's lanky frame. There they held him, despite his struggles.

"You heard Caitlin." In the candlelight Beech's red hair held fiery glints. "She gave her permission."

"You've gone too far, Marais." Saiban was outraged. "They'll make us suffer for this."

Beech tugged Saiban by the collar. The fierce glint in her eye matched those in her hair. "Make us suffer? The Saps will make us suffer if we go down there with floral bouquets. Don't you get it yet, Saiban? Humanity is out to make us extinct."

Saiban shrugged himself free, then turned his back in disgust.

Paul maintained his customary medical professionalism. Despite this his heart clamored. Humanity was a separate species now. Even so . . . when he touched her: a beautiful human female . . . her skin had been so soft. OK, it was flawed with freckles and the common blemishes that affect every single human being—they didn't possess the flawless complexions of God Scarers. But there was a vulnerability about her flesh—the way the buckshot had ripped it—sweet creation, it made his heart ache. He knew she stared at his face with her pale blue eyes. That vulnerability all mixed with trust and fear shone through them. A heat spread through his body. An erotic heat. He'd glanced at the shape of her breasts pressing against the fabric of the nightgown. Just for a split second the superheated image burning itself through him revealed what it would be like to slip that nightdress up over her head to expose her nakedness.

As he worked with the sterile wipes to clean the wound Paul found himself talking—anything to take his mind off the sexual heat growing inside. "That's not hurting too much?"

"Not at all," she whispered. "I can't believe you're so gentle."

"We're well trained."

"My father told me that you monsters were ugly close up. You're not."

"This Pharos. What is it?"

"It was a castle that became a lighthouse. I told you a few minutes ago."

"Looks as though it's become something else. Some kind of hotel?"

"Oh, they restored it and put in a lot of reproduction medieval furniture. They had to close it a couple of years ago when the tourists stopped coming. My father said that you lot wrecked our economy."

"We didn't intend to."

"The Pharos closed about the same time as the oil refinery went bust. There's no work now."

"Nothing?"

"Well, hardly anything. Even the police are part-time. Mostly people sit round getting drunk on liquor they make themselves. They call it Coffin Paint."

"Snappy, but I don't see it being a household name."

She watched his fingers at work as they cleaned the wound with a swab. "Coffin Paint. Black humor, or what passes for it round here. I guess it means those who drink it die young."

"What does it taste like?"

"I don't know, Paul. I don't intend dying young."

Her pale blue eyes gazed at his face with an intensity he found unsettling.

Talk about taboo, he told himself as he wrapped the bandage around her elbow. *This is forbidden fruit. Caitlin's a human. That means she's out of bounds.* And yet . . . and yet . . . Paul Marais's surroundings appeared to slip away from him. It was as if a bubble formed around him and Caitlin. He noticed everything about her. Her bare legs that emerged from the loose skirts of the cotton night-dress. The smooth swelling of her calf muscles. A freckle on her right knee. He found himself counting the curls in her hair that fell in extravagant loops of black over her shoulders. And there were the pale blue eyes that watched his face so minutely as if she saw something there that fascinated her. The rest of the cafeteria vanished into a mist of his mind's making. His fellow God Scarers still sat at the tables. Behind them, soda dispensers that were already disappearing under cobwebs faded into the background along with units that housed the hot trays for pizza and tubs of fries.

He and Caitlin spoke in murmurs. "What made you join us?" he asked.

"Like I said, I didn't want to die young."

"It's really that bad?"

"You should see the figures for drug addiction and suicide round here. It's not just adults that take the easy way out. Kids are jumping from the cliff tops, too."

"Don't you think you've leaped from the frying pan into the fire?"

"Paul, it couldn't get any worse. Scaur Ness used to be pretty. Now it's hell."

"I've stopped the bleeding. The buckshot nicked your skin. There's no shot left in there. How does it feel?"

"Like I've been born again."

With her uninjured arm she reached out to rest her hand on his bare forearm. Skin on skin. For a moment that contact could have been an interface for a wild, turbulent power that was thunderbolts mixed with sunlight, fused with a hurricane.

"I do, Paul. I've been born again."

How do I respond to that one? Instead he found himself asking, "How's the pain?"

"Not hurting. I'm tingling."

"Use this sling. You need to support your arm."

As he finished easing her arm into the sling that he'd looped around her neck she smiled. "Thank you." Then she kissed him on the cheek.

That envelope of intimacy that had formed around the two of them exploded. This was the cafeteria of the castle that loomed over the dying town of Scaur Ness. Here were survivors from a massacre. Their assailants had been human beings, the species to which they had belonged before their deaths. Now one of their number had just kissed a God Scarer. Blasphemy. There was no hiding it. Everyone in that room gasped in shock.

Saiban tore into Paul first. "Nothing is taboo in your eyes, is it?"

"Saiban. Caitlin kissed me. I didn't—"

"You let it happen. You're worse than him." Saiban stabbed a finger at Dominion. "At least he's insane. He kills human beings, but he doesn't know any better. You're a doctor. As well as the rules of medical ethics you know our law."

Paul looked to the others for support. Instead he was met by hostile stares.

Beech's mouth was hard. "What were you thinking, Paul?"

West groaned. "Dear God in heaven. The world's gone mad. You shouldn't have allowed that to happen, buddy. If those Sapheads down there find out . . ."

"Caitlin will become an outcast, Paul."

"She's hardly damaged goods." Paul hissed the words. Their stare felt almost a physical burden upon him.

"I kissed him." Caitlin shrugged. "So what?"

Saiban snarled back at her, "No man will want you now. You've become a leper. And don't think none of your people will find out. Because they always do. You'll be shunned by society."

"I'm with you now, aren't I?" She tossed her head in defiance. "Nobody down there will have anything to do with me anyway."

For seconds no one said anything. All Paul heard was the thud-thud of his heart. In that dungeonlike place with the vaulted ceilings it could have been the thud of dead fists on the door of a tomb.

Eventually, Dominion broke the suffocating silence. "Tell me this . . ." All eyes turned to him as he stood there in the center of the room. "How many of us pass through the Transit Station?"

Nobody answered. The question was so out of joint with the taboo-shattering kiss that Paul doubted if half the people there managed to absorb Dominion's words. There was a sense of time becoming stagnant, toxic; God's own heartbeat slowing deep in the body of the universe.

Dominion spoke again. "How many of us pass through the Transit Station?"

Saiban clicked his tongue. "Now isn't the time for discussing body counts."

"How many?"

Caitlin became interested. "What's he asking?"

"He means," Saiban began, "how many of us are brought back to life there."

Paul glowered at him. "Saiban. You were the head of administration. Are you going to give Dominion an answer?"

"We were discussing your crime, Dr. Marais. Not medical statistics."

Dominion took a step forward. "Saiban? How many?"

Paul detected the aura of threat around the gigantic figure.

Saiban did, too. With a dismissive gesture he snapped, "So far this fiscal year, 3,486. Satisfied?"

"How many a year?"

"For what good the information will do you . . ." He shrugged. "Usually it averages ten thousand Transients processed annually."

Dominion finally asked the question, "These ten thousand people that are brought back from death every year. Where do they all go?"

15

THE VANISHED

This question of Dominion's was an obvious one. Elsa thought: *But why hasn't anyone ever asked it before?* OK, she could have made a pretty accurate guess at how many made it through the process from death to life. After all, Elsa worked in the team that nursed them back to health. But once those ten thousand men and women per anum left the Transit Station in the blacked-out buses where did they all go?

Paul said, "Dominion, why did you ask that question?"

He appeared deep in thought. When he didn't reply a buzz of voices started as the God Scarers began to talk among themselves. *Just where did the resurrected go?*

West spoke up. "There are ten Transit Stations in this region. Did you know that? Some of those stations are bigger than the one that you guys worked at."

Elsa frowned. "You mean, in all they were processing in the region of one hundred thousand a year? Minimum?"

"And they all vanish into thin air." Paul's smile was a

grim one. "One hundred thousand God Scarers—*fffttt!*" He clicked his fingers. "Makes you wonder, doesn't it?"

Saiban spoke coldly. "It's not our place to question what happened to them."

"But where do one hundred thousand of our kind go?"

"It's not in our remit to debate their destination," Saiban responded. "But we all know that once Transients are declared fit for service they are assigned work in other parts of the world."

Beech growled in frustration, "Why do you have to be so pompous, Saiban?"

"I'm in control of my emotions—that's not pomposity, Beech."

"Oh yes, you are." The nurse's red hair flashed in the candlelight. "In that patronizing way you shrug off the question, what does happen to thousands of our kind? You tell us that they're given jobs. But where? What doing?"

"After all," Elsa added, "all those people have a destination; they occupy a space. They need housing."

"Unless they secretly end up as fast food."

Saiban looked down his nose at Paul. "Even coming from you that's a sick joke."

"Yes, it is a sick joke." Paul became angry. "It sickens me that I've worked at the Transit Station for twenty years. Thousands of cadavers have come in one door, thousands of Transients have walked out the other. Have we been wasting our time? Have they all been dumped in the ocean? Or fed to pigs? Come on, Saiban, take that fucking pompous look off your fucking face and tell us the fucking truth."

"My. Three fucks in one sentence. Don't we know what's on your mind, Doctor?" Saiban's mournful face turned to Caitlin. "There's no stopping your friend, is there, miss?"

Caitlin met his gaze. "I'm sure you're very intelligent, sir. Although you—"

"Please, miss." Saiban was politeness personified. "You shouldn't address me as sir, if you will forgive my contradicting you. I am merely Saiban, if it pleases you to address me by name."

"Saiban. You're far more intelligent than me. You all are." Caitlin looked at each in the group in turn. "But you've been so isolated you're overlooking the obvious."

"Miss, you should really consider returning home. Your family will be—"

Beech clicked her tongue. "Saiban, let her speak."

Caitlin continued, "I don't know anything about your lives other than you worked at the Transit Station. We've never seen inside because of the high walls. Oh, there's rumors. That it's where grave robbers finish their business. I've seen kids painting graffiti on walls. *Frankenstein Factory*, that kind of thing. You people don't really know what goes on in the outside world, do you? I bet you're not even allowed newspapers." She shrugged. "What there is of them these days. You know paper's been rationed since January? No, you didn't, did you? We don't hear about your lives inside those places; you hear nothing about ours out here. You saw the state of the town. Tourists used to visit this old castle by the thousand. Now there's not one."

"I see your point, miss." Saiban nodded.

"No, you don't because I haven't even made it yet. You're using that polite way you have to shut me up." Her face colored.

Saiban couldn't argue with a human. It would be against his servile nature. All he could do was step back as if yielding the floor to her.

"As I was saying. You should have been asking questions. But you shut yourselves away in that place. Dominion asked the right question. What has happened to all those people that you brought back to life? Where have they gone? And no . . . I don't know the answer either. But I've another question that's just as big and just as important. This country became an outcast in the world when it was the only one to keep the Transit Stations. For years it allowed this Frankenstein thing to go on. Sanctions were imposed. No other country traded with us. They blockaded ports to stop fuel coming in. Last winter children died of starvation. I might be asking the obvious here. But why did we continue to keep the Transit Stations? What made our government decide it was better to allow the whole nation to go to ruin than shut you down? Every other country abolished the Transit Stations years ago. Answer me this: what was in it for our people? We let you God Scarers live. Why?"

Paul shook his head. "You can bet your bottom dollar it wasn't through any noble, altruistic notion of giving us Frankenstein monsters sanctuary." His gaze roved the room. "So why did they let us live?"

"They didn't," West said. "Forty-eight hours ago they wrecked the station. We were the lucky ones that didn't get slaughtered."

"See, you know nothing," Caitlin said. "Last week we got a new government. They agreed with the U.N. to destroy the Transit Stations. In return the embargos have been lifted. They say things are going to get better, and there'll be jobs for everyone."

Elsa frowned. Something didn't add up. "Caitlin. If the economy is going to recover, why claim that life in this town is still hopeless?"

"I don't believe it will change for years. Besides . . ." She rubbed her arm where the shot had torn her human flesh. "If you ask me, the rest of the world is still terrified of you."

* * *

Most of the people sat with their own thoughts, or they dozed at cafeteria tables. After a while those that couldn't sleep became restless. The first gray light of dawn had started to filter through the windows. With some light to see by they moved into the central courtyard to explore their surroundings.

Paul stretched himself. "If this is going to be home for the foreseeable future we should make sure it's secure. We don't want the townspeople walking in."

"If you'll take my advice," Saiban began, "we should make contact with the police. It's time we talked to them about our surrender."

West grunted. "Stuff it up your backside, Saiban."

Caitlin had lain down on a bench along one wall of the cafeteria. There, she'd fallen into a sound sleep.

Elsa knew it made sense to sleep, too, after forty-eight hours without, but a restlessness drove her to her feet. "I'll come with you," she told Paul.

"OK. I'll be glad of the company." He smiled. "Although some might suspect that monsters are afraid to go into the dark alone . . . wee timorous beasties that we are."

"Do you really have a strong Scottish accent, or do you lay it on thick for our benefit?"

"Oh, it's still there from my old life. Maybe it's a conceit—an attempt to be different—but I hang on to it. Now, after you."

They emerged into the courtyard. The dawn air was chilly. Their footfalls echoed from the towering walls that surrounded them on four sides. Two men and a woman climbed steps that ran up a wall toward the battlements. The woman and one of the men was from the physiotherapy department. The second man was a patient that had been scheduled to leave this week.

"What do you make of it?" Elsa asked as they strolled

toward the portcullis that had so grudgingly admitted them just a few hours ago.

"The castle. It's a grand pile of stone, isn't it? It'd have kept the invaders out and no mistake."

"Not the castle. Dominion's question."

"Ah, what happened to all our progeny?"

"Ten thousand from our station. At least a hundred thousand from the entire region. Nationwide there could have been half a million per year."

He nodded. "Impressive. They must have been harvesting the dead from across the entire globe. There must have been a roaring black market trade in fresh cadavers, seeing as other nations forbade that kind of thing ... you know, defying God, thwarting nature, laughing in the face of Satan."

"Don't you take anything seriously, Paul?"

"My terrible sense of humor is a defense mechanism inherited from the old me."

"Well?"

"I'm mystified as the next man. Where do they hide thousands of God Scarers? Caitlin's question is rather unsettling, too. The government was prepared to bankrupt its own industry and plunge its own citizens into poverty for what? So it could defy the United Nations by permitting Transit Stations to continue pumping out all us wee Frankenstein monsters. That wasn't noble charity on their part. They had a motive. They believed that self-sacrifice would repay them with interest. So, what's really happening, Elsa?"

They'd reached the portcullis. Through the lattice-work of steel they could see the dawn light spreading through Scaur Ness. A mist had crept from the sea to lie on the harbor waters. Derelicts floated there. A number of cargo vessels had even sunk at anchor, only funnels showing above the waterline.

"Ah . . ." Paul let out a sigh. "A sleeping beauty of a town. Waiting to be woken by a hero's kiss."

"It'll take more than a kiss. Have you seen the buildings? They're little better than ruins."

"Come on," he said. "Shall we take a turn around our new home? I live in hope of finding a well-stocked wine cellar."

The rest had the same idea of exploring. She caught glimpses of more of their group on the battlements forty feet above them. West's face appeared at a tower window. A smudge of blood still marked his cheek from the grenade injury yesterday.

The next moment the silence vanished. Shots rang out. Mainly single detonations but they were followed by the chatter of a machine gun.

"Damn." Paul broke into a run. "It didn't take them long to come after us!"

They raced for the staircase that rose across the inner wall to the battlements. There, they saw Beech, who was in the process of descending.

Elsa called up, "Beech? Do you know if there are any other entrances to the castle?"

"There's only the portcullis as far as I know." A ricochet whined by, making her flinch. "There might be another entrance at the back."

The gunfire slowed to a desultory snap of single shots; these in turn were punctuated by longer pauses.

Paul climbed the steps. "With luck they're letting off steam rather than launching a determined attack." Red tracers sped above the courtyard. "If the Saps could get in they'd have waited until they were inside before they started shooting." He clenched his fist. "I hope."

A moment later they reached the battlements. Elsa kept her head below the parapet. From here she could see most of the walkway that ran around the top of the

walls that in turn enclosed the courtyard below. More
people had spilled out from the cafeteria to find out
what was happening. Parts of the walkway were piled
with building materials—sand, slates, blocks of stone.
The owners of the Pharos had begun renovations before
the bank pulled the plug on the overdraft. Another bullet smacked into the stonework on the outward face of
the wall.

"Keep down," Paul hissed.

"I hope those old-time stonemasons knew their job."

"Have faith," he told her. "Places like this could keep
out cannonballs." They worked their way along the inside of the battlements. These rose above the walkway to
around six feet in height with the characteristic crenella-
tions that would allow the bowmen of old to fire back. By
now, they were at the far side of the castle.

"This part must look out onto the cliff top," Paul told
her.

"I'd suggest you wait until the shooting stops before
you risk sticking your head up above the stonework."

"Suggestion noted with thanks." He gave a grim smile.
"At least they are on the outside firing in at us. Which
means this place is locked up safe and sound."

Elsa tugged his arm.

"What is it?"

She motioned to him to crouch with his back to the
wall. "Across there. It's a Newborn and the guy from
physiotherapy."

"It's OK, they're keeping under cover."

"But Luna was on the steps with them." Elsa waved to
the two who crouched down on the walkway opposite—
a distance of perhaps eighty feet. "Hey . . ." She waved
again to attract their attention. "Where's Luna?"

What they said was buried by another wave of gunfire,
but their shrugs were an eloquent enough reply. As for

the salvo of bullets, they either cracked harmlessly into thick stonework or sailed overhead.

Paul rose from a crouch. "Probably a gang of hotheads that got themselves fired up on booze and decided to prove they're not afraid."

"Keep your head down. We might be hard to kill but we're not indestructible."

"My refrain exactly."

Elsa lifted herself to see over the mound of orange sand that blocked the walkway. "So what's happened to Luna?"

"She might have decided to return to the cafeteria before the shooting started."

"Wouldn't we have passed her on the steps?"

"Another way down, maybe? Look, there's a door set in the tower across the way there."

"What do you make of that, then?"

"Huh?"

"The sand."

Paul turned to look at the mound of builder's sand just a dozen paces from them. Its orange hue had been dulled by exposure to the weather. Moss had formed on the sides. Even shoots of grass had sprung from the top.

"What of it?" Paul asked.

"Where the mound is closest to the wall. It's been disturbed. You can see the bright orange where the crust has been pushed away. It's even been scattered right across the walkway."

"Those two will have done it. You have to walk over it to reach the other side of the walkway."

"They made a heck of a mess." Elsa felt a chill spread through her stomach.

"Elsa! Don't!"

Elsa took her chance. In a matter of three seconds she thrust her head between the raised elevations of the parapet and looked down. A second later she ducked back behind the wall. A crackle of gunfire proved that their attackers had been vigilant. Bullets screamed through the gap where her head had been. Chips of stone rained down on them.

"Good God, Elsa . . ." Paul's protest tailed away. "She's down there, isn't she?"

Elsa nodded.

"Poor girl. Poor wee girl." His voice was a whisper. "She was the one with the dogs, weren't she? The golden Labradors?"

Elsa could only manage that same grim nod.

Paul grimaced. "I used to see her walking them."

"When the soldiers attacked the Transit Station they killed the animals, too." She shook her head. "Now Luna."

"You sure she's dead?"

"Just take one look at her . . . when those bastards have gone."

"Shit." He turned to the mound of sand that was scuffed. "They must have caught her when she walked over that heap to get to the other side. A lucky shot."

"Lucky!"

"Elsa, you know what I mean. Poor girl must have lost consciousness, then toppled over the wall."

Paul shuffled along, then took his chance. His glimpse at Luna confirmed what Elsa said. "I'm sorry. She's dead. If the shot didn't kill her the fall did. Her neck's broken."

Despite knowing that taking another look wouldn't help in the slightest, Elsa couldn't stop herself. Just in case there was even the infinitesimal chance she'd be alive. No. There she was. Luna lay sprawled on the concrete roof of a single-story building at the foot of the wall. The awkward angle of her head in relation to her shoulders broadcast its own diagnosis. Spinal column snapped. Eyes wide open. Staring. No sign of movement, nor respiration.

On this occasion, when she raised her head above the protecting curtain of stone, no one fired at her. Both she and Paul risked another look. She counted seven figures moving between gorse bushes on the cliff top. The mist made it difficult to identify them, but they appeared young. Paul was probably right. A group of youths had made their way up to the cliff on the off chance they could pick off one of the monsters who'd been stupid enough to stick their heads up above the castle wall. Bingo. The Saps had struck lucky. One of their shots had found Luna. Now she lay dead. They must have seen her fall, but they couldn't reach the body to take a trophy. Just imagine how valuable a God Scarer ear would be to the prestige of the oh so brave hunter.

"We've got to retrieve her body," Elsa told Paul.

"It's a risk going out there."

"I'll do it, then."

"Elsa, you don't know if they've left someone behind. If they've got a rifle . . . you know what I'm saying?"

"Yes, the bloody obvious." The words came in a bitter flood. "You know as well as I do they'll hack her to pieces. They'll make souvenirs out of her to impress the local tarts."

"Come downstairs, Elsa." Paul spoke calmly. "We'll see what we can do. No promises. OK?"

Dominion learned about Luna's fate along with the rest of the survivors in the cafeteria.

"I'll go fetch her," he told them.

When they were satisfied none of the townspeople lay in wait they raised the gigantic latticework of steel into its stone runners. Dominion left the Pharos as the first rays of the sun touched Scaur Ness.

16

THE VARIOUS POSTURES
OF DEATH

And death shall have no dominion . . . The words of the poet ghosted through Dominion's skull. A rising sun slammed its bloody light onto the harbor town. Even the mist on the water seemed to bleed deep crimson.

As he followed the outside of the castle wall from the portcullis side that overlooked Scaur Ness to the rear of the building he murmured the words out loud: "And death shall have no dominion." At the back of the castle there were no houses, only gorse-covered hills that ran back from the cliff, which in turn rose two hundred feet above the ocean.

Dominion found Luna on the concrete slab roof of what must have been a wartime observation post. Gently he scooped up her body with one arm beneath her back and one beneath her knees. Her head lolled back; the break in the spinal column meant it swung in an exaggerated way. A flesh-and-blood pendulum. In moments he had returned to the others, who clustered at the gate of the Pharos. Their faces were drawn.

Beech was the only one who displayed anger as he walked beneath the portcullis. "As God is my witness I want to hurt the bastard who shot her."

Dominion paused as he looked down at the red-haired nurse. "Luna wasn't shot. Her neck is broken but not from the fall." He scanned the grim faces. "One of us killed her." With that he carried the body inside. Behind him, they watched, stunned to silence.

Paul knew his laugh was a grim one. "Three years at med school. Then twenty years of experience on the wards. Of course, I was treating God Scarers. Men and women who'd died once. But I was trained. I was confident of my own expertise. Now I feel an idiot and, dare I say it? A fool of monstrous proportions."

Caitlin watched him as he paced about the room in the tower. He'd wanted to come up here alone, then stare broodingly out of the tower and try and make sense of the crazy twists and turns the last forty-eight hours had flung in his face. Caitlin had followed. Her pale blue eyes locked on to him as she stood in the room that was furnished with reproduction feasting table and chairs.

Words flooded from his mouth in a sour tide. "I worked six days a week at the Transit Station. They wheeled the corpses in. I pumped drugs through their veins until their dead eyes stood out from their wee corpse heads. Then I locked them into the Regenerators. And I was there to rebirth them. You know, I got such a feeling of love— that's the only way I can describe it: a bolt of pure love roaring through me when I saw *life* come back into their eyes. The same love a father has when he sees his new-born for the first time. I always tried to identify that split second of transition when something that was dead became alive . . . when the light came back into their eyes . . . I never could pinpoint that death-to-life rebirth. But I found it endlessly fascinating. It was never dull routine. Damn it, it was God's work. Not the devil's. I really believed I was engaged flesh, blood, and soul in making the world a better place. We defeated death. Nobody should ever be afraid of dying again. We would fill the world with immortals." He sucked in a lungful of air. "I couldn't see what was happening. It took Dominion—a freak of science—to ask what happened to all of those thousands we worked our Lazarus procedures on. Where did they go? I don't know. Then you asked why the government sacrificed the prosperity of its own people keeping the Transit Stations going when the rest of the world had destroyed theirs. Why did your country allow Scaur Ness to become moribund in order to keep my kind alive? Now Dominion has announced that one of us murdered Luna? Is he right? Dear God. I thought I was smart . . . I know nothing, I know nothing."

Paul felt the slap of her body against his. Caitlin's fragile human lips pressed against his muscular mouth. Her kiss had all the passionate, yet terror-filled fervor of a drowning woman clinging to the wreckage. Her kisses came in surging waves. His nerves seemed to detonate until bursts of incandescent heat filled his entire body.

"You know this is wrong," he panted. "It's not allowed. Nobody will talk to you if they find out . . . you'll be an outcast."

She hissed, "Then we'll burn in hell together."

With that Caitlin pulled the sling from her arm so she could embrace him. Her passion was relentless. Even though a voice in his head begged, *Leave now. Don't do this to her. Leave. Leave,* he couldn't; any more than he could order the ocean tide not to turn.

Perspiration drenched his back. "Oh God, this is wrong. I know it is."

"Because they told you?"

She caught hold of the hem of her nightdress. Smoothly she raised it to expose her naked body. To him it shone like a star. Every curve fascinated him. When he touched her bare skin it seemed lightning flashed through his limbs. His heart was its thunder.

Then she whispered the word in his ear: "Now."

Elsa stood at one end of the storeroom with Beech and Saiban. Luna lay on a trestle table. Now that Dominion had straightened her limbs and her head she appeared to be sleeping on her back. Shafts of gray light fell from the window to alight on her temples.

"I think," Saiban began, his mournful eyes regarding the corpse, "you should strip off her clothes."

Beech hissed, "Show Luna respect. Or get out of here."

"I mean,"—Saiban kept his voice under control—"those clothes are dirty. She doesn't deserve to lie on view like that. If I can find clean fabric, will you and Elsa remove her clothes? Her body should be washed. I've a comb for her hair. Then you can cover her with the fabric. She should be beautiful."

Elsa felt a lurch of surprise in her chest. Was this really Saiban speaking? He was such a cold snake—at least he was . . .

Saiban nodded before backing away, his head bowed. "Trust me. I'll find something worthy of Luna."

When the door closed she and Beech set to work without a word. Elsa eased the zipper down on Luna's uniform. Her smooth, naked skin beneath could still have been alive . . . then it would be. God Scarers were hard to kill. Hair, fingernails, and eyelashes continued to grow after the second death. Even the cells of the body continued to reproduce. It seemed as if physical corruption, having been denied access to the flesh once, was reluctant to return a second time. *If electrodes are applied to the head it will reveal electrical activity in the brain for some time to come. Our dead really do dream on their return to the grave. What dreams fill that cold brain?*

Paul knew this was impossible. It couldn't happen any more than wings would unfurl from his back to carry him into the sky. This emotional barrier could never be breached. It was impenetrable as the mind of God.

"Please," she whispered into his ear as she sat on the table with her legs wrapped around his waist. "Try again."

"I can't."

"Push your hips."

He pushed. His mind spun. This was the same as pushing a hand against a solid wall. *You know resistance will be total. Your hand can not pass through a solid barrier, yet that's exactly what happened; it was as if you found your fingers slipping through the brickwork as if it were mist. I'm doing the impossible*, he told himself. Excitement mingled with revulsion. Not disgust at this beautiful, naked human woman. No . . . this was revulsion at his own lust. He could barely bring himself to believe he'd commit this act that was pure blasphemy in the eyes of Transients and humanity alike.

But here it was. The irrevocable had happened. He'd pushed his hips against Caitlin. He entered her. An act as old as humanity itself. Only the circumstances together with *what he was* rendered this simple act of nature shockingly new. He'd broken one of their ultimate taboos. Paul's life could never be the same again. This knowledge seared itself into his mind. The act could never be erased. But he could never have dreamed of the beauty of this. His eyes fixed on her face that was framed with dark curling hair. Her dark eyebrows arched above her closed eyes. Her pink lips formed an O shape as she inhaled and exhaled to the rhythm of his body pulsing against hers.

Dominion dragged open an iron door set in the side of the chapel, which in turn was located beneath the tower that had acted as a lighthouse centuries ago. Relying on the light falling through the doorway alone, Dominion passed down the flight of steps into a crypt. There, lining the walls of the gloomy vault, were the stone sarcophagi of the lords and ladies who'd once ruled this province. He approached one tomb of gleaming white alabaster. On top of it, as if sleeping, reclined the marble statue of a regal woman clad in a gown, through which pink veins ran so it resembled the silk of a real dress.

Dominion gripped the lid of the tomb before sliding it to one side. Stone grated on stone with a sound like an agonized shriek. When the aperture was big enough he reached in one massive hand and tore the bones from their resting place.

The orgasm had built deep inside her. At first the sensation had been distant. It seemed to be buried so far down it would never struggle to the surface. Then all of a sudden it rose, expanding as it did so. The orgasm was so intense all she could do was utter a series of gasping cries as the explosion of sensation expanded within her Caitlin opened her eyes. Paul thrust into her. His eyes were closed. His lips pressed together. A sheen covered his powerful arms.

As she lay on the table her head rolled to one side. Looking at them both through the doorway that led to the spiral staircase was a man. His cold eyes locked on hers. There was no expression on his face. Nothing to reveal what he might be thinking. He merely looked, without moving. She remembered his name.

Saiban.

When Saiban's doleful face withdrew she wrapped her arms around Paul as he came. A burst of heat filled her belly. Then he was motionless apart from the rising of his chest.

When she reached up to put her hands around the back of his neck she noticed the gunshot wound had broken open again in her arm. Fresh blood stained the bandage a glistening red.

17

DEMANDS OF THE DEAD

"You can look at her," Elsa told Beech as they stood together in the storeroom. "There's nothing repulsive about her."

"I've washed bodies before. But they were always failures in transit. Never someone I knew."

Beech turned to where Luna lay on the trestle table. Her long slender body gleamed in the morning light falling through the window. There was bruising on her neck, but apart from that green mottle her body was unmarked. *Hard to kill . . . despite death her body still automatically responds to the environment. When cool air strokes her flesh her skin turns to gooseflesh. Tips of breasts darken. Nipples become erect. It's in the textbooks*, Elsa told herself. *The anatomy of the risen dead who die again.* Rational thought gave way to the irrational as she murmured to herself, "Breath again, Luna. Please."

Elsa's words provoked Beech. "She's dead. Stop asking her to breathe. Can't you see those bruises? Those are the marks of fingers. Someone snapped her neck, then threw from the wall. She's never going to breathe again . . . stop asking her!"

"I'm sorry. I only said it once. It's just that she looks as if—"

"Luna's dead! That's the end of it!" A throbbing silence, then: "Where's Saiban? He promised he'd fetch something to cover her. It's not right she's left like this. Anyone could stare at her like she's in a freak show." Beech lifted her face to the ceiling. "Saiban! Where are you?"

In the tower room Paul dressed Caitlin's wound. The raw edges of the injury had split open. Blood spilled down her arm in crimson rivulets. Every nerve in his body sang out from his flesh. He'd never felt so ashamed at what he'd done. But sex with this beautiful human female had made him feel so *alive*.

Caitlin kissed him on the face as he worked to bind her arm with the bandage. "Paul. I don't mind having your child."

"You won't." He spoke matter-of-factly despite the torrent of raw emotion surging through his body. "It's a normal part of the transition procedure. But we're all . . . castrated is too strong a word. But male and female alike are rendered sterile. So—" He gave a grim smile. "No pitpatter of tiny God Scarer feet."

Saiban arrived at the other side of the door. "I won't come in. I'll pass you what I've found through the door."

Beech scolded, "You took your time, Saiban."

"I'm sorry. I wanted to find the best I could for Luna."

Elsa opened the door six inches. His sorrowful face appeared at the other side. Hell, the man could have been a professional mourner.

"I did my best," Saiban told her. "I found this in the

gift shop. It must have been used to display the souvenirs. It's not dirty. It was in the bottom of a drawer."

She nodded as she took the bolt of creamy material from Saiban. "Thank you."

Elsa closed the door as he said, "Luna deserves better. But I did the best I could."

With the door shut Elsa said, "Beech, I can do this by myself, if you wish?"

"No. I'll help."

When they unfolded the fabric it proved to be a sheet of a silky material fifteen feet long by about five wide. It proved ample as a shroud for Luna's body. When they were done they called everyone into the room. The group stood at one end in respectful silence in the presence of the supine figure bound in white fabric.

Breathe, Luna, breathe . . . Despite her best efforts Elsa failed to prevent the mantra running through her head. She glanced at the others as they stood with their heads bowed. West, Paul, Saiban. Xaiyad and the rest. The human girl, Caitlin, hung back as if unsure to be part of the group of monsters mourning a death of one of their own. Another thought chilled her through. *We're all here*, she told herself. *That means Luna's murderer must be in this very room.* She glanced at Dominion's impassive face. *If he's right*, of course. It could have been an accident. Luna might have slipped. The bruises to her neck might have resulted from the fall. Could it have been suicide? A God Scarer killing themselves wasn't unheard of.

The mourners only stirred when Dominion picked up the body encased in the pale fabric. He carried her as a parent might carry a sleeping child to bed with an arm cradling her back and another under her legs. Instead of Luna's head swinging down this time he positioned her shrouded head so it rested against his chest.

Paul blocked Dominion's way. "Where are you taking her?"

"She must have a grave."

Paul stood aside. Dominion exited the room with the bundle in his arms. Wordlessly everyone followed. No one protested. Elsa sensed they all knew that Dominion would treat Luna with respect. Moments later they entered the medieval chapel at the base of the tower. It was a vaulted chamber with stone columns that must have been ten feet in diameter supporting the structure above. Beyond the dozen wooden pews was an altar. Beyond that, a cross had been painted in gold on the wall. It was depicted floating in a blue sky streaked with clouds.

Dominion carried Luna to the far side of the chapel; then he descended a set of steps into the crypt. *This is how we monsters bury our dead*, Elsa thought. *We have to invent our own ritual. No human priest would conduct our funeral rite, because in their eyes we already died a long, long time ago.*

Into the gloom of the crypt the muted survivors filed between the stone boxes that were the sarcophagi. One of the tombs had been opened. Dominion's work? Elsa saw the alabaster coffin was empty. On its side a tablet of carved limestone stated: *Rachel, wife of Zellerby, Earl of Holderness. Departed this life the seventh day of August, 1588. Eternal Rest.* In silence Dominion gently laid the white-shrouded body in the maw of the tomb. Then he hauled the marble slab that bore the statue of the long dead Rachel, wife of Zellerby, until it sealed the tomb shut. In the gloom of the crypt silence pressed down on them. With that weight of silence came the weight of years. This funerary chamber had presided over dozens of entombments down through the centuries. Even the inscription on the floor slabs revealed that men, women, and children had been interred beneath their feet. *Of Rosedale, sweet Annie, pure of thought and deed, ascended to heaven Christmas Day, 1726.* Another, beneath the etching of a skull: *Squire Apollinus Ewart-Brigg died as a result of a visitation of our Lord God, 1822. Peace Unto You Until You Follow Me Into Everlasting Night.*

Surrounded by death, treading on death—we are death. Elsa closed her eyes as tears pricked them. With the smell of dust she caught the faint trace of spices buried with the corpses long ago in the hope it would purify the air of the tomb. At that moment, Elsa heard the song of the ancient dead. Haunting voices ghosted through the atoms of the walls. The elegiac notes reached out to her from another existence in another universe. *They're calling me from the Land of the Dead,* she told herself. *I cheated them. I should have joined them there. I have no right to be in this world of the living. The dead are calling me back. . . .*

Behind her closed eyes dark forms rose from a deeper darkness. Indigo patterns blossomed. Faces resolved . . .

"Elsa? Elsa, are you all right?" She opened her eyes to find herself sitting in the cafeteria. Paul crouched down beside her. His eyes were large with concern. "You fainted in the crypt." He gave a reassuring smile. "It's a wonder it isn't happening to all of us. We haven't slept in days, never mind eaten anything. OK? No blurred vision? Headaches?"

Elsa shook her head. "Just light-headed . . . Luna . . ." She couldn't articulate the emotion. "It's shock. That's all." Elsa caught Paul's hand. "Luna was murdered by one of us. We've got to find out who's responsible."

"We can't be sure about that."

"Her neck was bruised. Someone snapped it."

"Before you do anything you need to rest awhile. OK?"

She nodded.

"Promise?"

Her lips tightened into a tired smile. "I promise."

She cradled her head on the table. How long she slept she didn't know, but when she opened her eyes Dominion stood over her. Drowsy, she stared up at his dark head with the sheen of short blond hair covering the massive skull. His eyes had a glossy blackness to them. They were like orbs of polished black marble.

"You remember your old life?"

"I can," she assented. "But I do my damnedest not to."

"Your family?"

"I remember them. Also I know I lost them just as much as they lost me when I made the transition. You can't return to your family in a physical way. To return to them through memory is just too bloody painful. Take my advice, Dominion. Even though you can't forget the people you love, don't think about them. Especially not when you wake up in the middle of the night. That's mental torture of the worst sort."

Dominion's dark gaze held her. "Elsa. I don't remember my family. Or who I was before I died. I'm frightened, Elsa. I know I'm different from the rest. I think I am the first man."

"The first man? What do you mean?"

"The first man. That's what I am. I know I have to do something that you and your people will hate."

"Dominion. It's an effect of the transition. Remember, you should still be convalescing. All the connections in here." She touched her temple. "They aren't complete yet."

"I'm the first man. I never existed before my transition. I have no past." His dark eyes seemed to grow even larger. They were mesmerizing and terrifying all at the same time. "I'm going to act in a way that no one can predict. That scares me, Elsa."

"Dominion. I'll fetch Paul. You're confused. It's a reaction—"

He loomed over her. "Elsa. I know you and your kind were once dead. I'm not dead . . . I am Death."

The armed force laid siege to the Pharos in the afternoon. Paul saw them scaling the four hundred steps from the town up the cliff face to the fortress. He took a moment to count the men and women who were armed with rifles and shotguns. He saw no military uniforms, but there were half a dozen police in that crowd of thirty or so.

He called to West, who walked across the courtyard, "West. There's a bunch of Saps coming up the steps. They're armed so keep out of sight."

"We need to lock the portcullis down."

"I've already jammed some timber into the hoist. They won't be able to shift it in a hurry. Can you pass word to the others?"

Of course, it had only to be a matter of time before they came. The citizens of Scaur Ness wouldn't rest with a gang of God Scarers taking up residence in their castle. Bang goes the neighborhood, was his sour thought as he returned to the cafeteria. He found Saiban in the doorway.

"So you've seen them?" The man's sad eyes fixed on him. "If it comes to surrendering peacefully or waiting for them to force us out I know which I'd chose."

"And I know which you'd chose, Saiban."

"Then accept my advice. Negotiate a peaceful surrender with these people before they attack."

"If they capture us they'll kill us anyway." Paul met

Saiban's cold stare. "Are you going to let me through the door, Saiban? Or don't you want me to warn the others?"

"After you." Saiban stood back to allow him through.

"Thank you, Saiban. You've got a heart of gold."

A sneer curled Saiban's lip. "I know you don't like me, Marais. But I am the most senior member of staff here. We must discuss a peaceful surrender. If we wait the army will arrive and then they'll dynamite this place with us in it."

"Go ahead, Saiban. Hand yourself over to the Saps. Nobody will mind. But close the gate on the way out, won't you?"

With that Paul went into the cafeteria. Most of his sorry band were there, including Dominion and Caitlin. When he saw her there in the nightdress the blood tingled in his veins. "Can I have your attention for a moment, please?" He clicked his tongue. "That sounds crass. Like I'm calling a meeting to order. Anyway, I've got to tell you that there's a group of people coming up from the town. It's mainly civilians with a handful of police. They'll never be able to raise the portcullis, although they can fire through it of course, so keep out of sight and we'll be fine."

West walked into the cafeteria with the rest of the God Scarers. Saiban crept in behind them with all the poise of a phantom.

Paul continued, "My proposal is we stay here inside the castle. We're relatively safe. It would require artillery to make a dent in those walls. But I know there might be some of you who prefer a different course of action. Now's the time to ask the question: does anyone want to surrender themselves to the people out there? A show of hands, please?"

No one raised their hand. Paul turned to Saiban. His hand wasn't raised. "I thought that's what you wanted."

"What I believe is right," Saiban began, "is safe passage for all of us out of this place. But more importantly, I have a duty of care to those human beings out there. Dominion here has proved he is capable of harming our mortal betters. I have to ensure that he passes into the care of the police without committing any further violence."

Elsa spoke up. "Saiban, if you think Dominion will just walk out of here to give himself up you're out of your mind."

Paul turned to the giant figure. "Dominion?"

"I will speak to the townspeople."

"There. You underestimated him." Saiban sounded pleased with himself.

Dominion began to move. Instead of heading for the door he went to the trestle table against the wall where the drape had been left last night. He opened it up to tip out the food he'd taken from the grocery store. Cans rattled down onto the tabletop.

"We don't have enough food," Dominion told them. "We also need clothes. They can give us more candles, too."

Saiban's chuckle was a dry one. "Dominion. You'll get nowhere making demands of the townspeople. Offer to surrender peacefully."

"We're staying here," Dominion responded. "This place belongs to us now."

Saiban shook his head, his lips pursed in disapproval. "I think you'll find the property is vested in the—"

"We're stronger, Saiban. We took it away from them. That makes it ours."

"Dear God," Saiban breathed. "He is insane."

Even Paul tried to block Dominion's exit. Not that he could delay the giant for more than a moment if he decided to keep walking. "Dominion. We need to discuss this first."

"I'll talk to them." Dominion continued moving.

Paul backed off, yet he still kept himself between the man and the door. "Dominion. The Saps'll open fire the moment they see you."

"I want them to see me. They won't have forgotten what I did to their town in a hurry."

West clapped his hands together in triumph. "See, Dominion wasn't acting crazy last night. He had a plan."

"That won't stop them from firing on you," Beech called out. "OK, they might not kill you, but they can make a hell of a mess of your head."

Caitlin ran forward. "I'll come. They won't dare shoot if I'm with you, in case they hit me."

Beech grunted, "Don't bet on it; it didn't stop them last night."

"Then I'll go first." Caitlin ducked through the door before anyone could stop her.

The rest followed at a distance. They were wary in case their presence in the courtyard was greeted with a hail of lead. Paul emerged from the doorway to see Caitlin run barefoot across the cobbles to the crisscross structure of the portcullis. Through the spaces in the woven steel he glimpsed the armed phalanx of citizens, including the face of the man who owned the grocery store. Caitlin stopped twenty paces from the portcullis; she deliberately put herself in the firing line. More than once she glanced back to make sure that she'd interposed herself between the gate and Dominion.

Voices rose from the far side of the gate. "Caitlin."

"Come out."

"What are you doing in there, girl?"

"Your father's here. Tell him you're all right."

Caitlin called out, "Dad. I'm fine."

"Come out here, Caitlin. Tell them to open the gate."

"I'm staying here, Dad. I want to."

The buzz of voices sounded angry.

"Caitlin, I understand you're not yourself. You're not thinking straight. Come home with me."

Dominion walked slowly to stand by Caitlin. With a determined sidestep she put herself in front of him, her head protecting his heart. Even so, Paul heard rifle bolts being drawn.

Caitlin called back to the others, "This man is my father." She pointed at the face beyond the gate. "He's the mayor of Scaur Ness. Tell him what you need."

"They'll get nothing from us, Caitlin." Her father grew angry. "Now leave there while you still can."

"No."

"Don't you know what those things are? They aren't even alive. Scientists take corpses and inject them with drugs, fill them with radiation and God knows what. They only appear to be living."

"You don't know them. They're kind and gentle."

"They're monsters, Caitlin. Even Jesus Christ Himself would turn His back on them. They've brought ruin on this country. Why do you think the town is a shambles?"

Dominion took a step forward. Despite the people being armed they flinched backward. Dear God, they remembered Dominion all right. And his violent entry into the town.

Once more Caitlin used her body to shield Dominion. "Dad. Listen to what he wants."

"Caitlin. No. You tell them to come out of there without causing trouble or we'll destroy every last one of them. They're parasites, don't you see that? Last winter our own people were starving—"

"Listen to me." Dominion projected his voice at them as if it were a weapon. Caitlin's father clammed up. Clearly, Dominion's explosive entrance into his store a few hours ago was still raw in his mind. "We need food, clothes, candles. For a while we intend to stay here. You will not attack us."

A woman's voice rang out. "You bastards. Who do you think you are to make demands of us?"

Rifle muzzles appeared through gaps in the portcullis.

Dominion didn't even appear to notice them. "For your own safety listen to me." His booming voice echoed from the castle walls. "I'm going down into your town. You will give me what we need."

"You can't make us."

"My name is Dominion. If any of you attempt to stop me I will hurt you. If you refuse to give me what I ask for I will take the youngest child I find and drown it in the ocean. Then, if you do not yield to my demands, I will take another child and do the same. I will keep drowning your children until you give us what we need."

Paul's heart lurched painfully in his chest during Dominion's speech. He could hardly breathe. The group beyond the gates blanched in shock. In here the God Scarers were equally stunned.

One of the God Scarers stammered, "Dear Lord, he can't be serious."

West was grim-faced. "You saw what Dominion did last night. He told the town to 'Wake up.' They saw what he's capable of. And I believe he's capable of anything."

When nobody spoke beyond the portcullis Dominion advanced until he was face-to-face with the Saps through the gridiron. "So? Whose child is going to be first? Will it be one of yours?"

Paul watched the portcullis being raised. Most of the townsfolk that had marched on the Pharos had vanished back down the steps into the town. A group of policemen remained on the walkway, perhaps there to monitor what happened, then report back to the mayor later.

Saiban stood beside Paul. "So the almighty Dominion got his way."

Paul found a smile breaking on his face. "Something told me he would."

"I wish I could say 'be it on your head' when it ends in disaster, but it will be on all our heads." With that Saiban turned away.

Paul watched Dominion stand at the top of the steps. He gazed out over the town as if he'd conquered it.

A moment later, Dominion began the descent. Behind him followed West, Elsa, and Caitlin. Paul had argued with her not to go, but she possessed a steel will. She said she wanted to choose her own clothes. After all, she couldn't live in her nightdress. Paul began to wonder about her. Was that the real reason for accompanying Dominion? Or did she want to strut through her town in the company of the giant?

18

SCAUR NESS

That afternoon the air was still. The water beyond the mouth of the harbor didn't have a wave on it. As they walked down the four hundred stone steps that led from the Pharos to the town, the sky was a misty gray. An uncanny silence pervaded the scene. Dominion led the way. Then Caitlin walked barefoot. She still wore the bloodstained nightdress, her arm in the sling. Then side by side came Elsa and West.

Despite the equilibrium of her surroundings Elsa's mind boiled with random thoughts. *Why are we doing this? They're bound to ambush us as soon as we're in those narrow streets. It's madness. But if we don't get food, how long before we starve to death? OK, we're monsters. We're hard to kill, but we're not indestructible. Just look at what happened to Luna. Good grief, what did happen to Luna? How did she fall off the castle wall? Did someone throw her over the side? Who could have done that to her? Why? The only one capable is Dominion. Where was Dominion when she died?* Dominion descended the stairs with a slow, deliberate step. The gold stubble shone against his dark scalp. *What's really happening inside that head of his? Did Luna refuse to do what he wanted, so he snapped her neck and threw her body away as if it were trash? Is he deranged? As the mood takes him, will he kill us all one by one? If that's the case, what can we do about it? If we leave the castle the townspeople will kill us. If we stay locked inside* . . .

From the town came the tolling of a church bell. A melancholy sound that seemed to count down the moments until their destruction. West appeared to feel the weight of her sense of doom. His eyes were grim as he scanned the desolate-looking town. Only Caitlin had a spring in her step. This could have been the return of the prodigal daughter. One who'd found riches in the outside world. Now she was going home to show off her acquisitions. *So what's your story, Caitlin? Why does a human being side with monsters? Why are you so upbeat?* Those questions joined the swarm buzzing inside Elsa's brain.

When the four reached the bottom of the steps they followed the road that took them over the bridge to the main part of the town. Garbage rotted in the streets. A dead cat lay on the pavement—a bloated, puffball of ginger fur. In the daylight the houses presented an even more squalid face to the world. Tiles were missing. Windows cracked. Paint came from stucco walls like peeling scabs. Most of the stores were boarded up. Listless seagulls squatted on railings that ran along the harborside. And all the time the bell tolled from the hillside church. *It tolls for thee* . . . The toxic thought only served to darken Elsa's mood.

"What? No welcome party?" West grunted. "I expected a warm reception."

Caitlin joined them so the three walked abreast behind Dominion as they entered the main street. "They've seen what Dominion can do," Caitlin told them with a glint in her eye. "They're nothing but cowards. You watch, they'll keep out of sight until he's gone."

West shook his head. "I hope you're right. Because if they decide to take an axe to us there's not a lot we can do to stop them."

"So it's true," Caitlin said. "You really aren't allowed to harm us."

"That's our law," Elsa responded. "We're psychologically incapable of harming a human being; or allow harm to befall a human being through our action or inaction."

"So I could slap your face and you could do nothing?"

That grunt of West's again that was loaded with so much emotion. "Miss. I could advise you not to strike me lest you injure your hand in the process. Other than that . . ." He shrugged.

Caitlin laughed. Dear God, she enjoyed this. "And are you really like the monsters from the Frankenstein story? I mean, are you stitched together from dead bodies?"

"No. The transition process only works on a complete individual who is deceased." West kept a wary eye on the surrounding alleyways. "We're more like Lazarus. A whole body raised from the . . . you know what."

"And there are no lightning bolts involved," Elsa pointed out. "No hunchbacks in the tower, no grave robbers, no neck bolts. Any resemblance our existence shares with Mary Shelley's Frankenstein is entirely coincidental."

"But in the eyes of human beings you're still monsters."

"Monsters, God Scarers; there are plenty of names for us." Elsa shrugged. "When the first were brought back to life we were hailed as miracles."

"From miracle to monster in forty years." West's gaze roved over the soon-to-be ghost town. "That's what I call a backward step."

Caitlin could barely stop herself from skipping along. "And you call human beings Sapheads?"

"Not officially," Elsa said.

West added, "Saphead derived from Homo sapien. It's frowned on, but lately we've tended to refer to you— well, to human beings as Saps."

"Fucking bastards!"

After the boy shouted, a bottle shattered on the road twenty paces from them. Dominion continued walking. He merely glanced in the direction of a boy running away along an alleyway.

"Bastards." The child's voice echoed back at them.

"At least the kid's got some spine," West murmured.

From the hill the tolling of the church bell grew louder. The melancholic peals rang out across the harbor with its sad assembly of derelict ships. Draped over railings were seemingly acres of fishing nets. Clearly they hadn't been used in years. All they caught now were scraps of windblown newspaper. When the four were just yards from the grocery store where Caitlin lived an old woman appeared at an upstairs window of a cottage. She shook a fist that resembled a wizened plum.

"Caitlin Jackson! You're a wrong 'un. Ever since you were six years old and you threw bleach in that lad's eyes I knew you'd be nothing but trouble, you little bitch." The woman's voice cracked as it rose in volume. "Pregnant at fifteen! Thievin,' breaking windows, runnin' away from home. You drove your poor mother into an early grave. And we know the rest. All that dirty carrying on! You'll be sorry . . ."

Caitlin hissed, "Take no notice. She's always been like that."

The woman's voice rose until it screeched like a knifepoint dragged across a plate. "Now you run off with those things. Everyone knows what they've been doing to you. A real man won't have anything to do with you now. You might as well be lying dead at the bottom of the sea. Corpse meat, that's what you are, you—"

Caitlin snapped. "What's the matter, Mrs. Wragg? Wake up with another hangover!"

"You little bitch! Just you wait . . . We'll settle you once and for all!"

"Oh yeah . . . like Mr. Wragg wanted to stay with you? Whose bed is he sleeping in these days?"

The old woman slammed the window shut.

Elsa took a deep breath. "It might be wise to avoid confrontations, Caitlin."

"That woman makes me sick."

"We're here for clothes and food; we don't want to be provocative."

"It's easy for you to be calm about it." Caitlin's eyes glittered with rage. "Yes, I had a daughter when I was fifteen. But it was her son that did it—that was only after he got me blind drunk. What's more he never even turned up the day I buried her. Chrissie'd been born with her heart all wrong. But she was a fighter. She lived two years after the doctor told me she wouldn't last the week out. The night she died—it was right on the dot of midnight—I wanted to take her to that Transit Station of yours. They wouldn't let me . . . even though I wanted her back so much I was . . ." She used the heel of her hand to scrape away a tear. "Look. You wait here while I pack my bag." When she entered the store she paused. "They've cleared out the place. You'll have to get them to bring you food from somewhere else." With that she disappeared into the back of the building. Of her father there was no sign.

Dominion stood on the pavement outside the store. The bell still tolled . . . a monotonous, one-note lament for the pathetic town. Fumes from blocked sewers floated in a miasma among the houses as if the place were possessed by a foul-smelling spirit. His sharp ears picked up snatches of conversation muttered behind the walls.

"You know what that Jackson girl has let them creatures do to her?"

"Even if her father is the mayor, he'll have get rid of her . . ."

". . . the big one with the dark skin and the yellow hair . . . that's the one that broke Anthony's arm."

"They say the best way to kill them is burn them. There's plenty of lumber in the railway yard."

"Call in the army. That's what Jackson should do . . ."

"It's the big one. He's not like the rest. He's got the devil in him . . ."

West had grown edgy as they waited. "We should go back to the castle. They might bring the food to us."

"No," Dominion told him. "They won't offer anything. We'll have to take it."

West shrugged. "Either the store's been looted since you paid it a visit or they've emptied it out. So, where now?"

"Most are in the church." Dominion gazed up at the stone building on the hill. "We'll go there."

"What happens if they don't want to play along?"

"Then there'll be children there, too."

West gave a nervous whistle. "You really intend to go along with it? Drowning their newborns?"

Dominion started walking. "They'll learn. One way or the other."

Behind him West began to follow. Elsa hung back. "I best wait here for Caitlin."

West called back in a voice that would carry to Elsa but not the people skulking in their homes. "Elsa, if trouble starts don't wait for her. Just head back up to the castle."

"Take care, Westie."

"Haven't you noticed? I'm with the eighth wonder of the world. He'll look after both of us."

Dominion heard the exchanges between the two, but he made no comment. Forces were at work inside him. He knew that now. Even though he could understand that his kind had laws that prohibited using force against humans, there was a willpower that drove him, which refused to accept that. Overriding every notion of right and wrong was the single, overwhelming instinct to survive.

Now instinct drove him up through the graveyard toward the church with its endlessly tolling bell. The cemetery bore the scars of his recent handiwork. Tombstones lay toppled in the grass. He'd smashed the faces from stone cherubs. The marble angel still lay amid broken panels inside the store where he'd hurled it. Come to that, the burnt car still lay on its side with the cross protruding from its charred shell. His step became firmer as he surged through the unkempt field of bones. Acute senses merged with his imagination. In his mind's eye he saw the reverberations of his footfalls pass through the layer of grass and down through six feet of soil to shake the bones of the dead of Scaur Ness. From the dainty skeleton of Caitlin's baby to the hefty bone structures of fishermen who had fought the oceans for their livelihoods.

Wake up . . . Wake up . . . Wake up . . .

What would those hardworking men and women of centuries past make of the town today that was nothing but a shadow of its former self?

West followed Dominion until he was twenty paces from the twin timber doors set in the bottom of the church tower. Dominion didn't pause. As he walked he balled his fist, ready to pound on the door.

Before he could reach the doors, they swung open to

reveal a figure dressed in black. Dominion's gaze swept over the man. He was aged around eighty. His cheeks were hollow and the face so gaunt that the veins in his forehead stood proud of the taut skin. The skin itself, an unhealthy yellow, was mottled with pale brown marks. Dominion could smell the priest's blood. It slowly turned poisonous inside him.

Dominion intended walking past the man into the body of the church where the congregation prayed. Row after row of hunched shoulders were all he could see as the soft throb of voices uttered their holy verse. When Dominion was no more than a yard away from the door the priest raised his hand.

The priest spoke firmly. "I won't allow you in there."

"The mayor is inside?"

"He is. But this is a religious service. Neither he nor my congregation are to be disturbed. I know who you are. And why you are here."

"Then move aside."

"No."

"I warned them what would happen if they didn't give me what I need."

The priest's face hardened. "Yes, I heard about your threat. But I won't permit you to intimidate me . . . what is more, you can't hurt the part of me that is constant and incorruptible. Do you understand?" Even though exhaustion was creeping into every cell of the holy man's body he refused to back down. "Dominion, I've heard you're not like the other transients. You'll probably take pleasure in hurting me, but let me tell you this. You are a blasphemy. When I see you I don't see a big man; I see a corpse that has no soul. You've been made to walk and talk by a trick of science, that's all. You're an empty vessel. Nothing more. I pray that your soul is already with God. But you standing there are nothing but clay."

Dominion held eye contact. "You are dying."

"No doubt your kind can see death in my eyes, can't you?"

"How long?"

"I'll live as long as God wants me to serve my parish."

"What does it feel like?"

"Dying? You've experienced it, haven't you? So, why ask me?"

Dominion looked over the man's shoulder. The occupants of the church kept their heads bowed. Above the altar, Christ on His cross gazed down. Taking a step back, Dominion said, "Tell Mayor Jackson I'll keep my promise." In the congregation a mother held her baby to her breast as she prayed.

"Before you do anything, Dominion, hear me out." The priest raised his hand again, almost but not quite touching Dominion's chest where the bullets had punched through the fabric of his sweatshirt. "We've debated your demands. A car will deliver food and lamps to the Pharos this evening. Understand this, also, if you're not gone in forty-eight hours the military will be informed of your whereabouts. There, you have my word that you will have your supplies by tonight. Now leave us alone."

The priest's eye contact didn't waver. After a moment he stepped back across the threshold of the church. The doors swung shut.

"You done it again." West sighed with relief. "You've got what you want." He took a step forward. "Dominion? What's wrong?"

When he didn't reply, West moved closer. "Dominion? Anything the matter?"

Dominion took a deep breath. "Look at me . . . I'm changing."

19

WHITE HANDS

"Hello." Elsa pushed open the door to the hallway. Behind her, the bare shelves of the store shared a barren symmetry with the rest of the town. "Caitlin? Hello?"

When there was no reply Elsa moved into the rear quarters of the shop. A couple of storerooms stood nakedly empty, too. Right at the back of the building a kitchen with grubby appliances looked out onto a walled yard.

"Caitlin? Are you packed yet?" *Maybe Caitlin's bedroom is in the attic? That's why she can't hear me.*

After walking back along the passageway from the kitchen Elsa found the door to a staircase. Its carpet had seen more prosperous days. In the center, where the pile should be, years of passing feet had rubbed away the material to reveal the string backing.

"It's time we were going back to the castle," Elsa announced to thin air. "Have you changed your mind? Are you staying here?"

At the top of the stairs a gloom-filled landing gave

way to three closed doors. The first she opened revealed a double bed. Men's shirts hung from a rail by the window. She crossed the landing to what must be a rear bedroom. When she opened it the first thing she heard was a shout.

"*Shit.*"

"One of the things followed her up here!"

One glance told her the story. Three men were in the room. Their ages could have been anything from late twenties to thirties. Caitlin lay facedown on the bed. A man with a red sweaty face had one knee pressed between her shoulder blades. One of his hands was clasped over her mouth. His right hand gripped her hair. Another man, this one with a goatee, held her by the wrists. Caitlin's eyes were wide with fear. A third man stood with his back to the wall.

"OK," he called to the others. "Leave her. Come on."

Red-face snapped, "Chicken."

"She doesn't deserve this, Mel. Leave her alone."

Mel, the red-faced one, spat back. "Doesn't deserve it? Christ, by the time I've finished with the bitch, she'll never walk again." He tugged her hair so hard it lifted her head. Caitlin cried out in pain.

The one with the goatee wore an expression of alarm. "Wait. What if that big bastard's here? He's not like the rest. He bust some guy's arm last night."

"I don't see him, do you?"

"No, but—"

"Then shut up, you spineless piece of, uh . . . do that again and I'll rip your hair out."

Caitlin stopped struggling.

Elsa moved aside from the door. The stench of alcohol cut through her nostrils like a blade. This must be the coffin paint that Caitlin had mentioned. The liquor boiled up in backyard stills. She didn't doubt its potency from the slurred speech of the men. The one called Mel had a face that was redder than an overripe cherry, while his eyes were glazed with alcoholic madness.

The one by the wall pleaded, "Come on, Mel . . . we've got to get out of here."

"Wait until I've finished with Queen Caitlin here. Just because she's the mayor's daughter she thinks she's royalty. She fucks around with these—these monsters. And what is this one anyway? Is that one of the uniforms that they wear in the Transit Station?"

The other man started having second thoughts. "Maybe Karl's right, Mel. Have you seen the size of the fucker who smashed up the town?"

"These are God Scarers. You know what that means, Johnnie boy? They can't hurt humans like us."

"You slept through it last night, Mel. You were off your wallet! There's this big God Scarer. He's a giant. He set fire to a car, and when some guys tried to stop him—"

Mel climbed off Caitlin. "You two." He pointed at his buddies. "Learn from a master." With that he swung a punch at Elsa. The blow rocked her backward. From a sheath attached to his belt Mel drew a diver's knife with an eight-inch blade.

"Hold on, Mel." Karl held up his hand. "You don't know what you're getting into here."

"Listen, stupid. When the army blew up the Transit Station some monsters got away. Farmers've been rounding up these things, then burning them alive. No one cares anymore." Mel grabbed Elsa by the hair. "You've got to understand one thing . . . no . . . two things. Two things!" His voice slurred; the stench of booze made Elsa gulp. "Two things, Johnnie boy. Unos dos facts. One: These little darlings can't fight back. They're not allowed to hurt us. Two: The new government wants us to destroy these moldy bitches. They're dead anyway. You wouldn't leave a body lying in the street to rot, would you? S'not hygienic."

Caitlin lay on the bed held by the one called Johnnie, but she could speak. "Mel. Leave her alone. She hasn't done anything to you."

"Shut up, Caitlin."

"Please, sir," Elsa began. "If you let us go, we'll leave right away for—"

"Who asked you to talk? You're a fucking corpse!"

In a rage that made his face burn even redder he lashed out with the knife. Instead of stabbing her he cut straight down the center of her uniform top, then ripped it open to expose her breasts.

"I order you to stand still," he told her. "God Scarers must obey their human betters. Isn't that right?"

"Yes, sir." Elsa spoke in a whisper.

"You're my property now, aren't you?"

"Yes, sir." Elsa's mind whirled. He held her by the hair. If she hurt him by breaking his grip, then it would contravene the monster law. Elsa couldn't bring herself to break that taboo. *Do no harm to humanity.*

Mel grinned, the stench of raw spirit flooding her face. "Let's see how she responds to a bit of surgery." He laughed, then touched her nipple with the point of his knife. "A bit of beauty treatment will do her—*it*—a power of good."

Karl became agitated. "Mel. This isn't funny; leave her."

"No, she's an it—aren't you an *it?*"

Elsa was powerless. "Yes, sir."

Her eyes were drawn from the drink-sodden face to the glittering point of the diver's knife that lightly pressed against her dark nipple with just enough force to depress the flesh.

This was arousing Mel now. "I've gutted thousands of fish with this blade. Do you want to see how good I am with it?"

"If that's what you want."

"I'm a fucking expert with it. Swish—slice open the fish's belly. *Ffft*—out with its guts. All in a stinking pile on the floor. Now, what's inside you monster whores?"

He pushed the point of the blade against her nipple. She gasped at the pricking sensation. The tip of the blade slipped through her skin. Mel toyed with the blade. He moved it slightly so her breast moved with it.

"That doesn't hurt, does it?"

Johnnie stared in fascination at the bare breast. "A little bit of pain never hurt anyone."

Both Mel and Johnnie barked out harsh laughter.

Only Karl balked. "Stop it. You're hurting her."

"Shove it, Karl."

"Mel!" Caitlin screamed. "You'll pay for this."

"Ha, in your dreams. Wait a minute. I've got an idea now we're starting to get all scientific." Mel thoughtfully patted the knife blade against his cheek. It transferred a spot of Elsa's blood to his skin just below his right eye.

"This is going to be good, Mel." Johnnie chuckled. "You've got something planned, haven't you?"

"Yeah, call it a dilemma. A dilemma for this monster."

"Her name's Elsa," Caitlin snapped.

"This monster can't attack us. And it can't stand back and do nothing if a human is being hurt. So what happens if I cut off one of Caitlin's ears?"

"The monster can't do nothing to you." Johnnie grinned.

"But then it can't stand there and not help a human. Interesting idea, huh?"

Johnnie licked his lips as images that were pleasing to him ran through his mind. "Have a go, Mel." He pulled Caitlin's dark hair aside to reveal her ear.

"In the interests of science, Johnnie boy, I will. See if

little Miss Monster here blows a fuse over the dilemma. Can't hurt me. Can't save Caitlin. What does she do?"

Karl stepped forward with his fists bunched. "I'm not letting you hurt either of them anymore."

"You know you're really vexing me, Karl. What's got into you?"

"Karl loves Caitlin." Johnnie tugged Caitlin's hair to the rhythm of his chant. "Karl's going to marry the bitch . . . marry the bitch."

Caitlin groaned with pain.

"You two are off your heads." Karl took a step toward Johnnie.

Mel brandished the knife. "Maybe we should start with your ears, Karl?"

Karl suddenly put his finger to his lips.

"Hey! Who do—"

"Listen," Karl hissed.

"You lump of brown stuff. You're nothing but—"

Karl held up his hand to silence them. "Footsteps."

Mel's booze-sodden face suddenly changed its expression as he listened. The sound of footfalls grew louder downstairs. Then a pause. A moment later a *clump-clump* as heavy feet climbed the stairs.

Karl gasped. "Shit. I told you."

Mel's face hardened. "Karl. Hold on to this thing." He pushed Elsa toward the man.

She felt Karl's hand against her back. If anything, he wasn't restraining her. He steadied her after Mel's brutal shove. Johnnie still gripped Caitlin by the wrists. Only by now he had the look of a frightened sheep the way his head turned left and right as if he expected attackers to fly through the bedroom walls at him.

Johnnie whined, "Mel. This isn't looking good—"

Mel held his finger to his lips as he concealed himself

behind the open door. Quickly he changed his grip on the knife so he could stab the blade down into the neck of whoever walked through the doorway. His face blazed crimson. Ruptured veins in his cheeks showed like a child's scribble. Elsa glanced at Caitlin. From the look in her eye Elsa knew she was going to shout a warning. Her captor anticipated her plan too. He rammed her face-down against the mattress so she couldn't cry out.

Dominion materialized in the doorway. He slowly stepped from the gloom, allowing the gray light of that dull afternoon to reveal his huge figure that had to lower the shaved head to enter.

Elsa glanced at Johnnie. He stared openmouthed at the apparition that had ghosted into the doorway. Dominion appeared to move with agonizing slowness. His hand glided upward until the palm rested on one of the upper door panels. Then he pushed. One fluid movement eased the door backward. The drunk with the knife reacted with a clumsy jerk as if to retreat. Only the timber door pushed him back until he was sandwiched between the edge of the door and the corner of a closet. Even though the man was pinched between the two timber surfaces he aimed a blow at Dominion as he leaned into the room. The stab went wide. Before he could try again Dominion simply pushed the door harder. There was no exertion on Dominion's part. Mel, however, croaked in pain. The glass doorknob dug into the man's stomach. What's more, the force was so great it pushed the heavy closet so it tipped back a couple of inches. When the bedroom wall prevented it tipping back farther, that's when the drunk really began to feel the pressure. He tried to shout in pain, but the pressure on his chest was so great all he could manage was a gurgling sound. The red face darkened to a congested purple. Saliva trickled down his chin. His bloodshot eyes bulged. The knife dropped from nerveless fingers.

By this time Karl and Johnnie had seen enough. They scrambled through the bedroom window onto the outhouse roof. Elsa heard them land with a thump into the yard before they fled.

Caitlin leaped up from the bed; her eyes flashed. "Don't stop, Dominion. I want you to kill the bastard!"

By this time Mel's tongue poked out between lips that had become a swollen purple. Air spurted from his throat with a wet crackling sound.

"Crush him." Caitlin clenched his fists. "He hurt me in the past." Her eyes locked on Mel's bulging stare. "How does it feel, Mel? You've met your match now!"

Mel hung limp, trapped between the door and the corner of the closet. Dominion's face was impassive. He merely appeared to be standing with his palm resting on the door. Did he even know he crushed the life out of the drink-sodden bully?

Only when Mel vomited a black liquid that smelled of bile and neat alcohol did Dominion turn his massive head to his victim. Then he released pressure on the door. Amazingly Mel didn't fall to the floor. He stood there gasping. Strings of black fluid hung from his lips. Even though he kept his balance, just, his eyes were dim.

"You should have finished him," Caitlin yelled. She picked up a brass plate from the bedside table and slammed it into her tormentor's face. The blast of pain roused the man. Mel straightened, touched his nose, saw blood there from the injury Caitlin had inflicted. He moved off in a shambling run through the door. Then came a clattering as he half fell, half ran down the stairs.

"Dominion, why didn't you kill him? That bastard raped me when I was fifteen. I had his child. He never even came to Chrissie's funeral! You should have made him pay!"

Dominion said nothing. He stared straight into the bedroom wall as he took three steps, then stumbled forward onto the bed. He rolled onto his back; his chest rose as if he'd been running. With an effort he lifted his arms so he could examine his hands.

"What's happening to me?" he grunted.

Elsa and Caitlin rushed to him as West entered the room.

Elsa held her cut uniform over her naked body as she called back, "West. What's wrong with him?"

"I don't know. We went to the church—"

"He's been shot?"

"No . . . nothing. He became anxious about his hands."

"Did he say if they were hurting? Does he have cramps, or tingling in his fingers?"

"Check them yourself." West approached the bed. "See? The skin of his arms is dark, but the hands have turned white."

"It could be a circulation problem." Elsa touched Dominion's forehead. "Temperature's normal as far as I can tell."

"Take a look at his chest," West told her. "His hands are white but the torso's darker than his face and arms."

"And what are these marks on his skin?" Caitlin asked, pointing at pale lines that looked as if they'd been chalked there.

"They appear to be old scars," Elsa replied. "They weren't there before."

"Oh God." Caitlin put her hand over her mouth. "Is he dying?"

"I sincerely hope not," Elsa declared as she examined his arms, then his head and neck. Thick white lines encircled the wrists where the shirt cuffs would be. Another white line circumnavigated his neck in the same position as a collar.

Elsa studied the stark, white hands. "Any diagnosis, West?"

"Don't think I'm being flippant, but I'd say Dominion is coming apart at the seams."

As West finished speaking Dominion laid down his head with a sigh. A moment later his eyes closed.

20

A BLOODRED TIDE

Luna's cries brought Dr. Paul Marais back to the castle crypt. Beech went with him. As they descended into the crypt they heard thunderous pounding—a fist striking the inside of the marble tomb.

Saiban came partway down the steps into the shadow-filled void where a copse of stone pillars supported the vaulted ceiling. The man screamed: "*Marais. For God's sake, you told us she was dead!*"

Groans boomed through the stonework. A deep sound that throbbed with immeasurable pain. Paul approached the tomb in which Dominion had placed the corpse just hours ago. He could see that the statue carved in veined marble vibrated from the onslaught from beneath the slab. Saiban clamped his hands over his ears.

Paul caught Beech's eye. "Will you help me move the lid?"

"No!" Saiban's howl merged with the groans pulsing through the crypt. "For heaven's sake, don't let her out!"

Paul moved to the head of the stone tomb, Beech to the carved feet.

Saiban howled, "Leave her. Don't open it!"

"Saiban!" Paul had to shout above the groans that created a deep booming sound. "Saiban. This happens sometimes. Even though a Transient might be brain-dead, physical signs of life continue . . ."

"Leave her, then. Don't open the grave!"

"I've got to check. I might have been wrong."

Beech added, "We haven't any instruments. There's a chance she might be alive."

Saiban's long, mournful face became a deathly white. "You saw her neck. She must be dead. For pity's sake leave her alone."

Paul snapped back, "Saiban, you don't have to stay."

Saiban clutched at the wall. His eyes bled sheer terror.

"OK, Beech. On the count of three. One, two, three . . ."

Together, they slid aside the stone.

Beech gasped. The flood of cries erupted from the open tomb. At that moment Paul Marais believed that heartrending voice would resonate through the surrounding tombs to shake the dust from the bones before echoing down into the bedrock on which the castle had stood for a thousand years. Like ripples spreading out in a pool, the woman's death call would spread out through the earth to reach into graves both ancient and modern to ring the cold hearts of the dead like a bell.

Wake up . . . Wake up . . .

What he saw in the open tomb filled him with terror. Even the shadows of the tomb appeared to flow out onto his bare hands to infect him.

"*Oh God.*" He flexed his fingers, as he murmured to himself, "OK. Steady. Keep calm. You've got to do this."

Then he reached both hands down toward the occupant of the casket.

Even though cloud prevented any sight of the sun, Dr. Paul Marais judged it to be low in the sky. Dusk crept into the town below. A mean beggarly light that barely revealed the tangle of alleyways running between the cottages. The harbor resembled a lake of oil rather than seawater, black and viscous. He stood in the highest tower of the Pharos. It still housed the lamp that had signaled to mariners the presence of Scaur Ness, although the mass of cobwebs revealed it hadn't been lit in years. Even from this high point—as far from the castle crypt as he could get without actually leaving the building— he could still hear Luna's after-death groans. Closing his eyes, he took a deep breath. He'd come up here with the intention of waiting for the return of Dominion, Caitlin, Elsa, and West—especially Caitlin. They were overdue; they might have been captured . . . only the single thing that made demands on his attention was Luna. Textbooks on Transient biology warned this could happen. In his years at the Transit Station he'd witnessed similar conditions after the death of one of his kind. But nothing as extreme as this. *So what's all this telling you? You saw the evidence. What does it all mean? I moved away the stone lid. Luna is in there. Only she's not still. She's writhing as if she's in agony. She's beating the sides of the coffin with her hands. Wounds have opened up in her fists. Blood gushes from them. It's three inches deep in the bottom. It's like she's writhing in a bathtub of blood. Even though Luna is dead her nervous system still causes the spasms. These affect her diaphragm and vocal cords. Luna is groaning; sometimes it's a shout. Then there's Saiban. He's terrified. He's asking, "What's she saying?" And I reply: "She's brain-dead. It's a postmortem effect, that's all."*

Then I examine the body—it's hot to the touch. And, dear God, that smell? The neck's broken. The face is expressionless, yet she's moaning, she's squirming, her bare arms slap the side of the tomb. The lips move as if she's kissing the air; her groans become a cry as her back arches. Saiban is begging me: "What's she saying? I know she's talking. For heaven's sake, man, tell me."

"She's dead, Saiban." I keep repeating that like it's the chorus of a fucking song. "She's dead . . . she's dead . . . she's not articulating words. She's dead."

Then Beech and I hoist the stone slab back onto the tomb to seal Luna in even though she's croaking syllables like she's reciting the book of the fucking dead. And the stone lid tips because it's so damn heavy, and Beech sees what's on the underside of it.

She shakes her head as if she can't believe what's on the coffin lid. "Paul. Have you seen that? Those aren't just smears. Luna's written a word in her own blood."

A breath of cold air came from the ocean as if that saltwater body had just exhaled. Paul shivered. It tingled down his scalp to shiver to the bottom of his spine.

"Luna's brain-dead," he murmured to as he gazed over the town. "Her movements are after-death spasms. Purely involuntary." He took a deep breath. "Then why did she write on the inside of her tomb?"

In the castle courtyard that was enclosed by forty-foot-high walls the darkness was almost complete. After descending the tower Paul paused at the portcullis. Xaiyad, one of the guys from pathology, sat there on a crate.

Paul asked, "Any sign of Dominion?"

"Nothing."

"It's been six hours. They should be back by now."

Xaiyad nodded at the gate. "All I can say is it's been quiet down there. There've been no gunshots."

"Nevertheless, I'm uneasy about the delay. Will you call me as soon as you see anything?"

"Sure." Xaiyad nodded. "I heard about Luna. After all that's happened to her it's bad news that she can't even rest in peace."

Paul grimaced. "I wish there was some way of incinerating the body, but short of building a fire in the courtyard . . ." He shrugged.

"It'll pass eventually. Her nervous system will fail as the cells begin to corrupt. Sorry, Paul. That's what passes for small talk among pathologists."

Paul moved on. As he crossed the yard to the cafeteria entrance Beech caught him up.

"Paul."

He gave a sympathetic smile. "It was rough back there with Luna. Are you all right?"

"I'm a nurse. You take the good with the bad. And you?"

"Fine." He was anything but—then as a doctor he swallowed good and bad, too. "I'm going to open one of those cans that we looted from the store last night. I haven't eaten in days."

"Listen." Beech's green eyes were almost luminous in the gloom. "What did you make of the word Luna wrote on the lid?"

"Beech. It can't have been a word. It's impossible."

"But hasn't the impossible happened over and over again in the last seventy-two hours. A government that's in power for thirty years is toppled overnight. The army destroys the Transit Stations. Transients are slaughtered. Dominion breaks the unbreakable rule by killing human beings. And now Luna . . ."

"Luna's brain-dead."

"But she still wrote the name of the person who murdered her."

"Beech." Paul spoke gently. "We're in shock. Everything looks weird right now. Even the daylight looks as if it's leaking out from underground rather than coming out of the sky. Did you see how poisonous the light looked today?"

"Paul. I repeat: In her own blood Luna wrote the name of the person who murdered her."

"Granted, it looked *like* letters. *Like*. That's all. They're just random smears caused by involuntary muscle spasms—"

"That just happen to resemble letters that form a name." Beech folded her arms. "Open your eyes, Paul. Yes, we're changing. The God Scarers are evolving. Dominion kills human beings. We're fighting for survival rather than passively accepting our fate. And even though Luna is clinically dead she still wrote the name of her attacker."

Images seared Paul's mind. Luna writhing in a pool of her own blood in the coffin. Dominion crushing the soldier's skull on the bridge. Him and Caitlin naked. How he slid into her in that fusion of disgust and ecstasy. *Everything is changing.*

Beech challenged him to deny what she said with a "Well?"

"OK. The blood smears resemble letters. What did it spell out?"

"I couldn't tell exactly. But I believe I know which name Luna tried to write."

"So who murdered her?"

Beech bit her lip. "I won't say yet. Not until I'm sure."

Paul watched her face, wondering if she was bluffing. He thought: *Maybe she's doesn't know and is trying to provoke a reaction from me? Perhaps she hopes I'll guess the same name that's in her own mind?*

A seagull cried out across the castle, while all the time from the crypt came the groans of poor, dead Luna. The flesh had begun to decay, turning the groans into a broken, guttural sound.

Paul waited for Beech's nerve to break; then she'd utter the name she believed she saw painted there in blood on the white tomb.

Instead, Xaiyad called from where he stood at the portcullis, "Paul. You best take a look at this. Something's happening down in the town."

21

DOWNTOWN

In the hallway downstairs a clock chimed seven. They'd been standing in silence in Caitlin's bedroom where Dominion lay on the bed. The clock voicing the hour broke the spell.

"He's still alive," Elsa told them. "There's no doubting that."

Caitlin placed her palm on his forehead. "Do you know what's wrong with him?"

"Without diagnostic equipment we're only guessing. I've not seen anything like it." West turned to Elsa. "Have you?"

"Dominion's transition was only completed a few days ago. He shouldn't have been racing across the countryside. It could be a simple case of overexertion before he was physically fit . . . I don't know."

West crouched beside the bed to examine Dominion's face. "But these scars? They're all over the body. Have you seen anything like it before?"

Elsa should her head. "Then Dominion's a mystery.

He's the first to wake up in the Regenerator. And you know as well as I do what he did to the soldiers."

"It must be exhaustion." Caitlin stroked his face. "He's only sleeping."

"I hope you're right." Elsa knew Caitlin's verdict was borne by faith rather than any medical diagnosis. She remembered West's observation: ". . . Dominion is coming apart at the seams." The white scars that traced lines across his body were more pronounced than just moments ago. Instead of mere coloration in the skin, as they had been, they now; formed distinct grooves. Once more she checked his chest. The bullet wounds had almost healed. Then it wasn't those that interested her professional curiosity now it was his torso. The taut skin over the muscled body was dark enough to be described as black. The skin of his face was a golden brown, while blond stubble covered his scalp. The arms were the same brown, yet they terminated in white hands. Her eyes met those of West. An understanding passed between them. Both were beginning to make the same assumption about Dominion.

West began, "It doesn't help us staying here."

"We can't easily move him," Elsa pointed out.

"We mustn't carry him." Caitlin's voice was firm. "If the people in this place see he's lost his strength, then they'll tear you apart. We've got to make everyone believe that Dominion's ready to break their heads if they attack us."

"Won't they be suspicious if we sit here all night?"

Caitlin was thinking fast. "We've got to act as if Dominion's busy with some plan. So we need to go out into the town as if nothing's wrong."

West became uneasy. "Something is wrong. We're pretty vulnerable right now."

"Word will get around about Mel being hurt by Dominion. What with Dominion smashing the place up last night it'll make them wary." She shrugged. "For now anyway."

Elsa nodded. "At least it'll give Dominion a chance to sleep. If all he needs is rest we've nothing to lose."

"Only our heads." West gave a grim smile.

Caitlin went to the closet that had played its part in crushing Mel. "I'll change out of this nightdress. And Elsa needs new clothes as well."

Elsa looked down at her own medic uniform that had been cut open by the drunk's knife.

Caitlin said, "Dad gave up ordering new clothes to stock the store, but there's still some left over in the attic. There's got to be something to fit you."

Elsa turned to the unconscious giant of a man on the bed. His chest rose and fell with a steady rhythm. His eyelids remained closed without so much as a single flicker. "I'm not happy about leaving him here. What happens if those men come back?"

"I'll lock the door downstairs that leads from the store into the house. Then I'll push the key under the gap. If Dominion wakes up and wants to leave he'll find the key on the floor. Come on, what are you waiting for?"

Twenty minutes later all three stepped out through the doorway of the grocery store that Dominion had wrecked on their arrival in Scaur Ness. Dusk had infiltrated deep shadow into the alleyways. Even the open streets had become gloomy due to the approach of both sunset and heavy cloud. Nobody had moved the wreck of the car that Dominion had set alight. The wrought-iron cross he'd driven into the body of the vehicle still jutted from it to create a surreal automotive grave. A couple of little kids played under the fishing nets that had long ago been draped across the harbor railings. They stood up beneath them so they formed shrouds; then they made ghostly moaning sounds.

West murmured, "Do you think we've inspired some new games?"

Elsa watched the children as they peered through the reticulated rope work at the God Scarers as they walked by.

Caitlin told them, "We'll go to the Angel Tavern."

"Is that wise?" Elsa asked as the children renewed their *whoo-whoo* calls.

"That's where my father will be, along with the chief of police, plus what passes for the town's top people." A laugh escaped Caitlin's lips. "I was going to say, 'Act natural.' But, you know . . ." She shrugged.

"Don't worry," West murmured, "we're the most natural down-to-earth monsters you'll ever find."

Elsa caught sight of her reflection in a window. The only garment to fit her among the cartons of clothes was a summer dress. In shades of electric green it wasn't ideal. Short of walking with a blanket round her, however, it was that or nothing. Thin straps supported it across her shoulders. The design meant it hugged her figure. After all those years either in uniform or sweats, this was something close to a miraculous transition in its own right. The dress was downright sexy.

"Elsa looks beautiful." Caitlin made a point of addressing West. "Doesn't she?"

West nodded. "Definitely. It suits you."

"Bloody liar." Despite her jokey tone the new-look Elsa pleased her.

"I was going to add dazzling."

"In these greens I'm dazzling all right. I'd have been more at ease in what Caitlin's wearing." She appraised the jeans and sweatshirt. After the billowing nightgown the close-fitting clothes made the woman appear taller.

"The men in Scaur Ness are breast men," Caitlin told

her. "With that cleavage you'll get them fired up even though they'll pretend you disgust them."

"Oh, we'll disgust them all right." Elsa spoke with feeling. "We're monsters, remember?"

"You clearly didn't notice that you were giving Mel the thrill of his year."

"Nonsense."

"You take it from someone who knows these people. He was so hot for you he was ready to burn."

From high on the cliff top Paul, Beech, and Xaiyad watched the three walk along the street on the far side of the harbor. There wasn't much light but there was enough to identify them.

So could Saiban, who appeared beside him like a wretched spirit. "So where's Dominion?" he breathed.

"He might have been caught." Xaiyad leaned forward to peer through the grill of the portcullis. "There must be a town jail."

"I'd say not from their body language," Beech murmured. "They're confident."

"Are my eyes deceiving me?" Saiban stared at the three far below. "Or is Elsa wearing a dress?"

The three entered the Angel, a whitewashed building just twenty paces from the harbor edge. Its bar was a large one, although there was something oppressively low about its ceiling. A sign painted on the mirror behind the bar proclaimed THE ANGEL. LARGEST HOSTELRY IN THE BOROUGH. FIRST ALE DRAWN 1833.

West murmured so only Elsa could hear, "This accounts for the streets being so empty. The whole damn town's in here."

Elsa couldn't disagree. There must have been dozens of men and women in the bar. They either stood at the bar itself or sat at tables. All had chosen the same drink. A dark, cloudy ale topped with a thin scum. Elsa had a mental image of it being brewed in big old rusty vats in the cellar beneath their feet. West nodded toward a corner of the bar. On a timber platform raised above the floor was a long table. Behind it sat eight men in a row. One wore a policeman's uniform. She recognized the thin man in the center as Caitlin's father, Mayor Jackson. So those were the seats of power. This tavern must be where they held court. Even their lordly seating arrangements meant they looked down on the rest of the patrons.

"Seems medieval to me," West murmured. "Masters and commoners, isn't it?" His eyes roved the bar. "See the man in black sitting by himself? That's the priest Dominion spoke with earlier."

"He's the only one who isn't thirsty."

"Notice how gaunt he is? He admitted he won't be long for this world."

Elsa made a point of not staring, but she noticed the man's skull-like face. The wrists that protruded from the sleeves of his black coat were painfully thin.

Everyone in the bar stopped talking. They stared at the newcomers. The silence was so intense Elsa could have believed she'd hear the hiss of bubbles rising in the beer. None of the people there even seemed to be breathing.

Caitlin caught her eye, a signal for the pair of them to follow her. She walked along the aisle between two rows of tables toward where her father sat with his companions on the dais. Wraiths of blue tobacco smoke drifted over the dozens of watchful faces. Elsa sensed the rising tide of disgust—even sheer hatred for the two creatures that had invaded this haven.

As if it couldn't be suppressed any longer a woman's

voice slashed through the air. "What are you doing here? You weren't invited. Get out!"

This opened the floodgates.

"Bloody animals."

"Caitlin, your mother'll be turning in her grave."

"What do you think you're doing with those beasts? Stay away from them."

A drunkard's voice rose. "Get their stinking corpse meat out of this bar."

One hurled the dregs of his glass against West's face.

"How did the army let these bastards escape?"

"Last night they marched down that street like they owned the place."

"Burn the damn lot of them, then dump what's left in the sea."

A man with a red face stood up to block Caitlin's way. Elsa heard him shouting, but his voice was so slurred by drink she couldn't understand what he said.

"Joseph . . . Joseph. Let them through."

Caitlin turned to see that the priest had struggled out of his chair. He was clearly so ill that he had to steady himself by pressing one hand down on the tabletop.

"Joseph. Don't lay a hand on them," the priest commanded. "The authorities will deal with the creatures."

"But you know what they are, Father?" The man swayed from the effects of the beer. "These two are nothing but monsters. They aren't even alive."

"I agree. But we will not hurt them."

"Father, you can't be serious. And look at this woman. Caitlin Jackson. She's been whoring round with them up there."

Caitlin's father rapped his knuckles on the table. "Sit down, Joseph, or go home."

Joseph obeyed. The mayor was still a powerful figure in these parts.

"Dad . . ." she began, then opted for the formal. "Mayor Jackson. We've come to ask when the food and lamps will be delivered to my friends."

Friends? Elsa realized Caitlin's allegiance caused an angry stir in the bar.

The mayor's face flushed red, a mixture of shame and anger. "Caitlin. I want you to come home."

"Not yet. We've come about the supplies."

Mayor Jackson lowered his voice as if embarrassed to speak. "The supplies are on a truck. They'll be delivered to the Pharos soon." He grimaced. "Satisfied?"

"That's all we wanted to know."

As the three left the tavern Caitlin murmured under her breath to Elsa, "Now can we can go back to the others?"

Outside, the gloom had deepened. Even so, the cloud cover had started to break, revealing slashing rents of blue overhead. The children still played under the fishermen's nets, although when they saw Elsa and West they started name-calling.

"Ugly buggers."

"Freaks!"

"Get back to Castle Frankenstein!"

West murmured, "It won't be wise to hang around here. We'll see if we can wake Dominion and get out of here."

"I'm with you on that one. They weren't overjoyed to see us in the bar, were they?"

"They're cowards!" Caitlin insisted. "There's no work here, but they still haven't got the guts to leave Scaur Ness to find jobs."

"That makes them angry," Elsa said as they walked back to the grocery store. "They'll be wanting a scapegoat." Above them on its cliff the castle promised at least a temporary safe haven. The question now: *If Dominion is still unconscious, how do we get him back up there?*

When they arrived at the grocery store they quickly passed through the shattered entrance to the rear of the store. The door Caitlin had locked now lay wide open. West ran up the stairs to the bedroom.

He called down, "Dominion isn't here."

Caitlin nodded at the door. "The key's in the lock, so he let himself out."

"But where'd he go?"

West came down the stairs. "If he's back at the castle, that solves one problem."

Elsa clicked her tongue. "But that leaves us in a vulnerable position."

When Elsa emerged into the gloom of the dusk she realized her words were more prophetic than she thought. The occupants of the Angel Tavern had emptied out onto the pavement. Some must have been drinking hard all afternoon, because at least a dozen men were swaying from the effects of the alcohol. A few had pulled half-pint bottles of a coal-black liquid out of their jacket pockets. Whatever had brought them out of the bar wasn't going to interrupt their liquor intake if they could help it.

"Coffin Paint," Caitlin told them. "The beer's bad enough. That stuff sends them crazy."

"Just what we need," West grunted. "A mob pumped up on Dutch courage."

"Only they aren't interested in us." Elsa looked over the heads of the crowd.

"It must be Dominion," West ventured.

Elsa stood on tiptoe to see more. "What's he doing?"

West became uneasy. "God help us if he's decided to fight everyone who was in the bar."

"He's not fighting . . ." Elsa moved toward the crowd. "He's pulling the fishermen's nets off the railing."

"What on earth does he want with them?"

Elsa didn't like this one bit. "Maybe he's suffering a psychological reaction to the transition."

"You mean he's gone crazy?"

Elsa gave an unhappy shrug. "There are physical problems; his body changing color and the scarring. It could affect his mind as well."

Caitlin still had faith. "No. He's not mad. Dominion's got a plan. Come on!"

22

A MONSTROUS HUNGER

Elsa asked herself in astonishment: *What the hell is Dominion doing?*

The crowds were watching the giant of a man as he worked. He was alert again, and appeared none the worse for collapsing unconscious in Caitlin's bedroom. On the horizon the sun had broken through the cloud. It cast its red light down the street to lend the short blond stubble on Dominion's head a copper glow. She saw his hands were the color of white marble, while the skin of his arms was the same gold as freshly toasted bread.

West folded his arms as he watched Dominion's endeavors. "He really is insane."

"No, he's not." Caitlin watched him in rapture. "Don't you see what he's doing?"

For one dreadful moment Elsa had thought he was in the process of carrying out his threat, that he strangled the children that had been playing in the nets. Now she saw the children watched him from across the street as he hauled what seemed an acre of net from where it had hung over the harbor rail. The netting must have been ancient. It was patched up with nets of different gauges and colors—blue, orange, gray, yellow. Windblown newspapers, carrier bags, gum wrappers, the flotsam and jetsam of the streets had become tangled up in it. Not that the sorry state of it bothered Dominion.

The crowds watched as he pulled the net off the rail, then hoisted it onto a massive shoulder. On the whole the crowd simply watched him without comment. Mayor Jackson was there along with his coterie of senior police and local bigwigs who witnessed Dominion's labors with disgust. Once he had the net over one shoulder, a mountain of frayed mesh with around twenty yards more of it dragging behind him, he marched away down the road.

"Watch out," squawked one of the men who'd been drinking Coffin Paint. "He'll carry you off in that if you're not careful!"

The Saps fell back when they heard his warning. The children, however, ran beside the folds of net he hauled away in the light of the setting sun. It didn't take long for the crowd to follow. More came out of their cottages; their questions about what the monster was doing were met by puzzled shrugs from bystanders.

Elsa glanced at West. "We best find out what he's up to."

Caitlin already followed in the giant's wake, along with what seemed most of the town. Even Mel wearing a bruise on his face from his earlier encounter tagged along in a staggering walk, a half bottle of coal-black Coffin Paint clutched in one fist.

Dominion's activities attracted the attention of the occupants of the Pharos. Paul stood alongside Beech and the others as they looked out through the grid of the portcullis. The setting sun engulfed the town with a deep red light.

"What's he doing with the net?" Xaiyad asked.

Paul shook his head. "He threatened to drown the youngest children in the town if they didn't give us food. I only hope to heaven the net isn't full of babies."

Beech angled her head to see through the steel bars. "I watched him take the net of the railings . . . it's just a fisherman's net. There's nothing in there."

As they watched, a rising wail sounded behind him. He turned to see Saiban run out of the door at the base of one of the towers. The man panted as if his lungs had failed him; he could hardly stand up by himself.

"Marais!" Saiban screamed. "Marais. I told you she's not dead. She's managed to get out!"

Paul's heart thudded . . . *She's managed to get out.* He knew exactly what Saiban meant. Paul ran across the courtyard toward the base of the tower that was now shrouded in shadow. Beside him ran Beech and Xaiyad.

Saiban pointed an accusing finger. "Marais! You lied! You said she was dead!"

Paul barreled into the chapel, then headed toward the crypt door that yawned open. The stairs beyond it led down into a pit of darkness. More by luck than judgment he managed to descend into the subterranean vault without falling. The sight that met his eyes at the bottom made him falter.

He took a breath. "Damn them for making us like this."

The pair behind him paused on the stair. Paul took another step into the crypt. Along the walls stone sarcophagi held the bones of the dead captive. In front of him, however, in the sun's bloodred light falling through a vent in the wall, was a scene of such ugly proportions he felt as if he'd blundered into a nightmare.

The stone lid of the coffin had been slid far enough to one side to create a gap. Luna had somehow crawled out of it. She now lay partway out of her coffin, the top of which was perhaps four feet above floor level where it rested on a slab. Her thighs rested on the edge of the coffin, while her hips and torso hung down the outside. Her chin rested on the crypt floor. The break in her neck meant that it was as supple as a snake. The head was raised so even though her body hung vertically from the open coffin, her face was horizontal. The body was naked after dragging itself from its shroud.

Beech gave a sob. *"Look at her eyes!"*

Dominion drew the crowd of onlookers behind him to where the harbor wall formed a granite pier that ran out fifty yards into the open sea. There, he walked out along the top of the structure. When he reached a lamppost near the end he shrugged the net from his shoulder. He tied one end of the net to the steel post. Then he threw the huge bundle of mesh into the water. That done he stepped off the edge of the walkway to drop into the sea that had now taken on the aspect of black chrome as dusk closed in.

"Look at him!" Caitlin's excited cry burst from her lips. "Dominion's fishing!"

Whether it was awe or disbelief, Elsa didn't know. The crowd, however, watched in silence as Dominion seized the other end of the net in one hand and began swimming out to sea. The weight of the net had to be enormous. The force of his arm and legs pummeling the water was like a never-ending sequence of depth charges. When the net pulled taut, there was a good thirty yards of it that linked the swimmer with the harbor pier. Then he swam back toward the beach, keeping the net straight.

"He really is fishing." West let out a whistle. "See how he's closing the trap on them?"

Just what he'd caught was soon answered by the sight of silver bodies breaking the surface inside the arc of the net. One or two fish leaped over the mesh to escape; most, however, were confined to an ever-diminishing area of water.

"Mackerel!" Caitlin hugged herself with delight. "Dominion must have caught a whole shoal of them!"

In the crypt beneath the tower the light had almost gone. Paul walked across to where Luna lay halfway out of the tomb. Her naked body gleamed as if it had become luminous. She lay with one arm stretched out in front of her. He grimaced. The sight of her head tilted so cruelly back like that revolted him.

"Oh, bless her. Why can't she rest in peace?"

Xaiyad, the pathologist, crouched down to examine the corpse. "This can happen, I'm afraid." He shook his head. "Ideally, the body should have been cremated immediately after death."

"I am right, aren't I, Xaiyad? Luna is brain-dead?"

"Undoubtedly."

Beech reacted angrily. "But is she?"

"There'll be no electrical activity in the brain stem."

"But just look at her eyes. You can see for yourself they are alive!"

Paul found it hard to disagree. As they'd approached the body the eyes had been staring forward. They'd been dull, lifeless. There had been an absence of spirit there, merely a pair of gelatinous orbs that were covered in dust. Paul had been struck by the sadness in them. As if Luna was saying, "I tried so hard to stay alive . . . in the end I failed." Only, as they approached, the eyes had swiveled upward to look at them. That's when a fierce intelligence had seemingly roared from them. The three had reeled back as if struck a physical blow. So much emotion fueled by anger had been transmitted from those two gray eyes.

Then, of course, Beech had noticed Luna's arm. The way it stretched out on the floor as if pointing toward the stairs. "Luna's trying to tell us who killed her." Beech was matter-of-fact. "First she writes the murderer's name in her blood on the inside of the coffin lid. Now she's tried to show us who threw her off the wall."

Xaiyad was astounded. "That's not possible. Luna will have no mental function. These movements are purely automatic reflexes. Look at the pallor of the skin. The hands are blue. Her internal organs are shutting down."

"As I keep saying." Paul shook his head. "We're so fucking hard to kill."

Beech paced the floor. "I don't know why Luna's different. Then we all seem to be changing . . . I don't know: evolving!"

Xaiyad kept shaking his head. "We can't evolve into becoming immortal."

Paul agreed. "All God Scarers die a second time. It's inevitable."

Xaiyad looked at Beech. "I'd be interested to know what you think Luna wrote on the inside of the tomb."

Beech glanced at Paul as if daring him to contradict her, or make her look foolish. Paul held out a hand, inviting her to speak.

With an air of defiance Beech said, "I couldn't make out the word—but they were definitely letters."

"How can you be sure?"

"I'm certain the last one was the letter n." Again she gave a defiant toss of her head. "Yes, the letter n."

"A name of one us that ends in n." Paul felt a growing sense of unease.

Xaiyad voiced the name that all three must have been thinking. "Dominion."

* * *

A remarkable event took place. Elsa couldn't believe her eyes.

As Dominion waded through the surf into the shallows the crowd of Saps went wild. Even though the town's ruling elite glared their disapproval, men and women raced into the surf, their feet splashing the water into gouts of spray.

"Fish!" Caitlin was ecstatic. *"All that fish!"*

Elsa watched in astonishment as the people laughed and called to one another as they grabbed at the mass of mackerel trapped between the net and the beach. The water swarmed with fish, their tails slapping the brine into a creamy froth. The noise of the locals' jubilation stunned West.

"Look at them. You think they'd never seen fish before."

"Never this much," Caitlin shouted above the laughter of people reveling in the shoal that Dominion dragged shoreward in the net. "Not for years. None of the fishing boats are any good now."

"They look happy enough," West said. "But it might not last. As soon as Dominion's done his fisherman act we should get back to the castle fast."

"I agree." Elsa caught Caitlin by the arm. "Caitlin. Where's the bag you packed?"

"Back in my room. I'll get it in a minute. I want to watch this first. Ha, see Dad and his cronies? They hate this, but they can't stop all these people having fun . . . just look at how much fish they're getting. Half this lot haven't had a square meal in weeks."

Elsa watched the frenzy of people scooping fish out of the sea with their bare hands. The expression on their faces was the same as kids unwrapping presents on Christmas Day.

"Caitlin . . . I'll run back for your bag."

"Are you sure?"

"Stay with West. I'll be back in five minutes."

Elsa raced through the deserted streets. It was almost dark now; only a pink after-light clung to the underside of the clouds. She knew they had to get out of here and back to the Pharos. The townsfolk's good humor might not last. In barely sixty seconds she reached the grocery store. She raced upstairs to the bedroom. It took a moment to find the bag that Caitlin had packed with clothes. When she turned back to the bedroom door a figure blocked her way.

The man's eyes locked on to hers. "Do you remember me?"

In the crypt all they could do was return Luna to the tomb, then slide the lid until it covered her. Her limbs made fluttering twitches now. At last death—a full, motionless death—had begun to creep into her body.

"Luna is over the worst," Xaiyad told the pair as the stone slab clunked into place. "The thrashing of the body has stopped. She isn't screaming. By morning she'll be completely inert."

Beech kissed her fingertips, then placed them on the sealed tomb. A moment later she said, "What about Dominion? Who's going to confront him about Luna?"

Elsa held her breath for a moment before releasing it with a groan. She pressed her lips together, trying not to shout out. Then she looked down at him.

"Am I hurting you?" she asked.

"No."

"I thought I was. You were closing your eyes as if you were in pain."

He shook his head.

She saw the pair of them reflected in the dressing table mirror. *Am I doing this or am I dreaming?* She asked herself. *How can my world turn upside down so quickly?* Once more her eyes were drawn to the mirror. There was her reflection. She was naked as she sat astride the man. He lay on his back on Caitlin's bed. He was naked, too. His dark hair was ruffled from where she'd held it as she kissed him. Now his eyes were closed. This was Karl. He'd tried to stop the other two hurting her that afternoon. When he appeared at the door he'd told her he was concerned she might have been seriously hurt by the knife injury Mel had inflicted on her. It was almost small talk. Far more was said with their eyes. She'd felt emotion run through her like electricity. Then she couldn't stop herself; she'd kissed him. After that, a frenzied battle to rip away their clothes before falling on the bed.

Now she sat astride him and groaned with a hungry, lascivious pleasure as she lifted her hips before sliding down onto penis. This was forbidden. Monster on man. Maybe that's why the erotic thrill of it all electrified her.

I am hurting you, Karl, she told herself. *The muscles inside me are crushing your cock. But then the barrier between pain and pleasure is a delicate one. So very easily penetrated.*

She kissed his face. The salt of his perspiration tingled on her tongue. When she bore down on him he moaned.

Elsa whispered, "I am hurting you, aren't I?"

Whatever his reply would be didn't matter one way or the other. She had a monstrous hunger to satisfy. Come what may, she would satiate the emptiness she'd harbored inside herself for too many dry and lonely years.

23

SLAUGHTER MAN

Night had fallen by the time the supplies arrived at the Pharos, and Dominion had climbed the cliff steps to the portcullis. Nothing less than a posse delivered the truckload of food, lamps, candles, and soap. The vehicle negotiated a narrow roadway that ran between the high wall of the castle and the edge of the cliff that plunged two hundred feet to Scaur Ness. With the truck came five cars. These carried the mayor, chief of police, three more police officers with civilian deputies armed with shotguns. After inching along the narrow road the truck halted just short of the portcullis. The cars stopped two abreast some fifty paces behind the truck with their headlights blazing to illuminate the delivery point.

Elsa saw all this as she and her little band reached the top of the steps. Dominion said nothing. He merely watched the men throw boxes of food from the truck onto the pavement outside the portcullis gate, which was still locked down against the outside world. Behind the portcullis her fellow God Scarers witnessed the deliverymen's none too gentle approach to unloading the cargo.

Dominion spoke. "Be careful with the boxes." There was thunder in his voice. "Pass them down. Don't throw."

The men weren't going to argue with the giant. One jumped from the back of the truck while the second man handed over the boxes.

With a creaking the portcullis winched upward.

One of the deliverymen shouted toward the cars, "We could use some help here."

The posse weren't eager. Their reluctance showed in their lack of speed as they climbed out of the vehicles before moving into the light of the headlamps. All this passed in a daze for Elsa. Most prominent now were memories of being in the bedroom with Karl just minutes ago. She'd ridden the human hard. Had he expected a God Scarer to be passionless? Hell's teeth, was he mistaken! She'd fucked the pair of them into a storm of sexual excitement. Monster taboos were ripping themselves apart. Dominion killed. She fucked mortal man. Here they were in a castle they'd stolen from the town. And here comes food that Dominion had extorted from the Saps. If they hadn't delivered, Dominion would have killed their children one by one until they'd relented.

Good one, Dominion. And, good God, yes . . . Good one, Elsa. I'm glad what I did with Karl. It's the first time in years that I feel as if I'm a living, breathing woman. I've no regrets. None at all. She craved the taste of his mouth on her tongue. The heat of his fire still burned inside her belly.

What's that? Elsa heard an angry voice. One of the posse, a white-haired man, was pointing at the stack of food beside the portcullis. "Do you know something, you bloody shower of shits? We can't spare this. Do you know what it's like to hear children crying with hunger?"

Mayor Jackson approached. He was unarmed but the rest held their shotguns in a way that suggested it wouldn't take much to provoke them into letting fly a storm of lead.

The white-haired man wasn't letting this drop. "We shouldn't be feeding this pack of corpses. Why don't we get this food back on the truck and leave these things to rot?"

Mayor Jackson spoke. "I gave them my word."

"Break it. Look! They're monsters . . . just a bunch of Frankensteins. They—"

"Harold. You know we've no choice. You heard what they'd do to our children if we didn't comply."

"You think this shower of shit would have the guts to kill our babies?"

"Harold, go back to the car. We'll deal with this."

So it goes, Elsa told herself. *These humans hate us. Yet they're compelled by Dominion to feed us. And they've barely enough food themselves.*

The scene in front of her seemed as bizarre as it was tense. Lit by the cars' lights was the truck in front of the open portcullis. Her fellow God Scarers emerged from the castle to watch the Saps unload boxes of food. Dominion stood by the truck, making sure they did just that. Caitlin moved close to Paul. Her allegiance to these creatures—these freaks of science—must have enraged every one of the human beings present. Especially Caitlin's father, the mayor.

Paul tried to thaw the mood of cold resentment. "Thank you for the supplies. We do need the food."

The mayor glared at him. "Make no mistake, this isn't an act of charity. You've forced us to hand over food we can't spare."

"There was the fish," Elsa began.

"Paul, you should have seen Dominion," Caitlin gushed. "He took some old nets into the sea and caught thousands of fish. There must have been a shoal of—"

"Caitlin." Her father became even grimmer. "This *man's* spectacle with the fish doesn't impress me, nor the town's authorities."

"Most people haven't had fresh fish in months. Dominion caught enough mackerel for everyone. Aren't you pleased—"

"No, I'm not pleased, Caitlin. None of us are. This . . . Dominion . . . made a play of catching fish to deceive the town that he was somehow compensating them for the supplies. Not only that, he's trying to create divisions, so people will be saying, 'Oh, those Transients aren't so bad after all.' While making the authorities appear unfair in their treatment of them."

"All I can say is," Paul told him, "if your people can accept the fish as a token of our good intentions—"

"Good intentions." Jackson repeated the words as if their taste in his mouth disgusted him. "Damn your good intentions."

"OK, clearly we can't change your opinion. All I can do is promise we won't harm your people or damage any more property." He looked at the giant standing by the truck. "OK, Dominion?"

Dominion said nothing.

"There." Mayor Jackson nodded as the last box was lifted from the truck. "You've got the food I promised you. Now you can stay in the Pharos for the rest of the week. Then you must go. You leave, do you understand?"

"We've nowhere to go," Beech protested.

"That's not our problem." The mayor's eyes flashed as the anger he'd suppressed began to boil. "Just get out of here by Friday."

Saiban stepped forward out of the shadows as if they

somehow gave him his gloomy form. "Mayor. I apologize on behalf of us all. You have my word we will leave here by Friday at the latest."

Paul spoke before Saiban could make any more promises that the God Scarers couldn't keep. "Mayor Jackson. Surely you've no experience of Transients. Those that pass through the Transit Stations are immediately bused out of the area. So why do you hate us?"

"Look at the town. It's dying. The nation's economy is in ruins, and it's all because of you."

"But surely you are happy that some of your people who die go to the Transit Station and are restored again? Look at us. We're healthy. The procedure makes worn-out bodies brand-new again."

"Are you out of your damn mind?" This was the chief of police. "In the last forty years not one single person from this town has been taken to your precious Transit Station. Once our people are declared dead they go to fatten worms in the fucking cemetery."

Paul frowned. "I'm sorry. I thought—"

"Well, think again. None of us become monsters like you. We've never been invited; frankly, I'm thankful we never have."

West stepped forward. "Maybe not recently but you'll have had Transients serving your community?"

"The hell we have." The chief of police laughed in West's face. "We've never even seen one in years."

Paul shook his head. "I don't understand. The intention was Transients would serve you."

"It never happened here."

"Listen." Mayor Jackson held up his hand. "I don't intend to stand here debating what did and what didn't happen. You are corpses that through trickery have been made to look alive. You aren't as far as we're concerned, you're just disgusting pieces of dead meat. Now: Here's your food. Do what you want with it. Make sure you've left here by Friday."

Dominion spoke. "You can't make us move."

"If you don't go the army will come back and extermi-nate you. Got that?"

"I don't agree," Dominion told him. "The soldiers won't be back for weeks. They've moved north to destroy the other Transit Stations."

"You're very well informed," the mayor sneered. "Who told you this?"

Dominion paused. For a moment he appeared puzzled. "I know . . . that is the strategy. The army isn't coming back."

Elsa watched that odd meeting of man and monster on the cliff top as a nighttime breeze blew from the ocean. Both the mayor's people and the God Scarers appeared perplexed by Dominion's statement. At that moment a faint music appeared to float on the air. *It's the song of the dead*, she told herself. A shiver tingled through her body to run prickles of ice across her scalp. The music was beautiful as it was mournful. A sense of such aching longing ran through it. She glanced around the assembly there. No one else appeared to hear it. No . . . wait . . . Just for a moment Dominion's head tilted slightly as if he heard faint notes reaching out to him.

Somehow he knows the soldiers aren't coming back here. He knows things that no one else does. Perhaps he knows about that song . . . The breeze drew a long heartfelt sigh around the castle. She closed her eyes as shivers cascaded down her spine. *The song of the ancient dead. It's their way of calling us to return.*

Mingled with these thoughts that seemed so troubling yet had the ring of a Bible truth about them were images of Karl. Even the knife wound in her breast had faded to a tingle. Her head spun. She wished this handover of supplies would be over so she could find somewhere quiet in the Pharos and endeavor to work out what was happening. Sex, the songs of the ancient dead. *Sex.* The word throbbed with a crimson light inside her head. *Sex.* Elsa wanted to find Karl again. Sex wouldn't be a word then. It would be a muscular act.

The gunshot changed everything. A detonation so fierce its echo stung her ears. Everyone turned their heads, trying to see who'd fired the gun. The posse looked at one another, but they stood with their shotgun muzzles pointing at the ground. Then she saw one of the Transients slowly kneel down onto the ground before sagging sideways onto the ground. It was Uri, one the physiotherapists. What she saw didn't make sense. As he collapsed, like he was nothing more than an accumulation of softly empty clothes, the white-haired man who'd protested about the handover of food appeared to guide him downward by touching the back of his head. This silent paralysis of the group only lasted a second.

Paul shouted, "Jackson! We agreed there'd be no violence!"

The mayor responded with "I didn't order this. It's nothing to do with us."

From stillness to a confused melee took seconds. God Scarers rushed to Uri, who lay still, his eyes staring. His attacker stood over him, bent at the waist while pressing a device of some kind to Uri's head. As one of the policemen reached the pair, the old man straightened. In the light of the cars Elsa saw what the man held. It was a humane killer used by slaughter men. Approximately the shape and size of a pistol, it would be used to kill big animals such as cattle and horses. An explosive charge drove a captive four-inch steel bolt through the thick cranium into the brain. Whereas an ordinary bullet might bounce off a Transient's skull, this bolt had penetrated Uri's skull to gel his brain tissue.

Saiban once again appeared to materialize out of the shadows to stand beside the mayor. "I must apologize again, sir, for the disruption we have brought to your town. Our actions are inexcusable. I have done my best to persuade these Transients to surrender to your—"

Jackson stopped short of touching Saiban, but he gestured with a sweeping motion. "Get out of my way."

"Of course, sir. I'm sorry."

Then the mayor called out, "Don't touch any of us. We didn't plan any of this. Our police will deal with it. Just stay back."

Saiban promptly obeyed. He moved to a respectful distance from the humans with his hands clasped together in front of his chest, his expression more mournful than ever; his huge sad eyes fixed on the mayor as if communicating a heartfelt apology for breathing the same air as humankind.

Two clusters formed. One around the white-haired man as the police bundled him to the cars. The second cluster, this one of Transients, gathered around Uri. They picked him up and carried him through the gate into the courtyard. Dominion's shaved head swung left and right. There was a sense of gathering violence in the air. Elsa waited for the giant to lash out at Uri's attackers. Meanwhile, Paul talked to the mayor. From the body language both of them appeared to be struggling to find common ground despite their anger. Clearly, neither wanted Dominion to begin one of his bone-crunching displays.

Elsa stood beside Saiban. Behind them, a waist-high fence separated the road from the cliff top. Two hundred feet below, the town lay in darkness apart from lights shining through windows to leave a sallow daub on the harbor waters. Briefly, her attention was held by the scene in front of her as the mayor and Paul worked together for once to prevent the shooting of Uri leading to more bloodshed. Dominion glared at the car that held Uri's attacker. *Roll it over. Make it burn.* It didn't take a genius to figure what he was thinking.

A Sap crept away from the group. He was one of those thin men whose bodies suggested a brittle hardness, like the shell of an insect. His face bore the blue lines of burst blood vessels as a result of drinking that rough liquor the locals distilled themselves. The man's eyes fixed on her as he approached. She realized her back was to the fence, which was all that separated her from nothingness. In her mind's eye she saw the man toppling her backward over the rail. Already, she felt a clutch of fear as she pictured herself plunging into the streets far below. She thought: *I know I'm stronger than him. But I can't resist in case I hurt him. I can't break our law.* Instead, she took a step forward. The man changed direction. Maybe there was something in her eye that made him rethink his intentions. He breezed past, keeping his distance, but still close enough to envelop her with the cutting stench of alcoholic breath.

A moment later he stood pointing into Saiban's face. "Listen, monster."

"Sir?" That was Saiban. Polite as ever. "Can I help you?"

"It's true that your sort can't touch us?"

"That is true, sir. Our mission is to serve humanity. We'd never—"

"Shut it, maggot."

"Yes, sir."

"And you must obey us?"

"That is true, also, sir."

"Then climb over the fence, and jump off the cliff."

"Sir?"

"That's an order." The man leaned forward. He'd begun to grin so hugely his lips slid back to reveal large brown teeth. "Go . . . and . . . jump . . . off . . . the . . . bloody . . . cliff."

Saiban's mournful gaze strayed to Elsa before returning to the man. "Sir, I'm not being disrespectful. It's just that I don't see what purpose it would serve."

Elsa realized that nobody else on the cliff top noticed what was happening at this side of the road. The mayor and police chief were discussing the attack on Uri with Paul. The rest of the God Scarers either had carried Uri away or were watching Dominion in case he erupted into a fury of destruction.

It's up to me to solve this one, she thought. Not that there was much she could do. She couldn't even touch the human, nor was it wise to shout to the others to attract their attention. A sudden outburst from her part might trigger Dominion into attacking the humans. *So, softly, softly does it.*

"Saiban," she said, "come with me."

"Keep away from me," hissed the man. "Saiban's going to do what I tell him. Isn't that right, monster?"

"If you say so, sir."

"Then what are you waiting for? Step over that fence, and jump off the cliff."

Saiban's mournful eyes took in the course he had to follow. It was just a couple of yards. It would take only a second to climb the fence and step out into the cold night air.

"You don't have to obey, Saiban," she told him. "If a human tells you to hurt yourself you're not obliged to comply."

"Shut it, you bitch." The man's near-toxic breath made her eyes water. "He's going to obey me, aren't you, Saiban?"

"Yes, sir." With that he climbed the fence. Beneath him the town stretched out in a dull mass of smoking chimneys and yellow squares of light for windows at this time of night.

"Saiban?" Elsa clutched her fists. "Why are you doing what he says?"

"You know why. Since we left the Transit Station we have committed crimes. Because I failed to stop you I'm guilty as you all are. I'm no better than Dominion."

The Sap grunted. "Want to stand there spouting all night, monster? Jump. That's an order of a human being . . . your fucking superior."

Saiban nodded. "Of course, sir. My apologies." He stared down. The faint light reaching him filled his mournful eyes with silver glints. This wasn't what he wanted, yet his obedience to the human race overrode the instinct for self-preservation.

"Jump," the man hissed. "You know you've got to."

"Wait." Elsa stepped up to the fence. The breeze blew her hair back from her face; she felt chill currents run across her scalp. "Wait, Saiban. You mustn't jump."

"I have my instruction. I can't disobey a human."

"See, you little corpse bitch?" The man was pleased with his power over the God Scarer. "He's going to do what I say, and then I'm going to do some work on you."

"Saiban," she whispered quickly. "You must not jump."

"Elsa, you don't have authority over me. The gentleman does."

"Saiban. Listen to me, you will be breaking our law if you jump."

This gave him pause. "How?"

"Saiban, just look below you. There are houses."

"But I have my instructions."

"What if you fall onto a house? You'd go right through the roof. There's a real chance you'd kill people inside."

"Fat chance of that happening." The Sap belched. "Now make like a bird. Understand?"

"Sir, there's a problem." Saiban gulped as conflicting ideas struggled for supremacy. "Yes, I must obey you. Especially in the light of my failings recently."

"Do it, then. Fly."

"But if I jump, there is a real risk of hurting a human being. To even damage human property would be a greater crime than disobeying you, sir."

"Thatta boy, Saiban." Elsa felt a surge of relief.

"Aw, go screw yourselves." The man knew he'd been beaten but disguised it by walking away as if bored.

"Saiban. Give me your hand." She reached out to help him back onto the road.

"Why did you save me, Elsa?"

"Oh, why do you think? Come on, move it, before he has any more bright ideas."

"OK," Paul called to his own kind. "Listen to me. I've reached an agreement with Mayor Jackson. In consideration of what happened to Uri we can stay in the castle for a full week."

Beech stood in the gateway. Uri's blood stained her clothes. "Are they arresting the guy who shot Uri?"

"Yes."

The police chief stepped forward. "He's been arrested for operating a firearm in a public place."

"What? You mean you're not arresting him for murder?"

"In the eyes of the law," the policeman explained, "you are still dead. You can't kill what's already dead. You follow that, don't you?"

Beech howled in anger. "That bastard blew Uri's brains out. Look at me." She advanced on the cop. "Put your hand on my chest; tell me there's no heartbeat. We're alive as you are. You're denying us justice over a technicality."

The man returned to his posse; they had raised their guns now. "I will uphold the law. But I can only charge the man with the illegal operation of a firearm in a public place. That's all I have to say on the matter."

The only one of their kind who could do anything chose not to. Dominion turned his back on the outside world and walked through the gate where his massive form vanished into the shadows.

24

TASTE THE BLOOD AND COFFIN PAINT

Silence. Stillness. The dead weight of the events of the past hour crushed down on everyone in the castle. Paul stood alone on the battlements. Seaward, the darkness was total. As for the town, he couldn't bring himself to look at it. Uri was dead. The slaughter man's humane killer that dispatched cattle and horses with such efficiency dealt with God Scarers too. The bolt discharged into Uri's skull by an explosive charge had turned his brain to puree.

As Paul stood there with his hands resting on the stone wall the breeze ghosted around the towers to draw out a ghostly sigh. The sound chilled him to the bone. It was the same sound Uri had made as his lungs slowed.

"We're hard to kill," Paul murmured to himself. "But not that hard."

Is this going to be the fate of all of us? he asked himself. *Are we going to be killed one by one? And if we leave here, where can we go?*

Questions surged through Paul's mind. He still asked himself where all the men and women the Transit Stations had brought back from the dead had gone. *What's happening to Dominion? Why are parts of his body changing color?* What did the scars mean on his wrists, shoulders, and neck? How come he appeared to be remembering facts that no one else in this sorry bunch of refugees from death knew? Had Luna really written the name of her murderer in blood on the underside of the coffin lid? Had Dominion killed her?

At that moment vertigo tugged at him. All he could see was a blizzard of questions without answers.

"I could jump off the wall." The bleak prospect became enticing. "We're all going to die anyway. Why not exit at a time of your own choosing?" His hands gripped the wall. Air currents produced an unearthly cry around the battlements. Beneath him, surf pounded against the cliff. "Come on, Dr. Paul Marais. You know a fall from this height will break even our thick heads. You've died once. Doing it a second time should be a cinch." Paul looked down into the surf. "If the fall isn't fatal, the sea will finish you. Easy-peasy. Why don't you do it? It's not as if anyone will shed a tear over you."

The darkness beyond the castle walls appeared to flow into him. He felt a shadow pool in his heart. Its blackness spread through his chest into his head. This was a darkness of the soul. It became unbearable. A physical pain. He longed to rip it out of him, but the only release from its grip would be to climb up onto the wall; stand there for a moment, feeling the ocean breeze chill his face; then lean forward. Gravity would do the rest.

"Marais . . . Marais!"

The voice wrenched Paul from that flow of dark thought. He turned to see Saiban hurrying along the walkway.

"Dr. Marais. You must come and see what they're doing."

"Saiban. Drop the Dr. Marais. Paul works well enough these days."

"They've all gone mad!"

"Saiban, what—"

"I tell you they're insane!"

Saiban ran back down the steps to the courtyard. It was deserted; the portcullis had been locked down. Nobody from the outside could get in, so what was Saiban so het up about?

"Saiban? Hey, Saiban? What's wrong?"

"You've got to stop them, Marais!"

Paul followed Saiban to the cafeteria. What was on the inside knocked him backward. Heat, light, sound, movement . . .

Saiban gestured at the God Scarers. "See? They're out of their minds!"

"Hey, Paul . . . Paulie, Paulie!" Beech lurched round a table to throw her arms round him. "You came! I thought you were going to haunt those bloody battlements all night."

West grinned from where he sat at a table. "It's the Monster Ball. Welcome. Welcome!"

Caitlin emerged form a corner where she'd been hiding. "Paul." Her eyes flashed with anxiety. "It wasn't just food the men delivered. There were cases of Coffin Paint too. They've started drinking it."

"Damn straight, sister." Beech reeled away from her. "Coffin Paint. I put my bottle down somewhere . . ."

Caitlin grasped Paul's forearm. "They don't know what it'll do to them. They'll go crazy."

"We've a human being here." Saiban's mournful eyes locked on Caitlin. His voice was equally woeful. "If she is harmed . . . You can't let it happen, Dr. Marais. You must stop them."

He did a quick head count. Everyone appeared to be in the process of getting drunk with the exception of Saiban and Caitlin. As for Dominion, he was nowhere to be seen. For all Paul knew the giant might be in the town, drowning its newborns as he'd threatened. West bellowed with laughter for no obvious reason. He lifted a bottle that had an inch of that syrupy black liquor in the bottom.

"West." Paul held out his hand. "Give me that bottle."

West hesitated. He'd got a taste for the witches' brew by now.

Saiban joined in. "West. I order you to hand the bottle to Dr. Marais."

Paul walked to the table, where he pulled the bottle from West's hand.

"At last," Saiban purred. "Sanity prevails."

"Hey." West became peevish. "That's mine."

Paul shook his head. "Not any longer, Westie, my old pal." He held the bottle up to a candle. No light penetrated the dark heart of the liquor. "There's more than mere alcohol in here," he told him. *"Thank goodness."* With that, Paul put the bottle to his lips. The liquid hit the back of his throat like molten steel. It continued its burning path into his stomach. The smell was like nothing on earth. A cross between burnt apple, stain remover and chemicals left too long in a chemist's cellar.

West clapped. "Atta boy."

"I only wish there was more." Paul wiped his lips. "A lot more."

"Help yourself." West's wave of an arm was a generous one. "There's cases of the stuff under the table."

"Which table?"

"The one with Uri on it. We're combining his wake with our in-or . . . in-or . . . inaugural Monster Ball." West belched. "Be a best buddy. Bring me a bottle back when you get one." Another belch. "Coffin Paint. A taste of eternity."

Paul crossed the room to the long trestle table where Uri lay on a white sheet with another white sheet drawn up to his chin. Someone had wrapped a bandage round the top of his head to conceal the head wound. For God Scarers death isn't immediately total. Uri still twitched. His arms had been crossed over his chest in solemn funereal style. The man's fingers, however, still drummed up and down as if he typed at an invisible keyboard. A moment later an eyelid slid back to expose a bloodshot eye. The eye darted as if Uri was trying to see who was making all this noise.

"Good night and sweet dreams, Uri."

Paul crouched down, plucked two full bottles from the box, then returned to West, who drew pictures in the air with his finger. This appeared to amuse him mightily, because his laughter shook the empty bottles on the tables.

Caitlin put her hands on his chest to stop him. "Paul. There's more than alcohol in that stuff."

"Good."

"It's mixed with a fungus they find up in the hills."

"Excellent."

"It sends men out of their minds."

"Perfect."

"Paul, why are you being like this?"

He looked down into her anxious eyes. The dark curls that framed her face glinted in the candlelight.

"You're beautiful," he told her. "But I'm a monster. We live in different worlds."

"Paul, this isn't you talking."

"I know, my wee lovely flower." His Scottish accent became stronger. "But all of us here are in hell now. My life has been torn apart. Most of my friends have been butchered. My home's burnt. We're refugees trespassing in someone else's property. Luna died yesterday. A slaughter man blew out Uri's brains tonight. Your people don't consider that a crime. In a few days our deaths will come, too, and you shall be home again with your father."

"No, Paul."

"So, right at this moment, I want to get away from me. Understand? I want to get out of here." He tapped the neck of the bottle against his head. "This might be the last bit of fun we have before our graves finally catch up with us again. Because, you know, that's what it feels like. God Scarers to a man look behind them and they expect to see a hole in the ground following them. Bizarre notion, isn't it? But it's always there." His chuckle was a grim one. "*We belong dead.* That's the line, isn't it?"

West called out, "Is it my imagination? Are you actually receding into the distance with that bottle? Because you're not getting any closer."

Caitlin lightly stroked his arm. There was such a fond expression on her face when she looked up at him that it twisted his heart.

"Paul. If we're together I don't care what anyone says."

"If you'll excuse me, dear. I'm going to enjoy a wee dram with my friend." He shook his head. "Excuse the overdone Scottish accent. It's only my poor attempt to be disarming."

"Paul. Listen to me. If you drink that you'll end up doing something you regret." She stood back. "It's more than poison, it's evil. You end up hurting the people you love."

Saiban approached. "Dr. Marais. I forbid you to drink any more of that. There's a human being here with us. What if you do something you come to regret?"

"Saiban. Go away."

Paul sat at the table with West. They opened their bottles, toasted one another's health, happiness, and whatever else came to mind. Paul had drunk wine at the Transit Station. All things in moderation of course. Monsters are restrained, even frugal. Wine's warming glow was familiar. Coffin Paint, however, was different. Before the alcohol started work a narcotic shock wave raced through the entire nervous system. As Paul drank that liquid fire from the bottle, some part of him retained its professional detachment. He identified the alcohol content. The other flavors that seemed to progress from burnt apple to incinerated tire rubber must have been a gift of the fungus. Whatever variety that was, although it might well be psychoactive with the power to induce temporary psychosis. The liquor lit a fire in his belly. The fungus didn't waste any time, either. It ate his brain. That's when the Monster Ball got weird.

25

KISSING THE MONSTER

This is where the Monster Ball gets weird. Elsa told herself this when she was past the point of no return. Twenty minutes ago they had carried Uri's corpse into the cafeteria to lay it out on the table. Then they brought the food and drink supplied by the townspeople. For a spell there was utter silence. A depressing weight of absolute doom. Their misery crushed them into stillness.

From a box West plucked a bottle of the home-distilled liquor the locals called Coffin Paint. "Personally, I don't think I've got anything else to lose." He downed the stuff like he was drinking poison. By the third pull on the bottle he couldn't stop laughing. Then everyone began drinking. Everyone, that is, except Saiban and the human, Caitlin. Their pleas to stop drinking the stuff were ignored.

This is where the Monster Ball gets really *weird.* By now Paul had joined them. He drank, too. Meanwhile, Caitlin sat on one of the benches against the wall, where she stared at Paul with that clinical intensity of the lovesick. Saiban prowled the margins of the cafeteria with such an expression of disapproval it must have made his insides ache. In the center of the cafeteria the Monster Ball consisted of God Scarers upending bottles of black syrup into their mouths. *And I'm one of them,* she thought. *Even though it feels as if I'm standing outside myself looking at that waif (which is me) in a pretty summer dress, bare shoulders, shining legs. Oh, where are your surgical scrubs, child?* She giggled. The others laughed, too. Some at bad jokes that were being tossed around the room. Some were hallucinating. She knew that for sure. West drew cartoons in the air. Nothing there, of course. Well, sometimes . . . Sometimes she saw his finger trace multicolored swirls in the atmosphere. Then, again, she saw pinks and blues flowing across the tabletop.

"This Coffin Paint isn't just alcohol. I taste fungus. That must contain halucogens. I am beginning to hallucinate—both visual and auditory. Oh, sorry. I mustn't speak to you, Uri." She shielded her hand as she whispered at the man lying beneath the white sheet. "Psst. Someone killed you. You might not have realized it yet, seeing as you're still moving." She broke off into bubbling laughter.

Dead man Uri rolled his eyes toward her. "Thanks for the heads-up."

Nice example of auditory hallucination. Her observation made her howl with laughter; she slammed the tabletop with her fist. The others joined in. They rocked in their chairs or buried their faces in their hands.

Saiban raged, "Stop this. You don't know what you're doing to yourselves!"

Saiban's anguish brought more laughter—salvos of it.

Dominion entered the room. He stood watching the party without saying anything. Dead Luna glided after him. "My murderer's name," she said, "ends in *n.*" Then she melted back into the floor.

Visual hallucination, methinks... Elsa found herself running across the yard. An urge to vomit pressed at the back of her throat. Yet everything was hilarious. The way the sky pulsed with purple lights. Elsa screamed with laughter when she saw Luna's moldering corpse beckoning her toward the chapel.

"There's space in my tomb, Elsa." Luna's face turned a luminous green as yellow puss oozed from beneath her eyelids. "Won't you sleep with me tonight?"

Elsa bit the back of her hand to stop her shrieks of merriment.

"Elsa," Luna's corpse pleaded. "I'll hold you tight. You'll never be lonely again."

The steps lurched out of the gloom. Elsa fell onto them; there she lay facedown, unable to move.

Luna's dead hand caressed the back of her leg. "Elsa. You can be with me. I'm a wonderful lover."

With a breathy giggle Elsa scrambled up the staircase to the battlements. There, the wind whipped from the sea to tug her hair. She raced around the walkway, first of all looking out at the fluorescing emerald hues of the ocean, then finding the best vantage point to gaze at the distant hills. Up there were the Nine Sisters, the ancient standing stones, that had loomed over the valley for three thousand years. She glanced back at the stairs. Nobody there. Maybe it was too chill up here for poor dead Luna. She must have returned to her snug little tomb belowground.

"Nighty-night, Luna." A giggle spurted form her lips. And as she turned to gaze at the hills the ancient dead began to sing again. Although it was far away she saw their spectral fire on the hilltop. A blue-white light that formed an envelope around the stone circle.

They want me to go sing with them, she told herself. *I should go join them. I'll be safe there.*

"Elsa."

She turned to find Luna there. Her dead flesh had begun to break open. The eyelids slid back, releasing rivers of puss down the ruined face. Luna opened her mouth. Something like a rotting fish moved in there. It was the remains of her tongue. But it was Luna's eyeballs that stopped Elsa laughing. They were so deeply wrinkled they resembled some sickly, pale version of a walnut . . . all pronounced ridges separated by deep gullies.

"You ran away from me, Elsa." Luna's voice became suddenly deeper. "I won't let you run away from me again."

Luna lunged forward with both hands to grab Elsa by the throat.

Xaiyad sat at the table. Coffin Paint filled his veins now. He sang happily. They were a million miles from danger. They were safe. As he emptied the second bottle the door opened. A little boy with a broad face and solemn eyes ran to him.

"Dad." The boy tugged Xaiyad's sleeve. "Why did you have to die, Dad?"

Xaiyad smiled. "It wasn't up to me, Son." He slapped his chest. "Bad ticker. I'm fine now."

"But Mummy went and married a man who was bad to us, Dad. He got angry every night. Then he used his belt on Timal and me."

"I'm sorry, Son." The smile on his face faded. "What could I do?"

"If they made you all right with that Frankenstein stuff, why didn't you come back for us?"

"I'm not allowed."

"The man whipped Timal. He'd done nothing wrong."

"Son—"

"Dad, look what the man did to me." The boy pulled down his sweater to reveal a band of purple bruising running around the neck.

"Oh God, I'm sorry." Xaiyad reached out to the boy, but all he found were shadows that ran through his fingers.

Xaiyad called out to Dominion, who stood there, motionless. "Dominion. I want to go home. Do you hear? I want to go home!" Xaiyad threw the bottle at the giant. It smashed against his chest. The massive figure didn't flinch. Xaiyad opened another bottle. With luck he'd find the answer to all his questions in the sediment at the bottom.

Paul worked his way through a second bottle of Coffin Paint. It tasted like the ruins of the torched Transit Station. "If I ever go back and taste them," he said to Beech, who laughed without knowing what he was talking about. "If I ever taste a burned morgue. This is it." He held up the bottle of black ruin to Caitlin. "Caitlin, my dear. This is formaldehyde, disinfectant, with just a dash of incinerated cadaver." Unlike the God Scarers, who were juiced up enough to laugh at anything, Caitlin merely awarded him a stare that was as cold as Luna's tomb.

"Saiban? Where are you, you old goat?"

Beech threw back her head with a huge, lascivious smile on her face. Candlelight flashed against her red hair. She was haloed by the most beautiful sunsets he'd ever seen in his life. Dozens of them. After gulping down another mouthful of that firewater she dragged her hand across her full red lips; then they began their conversation that went something like this:

"My death." She curled her red hair in her fingers, while smiling brightly at him. "My death was violence. Hitting a garden wall at ninety on a motorcycle is the ultimate violence, believe me. They said I was cold by the time they found me. And you know something, my dear, what I always feared is true. When you die you are aware for hours afterward. You can hear. I read it in a textbook.

Within twenty minutes of death, hearing resumes. *Boy, it resumes . . .* for anything up to seventy-two hours. It didn't hurt when they dropped my body with all its broken bones onto the slab in the morgue . . . the sloping one with the drainage holes. I heard the assistants talking about my tattoos, and that the branch of a lilac tree had pierced my throat and exited between my shoulders. I heard my family discuss me when I was laid out in the funeral home. *Are her fingers stiff? Did the undertaker glue her eyelids shut? She'd never have worn that blouse when she was alive . . ."*

"What an inappropriate subject at a party." Paul grinned. "Drink?"

"Thank you. Everyone that paid their respects had something to say. *Did she have life insurance? Uh, what's that smell? Will they pull the rings off before the burial? Isn't it true they have to break the fingers? Who did her makeup? To kiss the dead . . . is it lips or forehead? Does the skin feel very cold?"*

"This Coffin Paint works the magic. I prefer the flavor of malt whiskey. The peat, the water from the burn. *Burn's* Scottish for 'stream,' by the by."

"Then came the funeral." Her smile was more vivacious than ever. Paul felt a growing sense of enchantment. What would it be like to run his fingers through her beautiful red hair? She stroked the back of his hand as her voice dropped to a husky purr. "They put lilies across my chest, a teddy bear by my head, then nailed the coffin shut. Oh boy, oh boy, I could still hear. And there I was: this pouch of skin, full of broken bones—nothing more, but my ears still worked. The ropes creaked as I was lowered into the grave. After the soil had been shoveled back, that was real silence. Then I listened hard for the worms. I imagined they'd move through the earth with a whispery sounds. Ssss . . . sss . . . sss."

"We should have a funeral for Uri."

"You're right." Her laugh was bright as spring water. "A cremation. Luna couldn't keep still underground." Suddenly Beech paused. "I was buried in the ground and they dug me up. Someone stole my body from the grave, and then they made me live again. That's illegal, isn't it?"

Paul began to respond to the question, but Beech clapped her hands loudly. "Listen. Attention please. We have work to do, ladies and monstermen. Uri must have a funeral. I say we cremate his body on the cliff. What do you all say?"

The God Scarers signaled their agreement by applauding. Saiban would probably dissent. Paul noticed, however, that he'd vanished from the Monster Ball.

"It was the custom in my country," Beech told them, "to kiss the body before dispatch of mortal remains." She waved at the trestle table where Uri lay, then downed another gulp of the quaintly named Coffin Paint. "The custom is called Kissing the Corpse. Who wants to go first?"

On the walkway the cold night air roused Elsa. She recalled the wild party. She must have downed a couple of pints of that potent liquor. All she could hear now was the moan of the breeze around the towers. Confused nightmare images splashed through her mind. When she'd begun drinking the evil-tasting stuff colored lights had sprung from the furniture. She'd experienced hallucinations: the songs of the ancient dead, calling her. Luna pursuing her onto the castle walls. Then attacking her. *If I'd imagined it, then why is my neck so sore?* She tried to move her arms. For some reason they were restrained. The sense of *now* struck her with the force of a fist. Suddenly, she was wide-awake. Here she was on top of the castle wall. Nighttime locked the place in darkness. Air currents cried through the battlements. Her neck hurt. She couldn't move. Someone gripped her from behind. Their breath hissed in her ears.

Luna? No, Luna's lying dead in her tomb. At that moment she realized another powerful truth. Whoever held her was lifting her toward the top of the castle walls. In another moment they'd push her over. Nothing would stop her plunging to the ground far below.

Kissing the Monster. The perfect climax to the Monster Ball. Beech giggled.

"No pushing. Keep in a line. No cutting in. OK?" Beech swayed by the trestle table. "Me first."

Beech kissed Uri on the mouth. The corpse lying there on the table responded with a writhing of limbs that slapped against the white sheet that covered his body. A whistling started from the dead nostrils as spasms forced the lungs to contract. Blood ran from the nose.

One of the physiotherapists kissed him next. "His lips don't keep still," she exclaimed. "They keep moving like this." She mimicked a goldfish.

The next announced that Uri's tongue had entered his mouth the moment their lips touched. The man had tasted Uri's blood. It was astonishingly sweet, the man added. Sweeter than ice cream.

Kissing the Corpse. Paul swayed. A pleasant bubble of well-being surrounded him. The deliciously energizing Coffin Paint was a generous spirit. Its warmth flowed in his veins. He was scrumptiously happy. Now it was Paul's turn to give Uri his good night kiss, before they launched the dead man on his voyage into everlasting night.

Paul took his turn beside the corpse with the bandaged head. The arms still jerked on the chest. Fingers flexed as if trying to chase away the stiffness that must be creeping into them. The eyes were closed but the lips pressed together in a pulsing motion. It gave the appearance of the cadaver chewing on tough meat. Paul used his tongue to moisten his own lips.

The crash of the door made everyone turn round. Caitlin stood there, her chest heaving as she caught her breath.

"You've got to do something! He's going to murder Elsa!"

26

THE FALL

"Dominion! Leave her alone!" Paul came to his senses as he shouted at the male figure that struggled with Elsa up on the walkway. They were forty feet above the courtyard; the darkness meant he could see little more than the green dress that Elsa wore.

"Dominion! Stop it!" Paul raced for the steps that led to the walkway.

"Dominion!"

Elsa heard the name being shouted from below. But when she turned in her attacker's grasp so she'd be face-to-face she knew exactly who it was.

"Saiban?"

Perspiration soaked his cheeks as he struggled to heave her over the wall.

"Saiban, what are you doing? Let go of me!"

Saiban gasped, "I'm not going to let you, or the rest, ruin everything."

As she forced his head back with her hand under his chin she hissed, "You killed Luna, didn't you?"

"You've all got to die anyway. Why prolong your agony?"

"Saiban, stop it. You're hurting—"

"They'll destroy you in the end."

His huge, mournful eyes with their downturned corners gazed into hers. Despite his fight to lift her over the battlement they appeared strangely still, as if he'd abandoned himself to the inevitable a long time ago.

"Saiban. You're out of your mind!"

"No. I'm not mad. I'm loyal. Forgive me, Elsa, I'm working for a greater good. Now please submit. Be merciful on yourself."

"No."

"If I don't kill you the townspeople will."

"What do you mean? Greater good? What is it you know?"

"Hush. Let it go, Elsa. Give in."

"What is it, Saiban? You know something we don't?"

"I know *everything*."

For the first time ever Elsa saw Saiban smile.

"Just as the powers that be made Dominion different, so they entrusted in me the capacity to . . . No, not telling. Never shall. Everything you want to know is inside my head—and that's exactly where it's staying." The smile became a deranged leer.

At that moment, Elsa knew that the nervous strain on Saiban had overwhelmed him.

A voice rang out nearby, "Saiban. Let go of her."

"Paul . . . please, he's breaking my arms." As she said the words she focused her eyes as if looking at a face just behind Saiban's shoulder. It worked. The expression on her face forced her attacker to glance back. Paul, however, had just scaled the steps on the far side of the castle. It would be another forty seconds before he reached them. She used the distraction to head-butt Saiban as hard as she could in the back of the skull. Even someone as bloodless as the melancholic Saiban feels pain. He grunted. One hand slipped away from Elsa's upper arm as instinctively he clutched the back of his head. Elsa's vision blurred from the force of the jolt against her own brow, but she gritted her teeth, then wriggled free of his grasp.

She yelled, "Now it's time for you to give up, Saiban!"

His eyes blazed with fury.

"I'm going to tell them you killed Luna." She shook her head in disbelief. "Why did you do it, Saiban?"

"You've clearly not been listening to what I've been saying, Elsa. All you're getting out of me is this one nugget of information: All of you here are surplus to requirements. Nobody needs you. Can you absorb that? Now I shall demonstrate my loyalty. If you're at least half as intelligent as you pretend to be, *watch*, you might learn something."

Saiban always moved slowly, as if he took part in some stately procession. This time his movements were a blur as he scrambled onto the wall. He stood there on the coping stones with the cold night breeze running through his hair. He faced in toward the courtyard where the God Scarers stared up at him. By this time Paul and West were perhaps ten paces from Elsa; they slowed; they knew running would do no good.

"Listen to me." Saiban's cold voice was as much a drone as the noise of the wind flowing from the ocean. "You haven't the courage, I know that. But you could do worse than follow me." With that he allowed himself to topple backward.

27

BODY TALK

Saiban was easy to find. After winching up the portcullis the God Scarers walked around the foot of the castle walls to the point where Saiban had jumped. With there being no flashlights, they'd improvised by setting lighted candles in empty glass jars. The shock of recent events had sobered them up fast. Elsa no longer felt the effects of the Coffin Paint, but her neck was still sore from where Saiban had tried to snap it.

Beneath them the town lay sleeping. Scaur Ness nestled in darkness, the harbor pool glistening in its midst with its sad array of derelict ships. What would the population make of this bizarre candlelit procession? Elsa asked herself. They'd say their monster neighbors had gone mad. Or they were conducting a satanic rite.

Dominion emerged from the shadows to join them. He'd been nowhere to be seen during Saiban's attack on her. Perhaps the giant had been brooding in secret over the way his limbs had been changing color. Or how scars had formed deep red gullies in his flesh. He was different from the get-go. Now he was changing . . . or evolving . . . further away from the nature of a Transient: the beings resurrected by humankind to diligently serve humankind. Only humanity had become disgusted by their creation. Now they turned their collective faces from their dead that they'd dragged back into the world of the living.

The cool breeze whispered out of the night. Above them there were no stars. All she could make out by candlelight, apart from a few yards of road, were her fellow refugees—Dr. Paul Marais, Beech, Xaiyad, and the rest. Oh, and the human guest, of course. Caitlin walked beside Paul. You only had to look at them, and the word *couple* presented itself in your mind.

Anyway, Saiban . . . The mournful spook of a man was easy to find in death. His body had fallen on a low outbuilding, not far from where they'd found Luna—his victim. Well, strictly speaking Saiban didn't lie on the roof. Projecting vertically from the side of the roof was a steel fence topped with foot-high spikes to prevent vandals from scaling it. Saiban had crashed onto the spiked barrier lengthways. The first spike skewered his left thigh above the knee. Its bloody point stood above his leg by several inches. Then at intervals of six inches were a line of another half a dozen spikes. Saiban's body had impaled itself so neatly it looked as if a row of mutant steel spines ran up the center of his body as he lay there on his back; his right leg and arms hung limply down at each side of the fence. For a moment they stared at Saiban's bloody body, the spikes erupting from his leg, stomach, and chest. Damage to internal organs had been catastrophic. In Elsa's mind's eye, she could picture the metal blade that punched right through the center of his heart, to rip through its blood-filled chambers, arteries, and muscle wall. Death would be instantaneous. Of course, his God

Scarer biology meant that the body still twitched. The mouth formed an O shape in a rhythmic way; as if the pulsation of the lips struggled to compensate for the lack of heartbeat.

"Burn him," West told them. "Before we cremate Uri, burn this bastard. With luck he'll still feel the fire before it incinerates him."

Beech shook her head. "I say we shove him over the edge of the cliff. He's trash anyway."

"No." Elsa was emphatic.

"Why ever not? You know full well what he did to Luna. For God's sake, he nearly did the same to you!"

"Saiban knew the truth about what was happening to us." Elsa nodded at Saiban. "Take him inside."

West glared at the body in disgust. "He's dead. He's not going to talk, is he?"

Beech agreed. "Just drop him into the ocean."

"Look, what he knew might be important. Don't we still want to know about the thousands of people who we processed at the Transit Station? All the dead we brought back to life only for them to vanish the moment they left?"

Paul said, "We'd like to know that, Elsa, and a good deal more, but Saiban made sure we'd never find out when he took a dive off the castle wall."

Saiban gave a weird grunt as if in agreement. Xaiyad reached up to grip the corpse's jerking wrist. After checking the pulse—or lack of it—Xaiyad nodded. "Saiban is dead. What we're seeing are the usual after-death convulsions."

"Throw him off the cliff," Caitlin shouted

"And the sooner the better." West was angry. "He tried to persuade us to surrender so we'd be killed by the humans. When we refused he tried to finish us himself."

"No," Elsa shouted. "It's more than that. He said there was a plan."

"What plan?"

"I don't know." Elsa gestured in frustration. "Take him inside. Go through his pockets. We need to find out what's really happening. Saiban knew; that's why he killed himself rather than allow us the chance of finding out."

"Well, we're never going to know." Beech folded her arms. "He's dead."

Dominion stepped forward. "I know what to do. But I'll need your help."

With that he reached up, tugged the corpse free from the spikes, then carried it back to the Pharos.

An insane night is the ideal breeding ground for wild, mad acts. First, they cremated Uri's body on the cliff top on a huge funeral pyre built from wooden bed frames found in a storeroom. They covered their ears when the burning corpse groaned. A mournful music that ate its way into their hearts.

Dominion locked Saiban's corpse in the storeroom emptied of bed frames. Saiban made excited sighing noises as if he predicted extraordinary times ahead for the God Scarers. After that, Dominion vanished into the night. *Maybe he's gone night fishing*, Paul told himself with a stab of dark humor, *but something tells me he's got other plans in mind. God help us all.* Some of the God Scarers returned to the cafeteria where the Coffin Paint waited for them. Within half an hour Beech stood naked on the castle walls with her arms and legs outstretched to form an X-shape of naked womanhood—all curves, softness, with glints of red hair in the darkness. Paul could only guess at the hallucinations that roared through her mind. Maybe she called on some ancient god to take her. Did she see a vast luminous face rising from the ocean? Anything was possible with Coffin Paint.

As he passed Elsa in the courtyard she showed him her bruised throat. The liquor had left her elated. "Saiban knows everything, you know? Where all those tens of thousands of Transients went. Why Dominion is different from the rest of us." She giggled; her alcohol-fueled breath cut through Paul like a knife.

"Elsa, you've been through hell tonight. Why not get some rest?"

"Are you going to lie down with me?" Her eyes grew large. "No, you won't keep me company, Dr. Paul; bedside manner not included." She swayed.

"Take it easy, Elsa."

"Take it easy? That's what Saiban said to me. Take my second death easy, that's what he meant, didn't he?"

"Look, that stuff you've been drinking—"

"Grants us revelations, I know." She snorted; the smoldering eroticism flared into anger. "Not only Saiban knew things. I know things. Hard facts. Dominion is different."

"That's because his mind woke too soon. It must be the—"

"It's not his mind!" Her voice echoed from the walls. "It's physical. His body. You've seen how it's changing color. Arms paler than his head; torso darker than his neck. You can figure out what Dominion is as well as I can."

"Elsa. That drink is potent. You should—"

"Shut up, or you'll throw me from the fucking tower?"

"No. All I want—"

"Dominion is . . ." Her eyes blazed as she swayed there. "Listen to me, Paul. Dominion is a Frankenstein. A real Frankenstein monster. He's not like us who were brought back in one piece. You saw his scars, the different-colored skin? Dominion has been glued together. He's a hundred different body parts. He's a kit monster. An amalgam. A jigsaw. *And that, Paul, is why Dominion claimed to be the First Man.*"

"Rest, Elsa. Then we'll talk."

"No. I'm going up there." She raised her eyes to the highest tower. "Up there I can hear the dead sing to me. No, not our kind. The old, old dead. The people who built the stone circle up on the hill. You know something, Paul? They want me. Do you think I should go up there and find out what they want? Hmm?"

When he gently suggested she sleep off the liquor he found himself talking to the night air. She'd run for the tower. Hell, what a night. Gales of laughter came from the cafeteria. Rather than God Scarers in there it sounded like a student party going into overdrive. Calls, laughter, hooting, you name it.

Paul couldn't face that sober. He went in search of Dominion. The last thing they needed was their very own Frankenstein monster ripping up the town. If that's what he intended. But what did he intend? He seemed to work to his own hidden agenda. As he made his way to the portcullis a voice called to him from one of the doors that led from the castle buildings into the courtyard. He turned to see a door part open with a stark-white face behind it.

Luna? He blinked as the image came to mind of the woman Saiban had killed.

"Paul. Please come here for a moment."

He craned his head forward to see into the shadows. "Caitlin? Are you all right?"

Quickly, Paul crossed the courtyard to the doorway. Beyond it was a gloomy office with maps of the coastline on the walls. As he entered she closed the door behind him. Even though the darkness was almost absolute her eyes gleamed at him. They appeared as huge shining orbs in the darkness.

"Paul. That stuff you and the rest have been drinking. You've no idea what it's like."

"I guess they don't call it Coffin Paint for nothing."

"Every week someone drinks themselves to death with it."

"You might have noticed our own prospects for a long life aren't favorable."

"It's not just the physical damage. There's a fungus in there that sends people insane. There's a man in our street who's convinced his hands have become mouths filled with sharp teeth. He's terrified that they're going to eat him in his sleep." The eyes narrowed. "It's not funny, Paul."

"I know. I'm sorry. Put it down to the stress of tonight. Maybe a wee bit of your witches' brew as well. To me the whole wide world is a bit wacky and off-kilter."

It was so dark that when Caitlin closed her eyes she vanished. The next moment, however, he felt her arms around him. In the darkness she found his mouth with her own. That's when it hit him. A burning desire. His blood seared him like molten metal, igniting nerve endings. Her body felt so delicate as he touched her. In his mind's eye he saw the fragile skeleton beneath her skin. And this time he didn't beg himself to stop. He was a monster; he came from a coffin, not a womb. She was human, a Sap. So what? So bloody what? This time it didn't feel wrong. In the darkness they ripped away their clothes. *She feels so beautiful*, Paul told himself. *I love the touch of her.* His fingers mapped her anatomy, while all the time that heat grew inside him.

Caitlin whispered, "You can have me, you know that, don't you?" Her word "you" became a delicious tickle as she exhaled against his chest.

Alongside the wonderful sensation he heard a crash of breaking glass, followed by a shout.

Paul groaned. "I should really see what that was."

"Let someone else deal with it." She kissed his bare chest.

"Something might have happened."

"They're drinking Coffin Paint; something *will* happen. That stuff is a curse."

"Then I should check that no one's hurt."

"Believe me. They'll hurt themselves. And they'll do things to each other you can't even begin to imagine."

"Then, I have to—"

"Paul, you can't save them all single-handedly." Her voice became husky. "Take a night off."

In the dark he could feel her fingers on his bare arms. Then the cool, moist touch of her lips. She kissed his bare chest, then his stomach, as she worked her way downward to what at that moment burned like it was the center of the sun. At the first touch of her lips there, he let out a heartfelt sigh of pleasure.

In the storeroom Saiban's corpse lay stretched on the floor. Nobody had bothered to cover it. Nobody cared for him in life. In death he was reviled. Even though he was dead, blood still seeped from the line of puncture wounds. In the darkness a brain-dead Saiban jerked his limbs. His lips smacked together as if he muttered secrets. His eyelids would suddenly draw back to reveal eyes that gleamed as brightly as balls of glass. Nobody was there to see Saiban's after-death convulsions. In the depths of that congealing brain, ghosts of thought still flitted through dying neurons: *Dominion is the First Man. All those cadavers of men and women wheeled into the Transit Station in caskets packed with ice. Then after transition from death back to life they left the Transit Station. They aren't people, they are vast rivers that will irrigate the deserts of the world.* Saiban was too far gone to differentiate between fact and fable. All he could do was lie there, twitching on the floor, as his dead brain dreamed its last dreams.

Paul lost himself in a world where only he and Caitlin existed. This time there wasn't even a table for her to lie on. In the darkness they found a wall. He lifted her naked body until her hips were level with his, and then he gently sandwiched her between the wall and himself. For how long he pushed himself into Caitlin, her soft moans of pleasure sounding in his ear, he didn't know. This rhythm was the rhythm of the cosmos. At that moment it seemed as if it would last forever. The night must have been turning to dawn by the time his pace quickened. He could see Caitlin had scrunched her eyes together to concentrate on the sensations inside herself. Her lips had reddened. The black curls of hair tumbled down over her shoulder onto his arms as he held her with her back to the wall. Her legs were around his waist, the heels of her feet digging into the small of his back as he thrust himself into her. They both panted hard. Small cries began to escape her lips. This was joined with his own grunting, an involuntary primal sound.

That's when that slow-motion explosion started deep inside himself. A prickling sensation ran over his skin. He quickened the pace; Caitlin's breath erupted in his ear as she gasped. Then her eyelids snapped back. The way her eyes focused on a single point brought a shiver down his spine. *She's seen something that shouldn't be there.*

Paul turned his head. Even though he saw a figure there in the doorway, there was nothing he could do to stop himself. It was too late. Instinct had taken over. He couldn't break away if he tried. All he could do was continue to pound his own body against Caitlin's as Dominion stared in at them. There was no expression on the giant's face. He remained immobile. His eyes retained that impassive stare at the pair of them as Paul's orgasm ripped through him to vent itself into Caitlin's body.

Ten minutes later Paul confronted Dominion in the courtyard. He still dragged on the surgical scrubs as the giant gazed out of the latticework of the portcullis. A smudge of light appeared in the eastern sky.

"You shit!"

Dominion didn't even register that he heard Paul's voice. Paul glared at the wide back. Above it the shaved head gleamed as the dawn light caught the blond stubble.

"Dominion. What made you watch? Don't you know what privacy is?"

"We've got work to do. But I let you finish what you were doing."

"Oh, I suppose you think that's funny?" When Dominion didn't answer, Paul surged on in fury. "Or did it turn you on? We all know you're not like us. Your brain doesn't work the same. Your entire body is a patchwork quilt. You really are a Frankenstein, aren't you? A big ugly bastard stitched together from leftovers at the morgue."

"You might want to eat before we leave."

"Leave? I'm not going to anywhere with you!" No response. "Did you hear me . . . charnel house boy?" This time when Dominion ignored him Paul shoved him in the back. The figure barely moved. "Come on, let's see if I can take your bloody head off. It's probably glued on none too tightly anyway."

The shame of being watched as he had sex with Caitlin made him do it. He threw a punch at Dominion's head. This time the giant moved. As he turned round he grabbed Paul by the throat. Caitlin ran forward.

"Dominion, please don't hurt him. He's angry. You shouldn't have watched."

By now God Scarers spilled out into the courtyard to witness the commotion.

Paul managed to throw another punch into Dominion's mouth. The teeth were as hard as flint. A grunt escaped Paul's lips as the pain snapped up his arm.

Dominion's voice boomed out across the yard. "I must find out what's happening to us."

"We all want to know," West called out. "So leave Paul alone. For God's sake, he saved your hide."

Dominion shook Paul by the collar as if he were a doll. "You might be curious. For me it's imperative. Look at me! My skin is parting. It's breaking open. Literally I will fall apart. But learning what happened is more important than my survival. And it's more important than yours. In the last few weeks something huge has happened to this world. It's vital we find out what Saiban knows. He's the only person who could tell us the truth. Saiban has information I have to act upon. He is the key to all this. I feel as if I should know . . . and I should be doing something."

West stepped forward. "What do you know?"

"That's the problem, I can't recall it." Dominion released Paul. "And that's why we've got find out the truth from Saiban."

Paul rubbed the sore flesh where the collar had dug into him. "Dominion. Saiban's dead."

"I know." Dominion met his gaze. "But we can still make Saiban talk."

28

REGENERATOR

Dominion's speech silenced everyone in the courtyard.
The dawn breeze sighed around the towers. Elsa shivered
as she stood among the group. At times the night seemed
to have passed as if it had been a dream. The trauma of
Saiban's attack on her, that potent liquor. Now this. Dominion's speech about the need to discover the truth;
that and the need to make Saiban—*dead* Saiban—speak.

Everyone there knew what Dominion was suggesting.
Beech, who tottered down the steps from the castle wall
with a beast of a hangover, voiced what they were thinking. "Are you insane?"

"We must do it as quickly as we can," Dominion answered.

Paul flung out his arms. "But how can we? The Transit
Station was destroyed. Even if the equipment still works,
there'll be no power."

Dominion wasn't in the mood to be contradicted.
"There will be portable Regenerators in the stores.
They're self-contained."

"How do you know they haven't been smashed by the soldiers?"

"We'll take that chance."

Xaiyad stepped forward to join the debate. "Let me get this straight, Dominion. You're telling us to submit Saiban to the Regenerator?"

"Yes."

"That can't be done. We've all had two chances at life. No one has ever gone through the regeneration process a second time."

"Nevertheless."

Xaiyad continued, "You've seen the damage to Saiban. The spikes passed through the center of his body. Most of the internal organs were punctured."

"We'll fix him."

"How?"

Dominion's eyes swept round the group. "Paul will do it. He's a doctor."

"A doctor, yes." Paul's eyes widened. "Not a miracle worker."

"You can do it," Dominion insisted. "But the body will deteriorate, making your job more difficult."

"More difficult? It's impossible even now."

"No, it isn't." Dominion's voice became dark thunder. "Listen to me. It is vital that we learn what Saiban knew. That is my quest now. Nothing else matters. If any of you have to die in order for me to fulfill that quest, then so be it."

Elsa heard Paul murmur in his Scottish tones. "Well, that's reassuring. We're expendable." He cleared his throat. "But, Dominion, I take it you aren't. You're a major component in this mysterious strategy that Saiban knew all about."

"Once I've served my purpose, then I will be expendable, too," Dominion told him. "Until then I won't let anything get in my way."

"Dominion," Paul said, still clearly skeptical of Dominion's mission. "How do you propose we get Saiban to the Transit Station?"

"We're not. We'll bring the portable Regenerator here. That's why I need your help. I won't be able to move it myself. . . ."

"Come, come, a big strong boy like you?"

"I will need experts to check the unit as well as to collect whatever else we need to resuscitate Saiban."

"Dominion, we won't be resuscitating him. If this works we'll be aping God."

"Don't stand there talking, Paul. We're in a hurry."

"Another thing. Those so-called portable Regenerators are heavy . . . too heavy to pop onto your shoulder and stroll back through the countryside whistling a merry tune."

"While you had your fun I went out to find a truck."

"Did you kill anyone for it?"

"That's not important."

"And just one more thing," Paul called out as Dominion headed for the gate. The big man was in a hurry now; his patience had evaporated. "All the years I spent at the Transit Station we never, ever used one of the portable units. Even if they're intact they won't work anyway."

Dominion called back, "Elsa, West, Paul. You can help me."

Dominion had parked a refrigeration truck near where they'd found Saiban's body. His blood still smeared the walls of the building. Printed on the vehicle's flanks were the words CATCH OF THE DAY. OCEAN FRESH.

West grumbled, "Fish? I hate the smell of fish."

"All three of you get in the back," Dominion ordered. "None of you have slept, so get some rest before we get there."

"You'll find nothing but ruins, my friend," Paul called out.

Dominion climbed into the cab without answering. He'd already started the motor by the time they hauled themselves into the back.

"Hell. It still stinks of fish." West pinched his nostrils. "Keep the back doors open or I'll choke."

"If the worst that happens to us is you choking on the smell of cod, then I'll be happy."

As the truck rumbled away from the Pharos Elsa told herself: *We've been sucked into Dominion's universe now. Saiban lost his mind before he died. Maybe Dominion's gone the same way.*

The truck followed a road out of town. Through the open rear doors of the truck they watched houses passing. People had started to appear on the streets. These must be the few who had jobs to go to. Sitting with her back to the steel container that once transported the town's catch of fish to the outside world, she felt the vibration of the motor through the floor. The speed of the truck added to the sense of the inevitable. That they were rushing toward a revelation. What that was she couldn't begin to guess. Then, neither could Dominion. But, yes, he was different from the rest. He was the first Transient to wake in the Regenerator. He'd committed the unthinkable by killing human beings. At that moment she began to realize that there was something locked in the giant's head. Maybe what Saiban knew would unlock that secret truth. Of course whether it led to their salvation, or their death, was another matter entirely.

29

TASTES LIKE VIOLENCE

What remained of the Transit Station had been garrisoned by troops. These weren't the commando elite that had stormed the building just a few nights ago. The soldiers had stubbled faces. They wore hand-me-down uniforms. Their caps were frayed. Only one wore army-issue boots. The others opted for sneakers. They didn't know what hit them.

Dominion drove through the gate to the Transit Station that had been left flapping in the wind. A couple of soldiers eventually sauntered out of the residential block to challenge Dominion. They weren't expecting God Scarers, probably thinking the refrigerated truck was delivering supplies. By the time they realized that the truck's driver was one of the beings they'd be destroying it was too late. Dominion stepped down out of the cab in a way that was almost leisurely. Paul had already scrambled out of the back, so he saw the tragedy unfurl before his eyes.

The two soldiers were hungover; it took a while for them to understand that they were in danger. Naturally, they assumed if a God Scarer turned up at the door it wouldn't be to attack them. At last, one of the soldiers woke up to the fact that Dominion wasn't one of the submissive kind.

"Nik, I haven't brought my gun! You'll have to do it."

The second soldier managed to fumble a revolver from its holster just as Dominion reached out and snapped his neck. The other Sap turned back to shout toward the residential block. Dominion wasn't going to allow the man to warn his comrades. The giant caught hold of the guy by the back of the jacket. As the soldier opened his mouth to scream in terror Dominion simply pushed one of those weirdly pale hands into the man's wide-open mouth. Elsa and West turned away but Paul saw what Dominion did next.

The grounds of the Transit Station were as Paul remembered from just a few days ago. There were tall trees, a rose garden full of red and gold blooms. The morning sun shone on a pond where rushes waved in the breeze. Birds sang as if happy to report to the world it was going to be a beautiful day. *And here's Dominion. A hand in some guy's mouth. The guy's trying to scream but he can't. He can't make a noise. The poor bastard can't even breathe. That's Dominion's intention.* Just when Paul told himself this was as bad as it would get, it got worse. Dominion placed the flat of his hand behind the soldier's head. Then Dominion really turned up the pressure. He forced his hand down the man's throat. His victim's eyes were open wide; his terror blazed there like he'd got a thousand-watt bulb illuminating his skull. Paul saw Dominion's hand form what appeared to be a hugely bloated Adam's apple in the dying man's throat.

Dominion looked back over his shoulder. "Paul, hide the other man. Someone might look out of the window."

Dear God, what if they did? What would they make of this pretty little scene? Their buddy with a monster's giant fist shoved halfway down his gullet.

"Paul." The warning note was clear enough. Paul loped across to the corpse with the broken neck. Quickly, he dragged it beneath a bush alongside the driveway. By the time he'd emerged Dominion walked casually toward him with the soldier's body. The giant gripped the man by the back of the belt to carry him like a sports bag. Instead of hiding the corpse beneath a bush as Paul had done, Dominion simply flung him out of sight into the branches of a tree. Three days ago Paul would have howled in protest at Dominion's murderous actions, but now he was numbed to it. Dominion killed. That's the way it was. *Deal with it.*

"There's more inside," Dominion said. "They're cooking food. Which way to the kitchen?"

So Paul showed him. Elsa and West followed at a distance. On an upper floor Paul nodded at a door that led to one of the communal kitchens the residents of the Transit Station used. A strong smell of frying bacon filled the corridor. From the kitchen came the sound of male voices. A radio played upbeat music. This time Paul hung back as Dominion pushed open the door. Before the door closed again after Dominion passed through it Paul saw the soldiers in their shabby uniforms. He counted four of them. Three sitting to a table, drinking coffee, killing time; the third forked strips of bacon from a pan.

The soldiers' expression of surprise as that giant entered their cozy room should have been comical: all wide-eyed with jaws dropping. Then Dominion was the kind of beast they'd never seen before. A giant with hands that were white, his arms black. A blond stubble bristled across his formidable skull. From his coffee-colored face two enormous almond-shaped eyes that were as black as onyx fixed on them. Add to that the scars covering his body . . . *Mice see cat.* Paul felt immensely grateful that the door closed on whatever happened inside the kitchen; this time he wouldn't have to watch. When the sounds came they were so violent that he flinched. First were indignant shouts, even a "What the hell do you think you're doing here?" By the time they realized that Dominion wasn't one of the quiet, understated, submissive, oh so politely deferential God Scarers it was far too late.

Shouts of anger segued into screams of pain. The backing track to the Saps' expression of raw emotion was a sequence of crashes, thumps, snapping wood, shattering crockery. Paul glanced back to where Elsa and West stood in the corridor. They were mute with shock.

Paul gave a grim smile. "Hands up, anyone who thinks we've died and gone to hell?" They didn't react to his words. Their eyes were locked on the closed kitchen door as a cry ended in a rasp of agony. "Forgive my gallows humor. If I don't crack bad jokes I know I'm going to go out of my mind."

Still, neither of them spoke. The spell only broke when the noises stopped and Dominion emerged from the kitchen.

"They should have made it easy for themselves," he told them. "OK, time's short. If we're going to bring back Saiban we need to work faster."

The kitchen door began to swing open. Raw bacon lay scattered on the tiled floor. *No, that isn't bacon* . . . Before the door opened fully to reveal the room's occupants Paul turned his back on it. "Follow me."

* * *

The main entrance to the medical center had been burned to one almighty pile of crud. Even concrete walls had collapsed.

"Loading bay," Elsa told them. They skirted the outside of the building to the back. There, windowpanes had been blown out by the explosions; otherwise it appeared intact.

Paul looked through a window. "There's an automatic sprinkler system. It looks as if that was enough to stop the flames spreading."

"Hurry up," Dominion said. "You need to start work on Saiban by midday. Otherwise—"

"The rot sets in. I know." Paul began to wonder if Dominion might snap his spine if he was tardy. "This way."

Beside the loading bay doors that were big enough to accommodate a truck was a pedestrian entrance. This door had been blown off its hinges when the commandos had stormed the building. Someone had simply propped it against the door frame with a plank of wood. It would have kept the local rodent population out; not much more. West kicked aside the plank, allowing the door to topple onto the ground.

"What if there are more troops guarding the place?" Elsa asked.

Dominion replied, "There aren't any."

"How do you know?"

"I asked the men in the kitchen."

Paul exchanged meaningful glances with Elsa as they stepped into the loading bay. Light fell through the shattered windows to reveal tiled walls. The place retained its clinical air.

Elsa said, "This is where they brought those who'd been selected for regeneration."

West grunted. "She means, corpses are wheeled in here,

three weeks later they walk out through the front door."
He grunted again. "Good as new."

"Better than new," she corrected.

As they moved through the cavernous void of the
loading bay West sniffed. "This is why I don't like the
smell of fish."

"You're rambling, West," Elsa told him.

"I used to work with someone who incinerated the folk
you guys couldn't kick-start. By the time she got the pa-
perwork back from admin the bodies had started to rot.
She told me the smell always reminded her of sardines.
I've not eaten fish since. I can't even stand the reek of it."

"Stop wasting time," Dominion told them. "You need
to find the equipment."

West sniffed again. "The reason for my anecdote about
what sardines smell like is that I can smell it here."

Dominion's gaze roved the delivery bay. "It's important
we make Saiban talk. For now, nothing else matters."

Paul nodded toward casket-shaped boxes on a conveyor. "There's your sardine cans, West." He grimaced.
"They must have brought in a batch of lovely fresh stiffs
for transition. They never made it out of the bay; now
they're starting to ripen."

Dominion didn't appear to notice the aroma. "Where
will we find the mobile Regenerators?"

"Last time I saw one," Paul said, "which was years ago,
was in the storeroom next to the main Regenerator theater. We kept a couple as backup in case the main system
failed. Thanks to our diligence they never did, but
heaven knows what state they're in now."

"Find them for me," Dominion told him. "You need to
move faster."

Paul resisted the temptation to utter a flippant "Aye-
aye, Captain." Instead he pointed at a pair of steel doors.
"Through there."

To exit through the doors meant passing the caskets on the conveyor belt. One of the soldiers guarding the place must have been bored enough to unscrew the bolts that held down the lid. All caskets arrived packed with ice; that kept the corpse cool enough until it rolled along the conveyor belt to begin the procedure. What Paul saw as he passed was a casket full of melted ice. Floating in there, like in a bathtub, was a corpse still encased in plastic shrink-wrap. A green bloom of mold spread between the transparent plastic and the face of a woman. The eyes were wide open as if she was shocked to find herself in such a state. The soldier had also fired a bullet between the naked breasts, maybe to double-check this naked beauty was really dead.

She was dead—as deeply, truly, absolutely dead as you can get.

"Sardines." West pinched his nostrils with his fingers. "Never, ever give me sardines."

There was more horror to come.

"They had orders to trash the place." Paul gazed round the theater that housed the Regenerators. There were six lines of four. The cylinders that contained the body during the reanimation process were built from surgical steel. Seven feet tall, hourglass in shape, with narrow cinched waists, they stood upright in what had been a sterile environment. Although there was no electric light the sun falling through windows set in the ceiling revealed the extent of the damage.

Dominion ran his hand round the scorched fissure in the side of a Regenerator. Others bore the same kind of damage. "The soldiers used demolition charges to blow holes in them."

"Then the new government has no plans to restart the program." West examined the one closest to him. "This one reeks of sardines as well. No prizes for guessing what's inside."

They moved along the lines of Regenerators. Small observation windows were set in the top of the hourglass structure. West stayed clear but Paul noticed Elsa maintained her professional rigor as a trained nurse. She checked each one. Her face was like stone.

"Misfire." Dominion pointed at one of the vessels. A blackened smear radiated lines of soot. "The charge didn't penetrate the casing."

Elsa immediately ran across to check. Using her hands to block the sun's glare, she put her face close to the observation port. With a sharp intake of breath she jerked back. "*It moved.*"

"Forget it." West spoke as if a bad taste, possibly the flavor of sardines, formed in his mouth. "The power's been out for days. "Whatever's in there will have gone badly wrong."

Paul found that same bad taste creeping over his tongue. "All medical staff swore an oath never to neglect a patient. We can't simply stick our hands in our pockets and stroll away now."

"West's right," Dominion said. "Leave it."

Elsa rounded on him. "We've agreed to help you, Dominion. But we're not going to break our oath. Our laws mean nothing to you, but they still mean a hell of a lot to us. So fucking back off! OK!"

"I told you, you are expendable. What's important is that we make Saiban live again. He knows what's happening to us."

"OK, Dominion. Break our necks." Paul moved to help Elsa as she flicked open the catches that ran down one side of the upright canister. "If you do, then you'll have no one to help you load the Regenerator onto the truck."

"I'll give you ninety seconds."

Paul gave a grim smile. "We salute your generosity."

They worked together. Paul opened the vents to discharge whatever remained of the gasses inside the canister. These would normally be pumped out into catchment chambers beneath the floor of the theater, but with no electricity all he could hope for was they'd disperse harmlessly in the air. If anything the hourglass-shaped vessel that contained the body opened like an ancient Egyptian coffin that had been stood on end. Only the vertical "lid" of this cylinder swung outward on a hinged arm.

West groaned when he saw what was inside. "So this is what happens when it's left in the oven for too long."

Paul moved back as the last of the vapors poured out of the vessel. Standing there, restrained by a steel band across the waist, was what would have been one of his patients. Normally, after three hours of immersion in electroconductive gases the newborn Transient would be removed from the Regenerator. They'd still be unconscious; the moment of their waking for the first time after their deaths would still be hours away. Of course, after the attack on the Transit Station this individual had been left to bake in the gases untended by staff.

West swallowed as if whatever he'd eaten in the last twenty-four hours wanted out. "Dominion. Kill it."

The monstrous occupant of the Regenerator reached out its arms and screamed.

30

THE MONSTER'S MONSTER

Elsa stared. There, standing in the Regenerator with the restraining band around the waist, was a man who'd been left in that chemical soup for days longer than he should have been. The first thought that struck Elsa was: *He should be dead.* Second: *It would be better if he were dead.*

"Dominion, what are you waiting for?" West recoiled from the thing. *"Kill it."*

Dominion approached the Regenerator. His eyes absorbed details of that naked body in front of him. The addition of new flesh had been rampant. Where it should have produced a figure with an Olympian physique the morbid overgrowth had created a monstrous figure. A distorted head with massive brows sat on strangely bulbous shoulders that flanked its lettuce leaf ears. The skin was more like rhino hide with circular calluses spreading in a rash over much of it. One side of the head was bald, while the other sprouted lank rust-colored strands that hung down as far as the elbow. The chest heaved as the creature struggled to breathe. Its fingernails were a thick material that reminded Elsa of animal horn. They even emerged from the finger ends in a shape that was cylindrical rather than flat. Body hair sprouted as black spines rather than soft fibers.

It raised its head with a snorting sound that was more equine than human. She noted the eyes were so prominent that even though its eyelids were closed they were stretched so tightly red veins bulged from them. And despite the thing being on the brink of its second death Elsa saw that saw a desperate strength in the blood pumping through the veins. Whatever happened, this monstrous explosion of human flesh was determined to stay alive.

As Dominion moved toward the open Regenerator Elsa blocked his way.

"No. I won't allow you to kill him."

"Stand aside."

"He's one of our own kind," she told him. "You mustn't hurt him."

West cried, "For God's sake, Elsa. It'll die anyway. Dominion will be doing it a favor."

"He! Not 'it.'" Elsa's fury blazed. "You were like him, if you hadn't forgotten. You were carried in here a stinking corpse, you walked out alive again."

Paul spoke out, "We won't allow you to harm him. We dedicated our lives to giving people a second chance of life."

"Good grief!" West slapped his forehead. "What you going to do? Keep it as a pet? Look at it, man. It's a travesty. It'll be brain-dead."

Dominion reached out toward the man in the cylinder. Elsa knew she was no match for the giant, but she slammed her fists against his chest. "Leave him!"

Behind her came a gasp. She turned to see the man's mouth open. An overlarge tongue licked swollen lips.

Then he raised his head and opened his eyes. A shock snapped through Elsa's chest as she beheld those eyes that protruded from the head. They stood proud of the face as if the sockets could barely contain them. Larger than hens' eggs, the whites had that same chalky texture as eggshell, while the iris formed a hard blue disk centered with a large black pupil.

"See, all that shouting's woken the wee lad up."

Elsa turned on Paul ready to criticize his inappropriate comment, but from his expression of mortification he was struggling to maintain professional calm.

"No!" Elsa pushed against Dominion as he surged forward, his clenched fist raised in readiness to burst the monster's face.

What happened next caught them all by surprise. An excited snort vented the man's mouth as he stood there panting for breath.

The snorting became speech. "Dominion. I knew you'd come. Where's Saiban?"

Paul found the mobile Regenerators in the storeroom under dozens of packs of surgical gowns. The commandos must have put their heads round the door, then decided there was nothing to interest them here.

"There they are, Dominion. I'm making no guarantees whether they'll work. They've been gathering dust in that wee corner of theirs for the last thirty years."

West gave one of the timber cases an experimental kick. Inside, the Regenerator chimed like a bell. "Why on earth did they bother making them?"

"In the good old days, when monster and man lived in perfect harmony, every far-flung parish would have one."

"Paul's being flippant. The government's intentions were noble," Elsa said. "It was going to be the dawn of a new Golden Age. The end of death."

Paul agreed. "Indeed. No one need fear death. Because even if you didn't live near a Transit Station every community, no matter how remote, would have one of these beauties tucked away in a barn. Within minutes of old Uncle Barry or Auntie May giving up the ghost they'd be whisked into one of these. Then within days they'd be back in the pink again. Rosy-cheeked, brimful of life, ready to dance the Highland Fling at the next Hogmanay." He ran his fingers over a warning stenciled on the case that was now delicious in its irony: BEWARE. HIGH VOLTAGE! DANGER OF DEATH! "But no one appreciated how unfashionable it would become to be raised from the dead. Funny old world, isn't it?"

Dominion swept mounds of laundry from the cases. "We'll take two."

Paul shook his head. "I think you'll find we've only time to take one. These things are devilishly heavy."

"One, then," Dominion agreed. "What else do you need?"

"Full cylinders of M-stock and V-stock. Those work the necromantic magic when they're pumped into the Regenerator."

Elsa added, "We also need flush and primer. They come ready loaded in syringes."

"Find them," Dominion ordered. "We'll start here. West, move it away from the corner. Get down with your back to the wall; push it with your feet."

Paul caught Dominion's arm. "One other point. What do you plan to do with your friend back there?"

"If he's still alive after we load this we'll take him with us."

West gave an expressive shrug. "OK, Dominion, aren't you going to tell us?"

"Tell you what?"

"Beefy boy back there knows you. Do you know him?"

"I must have once. Now get to work. Time's running out."

West appeared reluctant to let it go at that. "You don't remember anything about him?"

A voice came as a sighing wheeze from the doorway. "It might come back to him . . . if I remind Dominion that we . . ." The monstrous figure gulped air as it leaned against the door frame for support. ". . . we were in the same plane when it was hit by ground fire."

Elsa frowned. "Ground fire. We're not at war, are we?"

"Not this country. But *we* are."

"I don't follow."

"No, because you've been kept in the dark here." The man sucked in a breath. "Your role was to keep this monster factory working day and night." He turned those bulging eyes to Dominion. "So, Dominion. Air crash. Do you remember me now?"

Dominion simply returned the stare—said nothing.

The man continued, "He wasn't always like this. Hardly garrulous . . . but Dominion was eloquent when the situation demanded." He coughed. "My God, I didn't think it would feel like this."

Paul shook his head. "You said the country wasn't at war, but *we* are?"

"You can see for yourselves, I'm in no state for explanations. If I can jog Dominion's memory, then he can tell you." When he coughed again blood ran down his chin. "But Saiban's the one who knows the plan."

"Saiban's dead," Elsa told him.

Dominion said, "That's why we need the portable Regenerator."

"You're going to bring Saiban back for a third term?" He gulped down more air. "I'd like to see the expression on his face when he opens his eyes."

"I'm not banking on success," Paul said. "For one, he's

messed up; internal organs destroyed. I can't guarantee the mobile units will still work after all this time. And last, but not least, I've never heard of anyone undergoing transition for a second time. There's no precedent that he'll—"

"No precedent?" The thing in the doorway quivered. It took several moments for them to realize it was laughing. "No precedent. Hear that, Dominion? No precedent! Here's some facts. Ah . . . I . . ." The man sagged as if collapsing. Paul moved to help him. "No. I'll be fine. Now, facts. I've undergone the process three times. Dominion's currently enjoying his fifth return to life. That's right, my fellow God Scarers. I've died twice before. Dominion, there, has yielded the spirit many times. That's because he's a warrior. I, on the other hand, lead the troops from the rear. That is, until last month when the plane took a pounding from ground fire. I survived for a few days after the crash. Dominion here was torn apart. See the different coloration of the limbs? We had prisoners on the plane. So our medics made good use of what was left of them to put Dominion together again. Same head . . . but as for the rest of him . . ." The man coughed. "He remembers none of this yet. Ah . . . I'm going to lie down and rest. But . . ." He held up a finger that was as plump as a child's wrist. "You asked if we were at war. Yes, we are. Mary Shelley had Frankenstein's monster turn on its creator. And so have we." With that the figure shambled away back into the corridor.

Paul, Elsa, and West waited for Dominion's reaction. He merely nodded at the huge timber case that housed the mobile Regenerator. "We're running out of time. Move this to the truck."

31

THE REMAKING OF SAIBAN

Noon arrived on the twelfth chime of the church clock in Scaur Ness. The sun raised the temperature of the garbage lying in the streets. That trash can aroma of sweet decay reached the Pharos. This is what Elsa exchanged for the smell of fish in the back of the truck as it stopped outside the portcullis.

Dominion beat the sides of the truck as he called out, "Hurry up. We don't have much time left."

As the occupants of the Pharos winched up the portcullis Elsa and West helped the creature that they'd found in the Regenerator.

"Hurry up," Dominion repeated. "You should bring the Regenerator out first."

Elsa disagreed. "We put the patient first."

"Thank you." The man's huge, misshapen head gave an exhausted nod. "You'll find I'm a rotten patient. By the way, I'm Brigadier."

"Brigadier . . . ?"

"Just Brigadier. My name became redundant a long

time ago." He grunted. "Warn your friends; I'm not a pretty sight."

Elsa said nothing, but it was hard to disagree. The man must have been as tall as Dominion, towering a couple of feet over the rest of the God Scarers, who could hardly be described as diminutive. Only where the God Scarers were aesthetically beautiful with their athletic physiques, flawless skin, and bright eyes, Brigadier walked with a stoop. The huge bulbous shoulders made him top-heavy. From the head blazed two protruding eyes that had the appearance of hens' eggs squeezed into a pair of eye sockets that were clearly two small. The rounded dome of the head was hairless, apart from that odd hank of long hair that sprouted above a lettuce leaf ear. The man was hardly complemented by his garb. In the rush to load the Regenerator there'd been no time to find clothes that fit him. Instead, Elsa had swathed the naked, lumpy figure in white cotton bedsheets that gave him the appearance of an ancient Greek whom the gods despised so much that they'd transformed into a living gargoyle.

Paul must have been thinking the same. "I'll let the others know . . ." He gave an awkward shrug. "That they should expect an addition to our happy clan."

When he'd gone inside, Brigadier turned his distorted head to Elsa. "Does your friend always have this trouble in expressing himself?"

Elsa forced a smile. "I like to think that Paul masks his sensitivity with humor. Well . . . a poor sense of humor."

Dominion strode toward them. "Get him inside. Then bring the others to help with the Regenerator."

"Can't you see that the brigadier is having difficulty walking?"

"You must hurry, Elsa. Saiban's body will deteriorate in this heat. He must live again. That's all that matters."

Brigadier murmured, "I prefer Paul's crappy sense of humor. Dominion isn't the same man anymore." The mouth formed a wide slit.

Elsa realized Brigadier was attempting a smile.

The croaking voice continued. "But do as Dominion says. He doesn't yet know why he's acting in this way." The man tapped a fat finger against his head. "Programming. Years of dedication to the cause has created an iron instinct. And if I know Dominion he won't even let his own death get in the way of his quest."

"Move faster," Dominion barked at them as they manhandled the Regenerator into the storeroom where Saiban lay. The men and women perspired as they lugged the vessel across the stone floor.

"We had to take it out of the packing case," West panted.

"You haven't damaged it?" Paul looked up from where he worked on Saiban's body, which lay flat on its back on a trestle table.

"Fuck knows."

Paul grunted. "Don't let Dominion hear you say that. He wants Saiban back in the land of the living. Nothing else matters. That includes your neck, Westie."

"Fuck him."

At that moment Dominion loomed through the doorway. West reacted with a start, then glanced at the others as if to ask, *Do you think he heard me?*

"Are you ready yet?" Dominion asked.

Paul nodded at the body. "It takes time to prepare for transition. We have to flush the circulatory system, then pump in the primer."

"Hurry."

Dominion's impatience prickled Elsa. "We're doing our best."

Paul eased a hypodermic needle into the anterior median vein in the forearm. As he did so he glanced at Saiban's face. The flesh was waxy now. The postmortem convulsions had stopped. *At least I'm not having to wrestle with a thrashing corpse,* he told himself. *Administering injections to a lively cadaver's no fun.*

He glanced at his fellow God Scarers, who stood there panting after shifting the so-called mobile Regenerator from the truck. In truth, it was no smaller than the static units they'd used at the Transit Station. It was seven feet tall. Wide at top and bottom with a narrowing at the waist. It resembled a gigantic hourglass as it stood there upright in the center of the room. Of course, an hourglass cast from glittering surgical steel. At the top were three small observation windows where medics could check on the progress—from corpse to newborn.

"Uh, he's spurting again." Paul wiped the sweat from his eyes. "Elsa, can you use the towel? Maximum compression, please."

Dominion prowled like an angry grizzly bear. "What's wrong?"

"It's the penetration wounds made by the fence spikes. There's no coagulation so the flush is leaking out as fast as I can pump it in."

"Close the wounds."

"Easier said than done, Dominion. I need a laser to suture the lesions."

"Improvise."

"That's what we're doing with the towel."

"It's not working."

"Full marks for observation, Dominion."

"Seal the wounds. You're running out of time. If Saiban isn't put in the Regenerator it will be too late."

"Dominion, we can't work miracles." Paul scraped away the persistent trickle of sweat. "One: We don't have the medical equipment. Two: We're in a bloody medieval castle, if you hadn't noticed."

"Seal the wounds, Paul, or I'll show you Caitlin's womb."

"You're a bastard, you know that, Dominion? You're a big, ugly, bullying bastard."

Paul reached across to a second table where there were instruments he'd been employing to prepare Saiban's body. One of which was a hefty carving knife from the kitchens. As he snatched it up the others in the room drew an intake of breath. Dominion locked those onyx eyes on him. The black stare was the entrance to hell.

Elsa watched the glittering blade in Paul's hand.

"OK, Dominion," Paul told him. "Watch how we doctors improvise."

He crossed the room to where a bunch of wooden dining room chairs had been left. In one savage movement he seized one and smashed it against the wall. Then he picked up the broken legs. Using the knife he shaved away the ends until they'd formed slender points. When he'd fashioned seven pointed stakes he returned to the table where Saiban lay.

"OK, Elsa, take away the towel, please."

Paul scanned the body. The steel fence had left seven puncture wounds that ran from just above the knee, up the thigh, then followed a center line up the torso, spearing belly and chest as far as the collarbone. Paul positioned the point in the wound beneath the collarbone, then tapped the end of the stake with the flat of his hand. The stake penetrated the wound. It made a wet sound as it slipped into the chest. Paul picked up one of the book-sized plastic cases that had contained the syringes, then used it to firmly hammer the sharpened chair leg into the wound.

"See this, Dominion? I'm improvising."

Paul sensed the giant's eyes burning into him. The comment about Caitlin's womb had been an oblique one, but he didn't doubt for one moment what Dominion had meant in a broader sense. *Make Saiban live or Caitlin dies.*

For the next ten minutes Paul drove the makeshift wooden stakes through the wounds. After each one he'd roll the body sideways to ensure that the stake had gone through. With the last one done he paused to wipe the sweat from his eyes once more.

"All right, Elsa. Now that we've plugged him up we'll inject more flushing agent."

Together, each using a full syringe, they injected the agent into the veins: femoral in the leg, axillary upper torso, jugular in the neck, then 100 cc blasted through the superior vena cava to flush the heart. Once that was done they set to work injecting the primer into a whole sequence of arteries from the minor dorsal artery in the foot to the arch of that great internal highway of the aorta in the upper chest.

"Have you finished yet?" Dominion must be close to grinding his teeth with impatience.

"We've flushed and primed Saiban's plumbing." Paul dropped the empty syringe into a bowl. "Now Elsa and I require some spare pairs of hands to help us move Saiban to the Regenerator. Xaiyad? Do you know how to open up?"

Xaiyad flicked the catches down the side of the hourglass-shaped vessel. A moment later he opened it up to reveal the gleaming interior.

Paul whistled. "Good. I expected cobwebs and a rodent's nest or two."

Elsa caught his eye. "It still might not work."

"And a wee birdy tells me the warranty expired a while ago." He beckoned the medical staff closer. "All right. I'll take the head. I need four people to take an arm and a leg each. Elsa, can you guide them in?" He grimaced. "And for heaven's sake watch my carpentry. If anyone dislodges the stoppers the primer will leak out all over the floor." He glanced at Dominion. "And that would annoy one of our gang, so if you value your necks . . . one, two, three. Lift."

With as much care as they could they carried Saiban's body to the Regenerator.

Elsa called out, "Wait!"

"What's wrong?"

"Leakage."

"Much?"

"Just a few drips from the thigh."

Paul gave a grim smile. "I can live with thigh leakage. Get him in the can."

After some anxious maneuvering they inserted the body into the Regenerator. It remained in an upright position. A metal band secured the waist. Clamps in the upper half took care of the neck.

Paul clapped his hands. "Good work. Elsa, can you help me with the lid?" Again, he was conscious of Dominion's watchful gaze. "It's OK, pal. I've done this hundreds of times. If it doesn't work it's not our fault; it's the machine. Understand?"

Dominion said nothing. At that moment Paul's confidence returned. He'd trained for this. His experience was second to none. Slipping into auto he helped Elsa fasten the clips. When he was satisfied the vents were closed he checked on Saiban by looking through a glass panel set in the upper section of the hourglass vessel. The face was as mournful in death as in life.

"Nurse, our patient is ready for a little gas therapy." He smiled at Elsa. She returned the smile. Doing what they knew was good therapy for them as well. It was like coming home.

Dominion asked, "What's in the cylinders?"

Paul screwed the threaded neck of a cylinder that was the size of a beer can into one of the Regenerator valves. "M-stock. Elsa's going to do the same at the other side with the V-stock."

"What's in it?"

"Ah, this is the witches' potion. The necromantic soup that will bring Saiban back to the bosom of his colleagues."

"What is the chemical exactly?"

"That's the beauty of it, Dominion. Frogs' eyes, blood of newt, essence of phoenix, a pinch of rainbow dust? Nobody knows. It arrives at the Transit Station in sealed canisters. We simply squirt it into one of these beauties once we have the cadaver nicely tucked up inside. Then bake for three hours until done."

"All we can figure out," Elsa added, "is that the two gases react with one another."

Paul nodded. "And they appear to release an electrical discharge—together with a number of other exotic properties."

Dominion gazed at Saiban's inert face through the glass. "How long until you know that it's worked?"

"We should register the first signs of life an hour from now. That's if this old lump of iron works."

"It must."

"And even if it does, Saiban here won't be winning any beauty pageants."

"As long as he lives long enough to tell us what he knows."

Paul didn't comment; he simply exchanged glances with Elsa that said clearly enough, *Heaven help us if this thing doesn't bring Saiban back.*

The gasses that hissed through the valves began to mingle with each other in the steel vessel. One vapor had a red tinge, the other was lilac. As tendrils of the two gasses met, threads of blue light ran inside them: lightning in miniature. Through the steel came a faint crackling. When one forked strand of light snapped against Saiban's waxy forehead it left a luminous patch of purple there, which took a number of seconds to fade away.

Paul folded his arms. "So far so good. All we can do now is wait . . ."

He addressed thin air. Dominion had walked out through the doorway into the courtyard.

32

SACRED V. PROFANE

Dominion went down into Scaur Ness. Midafternoon, the heat of the sun teased the stink from blocked drains. Garbage rotted in the streets. Scattered newspapers raised their listless corners in the rank air.

Dominion still didn't understand what drove him. Brigadier had returned with them to the castle on the cliff. Brigadier? He didn't recognize the name, though there was a resonance when he rolled the name through his mind. Brigadier? Impressions of urgency, noise, speed, violence. Now an instinct drove him down to Scaur Ness again. That near–ghost town on the edge of the sea, where ships lay rotting in the harbor. He didn't know why he was here any more than he recognized the searing need to return Saiban to life. The dour-faced man had to be the key to why he was here, and why he did the things he did.

The wretched town unfolded as he entered it. Cottages sagged in shabby profusion. Many of the cars that lined the street sat on deflated tires. Cats brawled with rats in overgrown gardens. Men and women that were as shabby as their homes skulked along the sidewalks. Some were drunk on homemade liquor. Vapor of Coffin Paint. It made his nostrils prickle. Most of the people melted away into alleys when they saw Dominion marching down the road. Some children, however, shouted insults before rushing away into the backyards. One youth threw a beer bottle. It struck Dominion on the chest. He turned to stare at the youth with such an intensity that the kid sank back against the wall as if the gaze crushed him.

Dominion entered the graveyard, the same one he'd stormed through the night he arrived in Scaur Ness. Ahead of him on the hill was the church. A tingle ran through his limbs. That deeply buried instinct guided him now. He passed through the field of bones; *smell the rot below my feet . . . death listens to me walk above it . . . we're old enemies . . . it longs to hold me . . . but death wants what it can't have*. Dark thoughts throbbed in Dominion's mind. At the church door he paused to look up at the tower. In his imagination it became a massive nail that fixed the buried corpses to the ground. *It nails man and woman to the cross of death. The church doesn't allow them the chance of escape*. But Dominion sensed change. A huge tidal sweep of change. He pushed open the church doors. Inside, candles burned. The priest sat in a wheelchair before the altar. On the front pew three old women prayed. Incense made the air heavy and sweet.

Dominion entered the church. "I am the First Man," he boomed. "I am the bringer of life."

When the priest turned his head to look at Dominion it was with enormous difficulty. Dominion saw the face had become bloodless as the old man's heart weakened to the point it failed to pump the fluid into the skin tissues.

The priest's voice was dry as dust in a tomb. "I forbade you to enter the church. I forbid it now. You are profane."

Dominion shook his head. "I am life."

"You are deluded. I wouldn't even describe you as a devil. I know you were dead. Science brought you back to some mocking appearance of life, but science is inadequate. You are mentally damaged. That's all. Anything else you might feel is a delusion of grandeur."

"I have a mission."

"Then leave this church and pursue it."

"You are part of it."

"No, creature." The priest smiled. "You might have noticed I am close to death. Besides, my purpose in life belongs with these people here in this town." The old women kept their heads down to pray, yet they shot glances back at Dominion as he walked toward the altar where the monstrance stood, a silver column that radiated silver rays in a sunburst effect from a silver cross.

"I once carried the monstrance," Dominion said. "A long time ago."

"In your first life you were a priest?"

"I don't know. But I had such faith. It was such a powerful force inside me. There were times I believed I could will an entire building to fly through the air."

"And do you still have faith?" the priest asked, his deep-set eyes locked on to Dominion's face.

"Yes, it's stronger than ever."

"But it's not faith in God?"

"Father." Dominion gazed at the monstrance. "I believe in a real life after death."

Dominion turned to see the ancient priest push down on the arms of the wheelchair to help him stand. "That belief," panted the old man, "is your own version of life after death. That's a blasphemy. If you deny death you must deny life. Life is an education for joy in the hereafter. When we are born we begin a progression. Each stage prepares us for heaven."

Dominion's heart thudded in his chest. The three women sat on the pew with their hands clasped together. They lived in terror of him. How they must have shuddered at his appearance—the dark head with its blond stubble, the pale hands; the scars that ran around his wrists and neck. He turned back to face the priest, who stood there in his black clothes as if they were now the strongest part of his body. The man's wrists were nothing more than twigs from which skeletal fingers dangled. The face was a death's-head.

The priest managed to point at the door. "Go."

Dominion shook his head. "I believe in life after death." He strode forward and seized the man by the lapels of his long black coat, then dragged him across the floor. The priest didn't shout. He gripped Dominion's hand in his own hand. His eyes never left Dominion's face.

When Dominion reached the stone baptism font he swept away the timber lid. By now the old women might have been screaming. He didn't care whether they were or not. Their reaction didn't interest him. Still the man didn't cry out when Dominion lifted the weightless husk of a body in one hand before plunging the white-haired head into the holy water. The font must have stood there for eight hundred years or more. Generations of babies would have received the church's blessing as they were christened. Gradually they grew into adulthood. They were married in this church. Their children were baptized here in this carved stone bowl that contained a gallon or so of ritually sanctified water. Then, eventually, the funeral. Hundreds down the centuries. After that, interment in the consecrated grounds beyond the church door. There, the men and women whom the Transients called Saps, a diminutive of Homo sapiens, would rot.

Now maybe this was a first . . . Dominion gazed almost

dreamily at the head of the priest beneath the surface of the holy water. A tiny drowning pool for one.

When Dominion was satisfied the priest was dead he lifted the dripping head clear of the water, and then slung the body over his shoulder. The three women clung to the altar as if they were adrift at sea and were clinging to a ship's wreckage. There they wept as they prayed.

Moments after Dominion left the church he climbed the cliff steps to the Pharos. The priest's corpse hung over his shoulder. One of its arms swung from side to side as if waving good-bye to the town that had been home for the past fifty years.

33

DEAD MOUTH—WHAT
SWEET MELODY IT SINGS

The moment Dominion returned to the Pharos with his
macabre burden Dr. Paul Marais thought: *He really has
gone insane.*

The sun cast a hard light on the pair as Paul and
Xaiyad winched up the portcullis.

"Dominion!" Paul shouted. "This is crazy. If the
priest's died you should have left him for the town to
bury."

"He wasn't dead," Dominion replied. "I killed him."

Xaiyad was stunned. "You what?"

"The old man would have died soon anyway."

Paul stared at the priest in the long black coat, his
body slung over the giant's shoulder as if he was nothing
more than a rag. Water dripped down the priest's skull-
like face. A shade of deathly blue spread around the lips.
"Dominion, don't you understand? You'll bring the
whole town down on us."

"Paul, once Saiban is out of the Regenerator you can bring the old man back to life."

"Dominion, you are a liar if you claim the priest wanted to make the transition."

"He believed the process was blasphemous." Dominion walked across the courtyard to the room that housed the Regenerator. "But I want you to show him how good it feels to come back from the dead to a new life. The priest will be living proof to the town that we aren't monsters."

Xaiyad rolled his eyes. "I wish I could believe you, Dominion. But you've just gone and made life difficult for us."

"Difficult?" Rage made Paul breathless. "That's an understatement. The people down there in the town are going to erupt!" His rage intensified when he saw how casual Dominion appeared. "They're going to rip this place down stone by stone to get us. *We're finished!*"

Dominion didn't even turn back as he carried the corpse over one shoulder. Instead he simply called out, "Once Saiban is out start work on the priest."

"You, bastard, Dominion. You great, mechanical, uncaring bastard!"

When Saiban opened his eyes he screamed. The cry blasted back from the walls, until it became a howl of human feedback. Beech jumped so violently at the sound that the bowl of disinfectant she held sprang from her fingers to shatter on the floor.

Elsa helped restrain the man as he convulsed on the table. "It's the plugs in the wounds. They're reacting against the new tissue growth."

Paul forced Saiban's shoulders down. "I can't remove them yet. The blood will empty out in seconds." He grimaced. "I'm sorry, Saiban, old pal, you're just going to have to live with it."

Dominion stepped forward. "Can he talk yet?"

"Not on your life. If the pain subsides he might be coherent sometime tomorrow."

"He's got to start speaking." Impatience flashed in Dominion's eyes.

"You'll get plenty of screaming before then, but mark my words, nothing sensible will pass his lips."

Brigadier sat on a chair against the wall. He was still swathed in sheets. "If he does have information, then we'll have to be patient, Dominion."

Dominion turned to Paul. "I'll keep him still. You start work on the priest."

Elsa said, "You know, I can't decide what's worse. That you killed the town's religious leader. Or that you want us to bring him back to life against his wishes."

Dominion's conviction was relentless. "Once they see one of their own has made the transition, then they'll change their minds about us."

Brigadier nodded his misshapen head. "Dominion has a point."

"Then I just hope you're right."

Most of the God Scarers were in the storeroom. Right then, close proximity to one another gave them a greater sense of security. *Even though that sense of security is probably an illusion*, Paul told himself. He glanced up as Dominion waved him back with his spade-sized hand.

"I'll take care of Saiban. You start on the old man."

"I just need to check my handiwork first." Paul examined each of the wooden plugs in turn. The chair legs he'd used to stopper the wounds in Saiban's body resembled spines. Around each one where it met the skin puncture was a pink collar of flesh. This was the new tissue growth propagated by the Regenerator.

"Hurry up."

"I've got to make sure that old Saiban here doesn't spring a leak."

"But he's going to live?"

Paul shrugged. "No guarantees. That Regenerator is positively geriatric. Saiban breathes, twitches, and yells . . . but whether there's any meaningful activity in that melancholy brain of his . . . well, that's another matter entirely."

"Make sure he lives. Now work on the old man."

Paul caught Elsa's eye. He knew what response he was tempted to make to Dominion's demands; however, he merely said, "Next patient, nurse." A smile played on his lips. "Just like old times again, huh?"

"No, Paul. To me it feels like we've all died and gone to hell. Will you pass me the syringe kit, please?"

As Saiban lay there he gave such a deep groan of pain that even Dominion grimaced in sympathy.

Paul glanced across at Dominion. "I hope Saiban's secrets are valuable. If he does wake, that poor devil is going to be in so much agony I pity anyone having to be in the same room as him as he screams the place down."

Two hours later Elsa went with Beech to visit Luna's tomb. At last the silence the crypt had enjoyed for centuries had returned. Luna was still now. Outside, the evening sun had shone so brilliantly it had hurt Elsa's eyes. Here, the gloom seemed to creep out of the graves to drown the crypt in shadow.

Yet the peace was something to be relished. Every time Elsa closed her eyes her memory replayed the sight of Saiban writhing on the table. That palely arching body, the jaws open wide, teeth snapping down on the tongue. Worse, was the sight of the chair legs that formed a surreal bristling spine down the center of his body. Even though the man was unconscious his vocal expression of pain had to be heard to be believed. During that outpouring of sound she and Paul worked on the corpse of the old man. The emaciated body revealed clear signs of being ravaged by illness. Dominion, however, had not damaged it more than necessary. Shock had killed the man as much as being immersed in water. Anyway, the preparations were complete. The priest had taken his turn in the Regenerator. What would that man of God make of being deprived of death? Elsa suspected that new experiences waited for all of them in the coming hours. None of them pleasant.

Beech broke the silence. "If only Dominion had decided to fetch one of the Regenerators earlier we might have been able to rescue Luna."

"But then Luna didn't harbor any secrets Dominion wanted. We're all expendable in his eyes, aren't we?"

"I suspected Dominion was insane, but now I wonder if we all haven't gone mad."

"We're surviving."

"But why do we obey him like he's some God or something?"

Elsa smiled; it felt more an expression of sadness than happiness. "We're desperate. Perhaps he's our only chance."

"But we were beginning to coexist with the townspeople. Now that he's murdered their priest there's no telling what they'll do in revenge." Beech flushed with anger. "Dominion is crazy."

"I've gone crazy, too." In the gloom she saw Beech's expression of surprise. "It's true, Beech. I've gone totally off the rails. Yesterday, I . . . how can I say it politely? Yesterday, I found comfort . . . no, gratification, in the arms of one of the men from the town."

"Elsa? A Sap?" Beech let out a breath. "You mean you . . ."

"I know I hurt him, but it was like I was ravenous. I couldn't stop myself."

"My God."

"And if I got the chance I'd do it all over again."

"Does anyone else know?"

Elsa shook her head.

"Then keep it a secret. Times are weird enough without causing any more complications." Beech checked her watch. "My turn to watch over Father Lazarus . . . uh, ignore me, I'm picking up Paul's dreadful sense of humor. Coming?"

"I'm going to stay. After the racket Saiban made I need the quiet."

Beech left the crypt. Elsa stood surrounded by the stone coffins topped with their ancient carved effigies. Here the dead stayed dead. The simplicity of their world exerted its appeal right now. Whatever traumas these long-extinct people experienced in life; all the dreams they had for the future; the tangled web of relationships—all that was gone. Where were the souls of the occupants of these tombs? Were they anywhere? Or was heavenly bliss, in fact, everlasting nothingness?

At that moment the sound ghosted through the walls to touch her. The song of the ancient dead that she'd heard before. Could they really call out to her? Were they beckoning her to cross over some great divide?

Paul had chosen to bask in the light of the evening sun. He stood on the castle's walls. The sea air chased away chemical and corpse odors. The screams from Saiban's mouth still reverberated inside his head. With luck another ten minutes up here would see the breeze chase those away, too. He gazed out over the town that had become submerged by shadow as it lay there between the cliffs that hemmed it in.

Today, he told himself, *Dominion pulled the lever. Things are happening. I don't know what those things are exactly. But he's set something in motion.*

And that sense of motion was quickening. It was as if

they'd become a runaway train that sped downhill where shortly it would smash into a gigantic obstacle. The thought had barely passed through his mind when he saw movement in the streets below.

"Here they come," he whispered as a chill crept up his spine. "You knew it would only be a matter of time, didn't you?" He gave a grim chuckle. "They've made up their wee minds at long last." He called to West in the courtyard, "Make sure the portcullis is locked down tight." He nodded toward the town. "The mob are on their way."

34

FINAL HOURS

Paul watched them swarm up the cliff steps, leaving the shadows behind to emerge into the evening sun. In a happier place this could have been the start of carnival night. However, Paul sensed the charge of fury that ran through the mob. *We've killed the man they loved*, he told himself. *What else could we expect? The priest was the only man in that godforsaken town that gave them hope.*

Paul leaned forward over the battlement to look at the roadway below, which separated the massive stone wall of the fortress from the edge of the cliff. So far, that was deserted. At least the army hadn't returned; he half expected to see tanks appear to batter their way through the portcullis. Once the gate had been breached it would seal the doom of all the God Scarers in the Pharos.

A body suddenly pressed against his. He looked down. "Caitlin. You should stay inside."

"My place is here with you," she said firmly.

"They've not come bearing gifts, that's for sure."

There must have been two hundred or more in that

mass of people that snaked up the cliff face. Most carried firearms—a motley collection of hunting rifles, shotguns, pistols. Most were civilian but he noticed a dozen or so in police uniforms. Even the cops had merged with that pack of hate-fueled humanity.

"Caitlin, it's not safe up here."

She gazed down at them. The setting sun illuminated her face. The combination of beauty and fragility tugged at his heart. At that moment he wished more than anything he could grow wings so he could carry them both away from here to safety.

"Just look at them," she breathed. "They're frightened as much as angry. So they want to fight. That's all they know. It was the same at school. They knew there was no work; they watched their relatives drinking themselves to death, so what did they do? They beat up the smaller kids, or fought one another. If they were punching out it felt like they were battling against what threatened them. All they were doing was making it worse. Now they find it convenient to blame Transients for their own lives being a mess."

Paul slipped his arm around her shoulders. "Dominion's focused their hatred. He should have left the priest alone."

"He would have died anyway. Dominion saw it as a means to prove that your people aren't monsters."

"Aye, but Dominion's mind works in a funny way." He pulled her closer to him. The need to protect Caitlin became a source of pain inside him. How could he save her if the mob broke into the castle? Images flitted through his mind of the woman fleeing along these walls as the men raced after her. Her father couldn't protect her now. Once they had their hands on her they'd savor their punishment.

"Ah," she sighed. "There's Dad with his old shotgun.

Behind him, the ones with the rifles, are Mel and Karl. You can see Mel's enjoying this. He'll be looking forward to raping me again." She gave a grim smile. "That's right. Scaur Ness went rotten years ago. Neighbors feed on neighbors, one way or another. Theft, rape, intimidation, bullying, cheating. The police ignore it." She tilted her head to one side as the Saps began to surge onto the roadway. "And there's nothing like an old friend for carrying a grudge. Those two in the short skirts are Fran and Magda. They were my best friends at school. We even formed a band and told each other all these stories how we'd be signed to a record label. Then we'd go to the best hairstylists, buy new clothes, tour the country. All the best hotels. Then a stretch limo to the arena." Her eyes became dreamy as if that flow of townspeople hypnotized her. At that instant it was strangely silent. If anything, all that could be heard was the soft roar of surf on the beach. "We even composed a song. It was called 'Out of Here.' That summed up our hopes of leaving for a new life. Some hope." Caitlin nodded at the pair of hard-faced women that she'd once spun daydreams with. "Those two will be among the first to stick their knives into me."

Whether someone gave the order or whether it was spontaneous Paul didn't know. The swarm raised their guns. Shots snapped out on the still evening air. Paul saw red flashes of tracer speed toward them. He dragged Caitlin back so violently that the air in her lungs came out as an *"uff."* The mob were at such an angle that they fired their weapons almost vertically upward. There was little chance of them causing any harm now that Paul and Caitlin crouched down behind the battlements. Nevertheless, this wasn't sharpshooting: it was an elemental discharge of sheer rage. Dozens of bullets smacked into stone. This Gothic fortress had been built to withstand cannonballs, so bullets from rabbit guns and revolvers wouldn't do much damage. Paul saw the danger would be real if, or when, the townspeople broke into the castle. The God Scarers wouldn't fight for their survival. They'd have to rely on Dominion to save them then. As more bullets ricocheted away in a piercing whine Paul beckoned Caitlin to follow him to the doorway in the tower.

In the storeroom that served as their own temporary Transit Station two figures were stretched out on trestle tables. One lay on his back with the pieces of wood bristling from his chest. He groaned as his eyelids fluttered.

Elsa watched Dominion and Brigadier stand over the half-alive wreck that was Saiban. They were waiting for him to wake so he could reveal his secrets. Their impatience was clear to see. Brigadier's sausagelike fingers fretted with the hem of the sheet that he wore like a Roman's toga. Dominion slapped his hand against his thigh. All the time his dark eyes burned into Saiban's face as he waited for the first flicker of true consciousness. Elsa reacted with shock, just like the rest of the God Scarers in the room, when the gunfire started. For the priest it appeared to be a signal. With a gasp he sat up on the trestle table. Rather than a dazed appearance, which was usual when one of the Newborn woke after their transition, the old man's gaze roved about the room. There was a keen intelligence in those gray eyes.

Old man? In years, yes, Elsa thought, but the Regenerator had opened to reveal that the disease-ravaged derelict of a human being had been reconfigured into a muscular man with aristocratic features. All signs of the gaunt frame had gone. Instead of clawed fingers there were now strong hands covered with smooth skin that was as flawless as that of his face. Where the black clothes had hung on him like rags on a scarecrow, the body had filled out into them perfectly. When he noticed his hands he studied the backs, then turned them to see smooth palms. The new growth of skin wouldn't have creased yet; there wouldn't be a line on it. His eyes absorbed the healthy pink of the nails; then he slid back a sleeve to reveal a muscular forearm.

That's when Elsa detected an expression of shock. Both his hands went to his face as he quickly ran his fingers over his lips, cheeks, forehead, then lightly rested the tips of his fingers on his eyes. The skull-like appearance had vanished. Instead, new muscle molded his handsome face. Where the eyes had been sunk deep into the skull they were now in perfect harmony with the rest of his features. She thought: *Say what you like about us, but one thing is true: We make beautiful monsters.*

When he took his hands away his eyes met Elsa's.

"Look what you've done to me," he hissed. "Have you no shame?"

35

SIEGE

Paul Marais arrived at the makeshift Transit Station to see the priest sitting upright on the trestle table. There was no doubt he was fully conscious. His eyes blazed with anger as he stared at Elsa.

Dominion and Brigadier stood beside the table where Saiban lay. Although he was still unconscious he twitched as spasms of pain shot through his nervous system. The rest of the Transients stood anxiously in the room as the sound of gunfire echoed about the castle walls.

Dominion turned to Paul. "Why isn't Saiban awake yet?"

Paul jerked his head at the hourglass-shaped Regenerator. "I told you that thing was an antique. I never guaranteed it would bring Saiban back."

"But he has important information."

Caitlin jerked her thumb back at the courtyard. "Forget Saiban. You've got the entire population of Saur Ness trying to break in here."

Dominion's face hardened. "Elsa, stay with Saiban. Let me know the minute he's conscious."

Elsa shook her head. "The priest is awake. I need to monitor him. There's always a danger that respiration can—"

"Elsa. Someone else can take care of the priest. Watch Saiban!"

Caitlin shouted, "If you don't do something soon you'll have the mob jumping all over you."

At first Paul thought she was frightened, but there was excitement in her expression, too. The prospect of her neighbors being paid back for all the abuse that they'd hurled at her through the years was Christmas come early for her.

"Elsa, I'll monitor the priest," Beech told her. "Do as Dominion says."

Elsa relented. She went to stand with Saiban. The wooden spikes in his chest moved in a tremulous way as his body shivered. A fever gripped him now. Without penicillin there was a chance Saiban would be dead within the hour.

"Remember." Dominion marched toward the door. "Call me if Saiban wakes."

Paul and Caitlin followed the gigantic figure.

When Paul spoke he found himself surprised by his own force of emotion. "For God's sake, Dominion, don't do anything rash."

"I can't allow them to fire on us. I have to teach them a lesson."

Caitlin joined in with equal passion. "Make sure it's a lesson that those bastards remember."

Paul sensed events were running out of control. "If you can see the portcullis, they can see you; then they'll open fire." *Dear God, all this is going nuclear; they're not go-*

ing to stop now. They want our blood. The words chattered inside his head, a weird monkey babble. *That's fear taking control,* he told himself. *Rather than being preoccupied with raising that bloody spook Saiban from the dead we should find a way of escaping this place. It's not a castle. It's a prison.* Even though he tried Paul couldn't stop the mind chatter. Nevertheless, he noticed that flares had been thrown through the bars of the portcullis. They burnt with bloodred flames on the stone cobbles. Why they'd bother throwing these, he didn't know. Nothing would burn nearby; it was all solid stone. *Perhaps the townsfolk think we're like wild beasts; because we're not human we'll be afraid of fire? Maybe we're all as insane as one another? This country's being going crazy for years. The economy's in the garbage grinder. The rule of law has collapsed. Politicians are crooks, or self-deluded incompetents.* A bullet smacked against a wall.

"Caitlin," he called out. "Keep back." Dominion scaled the steps to the battlements. For some reason he headed away from the side of the castle where the Saps gathered. "Dominion," Paul shouted. "Use the stairs in the tower. They lead out above the portcullis." Dominion ignored him. "Yeah, because you've gone insane, too." Paul saw a mad delight in Caitlin's eyes as she followed Dominion. *This madness is infectious. Townspeople, God Scarers, the entire fucking world. All gone loopy . . . because what's that saying?* He hissed the words to himself, "Those who the gods wish to destroy they first drive mad." *Words to that effect anyway.* He paused. *What the blazes is Dominion doing?*

Paul had anticipated that Dominion would position himself on the walkway above the portcullis, and above the mob outside the castle walls, then bellow down at them. Probably the same threat as before. That Dominion would kill their children. Only now, big, bad, stark-staring mad Dominion ran along the elevated walkway in the *opposite* direction to the portcullis. *Heaven preserve us. This is it: He really has flipped over into lunacy. What now? Punish the flagpole? Shout profanities down a chimney?*

"Dominion? Where do you think you're going?"

Dominion was a man with a plan. He ignored Paul. All that mattered to the giant was to run along the walkway. Caitlin had been ensnared by the drama of that headlong dash, too. And that was the moment that Paul thought: *Good God, they're going to throw themselves from the tower.* The image came with shocking brilliance—of the pair holding hands to swan-dive from the one-hundred-foot tower.

Idiot, he told himself, *this insanity's contagious. It's infecting you, too.*

By now the sun rested on the hills above Scaur Ness. It drenched the world in a light that was as red as blood. The sun itself became a titanic warning light that signaled danger to man, monster, and God alike. This route of madness led to the twin destinations of violence and death. Paul tried so hard to stop the weird mind chatter his head ached. In the darkening sky gulls hung there. Instead of appearing as white specks they were now black, as if they'd become transformed into a dozen black holes in the heavens. Into those black holes an infinitely powerful gravity sucked light and sanity from the world. *This is the end of the days. There will be no more tomorrows. Only the unending thunder of the apocalypse, forever and ever, amen.*

"Shut up," he hissed at that clatter of thought inside his head. Only it wasn't insane now. That inner monkey was a wise old soul. When he saw the sun lying broken on the hilltop as it hemorrhaged a bloody light he knew to the roots of his bones that this was the start of the end of the world. OK, the ocean hadn't evaporated, the town was still the town, the sky hadn't ruptured, the dead weren't rising from their graves ... And yet there was such a powerful premonition that the world had reached the end of its life that he felt crushed. The vision left him breathless. His chest ached. Every breath became a struggle.

And even though it seemed to him as if his body sagged under the pressure of that premonition, Caitlin didn't even notice when she glanced at him with such a radiant expression of glee. "You just watch," she shouted. "Dominion's going to make them suffer!"

"But why's he running away from them? They're on the other side of the castle, not ..." Paul stopped wasting his breath. No doubt about it, a vision unique to the giant man drove him. On the walkway were mounds of building materials that had been abandoned years ago. Sacks of cement, a mound of yellow builder's sand. There were also stone blocks against which a wheelbarrow rested; the steelwork of the barrow had begun to crumble before the onslaught of the elements; its single wheel had perished. Nevertheless, Dominion set the wheelbarrow upright. There were no tools there, but with hands the size of spades it didn't matter; quickly he filled the wheelbarrow with sand, using those giant paws. When the yellow mound had risen high above the lip of the barrow he grabbed hold of a sack that stood by the blocks. Even though the sack remained sealed a small hole in the side released a trickle of pebbles. These were the size of cherries and had probably been intended for use in reinforcing any cement works the long-departed builder had intended. Dominion hefted the bag onto his cargo of sand. For him it appeared to have no weight even though Paul guessed the bloated sack must have weighed a hundred pounds. The giant appeared to exude a ruddy glow in the setting sun as he wheeled the barrow on its single, rotten tire to the section of wall that spanned the portcullis. In the yard below a pair of road fares still sputtered crimson flames against the cobbles. The firing had stopped. Probably due to a lack of targets rather than a shortage of ammunition. If anything the crowd had grown. The Saps gestured with their firearms as they debated what to do next. Paul noticed Caitlin's father in the midst of the mob. They were so wrapped up in the argument they didn't see what Dominion did first. Instead, they felt it.

With those vast hands he scooped sand from the wheelbarrow, then pelted the people below. Even though they were forty feet beneath him the force of those particles striking bare faces invoked a burst of yells. Caitlin watched their discomfort with obvious enjoyment. Paul had to drag her behind the stone cornice before anyone started firing. Each handful must have contained the best part of five pounds of sand. What's more, Dominion threw with such force that it formed a fast-moving cloud of yellow that spread out to encompass the entire mob by the time it struck. From the shouts Paul realized that the sand hurt more than he could have imagined. If anything, the castle's attackers became a seething mass of shoulders as people ducked their heads as the sand struck. A couple of men fired off wild shots. One youth tried to fire a shotgun one-handed as he covered his smarting eyes with a free hand. The bird shot tore away an ear of the tall man next to him.

During all this, Dominion never said a word to the townsfolk. He could have been a farmer pelting stones at crows. When he'd used up the sand he tore open the sack of pebbles. They spilled out in a brown heap in the bottom of the wheelbarrow. By now a number of the people had recovered enough to fire off better-aimed shots at the battlements, although the angle made it difficult for them to hit anything, that and the grit in their eyes. Bullets ricocheted from the outer wall. More red-hot slugs of lead flew vertically into the sky. The gulls that were tiny black specks in the evening sky squealed in anger at this trespass into their domain.

Paul shouted, "That's enough, Dominion. They've learned their lesson." This wasn't strictly true. If anything, the accuracy became better. Those red-hot bullets zipped ever closer to Dominion's head.

Dominion said nothing. He now scooped up pebbles by the handful. This time when he threw the cries were real body pain rather than irritation. Paul risked a look over the parapet. With each throw more than a dozen of those cherry-sized pebbles blasted the Saps. They howled when struck. Paul saw trickles of blood running down faces. OK, those little stones weren't moving at the same velocity as bullets, but Dominion's muscular throw must have delivered them at close to one hundred miles an hour. This time the mob retreated in an untidy scramble. Some were knocked over to be trampled by their neighbors. The symphony of pain rose in volume.

"Just listen to that," Caitlin shouted. "Just listen! They're suffering! It's about time, too, after everything they did to me!" Then she shoved her head between the battlements to howl her glee at them. "See how you like it!" Her fists pounded the wall. "There! You felt that, didn't you, Magda? I remember how you treated me like dirt. I hope that knocked your bloody teeth out!"

Paul saw the one called Magda clamp her palm to her mouth as blood trickled between her fingers.

When the last of the pebbles left Dominion's hand in another blistering barrage he stood back from the wall. Beyond the portcullis the mob scattered. Some scrambled, half falling down the steps. Others fled along the road away from the castle. Caitlin exulted. A torrent of curses shot from her lips at her departing tormentors. Dominion simply watched them leave.

"They won't be gone for long," Paul told him. "You haven't killed anyone this time. You've left some walking wounded, that's all." He nodded across at the building materials. "There were some meaty stone slabs back there. Did you not think what kind of damage you could have done with those?"

Dominion met his gaze. For a moment his eyes were troubled as if on the verge of remembering an important fact. "I knew I could use the stones. I could have killed, only . . ." When he couldn't recollect what was important to him he let it go with a sigh. "Not yet."

"What do you mean, 'not yet'?"

Beneath them came the sound of shouting. They looked down into the courtyard to see Elsa waving up at them.

"It's Saiban." Her voice echoed from the walls of the Pharos. "His condition's changed."

36

DARKNESS DESCENDING

Elsa asked, "Have they gone?"

Paul's face was grim. "The mob? Dominion drove them off, but they'll be back. We killed their priest. We've given them a reason to unite against us."

Elsa paused as they crossed the courtyard. "Wait, do you hear that?"

"Hear what?" Paul tilted his head to one side.

That's the song of the dead. You must hear it. It's starting to sound like a storm . . . Elsa found herself framing the words; she had to talk to someone about that ethereal music that ghosted in from the ocean. There was an urgency now. It really did feel like a storm ready to break with devastating force.

Dominion urged her forward. "Hurry. You're exposed here; if they come back they'll fire at you through the gate."

Paul caught her arm. "Elsa? You said you could hear something. What is it?"

"It's all right." She spoke through gritted teeth as Dominion waved them toward their makeshift Transit Station. "I'll tell you later."

Only there is no sense of "later," she told herself. *"Later" has become a concept like that of an afterlife. It requires faith to believe in heaven.* Now even her faith in words like *later* and *tomorrow* was faltering. Events were reaching a climax.

Dominion bustled through the doorway, a gigantic figure on a mission. Curtly, he ordered West to keep watch outside in case the mob returned. Brigadier's monstrous form occupied a chair by Saiban's table. Saiban lay there with a white sheet draped across his waist. The pieces of chair leg that served as plugs in the wounds shook.

Elsa explained, "Saiban's condition has changed. Although he appears to be nearer to consciousness, there's a fever."

"Is it serious?"

"Might be." Paul touched Saiban's face that burned as if he'd stood too close to a campfire. "The wounds are infected. And we don't have the right drugs."

Saiban muttered. His eyelids fluttered but didn't remain open more than a second. The man's long fingers drummed with a fevered rhythm.

Brigadier regarded Saiban. "Don't Transients have a strong immune system?"

"Normally." Paul checked the pulse. "Rapid and shallow. Not looking good." He jerked his head toward the portable regenerator. "That thing is decades old. If you ask me it's a miracle Saiban made it this far."

"He'll survive?" Dominion gazed down at the trembling figure. "It's more important than you can know."

"We'll do what we can but it isn't much. I've said it before: We're hard to kill; we're not indestructible."

"You cannot fail."

"Is that encouragement or a threat, Dominion?"

Brigadier reached out a pulpy hand to grip Paul's wrist. "Make him live."

Elsa saw a grim smile turn up one side of Paul's mouth. "Brigadier. We're monsters, not gods."

The creature's voice rasped—dry as bones in a grave. *Do it. Make Saiban live.*

"Elsa. Keep pushing fluids into Saiban. The only medicine we have is good old-fashioned aspirin. If you dissolve a couple in water it might beat down the fever by a degree or so." Paul checked his patient. "See, gentlemen, reddened flesh on the lips of the wound. Inflammation. A seepage of pus. Smells like yogurt. Gangrene? Maybe, maybe not." Paul's accent grew stronger. The Scottish brogue always came to the fore as he grew angry.

"You're the doctor," Dominion told him. "You should have brought drugs from the Transit Station."

"The Transit Station had been looted. All the medication that humans could use was gone. They only left the witches' brew we use for raising the dead. And you know something, gentlemen? Even though I've pushed a corpse into a Regenerator and then pulled out a living individual I don't know what's in that stuff. For all I know it might really be made of bats' wings, blood of newt, and cobwebs found in graveyards when the fucking moon is full. My God, I've used it hundreds of times. I've seen how it works—but do I know *how* it works? Why haven't I ever asked myself that question? In the early days I'd chuckle when I saw it arrive in boxes labeled Lazarite—yes, Lazarite, how bloody witty is that? I'm a doctor. Yet I play God. I've brought hundreds of men and women back from death into the wonderful, shining province of life. My colleagues have done the same for the last fifty years. I don't know how I did it. No, what was important was the *why*. Science had vanquished the Grim Reaper. Death is extinct. Well, as near as, damn it.

So, my colleagues in Transit Stations throughout the country made the dead live again. We restored their health. They emerged the beautiful, athletic people you see around you today. But now I wonder what the real purpose was. It's not important *how* it was done. But *why* was it done? What was the *greater* purpose? The grand scheme? All those thousands of God Scarers, Transients, monsters? Call them what you will. What was the point?" His eyes blazed. "Where have they gone?"

Outside, the world lay gripped by darkness. Elsa heard the song of the dead rise in volume. A lyrical swell of notes that sent wave after wave of icy shivers through her body. Still no one heard it. Yet, Elsa's nerves throbbed at the haunting note of its call. At that moment she seemed to exist in two worlds. One where the unearthly music resonated throughout the entire cosmos. And a second world that became strangely unreal. In this one Paul railed against Dominion with his limbs of different hues, and the monstrous form of Brigadier with the pulpy body clad in a sheet. Paul's final question appeared to fix itself in the air. Not so much a question now, but a challenge: *Where have they gone?*

Brigadier turned to Dominion. "This is where I find myself saying, 'Gather round.' There was never any reason for you to hear the truth; you worked for the cause; but now there's no need to keep the truth from you."

"You mean we've been kept in the dark all along?" Beech's voice rose in disbelief. "Why didn't anyone explain the purpose of all our work?"

"The reason," Brigadier continued in that grave voice of his, "is explained by what happened a few nights ago. Government troops destroyed your Transit Station. Most of the staff and patients were murdered. No doubt some, however, were taken away for interrogation."

"So you couldn't trust us with the truth?"

Brigadier continued, "Transients are not permitted to harm human beings through action or inaction. It's our monster law. We're also obedient to humanity's wishes. How long would it be before you told the humans everything you knew?"

Paul was still suspicious. "And you're going to reveal the truth now, because?"

"Because, the Fates willing, you will escape here with your lives. You should have faith in your future."

"If we escape there's nowhere to go. All the Transit Stations will be wrecked. No government on earth is going to offer a single God Scarer asylum. Wherever we go we will be hunted down."

This time it was Dominion who spoke. "That's not true. There is a place . . ." He rubbed his forehead as his eyes appeared to gaze at some distant horizon.

Brigadier nodded. "Dominion is starting to remember. I wondered how long it would take. But then again, he's been through more than any of us."

Elsa said, "You described Dominion as a warrior. And that you both lost your lives after your aircraft was shot down."

"And not only that," Brigadier told them. "Unlike you, we've been through the transition process more than once." He regarded Saiban, who muttered as delirium gripped him. "Largely, we've made it through the Regenerator successfully, although it didn't work out well for me this time." He held up a bloated hand with its sausagelike fingers. "So this is the truth. You know the history of our people. Originally, the intention was that once the dead were returned to life they would go back into the community; there they'd devote their second lives to helping humanity. We would be something like a latter-day order of monks and nuns. We'd renounce worldly goods; we are sterile so we wouldn't procreate;

nothing would matter to us but the good we could do in our communities. Of course, humanity resented us. They envied our healthy bodies. They were suspicious of what we'd do in the future. And, even on a basic level, there is an instinctive disgust. Human beings found it repellent to shake hands with a corpse. They found our presence sickening. You know what happened next. We withdrew from society to work in our communities. However, our priority was still to help humankind. But no matter how much we accommodated their wishes they continued to discriminate against us."

"And now they kill us," Beech said.

"Exactly." Brigadier sighed. "The United Nations have banned member states from regenerating their dead. This country permitted it under draconian regulations, but it became a pariah state. No other country would recognize its sovereignty. Trade with it was forbidden. Now the old government has fallen . . ." He shrugged. "You know the rest."

"Which means we'll soon be extinct."

"No. Not yet." Brigadier's gargoyle of a face managed a faint smile. "You've wondered what happened to all those thousands of people processed by the Transit Station down through the years. What happened to them? Where did they all go now that they've been rejected by their own homelands?"

Dominion looked up. "The desert."

"Indeed the desert." Brigadier nodded at Dominion.

Paul frowned. "You mean all the God Scarers have somehow wandered off into the wasteland?"

"Not wandered. Thirty years ago we did reach a secret agreement with the U.N. All Transients that weren't required for duties in Transit Stations would be shipped out to Africa. The deal was, we'd work out of sight of humanity so as not to offend them. Our goal was to settle in an area of absolute waterless nothingness—a barren hell-hole on the borders of Mali and Algeria. There we sank boreholes four miles deep until we reached water that had been locked down there in limestone aquifers fifty million years ago. There are billions of gallons of water. It's not fit for human consumption but adequate for us and enables our people to irrigate the desert and make it green and fertile. That area of land, fifty miles wide and two hundred long, is lush with crops, and meadows and new forest. Living there are twenty million individuals just like you. And that, ladies and gentlemen, is our homeland. It's what Dominion and I have been fighting to protect."

Elsa shook her head. "But the monster law dictates we can't—"

"Can't fight. Yes, I know." Brigadier smiled again. "But now that you've seen what Dominion can do you'll know that law no longer applies. We have our sanctuary now . . . our homeland . . . however, the U.N. has passed resolutions to drive us from it into another barren waste-land while they settled it with their own favorites. But why should we hand over a paradise that we made from dust?"

A hush settled on the room. Even those songs of the dead that haunted Elsa receded into the background. At last Paul broke the silence. "We knew nothing about any bolt-hole in Africa."

"If you'd been told, the knowledge would have been dangerous to us. The irrigation project was top secret. Most of the world's population didn't know about its existence either. Now we not only want them to know we demand that they accept the Transients' right to exist—"

"But the other countries don't agree."

"No, so we're embroiled in one of those dirty wars," Brigadier told them. "The kind that are invisible to the rest of the world. We're constantly attacked by special forces or bands of mercenaries. Dominion and I were engaged in secret negotiations with U.N. representatives when our plane was hit by ground fire. We'd even taken prisoners of war along with us to prove we were prepared to negotiate a peaceful settlement. And that, ladies and gentlemen, is the truth."

"That's part of the truth." The voice came as a hoarse whisper. Saiban rolled onto his side and pushed himself up on one elbow. He winced as he looked down at the wood protruding from his chest. "Were these necessary, or are they there to torment me?"

"They stopped you from bleeding out," Elsa told him. "You've Paul to thank for saving you."

"Thank? I curse him. I didn't want to live again."

"Saiban." Dominion didn't waste any time. "What do you know?"

"I know more than Brigadier, that's what I know." Saiban coughed.

Dominion slapped his thigh in frustration. "Then tell us, Saiban, it's important."

Elsa went to steady the figure on the table. "Can't you see he's too sick to talk?"

"He'll have to talk, damn him," Dominion snapped. "What Saiban knows might save more than our lives. Saiban?"

Saiban nodded; the mournful face sagged with exhaustion. "Yes, I know my duty. It used to be absolute devotion to humankind. Now I serve our cause. My abiding regret is I failed. When the Transit Station came under attack I sent a message to the Command Center. They didn't have time to reply before I had to flee like the rest of you."

"You mean you were in contact with these people out in Africa?"

"Let him talk, Beech." Elsa spoke quickly. "He's very tired."

Saiban managed a faint smile. "You mean I might not live long enough to get to the end of my little speech before I go and die all over again. For the third time. OK. Here goes. Dominion here is the First Man. The first of a new breed of Transient."

Brigadier added, "His body was rebuilt using the limbs and internal organs from the prisoners in the plane."

"No. You don't know the full story, Brigadier. When Dominion arrived at the Transit Station, Central Command had to have someone in place who knew what Dominion is. True, just like Frankenstein's monster he is an assembly of different parts from different bodies. He's stronger than us. Once the assembly of organs and flesh knit together he will be more durable."

Brigadier chuckled. "He will be a stronger warrior."

Saiban shook his head. "Wrong again. He's not intended to be a warrior. He's to be a thinker, a debater, a negotiator. The real improvements are in here." He touched his own head. "Not only is Dominion's body an assembly of disparate parts, his brain is an amalgam. A human brain weighs just three pounds. Dominion's weighs eight. Our scientists grafted additional mass to the frontal lobe. It's not just his body that has the stature of a giant. The cerebrum has, too."

Paul frowned. "Why didn't you try and save Dominion, after we escaped the soldiers at the Transit Station?"

"How could I? What means did I possess to carry him away to our sanctuary in the Sahara?" A fever sweat glistened on his forehead. "No. My orders from Central Command were precise. If there was a danger that Dominion would fall into the wrong hands I should destroy him. The surgical work on his brain is still raw. And yet he has vast amounts of information about our strategies stored inside his head. In his confused state he could have talked to the human authorities and ruined our chances of survival. It was better that I persuade you to surrender to those local peasants. They wouldn't have cared anything about intelligence gathering. They'd have burned us all alive. Dominion included. Then at least our most important secret would die with us."

Brigadier was troubled. "But I understood Dominion would fight our enemy. The plan was to force the U.N. to accept our right to a homeland."

Saiban sighed. "Twenty million of us against the entire population of the globe? How could we win? Our best option was to build ourselves the supreme negotiator, not the supreme warrior. Dominion is brain, not brawn."

Elsa gazed up at Dominion. His eyes were distant as if he digested what Saiban had told them. "So Dominion's purpose is to bring Transients and humanity together again?"

"Yes, and in that skull of his he knows it. He's just got to find the right mental connections. Once the intellectual circuitry is complete . . ." A coughing fit racked Saiban's body. The wooden spikes shook to the rhythm of the spasms.

"Does Central Command know that Dominion is still alive?"

"I saw Dominion myself when he ran from the building. I communicated that, too. Although whether they actually received the message or not . . ." The cough returned.

Elsa shook his arm. "But why did you kill Luna? And you tried to kill me."

"A mercy . . ." He could barely speak through the coughing fit. "A mercy, that's all. The humans would have . . . tortured you before killing you. Now . . . you should consider the same. Kill yourselves before you fall into their hands."

"No!" This was Caitlin. "They can't hurt us in here. If they try to break in Dominion will destroy them. Isn't that right, Dominion?"

Dominion's eyes snapped into sharp focus as they swept round the room. "What's happened to the priest?"

37

THE DAMNED

Paul followed Dominion as he ran out into the courtyard. Behind him, more God Scarers spilled out into the
night.

Dominion called back, "Didn't anyone see the priest
leave the room?"

Paul responded with, "If you hadn't noticed, we were
hanging on to Saiban's every word. Monsters at war with
humanity? A garden of Eden in the Sahara? This is all
news to us poor bloody fools! We're only the handle-
crankers at the cadaver factory!"

Dominion flashed him a look that clearly meant,
Don't start an argument now. "We need to find the priest.
He's our bargaining chip."

A figure emerged from the gloom at a run.

"West, have you seen the priest?"

"He was in the room with you," West retorted.

"You're meant to be keeping watch in the town."

"Yeah, that's exactly what I have been doing. Now I'm
coming to report that things are starting to happen."

Dominion's eyes had been scanning the courtyard in search of the vanished priest, but West's comment made him pause. "What kind of things?"

"Bizarre things. It's getting weird."

"Have they come back?"

"Sort of." West took a deep breath. "They've not used the steps. About a dozen vehicles have been driven up the cliff road. They're only advancing slowly. For some reason they've erected timber boards on top of them. They've also mounted searchlights."

"Boards to protect them against your stone throwing," Paul told Dominion. "Searchlights to dazzle us."

"Wait, there's more. I keep hearing an aircraft. Now, one thing you don't hear these days are planes."

"What kind of aircraft?"

"Apart from guessing it's military I haven't a clue. Maybe a helicopter. I'm not sure."

Paul caught Dominion's arm. "If these people have managed to interest the army in us, then they might be flying in one of their commando squads they used against the Transit Stations."

"Then we need to find the priest."

"Dominion, what the *fuck* will the priest be able to do?" Paul's rage boiled. "Is he going to send us away with his blessing? Those people out there are going to tie us to a dirty great pile of wood and bake the bloody marrow in our bones! Does that great thick head of yours understand what I'm saying?"

Dominion pulled his arm out of Paul's grip so savagely that Paul nearly tumbled onto the cobbles. "I intend to save your lives." Dominion's voice was cold. "We use the priest to negotiate our way out of here. We will exchange their holy man for a boat."

"How do you think one of those wrecks in the harbor will make it to the Sahara? Sprout wings and fly?"

"Where?" West's expression was the embodiment of amazement. "The Sahara?"

Paul nodded. "That's the God Scarers' Promised Land, isn't it, Dominion? All green and lovely. We stayed here to be martyred. For heaven's sake, why didn't you build Transit Stations out there?"

Dominion wasn't going to be drawn. "Listen. You must find the priest." He announced this to the others, who watched the argument in a daze. They were still trying to absorb tonight's revelations.

Paul added, "When you do, Dominion here with his eight-pound brain is going to talk the Saps into giving us a free ticket out of here."

Dominion grabbed Paul by the collar, then thrust his own face forward. Paul felt the giant's breath jet from the flared nostrils. "You talked about the strength of your faith in helping human beings. Redirect that faith into helping your own kind."

Caitlin called down from the walkway, "He's over there! By the tower!"

The figure appeared to be black on black—black clothes against black sky. For a moment all Paul could really see was the gleam of the man's eyes shining at them from the darkness.

"There's your bargaining chip," Paul told Dominion. "Go negotiate."

After releasing his grip on Paul's collar Dominion bounded up the stairs that led up the inner wall to the walkway. Paul followed with West just behind him. Even as he ran he heard a faint sound mixed with the hiss of the surf. A distant aircraft motor. A suggestion of rotor blades chopping the night air. It only lasted a second before the throaty roar of a truck motor killed it. As the surge of revs pounded the air a searchlight blazed. It struck the figure in black.

Paul saw the priest had managed to climb onto the coping stones that ran along the very top of the battlement. It must have required an effort of staggering magnitude on the part of the priest. He'd only emerged from the Regenerator a few hours ago. He'd be weak for days. Even standing would require a huge effort of will. Now he stood bolt upright in the glare of the light from below. His long black coat caught the night breeze—a raven appearance of wings flapping. His balance was imperfect as he teetered there on the wall, his feet clamped to the stone blocks. With one hand he steadied himself against the wall of the tower, which soared above him.

Paul called out, "Sir, you aren't fit enough to be out here yet."

"I'll never be fit enough," the priest replied. "My soul is already in purgatory."

Dominion moved ahead with Paul following. He was mindful of the vehicles below him in on the road. Their searchlights were trained on the priest, while the people sheltered behind boards that had been hastily bolted to the tops of the trucks. They resembled old-time sailing boats, only these men-o'-war boasted wooden sails. No doubt somewhere in the backs of the trucks dozens of Saps crouched safe from Dominion's stones.

Dominion held his hand out to the priest. "Come back indoors. We can talk there."

"You want to talk?" panted the man. "What with, this?" He struck himself in the face. "You won't be talking to *me*. You'll be addressing a slab of dead flesh that only bears a passing resemblance to me. I died in the church. What you see here now is a shell without spirit."

A voice called from the truck below. "Father. Tell them to release you. We'll take you back down into the town."

"Haven't you see what these creatures have done to

me? They've made my body into the same vile beast as they are."

The owner of the voice failed to understand. "Father. They are Transients. It's against their law to harm you. Tell them to open the gate. Then walk toward the vehicles. We'll take care of you."

"I know you will do that. That's why you must prepare for my funeral. Listen to me! Even though I might appear to be alive you must bury me in the graveyard."

His words were enough to coax the townspeople from the vehicles. They clearly saw that the old priest had been transformed into a youthful man.

"They have brought one of their machines to the Pharos. The ones that mock both God and nature. Oh yes, they'll tell you they've brought me back to life. Lies, of course."

"Sir," Dominion said gently. "Come down and talk."

"Never."

"Don't you feel young again? What does it feel like to have a strong heart beating in your chest?"

"I don't feel anything because I no longer have a soul to feel with." He turned back to his people that gathered on the roadway. "Don't you see? These creatures are playing a trick on you. I'm not real. This isn't alive." He slammed his fist against his chest. "They are mocking you. I am not your priest now. What you see up here is a monster."

The mayor appeared from behind a van. "Father, don't talk like this. There must be some way to—"

"There is a way. Destroy this abomination." He slapped his chest again. "Destroy this. Then destroy the other monsters in here. It's your sacred duty!"

"Father—"

"Do it. Then bury this carcass in quicklime!"

A pause. The silence that wasn't a silence. That absence of sound seemed to screech in Paul's ears. Then came a flurry of shots.

A dozen hooch-soaked kids raised their weapons and let fly with a motley collection of shotguns and rifles. Bullets knocked chips of stone from the wall. Then there were those that found their flesh-and-blood target. The man on the wall flinched as a hail of white-hot lead struck him. Even from here Paul saw how a bullet sped at the priest like a shooting star, struck him in the rib cage, then tore through the body to explode out the other side in a spray of blood. Yet, he only faltered on the wall before regaining his balance. *Hard to kill.* The drunken gunslingers would have to wreak far more damage with their guns before felling this new God Scarer. The firing, however, stopped as quickly as it began. The mayor waved the young guns back. He was furious that they'd fired on what most of the townsfolk still believed to be one of their own.

"Father," the mayor implored. "We can take care of you."

Blood ran down the priest's face from a gunshot wound. In the searchlight the smear against his skin glared a violent crimson. "I've told you what you must do. Put this monster in the ground. Cover it with quicklime. Bury it under rocks, so it can't dig itself out."

Dominion spoke. "Don't you see what you can do? You're healthy again. You're stronger than before. These people need your help."

The figure swayed on the wall as he turned to face Dominion. "You really think Scaur Ness will welcome a monster as their priest?" He placed the flat of his hand against the tower wall and pushed himself backward from the battlements. Paul witnessed the man's fall to earth. The long tails of his coat flapped in the slipstream. A black raven plunging earthward. The silence of the townspeople made the slap of the body striking the road as shocking as a gunshot inside a church.

Immediately those manning the searchlights on the trucks swung them down onto the fallen priest. The black figure lay there with the arms straight out in a pose of crucifixion as if he'd been nailed to the ground. Then the fingers twitched. A moment later he rolled onto his side before laboriously standing. He took three limping steps toward the truck. The body must have sustained broken bones, but it still remained upright.

"Hard to kill," Paul murmured. "What will his people do with a fractured priest now, Dominion?"

"More to the point, what do we do now?" Dominion clenched his fists.

"Didn't your eight-pound brain foresee the possibility that the priest would prefer his own extinction, rather than live on in a form he detested?"

The priest's voice rang out with such power it echoed back at him. *"Use your guns! Shoot me!"* The townspeople froze. Now in that incandescent light they saw what the man in black had become. *Hard to kill . . .* The first volley of shots hadn't killed him. The fall hadn't killed him. Paul knew what must be running through their minds. *What do we do now? Burn him alive?* But which one of those Saps had the guts to destroy their own man of God?

"Fire on me!" he boomed. "It's not your priest that commands it. Christ commands it!" As he advanced toward the vehicles the men retreated. They didn't know how to deal with this . . . phantom? Demon? Monster? This creature bathed there in brilliant light that resembled the priest they all loved.

"Fire your guns at me!"

"We'll take you home. There will be a way to . . ." A *way to what?* The mayor couldn't finish the sentence.

The priest held out his hands. "Those monsters in there have damned me. If you don't destroy what I've become, then you will have damned me, also." He looked down on the town from the cliff top. "If I should still move, disregard it. If I shout, cover your ears. Bury me as deeply as you can." Having said that he climbed the fence and stepped off the cliff. This time the fall was two hundred feet. The silence ran on for a long time before Paul heard the crunch. At that height, two hundred pounds of muscle and bone must have hit the buildings below with the force of a bomb.

The silence that followed was a painful one. Paul sensed the rising tension. For a moment there was this frozen tableaux. *Here are the God Scarers on the battlements that overlook Scaur Ness. A dying town that lies in the darkness. On the cliff top a bunch of vehicles. They still shine their lights on the spot where the priest stepped into oblivion. The vigilantes don't move a muscle. Yet emotion scalds them inside as their anger builds with a pressure that's nothing less than explosive.*

Paul's gratitude for the rugged steelwork of the portcullis that kept the Saps locked out became surreal. He could have kissed that gate. Because as sure as the sun would rise in the morning, that was the only thing that protected the God Scarers in here now.

The surf hissed in the distance. In some of the houses below lights burned. He turned to gaze down at the mob. They'd do something. Their hatred blazed from them in a way that was nothing less than nuclear. Yet they still hadn't moved. No one had shouted. There was only this lack of activity that somehow seemed worse than them screaming abuse and firing their guns. Then, when they did make their move, it was what Paul expected least of all.

38

HERE COMES A CHOPPER TO CHOP OFF YOUR HEAD

Paul stood beside Dominion on the castle wall as the trucks began to move. After the townspeople witnessed the fate of their priest, Paul had expected them to fire on the castle. Instead when the vehicles moved they retreated from the fortress. He glanced to his left along the walkway. Most of the God Scarers had climbed up here to watch events unfolding below. They exchanged puzzled glances, then shrugged; the behavior of the mob had them mystified. Elsa stood beside Caitlin. West hoisted himself up to sit on the battlements for a better view. Beech talked to Xaiyad; from their expressions they clearly had no idea what was happening either.

Paul spoke to Dominion. "You killed their priest. I expected them to attack, not for them to crawl back to their homes."

"This will end peacefully," Dominion told him.

"Really? But then how can my three-pound brain match your eight-pound brain for wisdom?"

"You detest what I am, don't you?"

"Until I met you," Paul said, "God Scarers were fortunate individuals who had been rescued in their entirety from death. You've been built from a scrap heap."

"I have the same senses."

"But only more so. You, Dominion, really are Frankenstein's monster. You're an amalgam. Even your brain is bolted together from a mishmash of other brains."

"I still feel pain and loneliness."

"We . . . these men and women here . . . we're devoted to the notion of serving humanity. You know something, I believe you were built with the express intention of being *more* than human."

"And that makes you hate me."

"Hate you? I should have destroyed you when I had a chance."

When Dominion glared it felt like the blow of an ax. Paul forced himself not to flinch, or show any sign of weakness. Dominion claimed there'd be a peaceful end to the siege, but how did that abnormal brain of his define "peaceful"?

West shouted a warning. *"Watch out. They're up to something."*

The vehicles' lights revealed what happened next. A breakdown truck lurched out of the darkness into the glare of the assembled headlights. In clouds of blue diesel exhaust it rumbled up to the portcullis. Paul expected it to ram the gate. But the narrowness of the road, flanked by the cliff at one side and the castle walls at the other, made it impossible for the truck to strike head-on; it would be a glancing blow. The nose of the truck swung toward the portcullis, then turned away again. With a squeal of brakes it skidded to a stop. The back of the truck had been covered by a messy conglomeration of old house doors; clearly a crude attempt at armor to protect anyone in the back of the truck if Dominion had access to any homespun missiles. But Dominion at that moment was empty-handed. All he could do was watch events unfold . . . or as time would show: unravel.

Paul saw that the breakdown truck hauled a car. A rust-covered wreck of a thing, the rear tires were flat, the hood had vanished, exposing a motor that had been deprived of usable parts. The machine had been dragged from a backstreet where it had lain unused for months, if not years. As they watched, the chain that connected it to the truck's winch went slack. Then the truck drove away to leave the car there alongside the portcullis.

"That showed us." West laughed. "They're dumping old wrecks at our front door."

Cold spider feet prickled down Paul's spine. He hoisted his upper half over the top of the wall so he could look down at the car forty feet below. Then he turned his head to see the Saps' cluster of vehicles a good two hundred yards away. Their engines had been idling. Now they began to rev them hard. Exhaust smoke hazed the headlights. He turned back to stare at the car. It lay there; an inert lump of metal, plastic, cracked windows. Then he noticed a thin trickle of smoke emerge from an open window. There wasn't much. No more than someone lounging in the backseat to smoke a cigarette.

Paul opened his mouth to take a deep enough breath to shout as loud as he could.

Elsa had seen what happened to the priest. She'd watched the tow truck dump the old car at the gate. The night breeze began to blow colder. Above the rushing sound of surf on the beach she heard a deep pulse of sound on that chill air.

What's a helicopter doing here? she asked herself. Elsa leaned over the wall to search the dark sky above the town. Surely with this mountainous landscape it would be dangerous to fly so low at night. Even as she asked herself the question about the helicopter she spotted a light in the sky above the hills. That was the moment, too, that the song of the dead returned. It rose in a chorus that shook her senses. In shock she glanced round at the others. Why couldn't they hear it? Instead they were staring down at the old car outside the portcullis. Elsa clenched her fists. The unearthly music worked its way into every fiber of herself. The notes expanded in her mind; they stretched her senses until weird purple blooms burst through the black sky above her. The taste of the sea ran across her tongue. In it was more than brine. Somehow her taste buds prickled with the atoms of everyone who had ever drowned there. The surreal notion took her back to her death . . . that first death of hers when she and Richard swam in the ocean. The currents had carried them too far out. They'd clung together in desperation as they'd become exhausted. Each one had tried to support the other as the riptide hauled them downward. The coast guard had found her. Within hours her lifeless body had been rushed to a Transit Station. Within days she'd been taking her first "newborn" steps round the station's rose garden. Richard was gone. Never found. After all these years the ocean would have dissolved his body. Now its molecules might be rushing in the surf toward this very shore. The voices of the singing dead called to her. Their madrigal haunted her.

They're calling me . . . Richard is calling me. And even though she thought the voices of the dead couldn't get any louder they did. She slammed her hands to her ears. Surely these people could hear the music now? When she looked at Paul he was moving away from the wall and he'd opened his mouth to shout . . .

* * *

Paul yelled the warning with as much force as he could. "Get down! There's a bomb in the car!" The explosion tore through the night air like a thunderclap. A second later the shock wave slammed him against the walkway. Simultaneously a flash seared his retinas. A yard from him the car's gearbox crashed down in a shower of sparks. Broken glass fell from the night sky with a faint tinkling, as if it were a fairy-tale rainfall that had been transformed into diamonds. Then he saw nothing. Black smoke that smelled of burning paint obliterated everything.

When the sea breeze ushered the fumes away he blinked. First of all he realized that Dominion had vanished. Then he knew why. The blast had knocked the giant from the walkway into the courtyard below. West had moved fast because he was already down there helping one of the nurses haul the unconscious man toward the room that housed the Regenerator.

So they packed an old car with dynamite? There are quarries nearby . . . the source of the explosive is obvious. Only we were too dumb to realize they'd do it.

"Caitlin!" He yelled her name as she ran toward him. "Get back inside. Use the tower doorway."

"Not without you, I'm not."

His head rang like a bell. "My hearing's taken a beating. What's West shouting?"

Caitlin helped him stand. "He says they've blown a hole in the gate."

"Uh." He groaned, not with pain, but because he knew what would happen next. "Caitlin, get yourself inside, please."

"No." Her eyes were calm. "Not without you, Paul. Either we both go or we both stay. OK?"

"OK. Get everyone inside and lock the doors. Xaiyad? Xaiyad, can you walk?" He coughed as smoke engulfed them again. The stink of burning plastic made him want to vomit. "Xaiyad!"

"I'm fine. You get the rest. Beech is hurt."

Paul risked putting his head above the parapet. The lights from the vehicles bathed the front of the castle in a brilliant light. Now the Saps left the trucks to run toward the portcullis. Although he couldn't see the extent of the damage from this angle, he saw the black smear on the road together with the burning wreckage of the car.

"Caitlin," he shouted as he scrambled over crumpled sections of the car's bodywork that had been hurled up here by the explosion. "Caitlin. I'm going down into the courtyard."

"West said they'd blown up the gate."

"There's a chance I might be able to block the gap."

"Paul! They'll be here any second. They're armed!"

"Even if I can't someone's got to make sure the doors from the courtyard into the castle itself are barricaded."

"No! They'll kill you."

"If I don't there's nothing to stop them from walking in and killing us anyway."

"I'm coming with you."

There was no time to argue. He managed a groggy nod before half stumbling, half walking across what had been the roof of the car toward the entrance to the tower.

Elsa lay flat under a sheet of metal. The shock wave had knocked the air out of her lungs. Even when someone walked over the debris that pinned her down, it was all she could do to breathe, never mind cry out. Elsa realized what had happened. Explosives in the car had detonated outside the portcullis. Yet she seemed to occupy two separate worlds now. One of noise, commotion, shouting. Then another one where ethereal music washed through her. With the aura of tranquility came a yearning to surrender to the inevitable as voices called to her across a vast gulf of absolute darkness. That resonant summons had become irresistible. *I'm coming* . . . Elsa knew she must find the source of the music. That's all that mattered to her now.

Disaster. The word thudded inside his head. *Disaster, disaster* . . .

Dominion, where are you when we need you now?

Still dazed, Paul crashed through the door at the base of the tower and into the courtyard. The cobbled area lay wreathed in smoke. Flames from burning fragments of car lit the scene with an angry red glow.

Behind him, Caitlin shouted, "There's nothing you can do. It's smashed."

She was right. A hole gaped in the crisscross steelwork of the portcullis. Through the slash in the gate he could see silhouettes moving. A shot rang out as someone fired a rifle. The bullet whined through the air to smack into the stone wall. At that moment the only thing stopping the mob rushing in was one of the car's axles wedged in the tangle of steel bars at the top of the gate. A burning tire at one end of the axle poured a stream of molten rubber onto the ground where the mob would have to pass. Any second now the tire would burn itself out, and then they'd flood into the courtyard. And now that mass of people displayed their fury. They hurled abuse at the occupants of the castle. There appeared to be no discipline. This was a bunch of enraged men and women who simply craved vengeance. They pushed each other so they could fire at the God Scarers. Bullets snapped through the air. Xaiyad clutched his back as a bullet smashed into his spine. He still kept running, though, to eventually duck through a doorway into the relative safety of the building.

Hard to kill . . . but not Caitlin. She tried to stay at

Paul's side. In turn he constantly strove to put himself between her and the hail of ammunition.

"Paul, there's nothing we can do with the gate," she repeated.

"OK, but we've got to secure all the doors at ground level. Once they're in the building there's nothing we can do to stop them then."

"Those doors won't hold them for long."

"I know." He heard the misery in his voice. "I know. But for now it's all we can do."

The Saps pushed at the portcullis. A second later they shook the burning tire free. It dropped from the axle in a flaccid mass. Greasy, orange flame licked the air as it fell. The mob was thinking on its feet now. The moment the molten rubber hit the ground a thickset man dropped a car door onto it. The rubber still burned but the people had a stepping stone to bring them over the threshold into the Pharos. First across was the mayor. For a moment he stood there with a crazed light in his eye as he pointed upward.

"Have you seen it?" His voice boomed in triumph. "The army has sent a helicopter. It'll have troops on it. But you know something? We're going to do their work for them. We'll cut off your heads and make a display of them before the soldiers get here."

Caitlin screamed at her father, "Get away from here! Leave them alone!"

"Caitlin, girl, you've got one chance. Come across here now. If you don't I won't be able to protect you."

"Go to hell!"

For once Paul had to agree with Caitlin's father. The Saps were rabid. Nothing less could describe it. Monster blood. Caitlin's blood. All was the same to them now. They'd slaughter everyone in the castle.

39

ASSAULT

The people of Scaur Ness poured into the courtyard. Vehicles pulled up outside that directed searchlights so what happened next was illuminated in brilliant detail. Paul caught as many of his fellow Transients as he could and directed them through the doors that led into the body of the castle. He told them to barricade the doors from the inside. He wished Caitlin would join his people in the relative safety of the building, but she insisted she stayed with him. Everywhere pools of molten plastic still burned on the cobbles. Acrid smoke stung his throat with every inhalation.

The Sap women yelled. They were ecstatic. There was something sexual about their pleasure in retaking the Pharos. Their gunfire was wild—more venting of emotion rather than accuracy. Some bullets found targets. Paul felt a sting on his forearm as a bullet from a revolver wielded by a silver-haired woman cut a red furrow across his flesh.

A crimson-faced youth howled at him. "Helicopters!

See 'em? You know something, they're full of our troops. They're going to butcher you fuckers!"

"Caitlin." A man leered at her as he reloaded his shotgun. "You're going to get some special treatment tonight. You should see what we've got planned for you . . . corpse whore."

Then Paul saw his world unravel. A group of townspeople had cornered one of the Transients—a guy who worked in physiotherapy. They beat him back against the wall with rifle butts. It was against the monster law to defend himself. All he could do was suffer the blows.

"Leave him," Paul shouted. "He's done nothing to harm you!"

The man looked across at Paul. There was such sorrow in his eyes. And at that moment Paul hated himself, and the God Scarers' nature—their relentless submission; their acceptance of whatever humanity chose to mete out. *Humans can do what they like to us. We can't even complain.*

From behind Paul as he shielded her from the mob Caitlin howled, "You bastards! Let him go!" They simply worked the rifle butts harder. A split opened above the man's eye. "Can't you see you're hurting him? These people have feelings!" Her voice became a torrent of rage. "They're not the ones who are dead. You are! It's all you from this fucking ghost town. You're dead but you're just too ignorant to realize it."

One of the women in the mob stepped forward to stop them from beating the guy. Paul felt a surge of relief. It was short-lived. She told their victim to open his mouth. *He's a God Scarer. What can he do? He must obey a human.* So he opened his mouth. She inserted a stick of dynamite between his lips, then lit the fuse, as if she lit a cigar for a friend. The mob thought this was hilarious. They howled with laughter as they backed away.

The man's sad eyes met Paul's. At that desolate, soul-destroying moment the only thing Paul could do was stand there; his heart pounded, his ribs were a cage that crushed his lungs until it hurt him to breathe. The Saps' victim remained against the wall. He'd accepted his fate. The man knew this was the way his life would end.

The people, meanwhile, enjoyed their twisted comedy. *A man with a fat stick of dynamite pushed into his mouth! The fuse burns toward the detonator! Sparks cascade down his chest! Head wreathed in smoke. Another five seconds . . .* How the rabble laughed.

Paul longed for Dominion to appear. *The monster's monster. Dominion is the only one who can save him. So where are you, Dominion?*

Caitlin slammed her hand into his back. "Paul! Do something!"

All he could do was shake his head.

"You can't just stand there and let them kill him. He's the same as you!"

"It's our law." Paul hated saying the words; his heart was breaking. "We must not hurt a human being."

Paul turned back just in time. One moment the man stood there in front of his baying tormentors. Then the fuse triggered the detonator. The dynamite planted in his mouth erupted in a ball of flame. A split second later the headless body fell to the ground. And the mob roared their approval. They laughed. Slapped one another on the back. Showtime.

"*Paul . . .*"

He turned to see that half a dozen men had grabbed hold of Caitlin. Already one of them worked with a pair of shears. Savagely, the guy hacked at her hair.

"Leave her. That's my daughter." The mayor tried to intervene, but this time his neighbors bundled him away.

"*Paul!*"

The others held her as one worked with the shears; already they'd nicked her skin. Blood beaded above her right eyebrow.

"Leave her," Paul told them.

They laughed in his face. "How're you going to stop us?"

The one with the shears showed him a pink glaze of blood on the blades. "All you can do is watch, monster. See . . . I'll take a nip out of her ear . . . there!"

Caitlin screamed.

"There's nothing you can do about it, can you?" The man with the shears leered at Paul. "We know that only one of your sort can use his fists on us—and he's dead. We saw them drag the body into the castle. You're fucked, monster. And so is your corpse whore." He worked the shears again. His attack on her mane of hair was ferocious. When it didn't cut he simply ripped at it. Caitlin's screams of pain echoed from the walls.

Once more Paul shot a forlorn glance toward the door where Dominion had been hauled. Was he dead? It seemed impossible that towering man could no longer help him. Now this? The men were right. How could he save Caitlin? First they were going to cut off her beautiful hair. Then what? A wave of nausea scalded him inside.

DO NO HARM TO HUMANITY

That's our monster law, he told himself. *The only one to ever break it was Dominion. That's because he's not really one of us. He's an amalgam of body parts. His brain is a bastardized construct. A dozen brains welded together before being dropped into his skull. Only Dominion can . . .*

"Paul!"

He heard her agony. Abandoning themselves to frenzy, the men twisted her arm. The man with the shears snipped away. Sometimes he stabbed the points of the blades into the tender flesh of her ears. She wept. Not just with pain but knowing this was the end. The town had finally won. They'd reclaimed her. She was theirs to degrade. Eventually, in the next few hours, their torture of her would claim her life. They'd bury her in the cemetery in the center of Scaur Ness. Then the girl who dreamed of leaving this moribund town would never, ever escape. She'd be imprisoned forever in the tomb they'd built.

THIS IS THE MONSTER LAW
DO NO HARM TO HUMANITY

When one man twisted Caitlin's arm with so much force it dislocated her shoulder her cries blazed their way to Paul's heart. He clenched his fists. This was more than he could endure.

"Paul!"

The pressure became too great. Something tore inside him.

The man with the shears attacked Caitlin's hair with a new vigor. "Keep watching, monster," he called. "Just see what we do to her next. You won't believe your eyes."

The men roared with laughter. Paul saw the mob had gathered to enjoy the spectacle of one of their own suffer. Their eyes were gluttonous. For a short while Caitlin's agony would make them forget their own dead-end lives.

One of the women called out, "Cut off the bitch's nose!"

The man held out his shears to show them to Paul. He snipped the air, savoring his act as showman. Youths shoved Paul in the back.

They jeered. "Go on, kiss her nose good-bye."

"Corpse whore!"

"If anyone's got the dynamite I know just where to stick it."

They roared with laughter. The shears moved toward Caitlin's face.

"Cut!" one of the woman shouted. The rest took up the chant: *"Cut! Cut! Cut! Cut!"*

Paul snapped. He felt no sense of wrong retard his actions. In a blur, he leaped forward, seized the man's hand that held the shears, then drove them point-first through the bulge of his nose into his skull. The fingers that held the shears' handles snapped under Paul's powerful grip. The last Paul saw of the man was as he staggered backward, his fingers wedded to the shears that were embedded in his face.

The mob lunged at Paul in a howling pack. The slaughter man was there; he attempted to push the muzzle of the humane killer against Paul's head. Paul's own hand closed over both the weapon and the slaughter man's hand. He crushed both with such force the cartridge detonated in the gun, turning the man's hand to shreds. In that tangle of bodies the ones with guns were jostled so much by their neighbors they couldn't squeeze off a targeted shot. Pistols and rifles blasted away, either uselessly into the air, or so wide of their target the Saps were more in danger than the God Scarer they were hellbent on destroying.

A youth with a long scraggle of red hair lunged forward with a knife; his slash scratched Paul's chest. What Paul did in return was far worse. It felt as if something nuclear powered him. He had no qualms in attacking these people now. What's more, their bodies seemed as insubstantial as tissue paper. When the youth slashed with the knife he simply grabbed hold of the kid with the red mane and snapped his head from his body as if the spine was no more substantial than a bread stick. The body vented blood from the hole between the shoulders. For a second it tottered there before slumping to the cobbles. Paul looked at the head in his hands. The eyes stared back into his with shock before the brain cells died. *Easy to kill . . .*

Now he gripped the head by the hair, then swung it like a mace. With each powerful sweep, either the mob retreated from the head that sprayed them with blood from the ripped neck flesh, or it impacted against them, knocking them to the ground. A Sap ran forward with a shotgun. Before he had time to fire Paul slashed the head so fiercely it split the air with a whistling sound. Skull struck skull. Whether it was the youth's dead head that broke or the guy's with the gun Paul didn't know. But Paul heard the loud *snap!* of breaking bone. Shotgun guy didn't even cry out. He flopped down to the ground where he lay still.

The mob moved back now. Partly out of respect for what he could do with the bloody head, partly so those with guns could get a clean shot. Paul looked round for Caitlin. For a moment he was sure he'd find her among the corpses on the ground. Then he saw a flurry of movement beyond the portcullis.

"Caitlin!"

Paul watched as Caitlin's father dragged his daughter to a waiting car. A moment later she was inside and being driven away from the Pharos.

Bird shot stung his side. Guns bristled at him like the spines of a porcupine. This time he hurled the mangled head at one of the gunmen. It struck the man in the chest, knocking him backward.

"Paul!"

He glanced back. Saiban stood in a doorway. Even though the wooden spikes in his torso made each movement agony he beckoned Paul to him. Paul longed to race after the car that carried Caitlin away, yet it was too late and he knew it.

"Paul. You can't defeat them by yourself!"

With one last glance at the shattered portcullis Paul ran at the door. Saiban insisted he go first. The man even shielded him from the blows as a burly guy launched an attack with a hammer. Seconds later Paul leaned panting against the storeroom wall. His skin burned where bullets had struck him.

"Hard to kill." Saiban shot the bolts across the door. "Not indestructible. Go let Beech take a look at those wounds." Saiban stood back as a volley of gunfire struck the door. The old timbers were hard as iron. Not one bullet punched through. "Thank providence that they don't have military weapons."

Paul nodded. "Rabbit guns, antique pistols . . . that seems the best they can muster."

"If they have dynamite that's a different matter. Here . . ." Saiban took his arm to help him to where the God Scarers took it in turns to patch each other up.

"Is it true Dominion's dead?"

Saiban nodded toward a trestle table. Brigadier sat in a chair beside it. "The bomb knocked Dominion off the walkway. He fell forty feet into the courtyard. Xaiyad has pronounced Dominion concussed. That's all."

Paul began, "I tried to stop them from hurting Caitlin." As he stared at his bloody hands the flow of words stopped.

"West told us what you did."

Paul looked into those mournful eyes of Saiban's. "Then you know I broke our law?"

"Our monster law died years ago. It was our fault that we inherited the Frankenstein syndrome." Saiban smiled. "We kept bringing the law back to life. It belonged dead. We should have left it that way." He turned to Brigadier. "Is he waking?"

The grotesque figure clad in the white sheet nodded. "Slowly."

Paul found himself in a chair with Beech dabbing his wounds with tissue.

She asked, "Where's Caitlin?"

"I tried to save her . . . they were torturing her. So I killed them."

"Good." Beech spoke with force.

"Her father drove Caitlin away."

"Then she's safe."

"I wish I could believe you."

Beech dabbed a graze on his wrist. "You're not only hard to kill, Paul. You're hard to even dent. These wounds are superficial."

He gave a grim shake of his head. "But how long until they break in here?"

West stood on a table to look through an air vent into the courtyard. "They're not doing anything at the moment. But when I went up into the tower I could see that helicopters have landed on the cliff top."

Brigadier spoke. "Then that bunch outside are probably waiting for their soldiers."

"Grenades, rocket launchers, armor-piercing ammunition." Saiban shook his head. "As to our fate? Draw your own conclusions."

Paul stood up. "We've come too far to simply hand ourselves over."

"You surely aren't proposing we fight our way out?" Saiban stared at him. "Only you and Dominion have the bloodlust. As for us?" He looked round the room. "In reality, we're still more sheep than monster."

Anger surged through Paul. "We can't wait here. You're surrendering to apathy before you even surrender to the soldiers. And when you do they'll slaughter you where you stand."

"I couldn't have put it better." Dominion sounded weak. Nevertheless, he swung his legs round to sit upright on the table. "Keep the doors locked. Don't let them in."

Brigadier stopped Dominion from standing. "You took a hell of a knock. Don't rush anything."

"I'm fine. I take it their troops have arrived to finish us off?"

"Three helicopters landed on the cliff," West said. "They're big enough to be troop carriers."

Paul regarded the giant figure as he sat there. "You might have a bloody big brain, Dominion, but I don't believe for a minute you're going to figure out an escape route for us."

"I'm starting to remember . . ." Dominion experimentally straightened his spine as if checking for damage. "There is something I am supposed to do."

"What exactly?"

"That . . ." He rubbed his face. "That I can't remember. Not yet. But it's close to the surface now. I can feel it."

40

ANATOMY OF A MONSTER

That's the moment Elsa could have become the filling in a sandwich. On top of her the steel roof of the car pressed down. Beneath her, the unyielding stone slabs of the walkway radiated the cold of the castle into her bones. For a while the gunshots had been a brittle clatter; then they faded. As they did so the music that only she could hear ghosted through the night air. More than once she heard footsteps nearby; this was the light feet of humans, no doubt searching the walkway for God Scarers to destroy. But they missed Elsa lying concealed beneath the car roof hurled onto her by the explosion. The music called to her. Common sense told her to find her own kind; yet when she managed to push the metal sheet from her she knew what she must do. Searchlights mounted on vehicles illuminated the scene below. The mob had gathered outside the doorway that led into the storeroom at the base of a tower. That was probably where Dominion, Beech, Paul, and the rest were making their last defiant stand. She estimated there were two hundred Saps laying siege to that little doorway. From what she could tell they appeared to be arguing among themselves what to do next.

At one point a man suggested something, but he was shouted down with, "Wait for the soldiers. The army's on its way!"

The mob were too involved with their own debate to worry about what happened up on the walkway above their heads. As stealthily as she could she picked her way across the debris to one of towers. The door lay open. With luck there'd be no one inside this part of the building.

This is suicide, she told herself. *They'll see me the moment I step out into the courtyard.*

What option did she have? To crawl back under the metal sheet? They'd find her soon enough if she hid there. Rejoining her own kind wasn't an alternative at the moment. As far as she knew the only way into the storeroom was through the door that the mob had besieged. Besides, the call of that ancient song of the dead was stronger than ever. She must answer it. Elsa descended the spiral staircase in the tower, then slipped out through the door. There she saw the headless corpse of a Transient. A splash of body fluids violated the stone wall. God Scarer blood was the reddest of all.

While she ran lightly across the courtyard to the wrecked portcullis a couple of Saps took experimental kicks at the storeroom door. Women shouted encouragement. Another voice, however, sang out that they should wait for the army to finish the task for them.

The stink of burnt plastic still hung on the air as Elsa passed through the hole in the gate. Here the light from searchlights was so intense she had to shield her eyes. Behind her, the mob still failed to notice the lone God Scarer escape the castle. Beyond the lights, there was only darkness. The music grew louder; it became a homing signal. Whatever generated those unearthly notes was guiding her to its source.

"Have they got the bastards out yet?"

She shielded her eyes to see who'd spoken. The guy had to squint against the glare, too. It took a moment, but then he recognized what stood in front of him.

"Hey! One's got out!" He yanked a revolver from a holster.

From the vehicles half a dozen men ran toward her. They unholstered sidearms, too, and slammed a volley of shots at her. She couldn't run back into the castle. All she could do was race along the wall of the castle in the direction of the seaward cliff. Once she turned the corner of the building she found herself in darkness again. A cool breeze that tasted of brine tugged at her hair. Behind her came the calls of her pursuers. An eager sound. They knew the pursuit would be a short one. No doubt other members of the posse would circle round the other side of the castle to cut off her escape. Already she began to slow her pace. To her right the stone wall of the Pharos rose into the air. At the other side of her, just ten paces away, the land ended at the cliff edge. There it fell away in a sheer drop to the ocean far below. At the bottom of the rock face surf flooded across boulders in a mass of boiling white.

Bobbing lights rounded the corner. Some of her pursuers held flashlights; one let fly with a submachine gun. The rounds snagged the back of her knee; another clipped her hand. From the far end of the castle a pickup rounded the corner. *This is it.*

The music swelled with unearthly splendor. *Of course . . . this is meant to be.* The words had barely slid through her when she walked forward. Then without a moment's hesitation she stepped off the edge of the cliff.

* * *

In the storeroom the surviving God Scarers sat without speaking. Every so often a boot would crash against the door. Following that would either be taunts, or promises of what torture the Saps would inflict, or sometimes a more cajoling voice.

"You can't stay in there forever. Give yourselves up before the soldiers arrive. Make it easy for yourselves. I guarantee it'll be painless." Then there'd be silence for a moment before a drink-sodden voice punctuated by belches came through the door: "You've seen them for yourselves. Helicopters have landed nearby. They'll be full of our soldiers. Won't be long now. We're going to build a fire . . ." Then silence.

At last, Dominion slid off the table to stand on his two feet. "Paul." He beckoned him, then placed a hand on his shoulder. "I told you I was going to show you Caitlin's womb. Do you know why?"

"One of your oh-so-distinctive threats, Dominion." Paul heard the bitterness in his voice. "Why return to that now?"

"Because I wasn't thinking clearly then." Dominion brought his face closer. "Don't ask me how I can tell . . . a sixth sense. I don't know, there's so much happening in here now." He tapped his head with a fingertip. "But I can tell you this about Caitlin. She has your child inside her."

That silence became a force in its own right—an intolerable one that pulsed inside Paul's head. "That's not possible," he hissed. "We're Transients. Transients are sterile."

Dominion shook his head. "Not anymore." Gently, he shook Paul by the shoulder. "We're changing . . ."

Elsa didn't remember hitting the ocean. The impact would have killed a mortal. Even so, the force of the fall drove her deep underwater. As Elsa sped downward into the black depths she marveled she was alive. She was convinced that at the bottom of the cliff there would be shallows where her body would be shattered on rocks. Instead she sank down and down and down into liquid darkness. *Darkness everlasting . . .* Her mind became dreamy. The rise and fall of that unearthly music mesmerized her. And at last she realized she was in the midst of the music. It didn't come from any other direction but here. It surrounded here. A phantom chorus of voices.

For the moment she experienced no compelling need to breathe. Instead her eyes searched the darkness for the source of the music. And when she found it she wasn't surprised. Perhaps subconsciously she'd known all along. Beneath her, a figure drifted up from the depths. At first it looked like a pale X shape in the gloom, but it resolved itself into the body of a man with outstretched arms and legs. The man turned in the body of the ocean. His eyes were open as he gazed up at her.

Her long-dead husband drifted there a hundred feet under the surface of the water. *I'm not dreaming*, she told herself. *This is real. Richard has come back to take me with him. He isn't making that music, he's become the doorway through which it pours. That's the song of the ancient dead. They're calling me to join Richard. We're reunited.*

Richard loomed upward toward her. As he opened his mouth his lips framed a word that he didn't speak. It came as boom that thundered through her. *"Live."* Then he sank back down into the depths.

The booming came again. Elsa coughed the water from her throat. It felt hard as stone there. Another boom, and then the surf grabbed her and sent her turning over and over. Another boom—one that seemed to shake dust from the universe itself. A wave carried her up the beach. To the accompanying boom of surf on rocks she pushed herself to her feet and walked clear of the water. When she remembered the vision of Richard she also recalled his command: *Live*.

Live? What is there to live for? She saw the gloomy block of the castle standing on its headland. Her friends were in there. Either dead, or soon to be dead. So why carry on?

Surf boomed across the rocks again. That was the only sound she heard. She turned her face to the cold breeze rushing in from the ocean. With all her willpower she listened for that unearthly music . . . the song of the ancient dead that had haunted her since her rebirth in the Transit Station all those years ago. When she eventually began to walk up the beach toward dry land she realized she could hear their song no more.

West ran down the stairs that led into the tower. He called out to the survivors huddled in the storeroom, "They've broken in through the windows!"

Dominion looked at Paul. "It's up to me and you now."

Elsa climbed the path that wound its way up the cliffs. At the top, on level ground she saw three black helicopters. Moving away from them, under cover of darkness, was a squad of soldiers. Even from this distance she could see they were heavily armed. Machine guns, handheld missile launchers—these were people committed to executing their mission to the full.

Even at that moment, when death stalked the countryside, the meaning of the vision she'd experienced in the sea revealed itself. *Live. Be alive.* Maybe it was a kind of dream she'd experienced all these years when she heard that music. But if the ancient dead could sing, what would be their message in the lyric? They wouldn't sing in praise of death. They'd sing about the glories of life. And the more she thought about it, that yearning in the melody resonated again. So if the dead could sing, what would they sing about? Yes, it was about the splendor of life, and being alive. Of relishing that fleeting, shooting star existence in a universe of lifeless matter.

Elsa had been fortunate enough to return from death once. She should make the most of her second chance. Now she wanted life so much her nerves tingled. She had to escape.

Moving quickly, with her head as low as possible so she wouldn't be seen by the soldiers, she ran downhill. If she could find the river in the valley she could follow it upstream away from Scaur Ness.

When she rounded an outcrop of boulders a light blazed in her face. Three men loomed out of the shadows to grab hold of her.

"So, you were running from the soldiers?" The man's breath stank of beer. "I reckon they'll be impressed by our trophy, don't you?"

Two men grabbed her arms. One was a cop. The other man was far younger. She recognized him as the man who'd held her and kissed her just hours ago. Even though he didn't let his tough-guy expression slip his eyes pleaded with her not to reveal their secret. She held his gaze for a second, then looked away in the direction of the distant hill, where the stone circle had stood for three millennia.

The man with the beer breath grunted, "Hold her still."

Karl didn't grip her arm as tightly as the cop. At the last moment she thought she heard him whisper, "Sorry."

That was just seconds before the man with the stale breath showed her the pistol shape of the humane killer used to slaughter cattle. He grinned as he pushed the muzzle against her forehead; a mechanism clicked as a lever moved. Even as the detonation filled her ears and she fell dying at humanity's feet she thought: *I want to live.*

Dominion raced upstairs to where the break-in had occurred. Two powerful thoughts jostled inside his head. One: to drive the invaders out. Two: that need to *do something.* The thought had been implanted in Dominion before his rebirth at the Transit Station. It was an act of supreme importance. Yet he couldn't catch hold of it. The memory swam through his head as slippery as a fish. Just when he hoped he'd grasped it and could shout: *Ah yes, this is what I'm supposed to do,* it would wriggle away again. But it was coming. Oh yes, it was nearly here. Any minute now he'd remember that important task he must perform.

Everything depended on it.

41

THE LAST DAY

The moment Paul entered the room in the upper part of the tower he glanced out the window to see the pale gray of dawn spreading through the sky. In the room were eight of the town's young bucks. They must have spent the night downing liquor and goading one another into doing something about "those damned monsters in the castle." Now they were in through a broken window. When they saw Dominion wasn't dead after all they screamed at one another in panic. One of them scrambled out of the window so fast he missed his footing. Instead of making it to the walkway he tumbled forty feet into the courtyard below. The mob parted as he fell, leaving plenty of space for the kid to make landfall.

Dominion pounced. That giant of a man with the scarred neck, wrists lined with deep crimson gullies, where the hands had been welded by surgical laser to the arms. His shaved head with its dark skin and golden stubble must have been the last thing the men saw. They were still too drunk to handle their weapons effectively.

Shotgun blasts knocked holes in plasterwork. A revolver slug grazed Paul's shoulder. There was movement, shouting, yells, gunshots—but mainly there was killing. Dominion simply reached out and crushed heads in his vast hands, as if he crushed soft, ripe peaches.

A Sap of around twenty swung an ax at Dominion. Paul snatched it out of the man's hands and drove the handle so violently into his breastbone it must have popped the guy's heart. He dropped to the floor with an expression of utter surprise. The last Sap standing pulled a knife. Dominion simply slapped it out of his hand, reached down, grabbed the knifeman by the ankle, and upended him. He carried the squealing man to the window, in the same casual way a child would amble about a yard with a plastic doll held by the leg. A moment later he thrust the kid out of the window. Puke spurted from this captive's mouth to spray onto the mob below.

Dominion called down, "Leave the castle."

People screamed when they saw Dominion dangle the youth by the ankle high above them.

Dominion pressed on, "If you go back to your homes there'll be no more fighting. We'll leave here within the hour."

Elements of the crowd shouted abuse. Voices rose; even though it wasn't easy to make out complete sentences, the meaning was transparent. Government soldiers were on their way. They'd landed in helicopters. They'd be here at any moment.

The baying of the pack grew louder. Dominion standing there in clear view as he dangled one of their own tormented them beyond belief. Some raised their guns and began shooting.

The hanging youth screamed at them, "No . . . no . . . no!" One of the shotgun blasts meant for Dominion ripped open the youth's face. A strange, gasping scream pulsed through his bloody lips. Dominion flung the injured man into the crowd.

Paul watched Dominion step back into the room. Bullets ricocheted up the wall outside.

"So," Paul said. "We really are trapped. They're going to keep us bottled here until the troops come."

Dominion's forehead furrowed into hard ridges as he concentrated on some problem. That eight-pound brain of his—more than twice the size of a human's—must be working fucking overtime. Bitter observations. But Paul's thoughts seared him. What happened to Caitlin? She'd been driven away by her father, so she should be safe. But no one would tolerate her in this town. Once they'd done with the God Scarers the mob would find Caitlin, tar and feather her, then . . . He groaned at mental images of the thugs torturing her. If only he could escape from here and find her? A clatter of bird shot against the window frame was proof enough those people wouldn't let him stroll out of here.

He watched Dominion. The giant's eyes glistened as he hammered thought through that overstuffed skull of his.

Paul asked, "Have you remembered what you were supposed to remember yet?" Sarcasm tainted his voice. "You know, the important quest? The great and glorious task that you were entrusted with?"

Dominion pressed his lips together with the effort of trying to recall what was so vital.

"I wish that big block of gray matter could have helped us before now," Paul continued in a bitter tone. "If you know Caitlin is pregnant maybe you could have fandoozled some clever way of saving her. Because you know what those Saps down there will do to her, don't you? They'll shave off her hair, pour molten tar over her head, then cover her in feathers. Then they'll probably drag her round the town while her friends and neighbors kick her to death."

"I'm trying to remember," Dominion hissed. "I'm trying." He cuffed the side of his own head. "In here . . . in here . . . there's something important . . . I have to do something. It's vital. Once I remember, everything will be all right."

"I wish I could believe you, old pal."

"I just need to remember. Then all this aggression between humanity and our own kind will be over."

"Perhaps you're really the dove of peace." Paul's laugh was a grim one. "Then when you remember . . . whoosh . . . happiness, prosperity, and tranquility for all."

"Paul . . . it's important. Stop playing the fool."

"But that's just it. I'm not joking. I'm sick to my stomach that I don't know where Caitlin is. The idea of being trapped here waiting to die nauseates me. And I can't believe that there's something inside your big bastard of a brain that will set us all free, and stop the killing."

"I will remember." Dominion's eyes narrowed as he struggled to catch that slippery thought. "I will remember. It's almost within reach."

A cheer rose outside.

"Sorry, mate. You should have tried harder." Paul nodded toward the window. "Just look at who's walking through the gate."

In the early morning gloom soldiers entered the Pharos.

"Big guns," Paul intoned. "Must be elite forces."

The townspeople applauded the arrivals. There were more cheers.

Paul clenched his fists. "We should let our people have the choice of surrendering, I suppose, or taking their own way out from the top of the battlements. It would have worked for Saiban if we hadn't decided to bring him back." He watched the soldiers advance across the courtyard. "A matter of academic interest, I know, but have you remembered what you were supposed to remember yet?"

Dominion shook his head.

"Then you've been no use at all, have you, Dominion, old buddy? All this running and hiding and fighting? You were merely a clever conjuring trick of science all along."

Dominion tilted his head down at the troops. "You've been too busy talking . . . you should have been looking."

Paul looked down. The townspeople had parted to allow the troops through. That was the moment the light from the rising sun fell into the courtyard. When it lit the faces of the soldiers the men and women flinched backward as if they'd been struck by a blast of withering heat. The townspeople began to shout to one another. They raised their guns. The soldiers did the same.

Dominion smiled at Paul. "Don't you recognize a fellow monster when you see one? Those people down there realized before you did."

What Paul intended to ask was: *Those are our troops?* The gunfire stopped that. The citizens of Scaur Ness might as well have armed themselves with toy weapons. Their shots did little damage. The squad of God Scarers, however, dealt out a devastating barrage of machine gun fire. The big-caliber rounds smashed into the mob. From the tower Paul watched as Saps burst under the impact of bullets. Arms flailed the air, mouths opened to scream, but the frenzy of movement only lasted seconds. As quickly as the soldiers started firing they stopped. Up here in the castle the only ones left alive weren't human.

The aftermath was eerily peaceful. The soldiers—an elite squad of men and women—reported their arrival to

Brigadier. After that they stood in awe as Dominion entered the room.

Brigadier confided to Paul, "In our little nation out in the desert Dominion is a legend." He smiled. "See how they salute him? You know, I think they'd rather worship him." He beckoned Saiban. The man walked holding the wooden plugs in his chest; he grimaced with pain. "Saiban," Brigadier said. "I thought you'd like to know that your last message from the Transit Station got through. HQ dispatched this brave squad of Transients via sea and air to rescue Dominion. If we ever start handing out medals, Saiban, you will be one of the first to qualify."

Saiban managed a dignified composure. "Doing one's duty doesn't require symbolic rewards. The act itself is its own reward."

"Good old Saiban," Brigadier chuckled. "Good old Saiban. Born to serve. Then reborn to serve again."

Dominion approached. "I'm told the entire town is in our hands."

"So." Paul shrugged. "Our commando God Scarers have captured the town. We're saved." He turned to Dominion. "Have you remembered what you were supposed to remember? Or isn't that important anymore?"

Dominion didn't answer the question. Instead he responded with, "Paul. If you come with me it will be better if I show you."

Together they climbed the steps onto the walkway where it overlooked the town. The early morning sun made the tiled roofs glow red. Gulls called out as they glided on the warm air. The streets of Scaur Ness were deserted. Then Paul saw why.

He leaned forward, resting both hands on the battlement wall, as he took in what was happening on the beach by the harbor.

"You've got your prisoners of war," Paul told him. "Though from here the population of this little shambles of a town doesn't look much of an army."

Dominion's troops had ushered what must have been the entire population onto the sands. "So, Dominion . . ." Paul watched the tiny figures in the distance. From up here they resembled ink spots on yellow paper. "At the risk of repeating myself too often: Have you remembered what you were supposed to remember?"

"My task?" He took a deep breath as he gazed at the captives on the beach. "My purpose is to reunite human beings with the men and women who were brought back from the dead."

"Monster and man in perfect harmony, hmm?"

"Yes. That's my purpose exactly."

Paul shrugged. "How do you propose to achieve that?"

"Watch." Dominion raised his hand. Somewhere on the beach a soldier must have been waiting for the signal.

Then Paul watched in silence as a perverse version took place of Dominion's great fishing spectacle of just hours ago. There was nothing he could do but stand there as the soldiers stretched out the old fishing nets, then swept the townspeople up in them before wading into surf, hauling the netted men and women with them.

"This is your solution?" Paul whispered. "To drown them?"

Dominion didn't answer. Not that there was any need. Events spoke for themselves. Soon those inklike blots of humanity had vanished into the ocean. The beach was clean again.

When he managed to speak Paul breathed, "I should have killed you while I had chance." He felt cold inside.

"Men, women, children. You monster. You filthy, disgusting monster."

Dominion's voice rang with clarity when he spoke. "I remember everything now. The commandos aren't here purely to save me."

"No, they came to murder a town as well."

"And not just the town, Paul. All of you die, too."

Paul felt a surreal calm steal through him. "Outlived our usefulness?"

Down in the courtyard Saiban, Xaiyad, Beech, West, and the other survivors from the Transit Station were hauled out by the soldiers. There they were strangled by lengths of wire.

Paul, whether in this life or his previous one, was always vulnerable to the stray thought, as if he was purely a commentator on life, not a participant. His next thought ran something like this: *Unless you've ever heard a monster scream before you can't begin to imagine what the sound is actually like. It's every pain you've ever endured, every act of humiliation you've suffered, it's everything that's made you cry.*

Dominion's blow snapped his spine. Dr. Paul Marais was dead before he hit the floor.

42

ONE YEAR LATER

In the domain of Frankenstein death isn't always the victor . . .

"She's coming."

"Does she have the child?"

"Yes."

"Good."

"Well?"

"What do you expect me to do, Saiban?"

"Go meet her."

"First things first, Saiban. There's a new God Scarer to reintroduce to the world."

"A Newborn can wait."

"Ah, that's why you're an administrator, Saiban, and I'm the medic. This wee lad's reached a rather critical stage." He helped the Newborn to his feet from a bench in the courtyard. The courtyard, itself, now served as the Transit Station. Blue awnings undulated in the summer breeze. Beneath the sheltering canvas sat a dozen Regenerators. All demanded his attention because in an hour a new batch of God Scarers would be entering the world from those hourglass-shaped vessels in gleaming steel.

He took the Newborn by the arm and walked him to the open gateway of the Pharos. "My name is Dr. Paul Marais. You're going to be sick of hearing my bonny Scottish accent, but I'm trying to wake up your mind. We must get all those neurological connections firing. You need to remember who you are . . . *what* you are. And you have to learn about the world and our place in it. Now . . . do you remember your name?"

The man stood there in the white gown he'd worn for the transition from corpse to Transient. His wide eyes regarded the gulls wheeling in the sky. Then he held up his hand to examine the smooth skin of the palms.

Saiban shook his head. "Dr. Marais. You should leave them to sleep longer."

"Ah, that's where you're wrong. The sooner their minds connect with memory, the better their mental equilibrium. This gentleman came to us as an eighty-three-year-old with heart failure and dementia. He needs extra care to coax him back into the world."

Saiban chuckled. "Have it your own way."

Paul guided the man to the gate so he could look out over Scaur Ness that was bathed in sunlight. The Regenerator had done its work well. The man didn't appear a day over thirty years of age. His broad face was unlined. His thick hair didn't have a single strand of gray. The physique was that of an athlete.

"Look, Saiban. Isn't it true? We do make beautiful monsters."

"You're delaying the inevitable." Saiban's smile was a caring one. "You should go to her now."

"I will," Paul said. "But first I need to fire up that brain in our friend's head. Now . . ." He pointed. "That town is Scaur Ness. A year ago it was in a hell of a state. Garbage littered the streets. Dilapidated houses. Rampant unemployment. A dispirited population. It's easy to imagine the town had fallen under a curse. Do you remember the town, friend? You lived not far away. Did you not visit it during your lifetime?"

The man gazed with those wide Newborn eyes, as if marveling at the cottages with their sparkling windows and neatly tended gardens.

Saiban laughed. "Shouldn't you have begun your story 'Once upon a time'?"

It was good-natured teasing and Paul knew it. He exaggerated his Scottish accent as he said, "Ah, Saiban, be off with you. There's a full bucket of water there by the wall and I'm not afraid to tip it over your bonny wee head."

Saiban grinned. "OK, I can take a hint. Don't forget your visitor. Have you decided what you'll say to her?"

Paul felt the old tension return. "I'll think of something."

"Think hard, Paul. She'll be here in a couple of minutes."

The man headed away under the canvas awnings. Saiban had changed now. His spirits were lighter, and he was good company. Funny how a man's death can be the making of him. In Saiban's case it was the third time of dying that produced the cheerful soul that Paul knew today.

"OK," Paul said to the Newborn beside him as he watched a fishing boat glide out of the harbor. "Where were we? Ah yes . . . Perhaps I should take Saiban's advice on how I start this story . . ." He glanced at the God Scarer, Transient, monster, call him what you will. The eyes were bright, but the man still didn't recollect that a few days ago he would have been a mere husk, gasping out his last hours in some remote cottage. Now everything had changed. "So, to serenade you with my charm-

ing Scottish brogue again: Once upon a time . . . a bunch
of God Scarers came to Scaur Ness in the dead of night.
The term *God Scarer* is a misnomer, for it was we who
were terrified. All of us bar one. He went by the name of
Dominion. A giant of a man on a mission to reunite humanity with the monsters they created from their own
deceased. I only learned very late in the day how he
planned to do that. He claimed he couldn't remember,
but I'm not sure if he was telling the truth or not. Anyway, as we were under siege back there in that very building we were rescued by our own kind. And just as you're
no doubt telling yourself that I conclude here by saying
that we lived happily ever after, that's not quite the case.
What happened was that our fellow God Scarers killed
all the townspeople. And as I stood on the battlements
Dominion killed me, too." He breathed deeply, catching
the scents of the ocean. "But of course, science gifted us
with the means to bring the dead back to life. So here we
all are again. And Dominion got his way. He reunited
humanity with its monsters by the simple expedient of
killing every human being in the town and resurrecting
them as God Scarers. You know something, friend? We
were only a tiny part of the process. This was happening
throughout the nation. Today, there is no prejudice because we're all monsters now. Ah, once we have that
brain of yours firing on all pistons you'll be showering me
with questions. Why does the rest of the world put up
with it? I'd reply: That's something to do with Dominion. Just what it is, I can't begin to guess. And where is
Dominion? Well, he's out there somewhere." Paul nodded toward a blue horizon. "What is he up to? Search me,
friend, but my guess is the age of Homo sapiens is at an
end. Now, do you remember your name yet?"

The man thought hard as the breeze ruffled his black
hair. Then he spoke. "Child."

"Ah . . . all the nurses call Newborns Child. You'll have to try harder than that." Suddenly, Paul's muscles tightened. His sensitive hearing picked up the approach of footsteps. They slowed as if the person who made them was afraid to approach the Pharos. Paul found himself staring at the gap in the wall where the portcullis had once been. Any moment now the maker of the footsteps would appear. After she'd been gone a full year he'd accepted that he'd never see her again. Now his heartbeat quickened as his chest grew tight.

He addressed the newborn Transient, "Not long now." He closed his eyes as the sound of footsteps from beyond the castle wall became more purposeful. Paul spoke quickly as if to erase the sound. "Elsa. You won't know Elsa. But she's part of my story. She died, too, at the hand of a human. But we're monsters. We're not only hard to kill, we're hard to stay dead, too. Our troops found her and rushed her to a Regenerator. Her attackers were killed, too. They didn't stay dead either. They've recanted their wicked ways and work with us now. See? The Good Guys and the Bad Guys all died. Now they're back in the land of the living and the best of friends. Isn't that the happiest ending in the world. No?"

So what does happens when she gets here? The question made his heart pound. The footsteps grew louder. Any second now she'd appear in the gateway. Any second . . . He found himself speaking nonstop to mask his anxiety. "And what do you make of our friend Saiban? It took several deaths for him to become the amiable man you see today. By heaven, he was a dour piece of work in the old days. When we've time I'll tell you how I had to plug wounds in his body with pieces of a chair. The carpentry's gone now, as you'll have noticed. Saiban's well but nothing will convince him to move to the Sahara where our people made their homeland. He won't admit it but he loves this town. He even cuts the grass in the grave-yard. It's his way of paying his respects to all those that have gone before, and who didn't have the opportunity of taking a second shot at life. And there's West and Beech; they're living under the same roof now. Didn't I promise you happy endings?" The footsteps grew louder. Each step produced a flash of recollection. *Dominion thrusting the cross into a burning car. Luna breaking out of her tomb. The time I stood on the walkway to watch the townspeople being drowned. Dominion's words: "And not just the town, Paul. All of you die, too." Then Dominion killed me. I woke up to see Saiban looking down at me. "Welcome back to the world of the living, Paul. Don't just lie there, you've work to do."* And how he'd buried himself in that work for the last twelve months. He installed the portable Regenerators in the courtyard. The God Scarer troops collected the dead from the neighborhood. Then began the process of bringing thousands of men and women back to life. *The end of the world as we know it.*

The footsteps grew louder.

Paul turned to the Newborn who'd just made that same journey—from death back to life. "So, friend. Remember your name yet?"

"Joseph."

"Welcome back, Joseph. Go rest for a while and I'll see you later."

Those footsteps could be a colossal pounding on a door between two worlds. He'd been expecting this for days, but now the time had come the tension was almost unbearable. He fixed his eyes on the gateway with the town shining behind it—the image of pristine cleanli-ness. There, its population of Transients lived and worked. All wore young faces; they were healthy, there was no disease, they would not age—

—*and, so you see*, he told himself. *Happy endings guar-*

anteed. Only there was one person who wasn't happy. And he was standing in that man's skin. Oh, he'd dedicated himself to his labors here at the Pharos, but sorrow had run in his veins as if it were a new form of blood.

The footsteps grew louder. He stood there in the courtyard, fists clenched.

Lately, Paul imagined what that moment of her return would be like, and here it was taking place before he could even plan what he'd say and do.

Then the figure appeared in the gateway. The woman's hair was shorter now. In her arms she carried a baby.

Paul took a breath. "Caitlin."

She met his eye as she placed a protective hand behind the baby's head.

Paul said, "Dominion told me you were having a child, but how he knew . . ." Shrugging, he tried to smile and didn't know if he'd succeeded in making anything close to one. "At times like this I can be usually guaranteed to make an extremely bad joke . . . but today?" He shrugged. "It's got me beat. I can hardly frame a coherent sentence. See? I'm—"

Caitlin moved forward and put her arm round him as she held the baby in the other arm. Paul hugged them both. This time he found he could laugh as he said, "Welcome to the monster factory." He looked down into both their faces—the woman and her child. "You know, it's a long time since I've clapped eyes on a human being. Never mind one that's the mother of my son." He touched her face. "So, is this simply a visit of mercy, or—"

"We're here to stay, Paul."

"And then so you shall." Those were the words he wanted to hear, and yet—

"But if you want us to be with you," she said, "then we've got to be like you. *Exactly* like you."

"Caitlin, there's no need for you to go through transition. We can live together as a family."

Her eyes held his. "We can only stay together if we become the same as you."

"Caitlin, you don't understand. A living person can't be submitted to the Regenerator. It just wouldn't work."

Caitlin whispered, "Then what are you waiting for?" She hugged the baby tight as she closed her eyes.

When Paul did what he had to do it was only the seagulls that screamed out over the town.

SIMON CLARK

THE TOWER

The Tower stands in solitude. What began as a seven-teenth-century manor house has grown over the cen-turies into something very different. Something evil. There are the stark walls, the shadow-filled rooms, the lonely corridors. But the Tower is haunted by much more than ghosts of the past, and it can do far more than simply terrify. It has a dark heart and it has grown rest-less. When five unsuspecting young people agree to stay there as house-sitters, they soon learn that visitors are not welcome in... *THE TOWER*.